Praise for Emily Hourican's Guinness novels

'*The Glorious Guinness Girls* has already been compared, and rightly so, to *Downton Abbey*. The two share a delicious comfort-blanket quality . . . with sweeping historical themes'
Irish Independent

'A captivating and page-turning novel about a fascinating family. Fantastic' Sinéad Moriarty

'Gripping . . . this dramatic novel takes us into the heart of their privileged, beautiful and often painful hidden world'
Irish Country Magazine

'The perfect glorious escape . . . the intimacy of a family drama, set against the most opulent of backdrops'
Sunday Independent

'An enthralling tale that will dazzle and delight'
Swirl and Thread

'A breathtakingly glamorous and escapist read with all of the natural drama of two wealthy dynasties set against a backdrop of war. Hourican pitches her sombre ending just right, and leaves us reflective and poised on the edge of much darkness yet to come' Edel Coffey, *The Irish Times*

'Engrossing and page-turning . . . I loved it' Louise O'Neill

Emily Hourican is the author of nine novels and one book of non-fiction. Her first novel, *The Privileged*, was published in 2016, became an instant bestseller and was short-listed for the Best Popular Fiction Award at the Irish Book Awards that year. She then published three more works of contemporary fiction, the last of which, *The Outsider*, is being developed as a six-part TV series with Treasure Films, with Emily as screenwriter, supported by Screen Ireland.

In 2019 she began writing historical fiction, and has since published four acclaimed, best-selling historical novels based on the Guinness and Kennedy families.

Emily is also an award-winning editor and journalist with the *Sunday Independent*, Ireland's biggest-selling newspaper.

She lives in Dublin with her family.

Also by Emily Hourican

An Invitation to the Kennedys
The Other Guinness Girl: A Question of Honor
The Guinness Girls: A Hint of Scandal
The Glorious Guinness Girls
The Outsider
The Blamed
White Villa
The Privileged

How To (Really) Be A Mother

A
KENNEDY
AFFAIR

EMILY
HOURICAN

HACHETTE
BOOKS
IRELAND

First published in Ireland in 2024 by
HACHETTE BOOKS IRELAND

I

Cataloguing in Publication Data is available from the British Library

ISBN 9781399733830

Typeset in Sabon LT Std by
Palimpsest Book Production Limited, Falkirk, Stirlingshire

Printed and bound in Great Britain by
Clays Ltd, Elcograf S.p.A.

Hachette Books Ireland policy is to use papers that are natural, renewable
and recyclable products and made from wood grown in sustainable forests.
The logging and manufacturing processes are expected to conform
to the environmental regulations of the country of origin.

Hachette Books Ireland
8 Castlecourt Centre
Castleknock
Dublin 15, Ireland

A division of Hachette UK Ltd
Carmelite House, 50 Victoria Embankment,
London EC4Y 0DZ

www.hachettebooksireland.ie

To the readers.
Your enthusiasm for these stories
is the fuel behind them.

Cast of Characters

Kathleen 'Kick' Kennedy
Joe Kennedy Jr – Kick's older brother
Rosemary 'Rosie' Kennedy – Kick's older sister
Rose Kennedy – Kick's mother
Joe Kennedy Sr – Kick's father

Lady Brigid Guinness
Honor Channon (née Guinness) – Brigid's older sister
Henry Channon, 'Chips' – American diarist and politician,
   Honor's husband
Prince Frederick George William Christopher of Prussia,
   'Fritzi'
Lady Iveagh, Brigid and Honor's mother
Will – patient at hospital where Brigid works

Sissy Maddington
Edie – Kick's fellow Red Cross volunteer or 'Donut Dollie'
Peter – friend of Sissy's

Maureen Hamilton-Temple-Blackwood (née Guinness),
    Marchioness of Dufferin and Ava – Brigid and Honor's
    cousin
Basil Hamilton-Temple-Blackwood, 'Duff', 4th Marquess of
    Dufferin and Ava – Maureen's husband
Caroline Blackwood – Maureen and Duff's eldest daughter

William 'Billy' Cavendish, Marquess of Hartington
Andrew Cavendish – Billy's brother
Debo Mitford – friend of Kick and Honor's, Andrew's wife
Edward Cavendish, Duke of Devonshire – Billy's father
Lady Mary Cavendish, Duchess of Devonshire, 'Moucher' –
    Billy's mother

The historical figures featured in this novel are based on fact but as imagined by the author. Apart from the documented historical figures and events, this book, its characters and their actions are the work of the author's imagination.

Part One

July 1941

Chapter One

Kick, Hyannis Port, Massachusetts, USA

The light was already as bright as a bare electric bulb although it was only seven o'clock. Kick threw off the covers and sat upright. She could smell smoke from last night's beach bonfire on her hair, and remembered the crackling flames that had flickered across the faces of her companions, those summer friends who were as much a part of holidays at Hyannis Port as sailing and swimming. Her brother Jack's face, lit up and merry as he told a story from his recent Harvard graduation; Joe, so quick to cut in and tell his own story – a bigger, better one. The girls on either side of those brothers of hers who had laughed and urged them on. One especially, newly come from Boston, a friend of a friend, who couldn't seem to make up her mind between them, flirting with both.

Kick yawned. They had come home when dawn was already

throwing out pinkish streaks, like grappling hooks, to attach itself to land and pull against the dark, but for Kick, used to being woken at six every morning at her convent school, there was still something decadent about lying in till seven. In any case, their mother would never allow anyone to sleep longer. Breakfast was at eight sharp, every morning, even Sunday. And if you missed it, well, Cook was under strict instructions not to slip you so much as a slice of bread. 'If you're late for meals, you go without,' Rose said.

Kick rolled her shoulders back. They were tight. All that sailing the day before. They would be even more sore by the evening, she knew. A race was planned – first to the gull-rock and back. They did it every year, had done since they each turned, what, eight? Nine? They'd set off in their separate sail boats, as many of them as were deemed old enough to go, rounding the rock as close and tight as they dared, then home again to where their father waited on the dock, ready to judge the winner and give his verdict on their performances.

'Rosie,' Kick called across to her sister, in the bed on the other side of the room. Rosie slept, as always, curled into a tight ball so that only the top of her head poked out of the crisp cotton quilt that was patterned with tiny pink and white flowers. Rosie slept later than any of them and was the grumpiest in the mornings. 'Rosie, we should get up.'

'You get up!' Rosie called back. She hadn't moved and the words were muffled. Her dark hair spilled from the top of the tightly bundled quilt.

'Come on, Rosy-posy. You know Mother will only be fretting and fidgeting, if we don't go down for breakfast. "I won't have any Lazy Susans in this house,"' she mimicked.

That made Rosie laugh, unwillingly. She pushed back the

quilt and heaved herself up. Her eyes were swollen and her face puffy. Rosie was by far the prettiest of them, but you wouldn't know it in the mornings, Kick thought, with a grin she hid carefully by turning her head towards the window. Rosie didn't like being laughed at. Not any more. Before, she would join in, eager for any joke. But this last year she'd been so touchy.

Rosie swung her legs over the side of the bed and sat, yawning and stretching, with her feet flat on the bare wooden floor. Sun from the window glanced across the top of her head.

Kick got up, put on her dressing-gown and threw Rosie's across to her. She walked to the window and pushed it open, breathing in the sea air that was as much salt as anything else. 'Those birds must have the same kind of mother we do,' she said, with a laugh. 'They're mighty busy.'

Rosie laughed too. 'It's a beautiful day,' she said, in the monotone she affected when she imitated their mother. 'We don't want to waste a second of it.' She stretched and yawned again. 'But it's too early for Mother's moralising. My head's telling me I should be asleep.'

'You can't be as tired as I am,' Kick said, trying to cheer her. 'I think I only slept about two hours.'

It was the wrong thing to say. She knew it immediately from the way Rosie's face scrunched up, cross and resentful. 'I wanted to go to that party!' she said. Older than Kick by nearly two years, she was almost twenty-three, and had come to resent all that Kick was allowed to do and she wasn't.

'It wasn't a party, it really wasn't,' Kick said hurriedly. 'Just a bonfire on the beach and a few of the same people we see every day. You don't even like them very much.'

'I like Glen,' Rosie said, her face lighting up momentarily. Glen was a friend of Joe's, handsome and sporty. Rosie wasn't the only girl who liked him, Kick knew. In fact, she had once kind of liked him herself. But that was before England. Before Billy.

'Glen wasn't there,' Kick said. It was a lie, and she felt hot under the arms as she told it. She would confess it later, she promised herself. Right now, it was the smart thing to do. 'No Glen, and no one interesting at all, really. Come on, we'd better hurry.'

They dressed and ran downstairs, arriving at the breakfast table just after their father. They were the last. All the other children were seated in their places and Rose was ready to say morning grace. She bowed her head as Rosie and Kick slid into their seats.

'Who's sailing this morning?' their father asked, when prayers were over. Only Bobby said yes. The race was that afternoon, and the rest of them decided to spend the morning doing other things: tennis, swimming. 'Who'll play rounders with me?' Jean asked.

'I will,' Kick said. 'If Teddy and Rosie do.' It was her way of trying to ensure Rosie *did something*. Too often, that summer, Rose had found fault with her eldest daughter for 'not doing anything'. More and more, Rosie wanted to spend her days just lying on a striped towel on the beach, sunning herself, 'Not even reading,' as Rose said in displeasure. She didn't have the same need as the rest of them to be always in motion, doing and proving themselves.

It wouldn't have mattered, except that it mattered to their mother. 'Idle hands, idle mind,' she would say, disapproving. She would chivvy Rosie to 'do something', and Rosie would refuse, and then there would be an argument. There had been more lately. Rosie was so stubborn, but Kick hated to see how upset she got, and how her rages would fly so quickly out of control. They all had tempers – they were Kennedys – but even little Teddy controlled his better than Rosie did. She let fly, and was so upset afterwards that she couldn't seem to calm herself down, pacing and ranting that things were 'unfair' and people 'mean', long past the time the argument should have been forgotten. Because while it was OK to lose your temper, bearing a grudge was not. That was 'unmanly', even for the girls.

'All right,' Rosie said now. 'I'll play.'

Kick smiled at her, and Rosie grinned back. 'I'm trying to get in her good books so she'll let me go out with you and the boys tonight,' she whispered, leaning close.

Kick's heart sank. She didn't think it would work but she didn't say so. 'Good,' she said.

They dispersed as soon as breakfast was over. Joe, for all that he'd said he was playing tennis, went to the beach club to meet Clarice, the girl from the bonfire. He made sure to tell Jack how she'd telephoned first thing to ask if he had seen a head-scarf she'd lost. 'I'll bet that scarf is in her pocket right this minute,' he added.

The morning was hot and bright and perfect. Kick, Rosie and the younger ones ran about the beach until they were exhausted, diving into the ocean to cool off, then flopping down onto the warm sand to dry.

'I'm going to wear my new dress with the blue stripes,' Rosie said. She had continued to talk about the evening – how she would do her hair, whether she might get away with wearing lipstick. Kick felt worse and worse. She resolved to talk to their mother privately, and try to enlist Jack to help her.

'If we say we'll look after her,' she said to Jack, when she got him alone, 'maybe Mother will let her.' They were in the downstairs cloakroom, good-naturedly jostling one another at the washbasin as they washed hands. The slanting window beyond Jack showed stripes of yellow and blue – sand and sea – and the wooden shutters were so warped by years of wet, salty air that they no longer closed.

'OK,' he said. 'But you have to say it to Joe and get him to agree.' Joe would be less inclined than Jack. He felt Rosie needed too much looking after, and she came out with strange remarks that made other people laugh, but sometimes fall silent in embarrassment. 'He's more against taking her out than ever since she made that pass at Glen.'

'She was only dancing with him,' Kick said. That had been at their house, maybe two weeks ago now. A small party, not even a party, just a couple of friends and some records.

'He said she put her hands all over him and he didn't know what to do,' Jack said, grimacing a little as he spoke.

'He just needs to tell her no, and not be silly about it,' Kick said. 'That's just Rosie.' She giggled. 'I think it's funny when she does it.'

'Glen didn't think it was so funny. Neither did Joe, when Glen told him. He said Rosie had better learn to behave or he'll start agreeing with Mother that she can't be allowed to do the same things as the rest of us.'

'But can't he see that the less Mother lets her, the more she wants to? If Rosie was allowed to go out with us – even Eunice is sometimes – she'd soon learn it isn't all that wonderful. Just a bunch of kids.'

'Is that what it seems like to you now, after England?' he asked, with a sly grin. 'I suppose after coming-out balls and being presented at Court, a game of baseball must seem silly all right.'

'Don't!' Kick said, drying her hands and leaving faint streaks on the blue-and-white striped towel. 'I get enough of that from Molly and my other friends. They all watch like hawks in case I say something that suggests England's better, and then they *pounce*.' She rearranged the towel to hide the stains. 'Anyway, I'll watch Rosie tonight,' she continued, 'if you help me persuade Joe.'

'Well, OK. But I don't think much of your plan. Rosie doesn't learn like other people, you know that. She's not going to tire of going out. Not when she's got Glen to put her hands all over.' He grinned and flicked water at Kick, who swiftly held up the striped towel as a shield. 'Any luck with England?' he asked.

'None.' Kick handed him the towel. 'I tried and tried again. They just will not let me go back.'

'I tried too. I told Pa I didn't think the newspapers would be half so mean to you as he thinks, with you being a girl and all.'

'They were real mean when we left – all those headlines about what cowards we were to run away from war,' she said ruefully.

'Sure, but mostly they blamed him for sending you away, not you for leaving. Everyone knew how much you wanted to stay.'

'I really did,' she said. Then, eagerly, 'Anyway, what did Pa say to that?'

'The same as ever – that part of our lives is done now. That he's no longer ambassador, and England is now at war, and that's nothing to do with us. That the best thing we can do, as a country and as a family, is to stay well away.'

'Oh.' She was glum after the momentary surge of hope. 'Well, thanks for trying.'

'Do you really want to go back?' he asked curiously. 'After almost two years? Isn't it all just like a beautiful dream now, and best left that way?'

'No. I know I'll go back. I'm certain of it. I just wish it was sooner rather than later. Now that all my poor English friends are so much in need of cheering up.'

'You mean Billy, don't you?'

'I suppose I do.' She had spent so many months, back in America, longing for Billy. Longing for London and her London friends, and for the person she was with them – somehow unlike the Kick she had grown up as: the wholesome girl who was, first and foremost, a sister and a daughter. From the very moment the family had disembarked at Southampton in March 1938, the English press had chosen her to make a fuss of. More even than her father, it had been Kick the camera bulbs flashed for, Kick who was written and talked about.

Billy had been the coming-together of all of it. His instant attraction to her had been flattering, and welcome, but she hadn't been terribly serious about him until she realised – when Debo Mitford told her – that he would never offer to marry her. 'He can't. Absolutely can't,' Debo had said, oddly precise for one who spoke mostly in charming riddles. 'It's not even that his family won't allow it, it's that Billy himself would never begin to consider it. He likes you – oh, we can all see that – but he won't allow himself to be serious about you. If you ask me,' she had continued, 'it's only because war is on the way that he's even let it go this far.'

'Like before a half-day holiday, when everyone gets real giddy?' Kick had asked. She had been curious, and a little insulted.

'Exactly.'

It wasn't just that she was Catholic, Kick had discovered, it was her Irishness too. Her father was so self-consciously 'Irish', marshalling the Irish Americans of Boston and delivering them to Roosevelt, proud as a cat with a dead bird. His Irishness was careful, expedient, like everything he was and did, so that Kick had never before thought there might be different kinds of Irish, even different Irelands.

Joe Kennedy was vocal about his Irishness, yet had only been there once. He spoke of Irish freedom as something tangible, to be chased, like a football, but always at a remove, watched over from the fastness of Boston and America.

Billy's family, meanwhile, had a home in Ireland, an actual castle in a place called Lismore. They visited often and talked of how much they loved it yet they seemed to see a country almost without people when they spoke of it, and recoiled from any mention of 'freedom'. Generations of their family had been appointed to positions of great power, there in a country that didn't want them, sworn to prevent the very thing Kick's father cheered for: Irish freedom. 'Romeo and Juliet are a matchmaker's dream compared with you two,' Jack had said when she first explained it to him.

The impossibility of it all was what made her really fall for Billy. It had made her certain where she had been uncertain. The knowledge that he would likely not propose had made her determined that he would. It was a game. Until it wasn't a game: it had become the most serious thing in her life.

It was when she realised that he loved her and would never ask her to marry him that she felt she understood him and loved him too. It had happened at the very end of her time in England, when the certainty of separation had made them both speak openly. Then war came, and they were roughly pulled apart.

Through the years that they had been on opposite sides of a wide sea, it was Billy she had come to long for. Not the victory that his proposal would mean. Not any more. Just Billy, with his quiet voice and clipped sentences, so much more eloquent when he wrote to her than he had ever been when they sat side by side or danced together at the Café de Paris.

His letters carried a great deal about how he missed her, how he thought of her, without ever suggesting what could be done about it. He said he would never forget her, but didn't ask her to come back, or propose ways for them to meet. Which was how Kick knew that if there was to be anything for them, it was hope *she* would need to ignite.

'Still?' Jack asked sympathetically now.

'Still.'

'Better start to wear a hat, then,' he said, looking past his own face in the mirror above the washbasin to hers. 'Those freckles are not at all the thing for English girls. Or girls who like English men.'

'They're the same as your freckles,' she said.

'Yes, but I'm not trying to marry a duke,' he said, only half joking now.

Kick chose her moment carefully. Her mother had finished her thirty lengths – breaststroke, her head held out of the water and a flowery swimming hat to protect her hair – and sat by the side of the pool on a reclining chair, with a pad of writing paper balanced on her knees. Standing above her, Kick caught the words *Bishop Spellman maintains that* . . .

'Mother,' she began.

'What is it, Kathleen?' Rose asked, looking up through dark glasses. Only her mother called her that.

'May Rosie come out with us this evening, to the Brightmans' party? Jack says he'll help keep an eye on her.'

'No, Kathleen.' Rose returned to her letter.

'But why not?' Kick was still standing so that Rose had to

turn her head again to look up. With the sun behind her she was a thin dark shape placed on a backdrop of blue.

'It's not suitable,' Rose said, clear and precise. Kick's younger sister Eunice had once said she thought their mother kept a tiny stone in her mouth at all times, and spoke around it. Kick had known exactly what she meant.

'But why? She won't be alone. I'll be there, Jack and Joe too.'

'You know very well how Rosemary gets. She's excitable. She can be too much. Especially nowadays. No, she's better off at home. Besides, you don't want to have to look out for her when you're with your friends. I believe Peter Grace will be there.' By which Kick knew her mother hoped Peter Grace would be there, and that Kick would let him spend the evening at her side.

'He might.' She shrugged. She kept her irritation hidden. Why must her mother – her father too – continue to parade Peter Grace, and other rich Catholic boys, before her, as though she were a kitten to be distracted by a piece of dancing string? They knew very well that she wrote to Billy, hoped to return to him. And yet they continued to suggest the sons of their friends as though her attention was as easily caught as a brisk wind with the correct tack of a sail. She clenched her teeth. 'But I don't mind looking out for Rosie. I know how to do it so she doesn't exactly know about it.'

'She's not going, Kathleen. There are things you can do that Rosemary can't, and you will both have to learn to accept that.'

'But Rosie isn't learning. It's making her unhappy.' Kick sat down on the seat beside her mother, pushing her faded pink hat off her face. She hoped that sitting would encourage Rose to talk to her, to explain things, rather than just issue crisp orders. 'You've seen how different she's been lately. We all have. She's angry about things she used not to notice so much, like everything that me and Eunice—'

'Eunice and I,' her mother corrected.

'– Eunice and I get to do that she doesn't, even though we're younger.' Kick clasped her hands – an appeal for her mother to listen. 'She just wants to do what we do. And she can if we watch her, surely she can. We can dilute her.' She laughed a little, mostly to see if her mother would laugh with her. She didn't.

'That's not what will happen. Rather than you all diluting her, Rosemary will tarnish you.' Kick flinched at the word. 'That's what your father says, and he's correct. She is altogether too forward now. She can't be trusted not to say and do things that are not at all suitable.' Rose smoothed a hand over her perfectly set hair. 'And everything she does reflects on all of you. Your father is very clear that she mustn't be allowed to go around in a way that will be bad for you.'

'But it's only Rosie. Everyone here knows what she's like.'

'They do not. And your father doesn't wish them to. Rosemary will have a different path,' Rose said, her voice softening a little. 'That will be a cross for her, but she must resign herself to it and bear it, same as we must all bear the hardships that come to us. You, Kathleen, I have noticed, have been trying very hard to bear your own cross.' Did her voice soften a tiny bit? 'You may think I don't see the effort you make, but I do. I have prayed that you would learn acceptance,' Rose continued, 'and you have.'

'I prayed for it too,' Kick said. She didn't add that, so far, she had learned only to pretend to have found it. That all her prayers had shown her was the unwavering determination she felt that she would get back to Billy somehow.

As if her mother caught the tone of her thoughts, Rose then said, 'I know how much you want to ask your father again to let you return to England, and I have seen you hold yourself back from that. It's admirable.' She patted Kick's hand briskly, her fingers knobbly with rings. 'Your friendship with Billy Cavendish took us all by surprise, Kathleen, all the difficulties of his religion and ours, the many obstacles in the way. It was no easy matter. And I have been impressed by your fortitude in understanding this.' *Fortitude* was one of Rose's favourite compliments. She reached out to grasp Kick's hand once again, then picked up her pen and repositioned the writing pad against her knees. Kick stood up. The conversation was clearly over.

She tried to find a way to tell Rosie but there wasn't one. Not when her sister was so excited. Rosie had seemed to think permission was certain. She'd talked about what she would wear, who would be there, what they would do, the music they would listen to, the dancing. Kick said nothing.

Bobby won the race, by 'a handspan' as Pa said, and because of that, Cook made her special fluffernutter cookies. Dinner was animated. Bobby, because it was his first win, was allowed to talk them through his every move on the boat. 'For the one and only time,' Pa said indulgently. He loved a new winner. 'There is nothing in the world so boring as the person who makes you relive every round, every stroke, every kick of the ball.'

Kick thought of her English friends, and how they would solemnly describe a day's hunting, every hoofbeat, every holdup, as though these were moves in an intricate ballet.

After dinner, as they cleared their plates, Rosie said, 'Well, I'd better go up and change. You too, Kick.'

'Change for what, Rosemary?' their mother asked. Already

her tone was chilly, and Kick wondered why she had to sound like that.

'For the Brightmans' party,' Rosemary said. Her lower lip trembled and she stuck it defiantly out. She knew, Kick realised. She knew what was coming. But being Rosemary, she tried to tough it out. 'We'd better hurry or we'll be late.' She started for the door of the dining room. Kick could feel her urgency, as though Rosie believed that if she could only get out that door and up the stairs, somehow her mother would let her go. She felt sick. She saw Jack, Joe and Bobby slide out of the room by the door that led to the kitchen and hated them for it, but could hardly blame them. She'd have done the same if she could.

'No, Rosemary,' Rose said. 'You will stay home this evening.'

'I'm going to the party,' Rosie said. 'I have a dress picked and everything.'

'You will stay home,' Rose repeated, voice icy now.

Pa, Kick saw, had followed the boys out the kitchen door. Of course he would, she thought. The rule was his; its enforcement was up to Mother.

'Kick, you say I can come, don't you?' Rosie appealed to her.

'It's not Kathleen's decision to make,' Rose said.

Kick stood helpless as Rosie looked pleadingly at her. Her eyes filled with angry tears that spilled out and down her cheeks, seeming to take the blue with them.

'Kick?' she asked, voice wobbling.

'I'm sorry, Rosie,' Kick whispered. 'We'll go somewhere tomorrow, just the two of us, I promise.'

'Stay home with me,' Eunice said, trying to make it sound like a choice Rosie might make. 'We'll have our own, better fun.'

'I want to go to the party.' Rosie looked at them all, one after another, finally turning to face Teddy and Jean, who stood behind their chairs, hands resting on the wooden backs, as though pinned there.

'No parties,' Rose snapped.

Rosie shouted, 'I will go, and you can't stop me.'

'Edward, will you call Kikoo, please.' Kikoo was the nanny who had minded all of them and now just had the care of Teddy and Jean. She was an Irish woman with great strong arms, as liable to slap as she was to hug, to bellow angrily as she was to sing snatches of 'Willie McBride'. Teddy ran from the room and Kick heard his feet thumping on the wooden stairs, driven by an urgency that didn't need to be voiced.

Rosie was still shouting, 'I will go.' She was trembling all over with rage and stared at their mother with a blazing anger that was almost hatred. Kick was relieved when Kikoo came thundering in.

She seemed to know exactly what to do, and wrapped her arms tightly around Rosie, in a way that must have been painful though loving too. 'Hush now, Miss Rosemary,' she said. 'Don't be upsetting yourself.' Rosie struggled, but not for long. It was useless and she knew it. 'Come with me now, *alanna*,' Kikoo said, and she began to walk Rosie from the room, still with her arms around her so that together they were ungainly, almost grotesque. Eunice followed them. Their mother stood still and straight as a flagpole and Kick wondered what colours would be run up – triumph or alarm.

When they were gone, Kick tried once more. 'If we only stay a little while . . .' she began.

'No, Kathleen, and I would appreciate it if you didn't give false hope to your sister. She cannot go and that is that.'

'Perhaps I won't go either,' Kick said. She was so tired, she realised. The sun, the swimming, rounders, the race. Most of all, Rosie.

'I know Peter Grace is particularly looking forward to seeing you,' Rose said. 'You should go.'

When she went upstairs, Rosie refused to speak to her. She wouldn't answer when Kick tried to tell her things they might do tomorrow – walks and picnics and even a trip to the drugstore in Hyannis – just lay silent on her bed, face down. In the end Kick did go, mostly because she couldn't bear an evening of Rosie not speaking to her. Maybe once Kick was gone, she would forget about it and go down to play cards with Eunice. Sometimes she did forget.

But the evening was spoiled. She asked Joe to take her home early, and insisted even when he tried to make her wait another hour.

'She'll be asleep now anyway,' Joe said, as they drove the winding sea road back towards Hyannis Port.

'Maybe. But I didn't want to stay out.' Kick tied her scarf more firmly under her chin. Joe's open-topped car was cold.

'Well, I'll drop you at the gate and you can walk the rest of the way. I want to get back to Miss Clarice of Boston. She wasn't pleased at all that you took me away.'

'No, I saw that,' Kick said. She didn't say it, but the girl had seemed silly and selfish. Joe wouldn't see that, not when she had such shiny brown hair and soft pale skin.

But when they reached the gate, the house that should have been in darkness was lit up. Lights were on in every window and shutters open so that the ones facing the ocean banged in the wind. 'Uh-oh,' Joe said. Instead of dropping her off, he drove to the back door.

Eunice must have been watching for them, so swiftly did she

appear on the porch. 'Rosie's gone,' she said, leaning over the wooden rail.

'When?' Joe asked.

'We don't know. It was only when Mother went in to say prayers with her and found Rosie wasn't in her bed that anyone noticed.' It was their mother's habit, after an argument with one of her children, to go in before her own bedtime – sometimes it meant waking them up – and pray together for reconciliation. 'Strategic,' Joe had once called it. 'No one is going to hold out when they've been dragged from sleep.' But Kick had always thought it beautiful, willingly kneeling beside Rose and asking forgiveness with her in the quiet dark of her bedroom.

'When was that?' Joe asked now.

'About forty minutes ago. We've looked all over the house and down as far as the beach.'

'You're looking in the wrong places,' Kick said swiftly. 'If Rosie's gone out, it's to town, not the beach.'

'We'll go into Hyannis,' Joe said. Already he was turning the car.

'Joseph.' Their mother's voice stopped him. 'Where are you and Kathleen going?' She had come out onto the porch and stood beside Eunice.

'Into town. To see if we can find Rosie.'

'I will come with you.'

Kick heard Joe breathe out, 'Darn,' audible to none but her. She knew what he meant. Without Rose they might have been able to find Rosie, get her home and maybe even cover up the exact circumstances of her finding. Now that was impossible. Whatever Rosie was doing, she would be caught.

The drive to town was silent. Kick kept her eyes on the sides of the road and then the sidewalks, hoping they might yet intercept Rosie. 'Turn onto Pleasant Street,' Rose said, when they reached the main street.

'But the drugstore's that way,' Joe said.

'Turn,' Rose repeated. Then, 'There.' She pointed to a bar that Kick had never been into. The yellow neon sign above the door said *Beer*. Or, rather, *Bee*. The *r* was broken. Joe parked and Kick nudged him to be quick. Seated in the middle between her mother and brother, there was no way she could get out before one of them did. She wanted it to be Joe first. Needed it to be Joe. But Rose swung her legs out of the low-slung car the minute Joe turned off the ignition, and Kick had to scramble after her. She reached the door of the bar at the same time as Rose and, by dint of pretending to open the door for her, managed to get inside first.

Shades of brown and yellow. Brown leather booths lining one side, with wooden stools along the bar on the other side, and dim yellow light from low-watt bulbs in tin shades. The place was mostly empty and it took only a minute to spot Rosie in the furthest booth. She was smoking a cigarette and laughing at something, head thrown back so her hair fell away from her face, which was lit up and glowing as Kick hadn't seen it for a long time. She was so beautiful. In front of her was a glass of beer, and opposite, a man in a brown check jacket, his back to Kick. As Kick watched, he reached forward and took Rosie's hand, the one holding the cigarette, and drew it towards him. Leaning down, he took a drag of Rosie's cigarette and exhaled into her face. The smoke curled, thick and possessive, towards her. Rosie smiled a flirtatious little smile. She lowered her eyelids. Where had she learned that? Kick wondered, half laughing.

'Rosie.' Kick still thought she could get there first; could wrap this up, fold it down and contain it.

Rosie looked up and saw her. 'Kick?' The small flirtatious smile grew broad and cheery, then dropped. Rosie's eyes flickered from her face, and Kick heard her mother.

'Rosemary. Your brother is in the car.' Had Joe really stayed behind the wheel? Kick wondered. What a coward he sometimes was. 'I'll thank you to take your things and come now.'

'But I don't want to.' Rosie opened her eyes very wide. 'I'm having fun. This is my friend. Say hi, Mike.'

Mike turned and waved. 'Hi.'

'Get into the car, Rosemary,' Rose said again. 'Go join your brother.'

Rosie looked at Kick, face pleading. 'I want to stay. Kick, you could stay with me and Mike.'

Mike nodded, affable. 'You could,' he agreed, moving over to make space.

Kick shook her head sharply, then inclined it towards the door, and the car. 'Rosie . . .'

'In the car, Rosemary. Now, please.' Rose had moved to stand beside Kick. Half a head shorter, twice Kick's size in polite ferocity.

'We were just about to have another drink,' Mike said. 'Me and Rosie. She's a nice girl. Where's the harm? She's twenty-three, old enough to be out. Tell you what,' he looked pleased, 'you tell me where you live and I'll have her home later.'

'My daughter may be twenty-three,' Rose placed the words carefully, 'but in some ways she is a child—'

'Doesn't look like no child to me,' Mike said, still affable.

'Mentally she is a child,' Rose said. Kick watched, helpless, as Rosie's face crumpled. All the knowing flirtation, the smiling invitation of moments ago, was gone. She looked, indeed, like a child. A sorrowing, lonely child. 'Which makes me wonder,'

Rose continued, 'why a grown man like you should want to be here in her company.'

It was Mike's turn to crumple. 'She don't seem like no child to me,' he said. But already doubt was there. 'I didn't know,' he continued, looking from Rose to Rosie. 'How was I supposed to know? She never said . . .' He shifted himself out of the booth but his path to the door was too full of Kick and Rose. He turned, awkward in the tight space, and went the other way, towards the back of the bar. What would he do there? Kick wondered. Hide until they were gone? Probably.

'Your things, Rosemary,' Rose said, turning away.

Squashed into the tiny bucket seats of Joe's car, Rosie's legs were jammed against the back of his seat. She turned them sideways for more space and leaned against Kick. 'You're wearing my cardigan,' Kick said. Not because she minded, only to take Rosie's mind off what had happened in the bar.

'It's nicer than mine.' Rosie snuggled further in towards Kick and put her head on her shoulder. Her hair smelt not very clean. Rosie wasn't so good about washing any more. That was another thing Mother complained about.

'You can keep it.'

'Can I really?' Rosie lifted her head and grinned. Already, she behaved as though the bar and Mike were forgotten. But they weren't, Kick knew. They were in there, along with the other things that had happened that summer. Times Rosie had been told no. Times she had disobeyed. Times she had run away. Never as bad as this. Never yet at night – by day to the drug-store or Dee's Café, bad, according to Rose, but not this bad. But those times had led to this time. Where would this lead?

When Rosie was in bed and asleep at last, Kick went

downstairs for a glass of water. Outside the night was clear and the stars were high, small and mean. In the kitchen she took a glass, filled it from the jug in the fridge. She turned to see her mother in the doorway. Neither of them had switched any lights on so it was only by the neatness of her silhouette against the lamplight from the hallway beyond that Kick knew her.

'I was just going to bed,' Kick said. She couldn't bear a conversation now, prayers even less.

'You must be tired,' Rose agreed. Then, as Kick passed her, 'Please do not feel that you are responsible for Rosemary, Kathleen. You aren't. I am.'

'But she seems so unhappy.'

'She is wayward, and that is making her unhappy.'

'I'm not sure it's that . . .' Kick tried to find more words, different words, to ask again for Rosie's freedom. To ask for kindness, tolerance. 'She's just Rosie,' she said. It was the best she could do.

'You are not to be concerned for Rosemary. Home is where she should be. This is where we will care for her. She will be all right in a little while, you'll see.'

'You'll look after her?'

'Of course we will. Whatever do you think?' There was an edge, again, to Rose's voice. 'You have to trust me on this, Kathleen,' she said, and Kick knew there was no more to be done.

Chapter Two

Brigid, London, England

Every morning was a reckoning. With damage. With loss. With what lay ahead. Brigid's walk from Belgrave Square – where she now lived at Number Five with her sister, Honor, and brother-in-law, Chips, because her parents' house had become the HQ of the War Refugee Committee – to St Thomas' Hospital took her past several ARP, air-raid precautions, shelters and at each she asked the same question, 'What news?'

'Quiet night,' was the response everywhere that day, from men and women whose gratitude was written in bright eyes and steady hands holding mugs of tea. For almost two months this had been the answer – 'quiet night' or 'fairly quiet night' – and because of that, these were no longer the men and women she remembered from the height of the Blitz. Then, exhaustion had been written grey and tight in every face. There had been mornings when Brigid had prayed that no spy was carrying tales back to Berlin of just how close the city was to collapse.

London would never surrender, they all knew that, but she had learned in the months of heavy bombing that it might yet sink beneath the impossibility of keeping going when every night was chaos and terror, and every day the hopeless process of trying to put things to rights. Sweeping up broken glass with battered brooms, piling fallen bricks neatly in stacks, she had stood close enough to strangers for them all to feel what no one would say: *How much more of this can we take?*

And then came a lull. Whole nights when the Luftwaffe didn't drone overhead and drop destruction on them. Yes, there were still bad nights, but they were no longer strung close together, like fat beads on a too-tight necklace. Now, the 'quiet' nights outnumbered the 'busy' ones. Even so they didn't trust the pocket of peace that had unfolded around them. Any night might be the end of it. The near ten months of bombardment had taken trust from them that two good months couldn't restore.

So, every morning Brigid asked everyone she met, 'What news?' Her question wasn't just to reassure herself of where the city stood in relation to the active proof of war – the tally of homes destroyed, buildings damaged, lives lost. It was also to prepare herself for what lay ahead at the hospital. St Thomas' had been bombed – six times by now – and whole wings were no longer in use, with wards moved down to the basement where it was gloomy even at midday. But around the damage, hospital life continued as usual, and Brigid needed to try to understand what kind of day she might expect.

A response of 'Busy night' from the ARP wardens would mean

beds already full of wounded – hurt by anything from burns and falling masonry to bicycle accidents in the treacle-dark of the blackouts – doctors who were under-slept and short-tempered, nurses harried and snappish.

'Quiet night' boded well, and meant she would have time to read the letter she carried in her pocket, handed to her by the butler, Andrews, on a silver tray earlier that morning. She walked slowly towards the back entrance of the hospital, breathing in the early-morning summer air, feeling the sun on her face. It would be the last she'd see of daylight for twelve hours.

Inside she changed her shoes and took off her jacket, putting her outdoor items in the locker with her name on it. She tied a clean apron round her waist and pinned her hair firmly back before putting on the white cap. Around her, girls she knew and half knew were doing the same while the night shift changed in reverse, buttoning cardigans and lacing on walking shoes.

'Morning, Brigid,' said a dark girl, with crossed front teeth, as she brushed her hair out from its pins.

'You must be glad to get off,' Brigid said, adding, 'Mary,' politely, once she had remembered the girl's name.

'You have no idea.' Mary sighed. 'Though I'm not going home to peace or quiet. Mum's back with the little ones . . .' Brigid vaguely knew that she had younger brothers and sisters who had been evacuated but had trickled back into London '. . . and they'll be that noisy, I may as well be up with them as trying to sleep. I bet you can hardly imagine the din they make.'

Mary knew that Brigid lived with her older sister, Honor, and brother-in-law, Chips Channon, 'to keep them company' while their eight-year-old son Paul was safely in America. She didn't know the house had ten bedrooms and seven reception rooms, many as lavish and stuffed with objects and paintings as a gallery, with quarters below stairs that were like the hold of a vast ship. She may have known that Brigid's last name was Guinness, but was certainly unaware that her father was an earl who thought mostly about new ways of dairy farming, nor that Chips was an MP who thought mostly about parties. She knew that Brigid's brother Arthur was with the Royal Artillery, because they talked sometimes about where he was stationed, but not that he was a viscount. She knew what was necessary and cosy – an address, a family duty, a brother in uniform – no more than that.

It was funny, Brigid thought, smoothing her apron, the illusion of intimacy between them all. They worked long hours together, chattering and gossiping about hospital dramas and their own lives – who was walking out with whom, who had got engaged, who hadn't. Mostly, they knew each other's home circumstances. But the wards were too busy, the breaks too short, perhaps the differences too great, to confide. She could have told anyone who thought to ask where Mary lived, about the little brothers and sisters, the dead father and the mother who worked in a canning factory. But she didn't know Mary's favourite colour, what songs she sang in her bath, what dreams she held for after the war.

She took out the letter she had carried without opening, and slit the envelope with the scissors she kept in her apron. She sat on the narrow bench under her locker and unfolded it. 'My dear Brigid . . .' *Fritzi.* She had known it would be him. By now, she recognised his handwriting, the way he formed the *B* and *g* of her name. That was why she had taken the letter with her, rather than read it at the breakfast table.

'Who writes to you so often from Hertfordshire?' Chips had asked idly, seeing the postmark.

'A school friend,' she had replied.

A school friend . . . Fritzi, Prince Friedrich of Prussia, had been the dearest wish of Chips's heart. So much so that he had first started hinting about a marriage five years ago, when Brigid was barely sixteen. At her coming-out ball, he had seated the prince beside her, and each time Brigid had looked up, there Chips had been, watching them, smiling and nodding like one of those toys that wobbles back and forth – positively sinister in his bland benignity, she had thought.

And so, of course, she had refused to speak to the prince, beyond the barest of politeness. And when Chips had engineered a week at his country estate, Kelvedon, that last summer before the war, with both of them, along with Kick Kennedy and her parents, Brigid had been furious and had started by haughtily ignoring Fritzi of Prussia. Except that a week together had shown her that, beneath his tediously polished manners, he had worries and fears as rough and uncut as her own. She had even felt sorry when he spoke of his father, still chasing the title his grandfather had given up, into the arms of Hitler.

But then war. And, with it, a recalibration of Fritzi's worth. First he had been arrested. 'Inevitable,' he had written, 'and I would scorn to return to Germany to avoid it.' That was the first letter he had sent to her in secret. 'May I continue to write to you?' he had begged. 'I do not know what will happen to me, but I should like to write, if I may?'

And Brigid had said yes, even though Chips was by then cautioning her to have nothing to do with Fritzi. 'We are exposed,' he had said nervously, almost looking over his shoulder as he spoke. 'It is known that we have been friendly – very friendly – with him.'

'*We?*' Brigid had asked, because who could have resisted. 'Surely you mean you.'

'All of us,' Chips insisted. 'And how could one not, such a dear boy? But it won't do. Not now.'

She had tried pleading with Chips to speak for him – 'He won't go back to Germany, even though he would be safer there. Maybe you could explain that and they would leave him alone.'

But Chips wouldn't. 'He is the King's godson,' he said. 'If that isn't enough, nothing I can say will make a difference.'

She had said yes to Fritzi, and nothing to Chips about the letters that came. After a spell in an internment camp on the Isle of Man he had been sent to Canada, to another internment camp. In both, he wrote to her proudly, he was elected camp leader. He had sounded prouder of that than of any of his titles. His letters had been full of the day-to-day of camp life – what they ate, the hours they spent logging and laying roads – and very few questions about hers. She knew he wrote carefully, conscious of other readers – every letter from the camps bore the oval stamp of the censor – but even so, there was a curiously impersonal quality to what he told her. She sometimes wondered if he even remembered her, or was writing just to feel that someone knew where he was and what he was doing. But, then, if she was truthful, did she really remember him?

When he came back to England, released somehow from the camps, he went straight to Hertfordshire, a place called Little Hadham, where he lived as simple George Mansfield, farmer. From there, he continued to write to her, details of crops, livestock, the tractor, animal feed. It made him more remote again, even more unknowable, so that when she wrote back, she never knew how much to tell him about Honor, Chips, her cousin Maureen who he had met that week at Kelvedon and who came and went from London so that she was still a constant in Brigid's life – Fritzi knew these people but George, perhaps, did not.

It was confusing.

But as those letters travelled back and forth, especially once he was settled back in England, they expanded in warmth and detail. Once away from the heavy scrutiny of the censor, he told her more of himself, and she reciprocated. Something grew between them. Kindness? Friendship? Whatever it was, it was more than could be just put away.

My dear Brigid . . . She leaned back.

But 'Better be quick,' Mary said, rubbing thick white cream into her chapped hands. The smell of lanolin made Brigid feel sick. 'Matron's on the warpath.'

Matron was always on the warpath. Brigid folded the letter, put it into her locker and filled her pail with scrubbing brush and cloth, carbolic soap and disinfectant. Her duties were cleaning – beds, floors, bathrooms, wounds – dressing injuries, taking temperatures, checking 'mood and morale'.

In the beginning there had been a sense of camaraderie, of 'all in it together' among the nurses, even when they were dry-eyed from lack of sleep after another night of bombs and the *akka-aka-ack* of anti-aircraft guns. But that was mostly gone now. Whatever giddy spirit had animated the first year of the war was buried under the rubble of falling buildings and behind sleepless nights in underground shelters. Now it was simply routine and duty.

'Morning,' she said cheerfully, as she moved from bed to bed. She straightened pillows, tidied lockers, pulled sheets taut and crisp. She picked up charts, scanned them, wrote in them, placed them back.

'What's it like out there?' The questions followed her. It was the same every morning, their eagerness to know what had happened to the city under cover of darkness.

'Quiet night,' she said, again and again, dispensing reassurance along with pills and glasses of water. She enjoyed the rigid order of the hospital, in contrast with the mess outside. Even the makeshift wards in the basement had order imposed upon them. Beds spaced at precise intervals. Identical pillows, identical blanket turns. The rooms were bleak but their organisation careful. She moved easily between them, allowing the rhythm and routine to take over and lull her. The days passed quickly, she thought, days that would once have been hard to fill – a lunch, a dress fitting, cocktails, all the hours in between with nothing much to do. Now the hours slipped by, like fields seen from a moving train. It was this, more than anything, she had sought when she began her training three years ago: Purpose. Intent. Days that ended with a sense of something done rather than a headache brought on by the chatter and laughter of parties.

She saved Will's ward for last. She hoped he would be awake. It was a gamble – go early in the day, certain he would be up, but she would have little time to spare him, or go later when her shift was almost done, but he might be tired?

His was more a half-ward. Only six beds in a space that had once been a place to keep spare bed frames, folded and stacked. These days, there were no spare beds. It was on the first floor and light came in through the windows. To her surprise, Brigid saw that it was a bright sunny day. The hours in the basement had made her think it must be dark.

Will's bed was the last in the room, over by the end wall. He was sitting up, reading. He smiled when she came in, then bent his head again towards his book. Once she'd checked the other men, taken their temperatures and noted the results, Brigid sat down in the chair beside him.

'How was your day?' He closed the book – one she had given him, *Martin Chuzzlewit* – and placed it on the locker beside the bed. He pushed himself up straighter and Brigid leaned over to pull the pillow behind his head into a better position. Not for the first time she wondered how he managed not to smell of hospital. The antiseptic and carbolic soap that lingered on everyone else seemed to find no purchase on him. He smelt of the warmth of sleep.

'Busy.' She pulled a face.

'Matron?' He smiled sympathetically.

'Matron,' she agreed. 'You?'

'As ever.'

'Has Dr Carr been?'

'He has.' Will shrugged. 'Nothing new to report.' Will was a puzzle to the doctors. He had been in the army, had been wounded in North Africa, and sent home after weeks in a makeshift hospital had shown that his leg would never mend enough for him to walk properly again. Back in England, he had quickly adapted to a limp and a walking stick, and taken a desk job at the Foreign Office. There he had been, he told her, 'perfectly happy'. Until a bombing raid caught him one night as he walked home. He had been trapped beneath a fallen wall for hours. When one of the rescue teams dug him out the next morning, he was as much dead as alive. Since then, most of his wounds had healed, except for the injuries to his damaged leg. Dr Carr's theory was that the leg, semi-paralysed, wasn't capable of healing itself so the gash had to be cleaned and dressed twice a day. Because of that, he had been there longer than anyone now, months in which Brigid had grown to depend on the time she spent with him, finding in his friendship something she missed from the rest of her life. It was, she thought, the *smallness* of their conversations: no grand schemes as there would be with Chips; no planning and preparing, in the way of Mama, nor Maureen's abrupt demands for entertainment. Not even the worries Honor brought to her, usually about her husband or her son. Just *How are you? How's your day?* Simple questions, with answers he listened to closely.

'May I?' She gestured towards the leg covered with the grey hospital blanket.

'Of course.'

She fetched clean warm water and iodine and gently peeled back the covers. The leg might be slow to heal, resistant to movement, but that didn't mean it didn't transmit pain. She had seen how Will's mouth set in a line when the gauze was removed. Every time, there was the yellow pus of infection. No matter how often they cleaned it, they couldn't get ahead of the disease that spread its sticky layer over the deep angry red of a wound the size of a powder compact.

Will sat quietly while she wiped and dabbed, then rebandaged. He never protested, never volunteered any information beyond what he was asked for – *Does that hurt? And that?* Rarely asked questions. Whatever ailed his body, there was something that ailed his mind, too. Brigid knew it, as clearly as if he had said so. She just didn't know what it was.

When she had finished and had disposed of the basin with its dirty water, they talked – quietly, so as not to disturb the other men – about the day's newspaper, which Will had read and Brigid hadn't. He made a gentle joke about the hospital food, but shook his head when Brigid asked eagerly, 'Can I bring you anything? A pot of apple jelly? Cook made some yesterday.'

'It would be too much like school,' he said. 'Hiding jars of jam in my locker, eating it with a spoon after lights out.'

'I tried to keep the newspaper for you,' he said then, 'but Mike-next-door wanted it.' He meant the man in the bed beside him. 'And then he was transferred.'

'Different ward or hospital?' Brigid asked automatically, looking at the empty bed beside Will's.

'Hospital, I believe. So I'll have a new neighbour.' Will had had many new neighbours. He was the only constant among beds that turned over 'faster than rooms at a cheap station hotel', he'd once joked, then apologised when he saw her blushing. 'The army,' he'd explained, 'makes a man's language crude.'

'More books?' she asked now.

'Not yet. *Chuzzlewit*'ll keep me going another few days.'

'Are you sleeping any better?'

'Not really.' He hated to say no outright, she had learned, perhaps because he saw how it disappointed her. 'But, thanks to your lightshade, I make do.' By which he meant that he was able to read most of the night, thanks to the Oriental screen Brigid had taken from the library at Belgrave Square. Made of wood and painted silk, it closed like a large hardback book, and folded out to a four-sided screen. It had been one of Chips's endless curios and objects – bought on a whim, admired, then forgotten. By balancing it on his locker, Will could shield light from the bedside lamp so it didn't disturb his neighbours.

'Is it very bad? Being so much awake?' she asked.

'Not at all. The hospital is always busy. People come and go through the night.' It was true. She sometimes did the night shift. 'And I have *Chuzzlewit* for company.'

'I thought someday I could get a chair and wheel you outside. The days are quite warm now.' Even as she spoke, she knew it was hopeless.

'Thank you. That's very kind. Maybe in a little while.' It almost sounded like yes but Brigid knew it was no. Will didn't like to go outside. She didn't know if it was because he hated not being able to walk anywhere, if he was in too much pain to wish to move, or something else. On a good day he might use crutches to get about the ward, but she couldn't persuade him to go further.

He never had visitors, never received or wrote letters. 'No one knows I'm here,' he said, when she asked if she could write to someone for him, adding, 'There's no one to know.'

Brigid began to blurt out, 'There must be someone,' but stopped herself. Before the war, she would have done so. Back then, she'd believed that everyone had someone, of course they did. But she had seen too many who didn't. Or no one they wanted to know where they were, anyway.

She had pieced together bits about Will's life. He was younger than her by a few months. There was a sister, older than Will and married, but mentioned only once and not again.

She sat beside him now, not speaking, and took out the things that had accumulated in her apron pockets. These she ordered, re-rolling two bandages and pinning them neatly, wiping clean the neck of a bottle of mercurochrome, then rubbing at the red stains it left on her fingers. Will picked up *Martin Chuzzlewit* and turned a few pages. After a while she stood up and said, 'See you tomorrow.'

'See you tomorrow,' he agreed, turning from his book to smile up at her.

Chapter Three

Sissy, Wicklow, Ireland

'You never said . . .' Theresa Molloy spoke resentfully, looking up at the house in front of them. Ballycorry lay in its usual slump, leaning forward as though it would escape from the wet hills behind it. Sissy couldn't blame it. She, too, longed to escape from those wet hills.

She had known Theresa would say that, or something like it. When they had turned in through the stone gateposts and trudged up the long potholed driveway, Theresa had gone silent. Her chatter about the mistresses at school and the cold of the recreation room had sustained them on the walk from the railway station but fell away to nothing before the stone and moss façade of Ballycorry.

She stared now at the six upper windows that frowned across the front, like a man with eyebrows nearly meeting in the middle, and the four long columns that held up the portico above the front door, and muttered, 'You could have said . . .'

She didn't see that the windows rattled in their rotten wooden sashes, that the columns were stained and weathered, so grimy that they were the same grey-brown as the mice that ran about the kitchens. Sissy thought of pointing out these defects to her, but realised there would be little point. Theresa was enjoying her resentment far too much.

'Let's go in,' Sissy said. 'Mother will be wondering where we are.' Mother wouldn't be wondering any such thing, but she wanted to get Theresa inside, where she couldn't see the full size of the house.

But inside was the same. It wasn't the bulging wallpaper or spreading damp that Theresa noticed, only the few paintings that hadn't been sold – stern ancestors who looked out of gilt frames – and the size of the drawing room where Sissy took her to meet Mother.

Mother was lying on a sofa with a shawl over her legs and a copy of an animal-feed paper in her hands. She smiled vaguely and said, 'How sweet,' giving Theresa a limp hand to shake. Theresa took it silently, staring, and Sissy knew that at school Theresa would tell everyone that Sissy lived in a mansion and her mother was as beautiful as someone in a storybook. There was no point in trying to tell her about Mother. How her beauty was a thing to be hoarded, pennies against a rainy day, and used only where there was advantage to be got from it. Theresa had been given a glimpse of it, because new people always were, but Sissy had seen the quick summing-up in Mother's eyes and knew that Theresa, should she call again, would get no more.

Any more than the damp and rot, Theresa couldn't see the coldness of the look Mother turned on Sissy, the silent enquiry

– *Who is this?* – even though Sissy had asked permission to bring 'a friend' home for tea, and reminded Mother when she set off for the station to meet Theresa.

Not that Sissy had any friends. It was just how she phrased it. It was what the other girls at school called each other. None of them called Sissy a friend but she had hoped Theresa's visit would help with that. Now that she was here, it seemed unlikely.

'The girl will bring you tea in the nursery,' Mother said, to get rid of them. *The girl* was how she referred to the maid, who changed so often – the girls from the village disliked working at Ballycorry, or having much to do with the Maddingtons – that Mother had long since stopped learning the new names.

Tea was a poor affair. Although she was sixteen, Sissy usually had hers in the kitchen – she had long since found that the maids had much better cake than the wan slices of sponge sent to the drawing room, and the new girl, Sheila, resented bringing the tray upstairs to the nursery. Now, the tea was lukewarm so that the milk sat greasily on top of it, and there was only bread and butter to go with it. When she asked, timidly, for cake, Sheila slammed the cups down and said, 'There's a war on, or didn't you know?'

'But not here,' Sissy dared. 'Only an Emergency.'

'My father says it might as well be war,' Theresa said importantly. 'He's a solicitor.' She didn't add anything else. She didn't need to. 'What does your father do?' she asked then.

Sissy blushed. What a question. It was the kind of thing Mother had warned her about when she'd started at that school ten months ago. 'I do hope you aren't going to become one of those people who talks about "summer holidays" and asks what people's fathers *do*.' She had placed the word like someone putting a winning card on a table. Then, to Sissy's father, 'I don't see why she has to go at all. There's plenty for her to do here.'

Briefly Sissy had wondered what on earth her mother could mean. There was nothing at all to do, even less now that most of the horses had been given away or sold, now that her brother Toby, two years younger, had been sent to school in England, and now that Sissy was deemed too old to ramble about the countryside alone as she used to.

In any case, her father had simply sighed and said, 'You know why. We've talked about it. She'll have to earn her living one of these days and she'll need an education.' Then he'd changed the conversation quickly. Everyone knew that needing to earn a living was because Father had turned out to be not very good at business, as well as unlucky. He had made the wrong investments, bought the wrong horses, or the horses went lame. Even the chickens died so that the poultry farm he started ended in the sickly smell of decay and a mess of limp, feathery corpses.

'Well, there's the farm . . .' Sissy said now, in answer to Theresa's question. Really, it was more a few empty sheds and barns but she had to say something.

'Oh. A farmer.' Theresa looked relieved. Sissy suspected that this information – *a farmer* – balanced out the house and its surroundings, evened the score as it were, putting Theresa and her solicitor father ahead.

After that, Theresa grew bolder. She compared the kinds of things they had for tea in the red-brick house by the green where she lived with the poor spread in front of them. When they had finished and went to walk about outside, she was alert to the dustiness of the motor-car in the garage. It had been so long since there was any petrol for it that it had become woven about by spiders. 'You should keep it under tarpaulin,' she said. 'Father gets an extra petrol allowance.'

Sissy quickly ran out of things to show her so she took her

to Mother's dressing room and let her look at the clothes. Mother's evening dresses and coats. Theresa exclaimed at how 'sweet' everything was, and tried on some of Mother's hats. Sissy watched her with a knot of fear in her stomach. Each time Theresa finished with something, Sissy put it back as exactly as she could. But she knew she would make a mistake. Impossible not to.

'Come downstairs and tell me more about your brother,' she begged at last. Theresa was now trying on Mother's amber brooch, pinning it this way and that on a silk shawl. Outside, the July afternoon had started to lose definition, blurring at the edges. Soon it would be time for Theresa's train.

Sissy had heard her talk about her brother before. He was training to be a solicitor, and would one day 'take over the family firm'.

'He's engaged to be married,' Theresa said, so swiftly that Sissy blushed for both of them. But she was still content to walk downstairs, telling of the difficult exams this brother must do, how he planned to go to London for a time.

London, Sissy thought wistfully. Imagine being able to swap this endless round of nothing for a place full of people. They sat on the front steps in the evening sun, the stone cold under them, and Theresa droned on about her brother. Sissy, arms folded around her bent knees, looked around at gardens and fields and hills that were as familiar as her own palms, and as dull to her. She had seen them in every guise – the fresh green of spring, the brown burn of summer, the greys of autumn and blue-white of winter frost, vanishing and reappearing through mist and rain. There was nothing they could do or show or offer her that she wanted to know or see.

The idea that she would never see anything else, never know

any roll of time beyond the rhythm of the seasons as they played out on this canvas of grass and gorse, appalled her. 'We'd better start for your train,' she said. She needed to stand, to move, to walk briskly away from the thought that lay on her: *It'll only ever be this. Never anywhere but here.*

Suddenly, for the first time, she was jealous of Theresa and her talk of the horse show, the weeks in Galway, a regatta her brother was to sail in. People complained that the Emergency had made life duller, but it hadn't changed anything at Ballycorry.

Sissy walked home the long way from the station. She hoped the house would be busy with its own affairs – washing up dinner, banking fires against the summer-evening chill – by the time she got in, and that she could slip upstairs to her bed. But her timing was off. Mother had finished dinner but had not yet drunk enough of the sherry she liked while she was playing her gramophone and thinking about the dances of her youth.

'You've been at my things,' she said, when Sissy went into the drawing room – ordered there by Sheila.

'It wasn't me, it was Theresa,' Sissy blurted out.

She knew immediately it was a mistake. Mother's face twisted in fury. 'You let that common little chit dip her paws into my things?'

Sissy said nothing.

'Come here.'

Sissy walked forward, moving her body obediently, leaving as much of herself behind as she could. The bit of her she detached stayed by the door, watching, as Mother, still sitting, reached around and took a window pole from the corner behind the sofa. 'Turn,' she said. Sissy did so. Mother hit her three times, drawing her arm far back each time so that the slender pole landed with crisp force. Watching-Sissy admired the elegance of her movements even as she saw herself flinch.

Afterwards, she walked down to the stables to look for Tom, as she had ever since the evening he had found her there, crying, after Mother had hit her with the poker. It wasn't the hitting that had made Sissy cry, just that the poker had been hot so she was burned as well.

Tom had put something on the burn that he used for the horses when the shafts of the carriage rubbed sore spots on their backs. It was an ointment he made himself. He wasn't much older than Sissy, and had been so slow to talk that people had thought him stupid. But he wasn't, Sissy had learned. He was just quiet.

She wasn't crying this time, and she said nothing about the window pole, but Tom seemed to know why she was there and put a soft blanket over the straw bale for her to sit on, just as though he knew how the backs of her legs stung.

Part Two

1943

Chapter Four

Kick, New York Docks, USA, June

Only her father came to see her off, and after a while Kick wished he hadn't. The activity around *Queen Mary* was so urgent, so unlike their first trip on that great ship, that it made her painfully aware of everything that had happened since that March, five years ago. How blithely then they had set sail, the Kennedy family, for an England that was unknown, scarce imagined, but friendly. Or so she had believed. And, indeed, so she had found it.

She thought, but only briefly – because here was too much clamour – of the year they had spent in London as family of the American ambassador. The people she had met, the friends she had made. She thought of Brigid Guinness, of Deborah Mitford. Of Billy. She mustn't think of Billy, she told herself. Not yet. When she had heard of his engagement to Sally Norton, she had tried to take her hopes and pack them tightly away. She'd even believed she'd succeeded, until the news that he had broken the engagement showed her she had put nothing away: she still thought of him with a swoop of her heart that was part elation, part alarm.

'You sure you want to do this?' her father said. His grey-blue eyes travelled the dock, sizing up the ship drawn alongside, the cranes that scooped and dropped, the vans that trundled past, and everywhere the sound of marching feet, men in step, who arrived and advanced up the gangplank in a khaki wave. So many that they filled every deck and corner of the ship, like the gulls that clustered, thousands to a rock, off the shore of Hyannis Port.

'You know you don't have to,' he continued. 'You could come right back to Washington and start again with the *Washington Times-Herald*. Frank Waldrop would take you back as his secretary in the morning. Why, I could ring him right now.'

'I know you could, and I know he would,' Kick said, 'but I guess that's part of why I can't.' She squeezed his arm. 'And you know exactly what I mean.'

'I do,' he agreed. 'And I like you the better for it, but don't tell your mother I said that or she'll say I didn't try hard enough to keep you.'

'You tried,' Kick said.

'I did. I just didn't try as hard as you did. All that not asking, why, I could hear you as loudly as if you'd shouted the words.' He grinned at her. 'I like your spirit, kid,' he said. 'You know how many travelled on this ship when we went over first?'

'How many?'

'Two thousand people.'

'And seven of them were Kennedys.' She smiled, the memory fond.

'You know how many are going aboard now? Eight thousand. Nearly all soldiers.'

'And just one Kennedy,' Kick said, a little sadly. She thought again of that first trip. Of walking the deck with Eunice. Of Teddy and Bobby, the Little Boys, as they were still known, even though they were now eleven and almost eighteen. Mostly she thought of Rosemary, of how beautiful she had been then, her skin made luminous by the wind and spray of salt water. Her excitement at the enclosed world of the ship where she could go about like any of them because there was nowhere for her to 'wander off' to. And because their mother, Rose, wasn't on the ship with them to stop her.

She shook her head a little. She wouldn't think of Rosie. Not now. 'Eight thousand,' she repeated instead. 'So many men.'

'A drop,' her father said. 'A tiny drop in a very great ocean.'

She knew he still opposed war, although he no longer said so aloud. Not since the attack on Pearl Harbor a year-and-a-half ago that had brought millions of Americans rushing to the defence of their country, her brothers among them. Now he was quiet where he had been loud. Even, Kick knew, he had tried to contort what he had said, to repurpose it so that the President might find something he needed in her father's understanding of the war that still gathered pace in America although it was already four years old for Kick's English friends.

But the President was resolute that he needed nothing from Joe Kennedy. That, Kick knew, stung her father greatly, and he had begun to talk all the more of what her brothers – Joe Junior and Jack – would do, even of what she would do. That was when he had agreed that, yes, she might join the Red Cross, might even go back to England. He said it was her persistence, the unwavering quality of her determination, but that was only half the reason. Half at best. Two sons in the armed forces, a daughter in uniform too – these things played well for Joe Kennedy. 'You three will be the ones to write the story of the next generation,' he had said. He spoke fondly, but also so that it wasn't something you could ask questions about. And Kick hated that he specified 'you three'. *What about Rosie?* she had tried to ask. *What story will Rosie write?* It had been useless, as she had known it would be.

'You can leave me here, Pa,' she said. 'I see some of the other Donut Dollies.' A group of girls in the drab blue-grey of the Red Cross stood at the bottom of a narrow walkway. Seven or eight of them, chattering and laughing. They looked older than Kick, more at ease. Perhaps they had a better idea of what they were being sent to do. Honestly, beyond knowing she was to make, fry and serve doughnuts to GIs, as well as provide the comfort of a familiar accent and some wholesome entertainment, she had very little idea.

'I wish you wouldn't call yourself that,' he said.

'It's what everyone calls us,' Kick said. '*Be healthy, physically hardy, sociable and attractive,*' she quoted from the manual.

'You are representing the United States on the world stage,' her father said stiffly.

'By constantly smiling, being always full of jolly talk. Oh, and not wearing too much make-up,' Kick said, with a laugh. 'Or earrings. Which reminds me.' She reached to remove the diamond clips she wore. 'I'd better keep these hidden . . . I wish Mother might have come to see me off,' she said, as she stowed the earrings in a pocket. But Rose would have hated the frantic pace of the dock, the loading and crowding. Kick had the rosary beads Rose had given her, blessed by the new Pope Pius XII, formerly their 'very own' Cardinal Pacelli, as Eunice called him.

Now that departure was so close, she missed her mother's hands, her voice. Suddenly, childishly, she wanted to ask, *Do you think I'm doing the right thing?* even though she had long ago decided that Rose must never be asked that. In case she answered no.

'Your mother would have come if she could,' Pa said.

'I know,' Kick assured him. 'Pa . . .' she began. She wanted to talk about Rosie.

But he interrupted her swiftly. 'London won't be what you expect,' he warned. 'No matter what you think you know.'

It was so hard to imagine London as Brigid and Debo had described it, almost casually: the bombs that rained down. The nights split open by fire and the *waah-waah* drone of the air-raid sirens. It wasn't that they didn't tell the full horror in their letters, only that they were so determined to be cheerful, to insist that the bombing was no big deal. And that made it hard to imagine as more than pantomime fear, the villain at the vaudeville show where everyone shouted, 'Look behind you,' and no one was actually scared. But surely a war was more than that?

That was why these last years of trying, failing, to get back had been so hard. It wasn't just Billy. It was all of it, a place she knew was rightfully hers, closed to her. Glimpses snatched through letters and newspapers. Scraps and crumbs. Brigid, bless her, was a faithful letter writer, diligent but unimaginative, Debo the exact opposite. Unreliable, erratic, but her letters were full of life and snippets of vivid story when they did arrive. So much so that there had been a time when Kick had been on the verge of asking her to stop, saying it was no good, she couldn't see how she would ever return, and that to keep hearing news of one's friends when one had no hope of seeing them was too much.

Billy had written too, often, continuing in his letters all the conversations they had had, so that even when she knew he was engaged to Sally, Kick had felt as though he were part of her. And when she knew he had broken it off, she had understood she had to get back. Fast.

'Dollie! Over here, with us!' One of the girls in grey-blue was waving and snapping her fingers at Kick. She wore the tailored trousers with her uniform jacket, whereas Kick wore the skirt. 'Over here, Dollie,' she called again, laughing into the early-evening air.

'I'd better go, Pa,' Kick said. He looked relieved. A quick goodbye would be far more his thing.

'Goodbye, kid,' he said, pulling her forwards into a hug that said so many of the things she knew he couldn't. Her eyes prickled. 'I'm proud of you.'

'Pa . . .' she muttered into the crush of him, into the warm smell of his cologne.

'No tears,' he said sharply, standing back and away.

'There'll be no crying in this house,' she recited dutifully. It was what they all said. It was what they had all been told, from the time they were babies. *No crying.* Sometimes, Kick wondered if she was even able to cry.

The first time she had seen Rosie in the dreadful room that was silent in all the wrong ways – silent of Rosie's chatter and laughter even though her sister sat right there, wedged with cushions on each side to keep her upright because she couldn't sit straight without them – Kick, dry-eyed and shaking, had wondered whether she would finally cry. She had looked at her hands, trembling violently, and wondered what it might be like to feel hot tears fall. Would they dissolve the cold horror she felt in watching Rosie try to mouth words? Loosen the binding on this thing she couldn't unpick or properly look at? But there was, she had discovered, no way to find out. Because the tears simply would not come. Too many years of denying them meant they had dried up.

'That's it.' Her father looked relieved. 'Chin up.'

'Pa,' she tried again, 'can I ask . . .' Already she saw his mouth drawing into a thin line. But she rushed on. 'Rosie—'

His hand rose sharp, convulsive, in the air. 'No, Kick. Rosemary is your mother's concern. I don't want you burdened with that. You think about your Red Cross duties, and your brother, Joe, who will soon be posted to England.'

'He'll get doughnuts, cigarettes and talk of home, just like any GI,' Kick promised. There was nothing else to say.

Why had she tried to ask about Rosie? she thought, as she hoisted her knapsack high on her shoulder. None of them asked about her. None of them talked about her. She winced and her father looked at her.

'Heavy?' he asked. Kick shook her head. The knapsack was heavy, even though her clothes were in a trunk in the hold, but it wasn't that. Somewhere deep inside her there was a sin so terrible that she couldn't even look at it. It was the evil thought that Rosie would be better off dead rather than the silent, drooling creature she had become.

The wishing-away of life was unholy, the most unholy of all things, and every time the idea flitted across Kick's mind, well, she sinned so terribly that she felt it must show on her face when her mother looked at her. She couldn't even confess it because to confess it would be to admit it. To put words on it.

'Not heavy,' she said, forcing a smile.

'That's my girl.' Her father squeezed her hand and walked swiftly away, swallowed in the crowds of soldiers.

Chapter Five

Kick

'I'm Edie and we're to be eight to a cabin,' the girl who had called to Kick said cheerfully, as they pushed their way along a deck so crowded it was like being at a county fair. Except that at a fair it would all be different – colours competing and clashing, each stall clamouring for attention. Here, it was the sameness of everything that struck Kick. The same uniforms, overcoats, kitbags, almost the same faces, repeated again and again as though they had been turned out of the same mould.

In her knapsack she carried a tin helmet, a first-aid kit, a gas mask and a water flask, identical in every way to the contents of Edie's and those of all the other Dollies.

'Be different,' she remembered her brother Joe saying to her. 'Be daring.' Kick had been about fifteen at the time, lamenting that she wasn't beautiful, like Rosie. 'Doesn't matter,' Joe had said kindly. 'The beautiful ones aren't always the ones men are mad about. Be yourself, kid. Your real self. It'll be plenty.'

What price different now? she thought, eyes flicking past endless rows of khaki.

'Eight,' she repeated, remembering the stateroom she, Rosie and Eunice had shared on their last trip.

'We're lucky to have a cabin,' Edie continued. 'Most of the men have to sleep in the hallways or on deck.' Edie was from Virginia and had never left America before. 'It was either stay and get married, or this,' she confided to Kick as they dragged their knapsacks along a crowded gangway. No one, Kick noticed, offered to help. The rules must be different in wartime. Or maybe it was the uniform, she thought, setting them apart, conferring competence and a kind of camouflage upon them. It was a relief, she decided.

'So why not get married?' she asked.

'He didn't ask me,' Edie said. 'He joined up, then came by the house to tell me, and I was so sure he'd ask then, but he didn't.' She laughed, a big deep laugh. 'Did I feel a fool! Almost as much as I felt relieved.'

'Would you have said yes?'

'No way. I would have pretended to think, and said how awfully flattered I was, but I would have said no. Especially seeing as I already knew about the Dollies. I mean, did you ever?' She stopped, putting her knapsack down, and brushed a few strands of hair that had escaped from under her boxy little hat. Kick saw she had a snub nose and blue eyes with dark lashes. She gestured at the chaos around them. 'Can you believe all this? I never thought I'd get to Europe. I never thought I'd get much beyond Richmond. And now . . . Well, here I am.' Her blue eyes opened wide. 'And if I still wanted a husband, there's plenty to choose from here.' She looked around at the men trudging everywhere, filing past them like water dividing. 'What about you?'

'What about me?' Kick asked. She was wary of saying she had been on this ship before . . . or been to England before . . . or, indeed, very much about herself. The last few years had taught her that in the wider world, being a Kennedy was a more mixed-up thing than she had imagined.

'What about you and marrying?' Edie asked. 'Is there Someone?'

'There might be,' Kick said. It was as much as she could say. After all, she hadn't told Billy she was coming. And was he really *Someone* when there was nothing between them that couldn't wear the label of friendship? No engagement, only endless circular conversations about why there couldn't be an engagement; Kick's mortifying sense that to be Catholic in the eyes of his family was to be somehow grotesque, not so much a religious matter as a matter of taste and decency. Why did they make her feel like that, she wondered, when no one else ever had?

'*Might be* . . .' Edie echoed. 'I see . . . Where is he?'

'With his regiment, in England. Waiting to be sent back to the front. More than that, I'm not allowed to know.'

'Of course not,' Edie said. '*Loose lips sink ships,*' she parroted.

'*Keep it under your hat,*' Kick responded. '*Free speech doesn't mean careless talk.*' The posters were everywhere, at once jolly and threatening. It was the way everything was now, since Pearl Harbor, she thought.

'This is us,' Edie said. 'Let's take the bottom bunk and share. That way we won't have to climb up over everyone at night.'

'OK,' said Kick. Not that there was space to climb anywhere, she thought. Two sets of bunk beds either side of a tiny table, everything fixed tight to the walls. A single mushroom-shaped lamp sat on the table between the beds and cast a yellowish glow. It was needed. There was a porthole – round and fishy-eyed – but the thick glass meant little outside light made it in. It was a beige-and-cream cupboard that must somehow contain eight girls.

'We won't be doing much sleeping anyway,' Edie said. 'They want us to start right now, talking and being friendly. They'll fix us up with cigarettes and gum.' Then, 'Was that your pop at the docks with you?'

'It was.'

'What does he do? Mine's a doctor.' Kick thought about what she might say. *He used to be ambassador and wanted to be President, but now he cools his heels and waits for Roosevelt to give him a friendly look.* Luckily Edie didn't wait for an answer. 'Have you anyone you know in England? Some of the girls do. One has an aunt who went in the last war, married an Englishman and never came back.'

'I do know a few,' Kick admitted. 'One friend knows I'm coming, but not when.' That was Brigid. She hadn't told any of the others. She was too afraid word would get out, and of what the newspapers would say. Not about her, but about her father.

'Well,' Edie said wisely, 'it's easy to make friends when there's a war on.'

Other girls arrived, crowding into the stateroom, hoisting themselves onto the higher bunks, chattering, laughing and smoking, their legs swinging into the pocket of empty space between the bunks.

They competed as to who could be the most careless, the most worldly, the least homesick and Kick understood how apprehensive they really were. They were like tough babies, she thought, determined to talk their way to comfort.

She took out her writing pad and settled herself against the headboard of the bunk. She started a letter to her mother: 'You wouldn't recognise this boat,' she wrote. 'Already we are hours later than the scheduled departure time and still the men pour up the gangplanks, thousands of them. They unroll their bedding and simply lie down in any place they can stretch out.'

Finally, when the ship was packed so tightly it felt as though not a single person more would fit, the engines rumbled to life and the loud, mournful blast of the horn signalled departure. Almost as soon as the lights of New York had faded behind them, the portholes were covered with blackout cloth and warnings were issued about lighting cigarettes on deck. The girls were told to stay in their cabins till morning: so dark was the ship that there was a real danger of tripping and falling.

'Not to mention the thousands of men out there,' muttered a girl with blonde curls. Kick lay in her bunk, trying to find spaces that didn't already have Edie in them. Around her, the girls talked and smoked, telling stories of home, of friends, family, even pets they had left behind: 'Just the cutest dog, she does tricks for fun, even without treats . . .' Talking into the darkness, trying to fill it with familiarity, comfort, making friends quickly, urgently, even though none of them knew where they would be posted once they arrived in England. Kick hoped for London – of course she did – but they all did, she realised, listening to the talk. Mostly because it was the only place they'd heard of.

'If I don't get London, I'm turning right round and coming home,' Edie declared. 'I want to be where the action is.'

'The front?' suggested a small girl with sharp white teeth, sarcastically.

'You know what I mean,' Edie said. 'The fun action.'

'Well, you'd better hope your luck's in,' the girl with sharp teeth said, 'because it's a lottery.'

But it wasn't, Kick knew. Or not for everyone.

'I suppose you'll be hoping to be in London,' her father had said, when Kick's training was complete and the date for departure set.

'I will,' Kick had replied. 'I am. I wish only there was some way to be sure . . .'

'There's no way to be *sure*,' her father had said, 'but there are ways to make it *likely*.'

Listening to Edie now, she felt a pang, knowing that to be a Kennedy was always to be dealt a little more than others. A lot more, if she was honest. That even lotteries inclined their way; magnets drawn, willing or not, to the Kennedy metal.

She fell asleep trying to puzzle out something her brother Joe had once said: 'Would you rather things were unfair and in your favour, or completely fair, which mostly means not?'

She hadn't found an answer at the time. And couldn't land on one now.

The next morning they queued for an hour with their mess kits for breakfast, which they ate standing and looking at the endless ocean. Edie had made a rule: 'No eating in the cabin, girls,' she declared, as they dressed that morning. 'It's bad enough that we're in here like sardines. Better if it doesn't start to smell like sardines too!'

Soon, Kick felt sick. Was it the crowding, the noise, the sight of men everywhere she looked – playing cards, rolling dice, reading? Their seemingly endless patience was a reproach to her restlessness.

'We're zigzagging,' Edie said. 'It's to avoid U-boats. We change direction constantly to make sure they can't torpedo us.'

Despite the lurch that 'U-boat' and 'torpedo' gave her, Kick laughed. No wonder she was sick, she thought. To combat the nausea, she ate cookies, crackers and chocolate bars, then, worried she would get fat, paced the bit of deck set aside for walking. 'It's about forty feet,' she told Edie, measuring it in comparison with the sailboats at Hyannis Port, 'so if I walk it one hundred and thirty-two times, I'll be getting a mile. And with this wind blowing, it's harder.' She pushed her hair out of her face, plucking strands from her mouth where the brisk wind blew it straight back. The ends were damp and tasted of salt.

'You're crazy, Kick,' Edie said.

After four days, the first promise of land was the seagulls – one and two, then many – that came to sit on the rails and rigging, cheered by the soldiers. After that, straining her eyes through the mist and drizzle, every cloud looked like land. And each time was a disappointment, until Kick wondered if they would continue to churn through thin grey water and thick grey sky for ever.

'There she is,' the man next to her said suddenly, nudging her arm with his. 'Glasgow.'

'What's Glasgow?' asked Edie, on Kick's other side.

'Glasgow is Scotland,' the man said.

'Well, I do think they might have told us,' Edie complained.

'There are trains to London,' Kick reassured her. 'It doesn't take long. You'll see. England is not so very big.' And, with a lurch of excitement, she realised it really wasn't. If Billy was in London, or at Chatsworth in Derbyshire, or indeed anywhere in England, she was close to him already.

All around her, men crowded the rails, eager for a first glimpse of this new world. They talked and laughed, animated by the end of the long voyage – four days of too much company, too little space. Overhead, four planes, dinky as toys, flew out from land, swooping over the ship in greeting, so low that Kick could feel the rough wind they stirred.

'Spitfires,' said the man beside her, almost reverentially.

As they steamed slowly into harbour, Kick heard the sounds of a marching band sending up a gay rendition of 'The Minstrel Boy'. She hummed along. Others did too, ready to be welcomed with arms wide open. But, abruptly, as they drew closer, silence fell. A silence that was like an endpoint.

All along the harbour, on either side, a tale was written in rubble. Hefty buildings listed crazily sideways, whole sections scattered to the ground in piles of brickwork so that what remained standing all but blew in the wind, so frail did it seem. Houses without roofs, or with roofs so pitted they looked on the point of collapse; whole sections of street littered with broken masonry, sometimes pushed to one side neatly, more often strewn about haphazardly. On one corner, she saw children playing on the heaps, chasing one another over them. One had a tattered flag made from a jersey or shirt – she couldn't quite see – that he had stuck jauntily into a chimney pot that sat flush with the sidewalk. Everything they saw was untidy, dirty and spoiled.

They had been told of war, had read of bombings and knew to say 'The Blitz' with confidence. But nothing, Kick thought, had prepared them for the reality. Certainly not her friends' letters, full of jokes about rationing, or neat litanies of shifts worked. Kick thought of Hyannis as it would be now: the warm light of July tossed about by sparkling waves, pavements hot under her sandalled feet, strawberry ice cream at the drugstore.

Across the mouth of the river she caught the smell of something scorched, then soaked; burned metal, wet wood. The man beside her shifted uneasily. Was this really what she had fought so hard to get to? Was seeing Billy again worth all the rest?

The child with the ragged homemade flag caught it up and waved it vigorously in the direction of the ship. The material – it was indeed a jersey – fluttered in the breeze. Kick raised her arm and waved back, although she doubted the child could see her. Back in Washington, it would soon be time for Frank's second coffee, to be delivered on a saucer with two biscuits by his new assistant at the newspaper office. The thought cheered her.

Yes, she decided. This, too, was what she had come for. Because, after all, just as she had said to Pa, if there was a war on and one's friends were fighting, wouldn't you want to fight with them, any little way you could? Ahead of them, the child with the flag tripped and fell.

'I do think they might have told us,' Edie said again. But she said it quietly.

Chapter Six

Brigid, London, England

The walk from Belgrave Square to her cousin Maureen's house at Number Four Hans Crescent took Brigid past the new Red Cross officers' club. A group of American GIs stood outside Number One, smoking. They saluted her politely as she went by. From inside, she could hear a gramophone playing 'Wishing (Will Make It So)'. The song reminded her of Kick – of the last time she had seen her, that September day four years ago, just after war had been declared. They had played the same record, lying across Kick's bed, and talked of all the things war must mean. Had they been right about any of it? And what would Kick be like now? Her last letter had arrived more than a month ago, with the jubilant announcement, *I am fully trained and will soon be dispatched. I may even be in England by the fall. You must keep Billy from Sally until I get there!* As if the memory of Kick hadn't already done that, she had thought.

But she hoped Kick wasn't coming just for Billy. Her friend never had fully understood the depth of resistance to the two of them. 'There has to be a way around it,' she had said, talking of 'dispensations' and 'permissions', of the willingness of her Church to 'accommodate', never quite seeing that it wasn't religion – not really, or not only. That it was *everything*: everything Billy was, his family were. Everything the Kennedys were. So she hoped it was for many reasons that her friend was returning, not just one.

The record ended and Brigid heard a burst of loud laughter before someone changed it for a jazzier tune. She quickened her step in time, thinking how different things had seemed since the Americans had joined the war. Cheery, almost hopeful. It was hard, now, to remember how desperate it had been. The thunderous nightly annihilation of the city that meant every morning had brought a patchy new skyline, landmarks that had stood forever, missing or fatally altered, their misshapen silhouettes spreading unease.

In contrast with the gay activity around the officers' club, Number Four, Maureen's house, looked gloomy indeed. The windows were shuttered and the smart red bricks seemed to breathe out something dispirited. Maureen had been in Ireland, at Clandeboye, her husband Duff's estate in County Down, for more than a month now.

Brigid thumped the brass knocker, hard. When no one answered, she thumped again. The door opened, not wide, but enough to see the child, almost a young woman now, standing there. Her cousin Caroline. Or, if one was strict, Maureen's daughter and therefore cousin-once-removed.

'Caroline, darling. May I come in?'

'There's no one here,' Caroline said. 'Only me.'

'And it's you I've come to see. It's your birthday, isn't it?'

The girl's face lit up. 'It is. How did you know?'

'It's July the sixteenth,' Brigid said patiently. 'The same day every year. You do know that's how birthdays work, don't you?' she teased.

'Well, no one else seems to remember much,' Caroline said. She was still half hidden behind the front door. 'Perdita telephoned, but the line was terrible. She said she would put Mummie on, but then the call dropped. Or perhaps someone rang off.'

Her head drooped, dirty blonde hair hanging at either side of her face. She looked, Brigid thought, thoroughly neglected. Dishevelled, wan, not very clean. She was twelve, but could have been ten.

'Well, Perdita is a dear sister. And I have something for you, so let me in, there's a good girl.'

Caroline stepped back and Brigid walked into the hallway, which was large and badly lit. A marble staircase in swirls of brown rose from it and curved to the upper reaches of the house. Somewhere a door thumped sullenly.

'Shall we sit?' she said.

'There are holland covers on everything, but I suppose . . .' Caroline said. She led Brigid into the smallest of the rooms facing the front of the house, a little study where Maureen sometimes wrote letters in the mornings. Unbleached linen sheets had been draped over the furniture. Brigid dragged at the end of one, exposing enough sofa for her and Caroline to sit side by side.

'Here.' She took the parcel she had brought from her bag and handed it to the girl. Caroline carefully undid the string and unwrapped the brown paper. There was no fancy paper, as they used to call it, anymore.

'*Lassie Come Home*,' Caroline read the title of the hardback book. 'You are kind,' she said. 'Thank you.' She clutched it to her chest, arms wrapped tightly around it, as though Brigid might try to take it back and she would have to fight for it. There was silence then, and Brigid remembered how very hard it was for Caroline to talk to any of them. 'Sits and simply stares at one, with those great eyes,' Maureen had said of her. 'No wonder the local families say she's a changeling. Not that Duff can see it,' she had added petulantly. 'I swear he likes her better than anyone else.'

'When did you get back from school?' Brigid asked. Caroline had spent much of the year in Essex at a boarding school for girls.

'Yesterday,' Caroline said. 'I'm supposed to travel on to Clandeboye, but no one has left any money so I can't take the boat train.'

'Oh, darling, did you really spend the night here all alone? No servants?'

'Not now.'

'Not even your father?'

'He isn't in London yet. Still at Clandeboye. But it wasn't so bad. Cosier – by far! – than school.'

'Well, I don't think you can stay here any longer. What are you doing for food?'

'Not much. The kitchens are locked.' Brigid looked out towards the hall, on the other side of which were two dining rooms, one with seating for forty people. 'There are some stale corn flakes.'

'What would you have done if there had been an air raid?' she asked.

'Stayed where I was,' Caroline said. 'I'd rather be alone here than squashed into one of those dreadful shelters with women knitting and singing "We'll Meet Again".'

'I know exactly what you mean, but all the same, I think you'd better come to Belgrave Square with me,' Brigid said firmly. 'Honor will be so pleased to see you.'

'If you like,' Caroline said. 'Anyway I can't go back to that school. Mummie doesn't know yet, although the headmistress said she'd write, but it's closing. Too hard to keep going during wartime, she said.'

'So what will you do?'

'I'm sure Mummie will find something,' Caroline said, in a way that was curiously blank. She went to gather her things and Brigid walked from room to room, looking for anything that would give a hint of someone different, softer, hidden behind her cousin Maureen's hard shiny exterior. Mostly, she seemed to Brigid like a person living on an island, in full view – often gloriously so – but so far away that no amount of shouting would carry to her. But maybe her things would tell another story.

They didn't. Some paintings, many photographs – mostly of Maureen, one or two of Duff looking handsome and cynical, none at all of Maureen's three children, Caroline, Perdita and Sheridan. Perhaps they were in her bedroom, Brigid thought hopefully.

'Ready.' Caroline came down the brown marble stairs with a small, scruffy case in her hand. 'The trunk can stay. It's mostly full of lacrosse sticks and tennis rackets anyway.'

'Jolly good, then we can walk. It's only ten minutes. And impossible to find a taxi, these days.'

*

They passed the Red Cross officers' club. A different group of young men stood outside, and with them three girls in uniforms of pleated skirts and stiff jackets. One girl had reddish curls pinned high on her head and was laughing loudly at something, head thrown back. From inside came the smell of something sweet, warm and fried. Caroline turned her entire body towards the front door, her thin shoulders lifting hopefully in the brown cardigan.

'Doughnuts,' Brigid said. 'The Red Cross girls make them for the GIs. It's to keep them from feeling lonely and homesick.'

'Does it work?' Caroline said. 'If so, perhaps they should have them at boarding schools too.'

'That bad?' Brigid asked.

'A bit,' Caroline admitted. 'Though I was usually top of my form.' Not something that would impress Maureen, Brigid thought. 'Not that *that*'s hard,' she continued witheringly. 'The lessons were terribly easy.'

'Chums?'

'No. In fact, the other girls rather hated me. They said I was strange. And dirty.' They had a point, Brigid thought. In daylight, Caroline's face was grubby, her nails positively filthy.

'The train,' she explained, following Brigid's eyes to the hand that was holding the case. 'Simply black with soot. And no hot water at Hans Crescent. Although I suppose I could have used cold. We did at school all the time.'

They turned onto Hans Place where one of the earliest bombing raids had destroyed a row of houses along the far side. It was, Brigid thought, very obviously old damage, almost re-assuring, so different from new. Debris had been cleared from the pavements and shovelled into fairly neat piles beyond the edges of ruined homes. The houses, though destroyed, no longer had the teetering look that more recent destruction left. Instead they looked settled into their decline. Weeds grew between tumbledown walls and in piles of battered bricks. Wallpaper, paintwork, the exposed innards of once-grand rooms – some of which she had visited for parties and dinner – had weathered to softly varying shades of brown and grey. In one, a house where she had danced at a school friend's coming-out, a sofa stood in an upper room that had walls missing on three sides and only enough floor for the sofa, perched above a mess of splintered wood and rubble.

Every time she passed it, Brigid remembered sitting on that very sofa, upholstered in a bright poppy-red that was now the colour of old blood, with her partner – a gentle, fair-haired boy whose name no longer came to her. She had stifled a yawn as he asked if she hunted, and watched the sunrise, waiting until she could go home without anyone saying, 'But it's so early!'

She wondered idly where the boy was now. In uniform, she supposed.

'It looks like the dolls' house in the nursery at Clandeboye,' Caroline said, pointing at the house Brigid had been looking at. 'The way it's all blown open. Our dolls' house has a front that swings open and you can move the furniture around. That looks like me or Perdita played with it, then left all the furniture in a big mess and the front wide open.'

'It won't last for ever,' Brigid said, putting an arm around Caroline's shoulders. That was what they all said. Mostly, she thought, because it was vague. *It won't last for ever* didn't make any rash and glorious prediction of victory – because who would dare such a thing? It simply described a basic truth. She said it to Will on her daily visits after her shift at the hospital. He would nod solemnly, but she could see he didn't believe her. Too many times he had been discharged – to convalescent homes, even once to his own flat – but each time the infection took hold again and he was brought back to hospital.

'Coal fires and damp,' the doctor had said, listening to Will breathe in and out. He had said it low, almost to himself, but Brigid understood what he meant. Will's lungs weren't strong. A childhood spent breathing wet, dirty air in a small cottage had made sure of that. She wondered if Will had even heard what the doctor said. He paid less and less attention during these visits, just waited for them to be over so he could get back to his reading.

After the doctor had left, she had dressed Will's bad leg. The hole was so deep now it was more like a tumbler than a powder compact. No matter what they did, they couldn't get the infection to yield. 'It's got its teeth into me good and proper,' Will said, peering at the sticky flesh. Even that didn't seem to move him much. 'I'm all right here,' he had assured her, after his most recent admission. 'As long as I'm not taking a bed from anyone who needs it.'

'You need the bed,' Brigid had responded firmly. 'That's why you're in it.'

At Belgrave Square, Chips greeted them. In the drawing room, they found Honor about to leave for a meeting. She hugged Caroline warmly – the girl merely submitting to it. 'Darling, I wish Maureen had told us . . .' it was clear she didn't expect her cousin to tell anyone anything; 'You could have come straight here. Now, you must have tea in the back drawing room where the fire is lit, but' – wrinkling her nose – 'perhaps a bath first?' To Brigid she said, 'A girl called Sissy, from Ireland, is coming tomorrow to stay for a few days. Or maybe more. I don't really know. She's one of Mama's waifs . . . I won't be here. I leave for Essex in the morning.'

So many of the girls came from Ireland, Brigid thought. There were Guinnesses spread right across the place, from Maureen's father Ernest through a variety of cousins, some grand, some humble. And through them, the chance of a move, an introduction, a new start, for so many young men and women.

One of Mama's waifs could, Brigid knew, mean anything. Sissy might be the daughter of a friend, or a destitute wife Lady Iveagh had come across through her charitable works. Perhaps an abandoned orphan. A runaway. On her way to something exciting, or 'stuck in a rut' with relatives who felt that Lady Iveagh's energy would be galvanising. Now that Grosvenor Place was occupied by the War Refugee Committee, the waifs were sent to Honor at Belgrave Square instead. At first, Brigid knew, Chips had been furious – anyone except Lady Iveagh and he would certainly have said no – but, in fact, the waifs rarely made much impact, often staying only a night or two, sometimes barely speaking. She had learned to ignore most of them.

After her bath, in a different jersey and skirt, hair washed and combed, Caroline looked less forlorn. Honor smiled more approvingly at her. 'You must stay till your papa arrives. Longer, if you like.'

When he came in half an hour later, Chips agreed. 'A delightful idea,' he said, several times. 'Perhaps your father will stay too, when he comes.'

'Daddy mostly stays at his club. But he doesn't mind Hans Crescent. He says he prefers it all shut up and without the servants,' Caroline said.

Chips looked baffled. 'Does he indeed?' Then, 'Brigid, you should go up and change. You'll be frightfully late.'

'For what?'

'Lady Ware's supper.'

'I've already declined. I told you that,' Brigid said patiently.

'Tony Rosslyn will be there.'

'Still no. I have an early shift.'

'Honor, don't you think Brigid must come with us to the Wares'?'

'There's no us,' Honor said. 'I'm not going. But certainly Brigid should. You can't just mope around at that hospital, you know.'

'Not moping. Working.'

'Well, you're not meeting anyone. Or, at least, no one of any use.'

'Must people be of use?'

'Yes, they must,' Chips interjected. 'It's one of the things you refuse to understand, although you're not at all stupid. Honestly, Brigid, time is moving *very* fast. You're, what, nearly twenty-three?'

'You know exactly how old I am.'

'Well, then. And you know it too. Twenty-three is *not* young.'

'We are at war.'

'Yes, and all around you people are still meeting one another and marrying.'

'He's right,' Honor said. 'Although I know you hate to hear it.'

'The world doesn't stop because there's a war,' Chips continued. 'I see Dina Bridges got engaged just the other day. Very suitably. There will be no one left if you don't hurry. Really,' he was getting crosser by the minute, 'I would think, in a war, you would be more urgent about this. War is not kind to young men.'

'Chips!' Even Honor, so used to her husband's ruthlessly narrow view of anything, was shocked.

'You know exactly what I mean and how I mean it. War is not kind to young men, and spinsterhood is not kind to women of any age.'

'I'm going up,' Brigid said. 'Caroline, you'd better come with me before he suggests you accompany him.' She found she was more than usually upset by Chips, and couldn't understand why. After all, this was what Chips did – plot and scheme and intrigue, so often with her marriage as the focus of his ambitions – and she had learned to ignore him just as she might ignore a horse butting against her for a carrot or sugar lump. But something about the way Chips had said war was not kind to young men . . . She thought of Will, of war that had been the start of his sickness, of all the other men she knew, young and old, how they came and went from London, on leave, always cheerful, then back to where death lay behind every hill and in every hollow. How could he?

'I don't know what's wrong with you these days, Brigid,' Chips said, as she left the room. 'You never used to be so dreadfully stubborn.'

Chapter Seven

Maureen, Clandeboye, Northern Ireland

Maureen heard Duff's feet along the corridor, the unmistakable brisk solidity of his tread, and sat up straighter on the sofa, putting away the copy of the *Tatler* she had been reading and tipping Pugsy off her lap. The pug had been sleeping, woke with a start and stared reproachfully at her with bulging eyes. She hoped her husband was coming to sit with her, even for half an hour, before setting off on one of his endless outdoor pursuits, the many activities of Clandeboye's two thousand acres.

'Did you know Caroline was on her own in London?' he asked, as he came through the door, with him the spaniels and lurchers that followed him everywhere when he was at home. Pugsy drew back in alarm.

When Maureen didn't answer immediately he crossed to the empty fireplace and stood in front of it so that his back was reflected to her in the tarnished gilt-edged mirror that hung on the wall above. 'Did you know,' he said again, 'that your daughter was alone in London?'

'Not alone, surely,' she said. 'A city of so many millions of people . . .' She knew how much it would infuriate him – how could it not? – but, honestly, storming in like that, what did he expect? she thought crossly. When it came to Caroline, he was simply ridiculous.

'Maureen,' he said, 'do not, I beg you . . .' Not so much *beg* as *order*, she thought.

'Well, you'll have to be more precise. What's upset you?' What indeed, she thought, when only last night they had been in such harmony. She remembered the glee with which he had told her that their dinner guests had cancelled – 'Not enough petrol, God bless rationing' – and how they had switched from the sombre dining room to the cosiness of the little sitting room. Dinner, just the two of them, with the fire lit because, even though it was July, it was Clandeboye and therefore cold. After dinner, a game of cards, brandy, his arm around her shoulders as he drew her close beside him on the narrow sofa, their own quiet conversations, his hand in her hair. And even when Sheridan had sneaked downstairs – she must speak to Nanny about that – Duff had simply said, 'Not tonight, old chap,' and sent him back to the nursery.

It had been, at the time and even more so when she remembered it this morning, *perfect*. And now this. She sighed.

'I've just had a telephone call from Belgrave Square,' he continued, 'Chips, brimming with eager malice, to tell me your cousin Brigid has "rescued" Caroline from Hans Crescent, which was entirely shut up, without food or money for the child. How is that possible?'

'She must have come back from school early,' Maureen said. 'I do hope she wasn't sent away.' If she had hoped to distract him with that possibility, she had failed.

'How early?'

'What?'

'How early? And what were your plans for the correct date of her arrival?'

'Well, I . . .' Maureen tried to remember what she had thought about getting Caroline home from boarding school. 'I assumed she would telephone me when she got to London,' she said. 'There was talk of her going to stay with a friend for a few days.' There hadn't been. Caroline didn't have any friends. 'She could have telephoned,' she said, adding, with some indignation, 'instead of whining to Brigid and Chips.'

'She didn't whine. I told you, Brigid found her in the house, all alone, sleeping on a bed she made up herself.'

'I'm sure she exaggerates. That would be just like her.'

'When was the last time you were there?' His voice was quiet now. That did not mean he was any calmer. When she didn't answer, he continued: 'The whole house is shut up. The kitchens are locked – on your instructions – and the telephone is disconnected. There are two rooms that I use occasionally when the House has sat very late and I don't want to go to my club. It is not a fit place for a child. Just thank God there was no air raid last night. As it was, she spent the night shivering under dust sheets.'

Maureen said nothing. The image was indeed rather pathetic. She imagined Caroline, so shy at the best of times, and how frightened she must have been. But why must Duff assume it was Maureen's fault? She was perfectly sure the child hadn't told her the dates. Or if she had, she hadn't reminded her. But Duff was so quick to blame her.

'Did you know it was her birthday today?' he asked then.

'Of course I did. I sent a parcel last week.' She spoke quickly. If she caught the early post tomorrow, something might yet arrive in time to make that seem true. But what could she send? She had only the faintest idea of what Caroline might like. She must be . . . Maureen ticked time off rapidly in her mind . . . Twelve, she decided. And she liked to read. She remembered a copy of *Treasure Island* she had seen about the house. She had an idea that someone – Duff's friend Betjeman? – had given it to Sheridan when he was five, too young for *Treasure Island*. It would be the perfect gift for Caroline. 'Some books and things,' she finished.

'Well, nothing arrived.'

'The postal system is so very disrupted.' She kept her voice carefully bland.

'Hmm,' he said. He picked a book off the shelf beside the fireplace and leafed through it. 'I should tell you,' he said stiffly, 'that I plan to resign from government.'

'Why?'

'To join the army.'

'But you already did that,' Maureen said, bewildered. 'When war was first declared. And they persuaded you to stay.'

'Churchill asked and I agreed. I believed then that I was more useful at the Ministry of Information. But now, after four years of fighting, I no longer believe that.'

'We've been through all this, darling. You're needed where you are. It makes no sense for you to go haring off to fight. Let younger men do that, while men of *experience*,' she smiled at him as she spoke, 'play their parts.'

'It's time now for everyone to fight,' he said. 'A further push is needed. Perhaps a final push.'

'Are you a child, to throw your toys to the ground and threaten to enlist every time we have a row?' She could no longer keep her voice calm.

'You do know that isn't why I'm joining up?'

'Isn't it?' Worry made her harsh.

'No.' He spoke more gently. 'I've been thinking about it for some time now. I tried to tell you last night, before Sheridan interrupted.'

'Yes, I must talk to Nanny. How dare she let him down at that time.'

'Poor chap. It's bleak enough up there, from what I remember,' he said, with a faint smile.

'Nonsense,' Maureen said. A memory came to her of torn linoleum, grimy windows and a strong smell of carbolic soap. But was that the Clandeboye nursery or somewhere else? Her own nursery as a child, perhaps? She wasn't quite sure. She didn't ever go to the Clandeboye nursery, which was on the top floor and far from her own rooms. She had ordered it moved when Caroline was a baby. Her constant crying – always, as Maureen recalled it, at a pitch of despair – had been too terrible to listen to. And what was the point of having a house with more than a hundred rooms if one couldn't arrange them as one wished? 'She has no business letting him roam around at night,' she said now. Sheridan must have travelled miles of passages alone, in the dark, to get to the little drawing room, she thought. 'We have time to talk about this.' She made an effort to speak pleasantly.

'I leave for London in the morning.'

'But why? The House doesn't sit until next week.' Maureen might be vague about her children's birthdays, even the exact whereabouts of the nursery in that vast house, but she knew the dates of her husband's comings and goings perfectly.

'To see Caroline. We've all missed her birthday, poor child.'

'But you said yourself she's at Belgrave Square so she's perfectly all right. And there will be other birthdays. There's a war on – even she knows that.'

That he was leaving her to see Caroline might be the hardest of all reasons to accept, she thought. So often, it seemed it was Caroline between them. Duff's devotion to his eldest child was matched by Maureen's remoteness from her. Where he doted on Caroline, Maureen found her sullen, indifferent, almost rude. Between her and her daughter, there was no bank of tender memories that either could draw on. But was that any different from Maureen's recollections of her own mother? When she tried to think of moments she and Cloé had spent together, she could recall nothing except the occasional silent car or carriage ride. Was it so strange that Caroline's company was something she endured rather than enjoyed?

There was no one to whom Maureen could have told her most secret thoughts about the girl, certainly not Duff. The confused mix of emotions that Caroline stirred in her – memories of the child's birth, the early months when she had cried and cried, all day and all night it seemed, and Maureen was unable to soothe her. Then the relief of accepting that, after all, she must be the nanny's responsibility and the start of long periods in which she hardly saw her so that Caroline grew wild and strange to her. But not to Duff.

Her cousin Honor had come closest to understanding, although in a funny sideways sort of way. 'After Paul was born, it all changed,' she said, perhaps a year ago now, when they sat alone together one afternoon. 'Chips simply adores that child, far, far more than he ever adored me.'

'Yes,' Maureen had agreed eagerly. 'Duff is just the same with Caroline . . .' She had been ready to tell how it hurt her to see the endless patience and kindness with which Duff behaved towards his daughter. Never any hint of the irritation, the anger Maureen seemed to provoke in him.

'It's wonderful,' Honor had continued. 'I feel I hardly need to be there any more, now that I've given him this new person to love. So freeing,' she concluded, with satisfaction, so that Maureen had immediately squashed everything she had been about to say.

She did not find it freeing. She found it intolerable. To fight with her daughter for her husband's attention – sometimes, to lose that battle – brought a sharp sense of pain and mortification.

'She needs me sometimes to pick her,' Duff had tried saying gently, but Maureen found no comfort in his explanation. Winning was necessary to her. Winning in the bid for him was vital. That it was strange, silent Caroline, with her huge eyes and wary expression, who sometimes supplanted her was worst of all.

'Stay,' she said now. She spoke coaxingly and reached out a hand towards him. 'Don't go. If we tell Chips to put her on a train, Caroline can be here in a day or so.'

'It's her birthday,' he repeated. 'And I need to be in London. I must talk to Churchill about my resignation.'

'Duff, no—'

But he left, whistling to the dogs. Pugsy watched them go

with relief. After a few moments, Maureen heard an outside door slam. He would not be home for hours. The house settled down around his absence, content to wait in a way that she was not.

She would go to London too, she decided. If that was where Duff was, that was where she would be.

Chapter Eight

Brigid

The next morning, Brigid was dressed and down for breakfast early. She was due at the hospital and hoped to eat and slip out before anyone else was up. But she was out of luck. Chips was in the breakfast room, wrapped in a purple and yellow silk dressing-gown. He was earlier than usual, Brigid thought. In front of him a newspaper was placed flat on the polished rosewood table. *Bomb Hits School, Kills Children; Others Trapped* she read on the front page.

Opposite Chips, hunched over a plate of toast, sat Caroline. Neither spoke and Brigid could imagine the doomed efforts both would have made – Chips asking politely how she had slept, Caroline volunteering as much information as she could bear, both then grinding to a halt. He looked up with relief when she came in. She had wondered if he would still be angry about

Lady Ware's, but that was the thing with Chips. He didn't waste time on grudges, only moved swiftly to the next plan.

'Best of the bunnies!' he said heartily. It was what he called her – mostly to annoy Honor, Brigid sometimes thought, because Honor clearly couldn't be the best of the bunnies if Brigid was. And it used to annoy her, but recently, Brigid had noticed, her sister was more abstracted, indifferent to Chips's barbs. War, she supposed. Bigger things to think of.

She took a bowl of porridge, even though there wouldn't be cream to go with it, and only a dusting of sugar, and thought back to the breakfasts of before. The silver dishes filled with scrambled eggs, kippers, steaming mounds of kedgeree, slices of fried bread, kidneys in mustard sauce, so much that it was never eaten, would simply be taken away and replaced the next day with more. 'Remember sausages,' she said dreamily. 'Real sausages, full of meat.'

'Bacon,' Chips agreed. 'Thick cut.'

'Sponge cake,' Caroline said solemnly. 'With butter and real eggs.'

Andrews came in then. 'A visitor,' he said. Chips put down his newspaper. 'For Lady Brigid,' Andrews continued. Brigid's first response was alarm. It was what they all felt now, at any unexpected call or appearance or – God forbid – telegram: *Something's wrong.* 'Miss Kathleen Kennedy.'

'Kick, my goodness,' Brigid said, jumping up. 'Here? Already?'

'Show her in, Andrews,' Chips said. 'And bring an extra cup.'

He went, and returned, followed indeed, by Kick. Brigid went to embrace her. 'How is it possible?' she demanded. 'I didn't expect you for weeks.' She looked, Brigid thought, the same as ever, except for a new fringe that didn't suit her. Merry, vital, brimming with life and energy.

'How indeed?' Kick said, with a laugh. 'Except that it is, and so here I am.'

Brigid took in the heavy grey-blue uniform and the neat red badge stitched to her upper arm. 'So you are!'

Kick took the cup Andrews had brought and poured coffee with one hand, splashing some unsteadily onto the saucer as she helped herself to a slice of toast with the other. 'The ship was like a floating lunatic asylum. You never did see so many people in one place. I still feel like I'm at sea. My legs can't seem to stop rolling, and I can't stop eating. No one was ever so hungry.' She took a bite of toast, then gestured at Caroline to pass the marmalade pot. 'Thanks. I'm Kick,' she said, taking the pot and extending a hand for Caroline to shake. 'Let me guess – a Guinness, right? With those eyes. Hardly a Channon.' She flicked her eyes at Chips, who smiled benignly back.

'My cousin – cousin-once-removed,' Brigid corrected herself, 'Caroline Blackwood. Maureen's daughter.'

'Maureen has a daughter?' Kick opened her eyes wide in exaggerated surprise and Caroline, to Brigid's surprise, laughed, and even laughed again when Kick said, 'You have much better food here than I expected. Although I bet not so good as at the officers' club in Hans Crescent.'

'Is that where you are?' Brigid asked. 'Why, we walked past only yesterday, didn't we, Caroline?' The girl nodded. 'At almost two o'clock,' Brigid continued. 'Were you in there?'

'I was,' Kick said. 'Playing ping-pong with a GI from Tennessee. They say we're supposed to let them win, but I find I can't, even when I try ever so hard to.'

'Is that what you do? Play ping-pong?' Brigid asked, curious.

'Ping-pong. Bridge. Gin rummy. Golf. I usually win at those too.' She grinned.

'I can't believe that of all the Red Cross stations in England you end up in the one opposite Maureen's house,' Brigid said.

'I know,' Kick said swiftly. 'I was as surprised as you.' Did she imagine it or was there a flicker of something in Kick's face as she said this?

'Where do you live?'

'At the club for now but only a few more days. Then I need to find somewhere else.'

'You need a flat?' Brigid said. 'You may be in luck . . . Chips?' Chips nodded, so Brigid continued, 'There's a place around the corner from Hans Crescent, only small and on the top floor so not at all grand. Chips was going to let my brother Arthur use it when he's in town, only Arthur has decided he'd rather stay at his club.'

'Would it fit two of us? There's an awfully nice girl from Virginia called Edie whom I met on the way over. She's at the officers' club too. She doesn't know anyone in England, so I thought it would be nice to show her around a bit.'

'I believe it has three bedrooms,' Chips said.

'You believe?' Kick asked. 'You haven't seen it?'

'Why would I?' Chips asked. '*I* don't intend to live there.'

'Right,' Kick said. 'Well, it sounds perfect for us.'

'I can take you round there later,' Brigid said. 'But why have you been so slow to call?'

'I wanted to get settled, and there was so much to learn, about how to use everything at the officers' club. You know we make the doughnuts ourselves? And the coffee?'

'I would have assumed so,' Brigid said. 'I mean, what did you think? That someone else made them and you just handed them out?'

'Something like that,' Kick confessed. Brigid remembered how quick she was to mock herself, how ready, always, to see the joke against her. 'In fact,' she confided, leaning close to Caroline as she spoke, 'I've started to think I might just have been a tiny bit spoiled.' She sat back and laughed loudly. 'But I don't intend to be any more,' she continued. 'I intend to work just as hard – harder! – than anyone else.'

'How is your father?' Chips asked. He turned over the newspaper so that the front page Brigid had been reading upside down – *. . . parents waited anxiously in one road in the London district for news of their children after a school there had received a direct hit . . .* – was hidden. 'And,' when Kick had answered that he was well, 'your mother? I think of them often you know, and that delightful week we spent at Kelvedon, how many years ago now?'

'Four,' Kick said. 'I remember exactly. Which reminds me, how is your prince, Brigid? Fritzi?'

'He's not *my* prince,' Brigid said, ducking so Chips wouldn't spot her blush. 'Anyway, it's all frightfully strange . . .' She paused. How to explain, when she only barely understood, the swift upending of Fritzi's fortunes?

'Do you remember we called him King Midas's son, because he was all burnished and golden and like a statue?' Kick said. 'But he turned out to be mighty nice, didn't he?'

'I suppose he did.'

'You know he did!' Kick grinned slyly at her.

'I must go to the hospital,' Brigid said quickly, before Kick could ask any more questions. 'If I'm late, Matron will murder me.'

'I'll walk with you. I'm already late. There'll be a queue of Doughboys all the way down the street.'

'Is that what you call them? Don't they mind?'

'Not at all.'

'No, not when you do it I suppose.' She smiled at her friend, remembering all over again Kick's easy, magnetic charm. 'Let me change my shoes. Wait here.'

In the hallway, Andrews glided up to her, a letter on a silver tray. 'For you, m'lady,' he said.

'Another letter from Hertfordshire?' Chips said beadily. He had followed her.

'My school friend,' she said firmly. 'A sweet girl. She's rather lonely.'

'Well, don't ask her to stay. And don't forget that chit of Lady Iveagh's arrives later. You will be back, won't you? I can't be expected to be responsible for all the flotsam . . .' He was starting to work himself up.

'I'll be here,' she reassured him. She started up the stairs to her room, only to find Chips continued to follow her.

'How capable you are,' he said. Then, in a conspiratorial voice, keeping pace, 'I hope Kick isn't back here thinking to marry Billy Cavendish. I've been thinking he might do for you.'

Brigid bit the inside of her cheek with irritation. 'Don't meddle, Chips,' she said. 'It's intolerable.'

Chapter Nine

Kick

'This is nice,' Kick said, tucking her arm into Brigid's as they set off along Belgrave Square.

'It is,' Brigid agreed. 'Though you might have given me more warning . . . So, does Billy know you're here?'

'Not yet. And he isn't the only reason I've come.'

'What else could possibly bring you?'

'The war effort.'

'Pure, artless sacrifice?' Brigid asked.

'Exactly. To be with my English friends at this testing time.'

'You sound like Mr Churchill: "Let us therefore brace ourselves to our duties . . .",' she quoted. 'And I don't think I believe you for a second. So, have you seen many of your "English friends"?'

'I've seen you, haven't I?'

'Don't be dull,' Brigid begged. 'Please.'

'No. I only got here a week ago and, well, I've been hiding out a little . . .'

'Why?'

'You know what the newspapers were like when we left. When Pa sent us home, how they jeered him: "Run, Rabbit, Run,"' she quoted bitterly. 'They were so quick to call him a coward, and all of us by extension.' She thought of her father's mortification, the grim way he refused to discuss what was written about him. 'Sticks and stones,' he had insisted. 'I don't know what they'll make of me being back,' she finished.

'They'll love it,' Brigid said wisely. 'We need all the friends we can get. Especially American friends.'

'Well, maybe . . . Also, none of the girls I came over with know about Pa, or any of us. They think I'm just the same as them.'

'Oh, wartime is a great leveller,' Brigid said vaguely. She sounded, Kick thought, as if she was parroting something she'd heard someone else say. 'No one cares who people's parents are any more. Anyway, none of your English friends think badly of you for leaving when you did. So, why hide?'

'It's been so long,' Kick said. 'I didn't even realise until I got here. Because it was all I thought of, back in New York, and even when I was working in Washington. I thought so much about coming back, and tried so many times, only Pa and Mother wouldn't hear of it. But it was almost like no time was going by. And then, on the crossing, I started to think how much can happen in that time. And then we arrived, and it just isn't the same place at all. I'd been thinking of one place, and the people in it, and I found somewhere completely different. So maybe these friends are different too.'

'You mean Billy, don't you?'

'I guess I do.'

'He was rather different after Dunkirk . . .'

'How so?'

'He never said very much, only that they should have stayed and fought, even to the death, rather than run away.'

'Hardly run away . . .' Kick said. She knew this – they all knew this: Triumph wrested from disaster; three hundred thousand men saved from a narrow stretch of beach by eight hundred boats, many of them tiny fishing vessels. That had been in the first year of the war, and her father had pronounced it the beginning of the end; 'the jig's up,' he'd written to them, suggesting that the end would come quickly. How wrong he had been. 'They were rescued,' she continued; 'evacuated, so as to regroup and fight again. Mr Churchill's "miracle of deliverance."'

'Yes, but Billy never saw it like that. And ever since, he's been cooling his heels, waiting in that training camp at Eastbourne for his regiment to be sent back to the front. It means he gets to London rather often, on leave,' she added, with a sideways look at Kick.

'And what about Sally?' The talk of Billy's army frustrations was interesting, but really, what Kick wanted to know was quite different.

'Well, he was engaged to her, and then he wasn't.' Brigid shrugged. 'His family didn't seem to care for that any more than they cared for you. Rather less, even, although she's not Catholic.' They winced a little at the word, Kick at hearing it said so bluntly, as if it was a stain, Brigid, she suspected, at having to say it at all. 'But that's finished now,' Brigid continued, 'and I suppose that really he is the same as ever.'

'Really?' Kick asked with a spurt of hope. 'On the boat,

coming over, I wondered if I was just crazy to come all this way . . .' Her normally strong voice faltered a little.

'It depends what you hope for,' Brigid said cautiously.

'I don't know,' Kick confessed. 'Oh, I know everyone says it can't be – and Billy's family look at me in a way that makes me feel . . . like I've got lipstick on my teeth and no one will tell me, though they all see it – but I just know I need to be where he is, whatever else happens.'

'So you do notice? I wondered . . .' Brigid said.

'Of course I notice. How could I not? When everyone is so careful not to say it, and so clearly can't stop thinking it,' Kick said, with a half-laugh. 'I know that being Catholic is way worse for them than if I was a murderer.'

'Some of those in the best families all right,' Brigid agreed.

'At first I thought they didn't like me. I'm not used to people disliking me,' she grinned, 'but, you know, it was OK too. I mean, I guess that happens sometimes . . . But then I realised it's not that.'

'They do like you,' Brigid agreed. 'I've heard Moucher say so.'

'And that only makes it worse. If they like me, but I still feel as if I've got lipstick on my teeth – worse, something on my shoe – when I'm with them, then it's not even anything I can change. If it was me, I could wear my hair differently, or different clothes, or eat differently, be more what they're used to. But this,' she touched the little gold crucifix that was always around her neck, 'it's what I am, more even than you can imagine.'

'But you still came back?'

'I still came back. That's them. It's not Billy. Or it is, but he doesn't make me feel like—'

'Like you've anything on your teeth or on your shoe?' Brigid said, with a smile, linking Kick's arm with hers.

'No, he doesn't. With him, I feel like I want to feel. Like we two can do anything together.' She looked around at the unsettled streets, the piles of sliding masonry and holes filled with dirty water. 'How is it possible any of you are the same when everything is different?'

Brigid nodded solemnly. 'I know it must seem very shocking to come upon it all at once. But for us, living here, it's different. There was a time we were like people speaking in code: "UXBs", unexploded bombs, "DAs", delayed action bombs. Even the moon turned against us – any full moon was called a "bomber's moon" because it meant the Luftwaffe could see us clearly. We walked round and round, dazed like ants in a disintegrating ant heap, just waiting for the end.' They kept moving, through streets that bore the visible scars of all that Brigid described.

Kick squeezed her arm. 'So what happened?'

'After a while, we began to get used to it. Strange as that may sound. And things got a lot more cheerful. Those dreadful air-raid shelters.' She shuddered. 'That was the turning point for me, deciding I wasn't going to spend another night down there. So dreary, darling, you cannot imagine – electric bulbs painted blue so there wasn't even light enough to read or play cards by. Long, long wooden benches and cold dank air, no matter what kind of a night it was up above. And everyone silent like in church, or non-stop singing "Knees Up Mother Brown". Sometimes seven or eight hours at a time, until the all-clear sounded. So I decided, no more, I'd rather take my chances above ground with the bombs.'

'Is that when you moved in with Honor?'

'Yes. Once I saw Chips had no truck with communal shelters . . .' She laughed.

'And what do your parents say?'

'Oh, they don't know. They're hardly in London and would be awfully disapproving – not so much for the danger, as for not doing what one is told "in a time of national emergency".' She laughed. 'But once I stopped scuttling underground like a rabbit at the first sound of an air-raid siren, I found so many others had come to the same conclusion. A whole second city, above the shelters, carrying on as though they hadn't a care in the world.' She gave a gurgle of laughter. 'Now, it's like the old days of one's coming-out. Endless parties in tiny flats. The *strangest* mix of people. And the nightclubs full every night. All one's chums. It might seem very foolish, even reckless, but it's that or go mad.'

'It doesn't seem foolish to me,' Kick said. 'I see exactly why. If the world is going to end in a hail of bombs, where would any of us rather be? In a nightclub, or dug down into some stinking shelter? I know which I'd choose.'

'I knew you'd understand. And one thing is for very sure. War does change one. All those awful nights showed me that if I keep on being as Chips, Honor and Mama expect, I might as well crawl into the deepest underground shelter and stay there.'

'I've never been in one but I know what you mean,' Kick said. 'After a while we realise that doing what we're told doesn't protect us at all, even though they pretend it will. All sorts of things happen anyway . . .'

'I knew you'd understand,' Brigid said. 'Now, there's a terrific system. Come eight o'clock, everyone who's in town, on leave or visiting, goes to the bar at the Ritz, so if you haven't any sort of plan made, you just pop along there.'

'I see, and can anyone come?'

'Anyone at all,' Brigid said. 'Does that mean I'll see you there later?'

'You might.'

'Sally and all those girls will say you're determined to be a duchess and that's the only reason you came back.'

'I'm sure they will. It's the kind of thing girls like Sally do say.' By which she meant girls brought up in the same way Billy had been, with the same rules, behind the same walls. Girls who never tried to look over those walls. 'But, as I said, Billy isn't the only reason I came back.'

'Of course – your burning sense of duty towards your beleaguered English chums.' Brigid grinned, but Kick didn't manage more than a half-smile in return.

'Lots of reasons.' She thought of Billy's freckled face, the smile that showed his uneven teeth, how she loved those teeth even though Joe, when he met Billy first, had muttered, 'What do they do with their mouths? Chew steel?' She thought, too, of Washington, of placing cups of coffee on Frank Waldrop's desk and taking away the half-drunk cold ones. And of Rosie: the rages that had filled her, then the terrible ugly emptiness when those rages were gone. 'Mostly, it was time to go,' she said. 'I'm just lucky Mother finally gave permission.'

'Hard to resist the call of duty,' Brigid agreed. 'But does that mean she's changed her mind about Billy?'

'Lord, no. But I don't think she thought very much about him at all. Mother has a way, when there's something she doesn't like and has decided on, of assuming that everyone has decided the same thing.'

'I see,' Brigid said. She looked at her, waiting for more, and Kick realised that the way she'd said it had sounded odd. But she didn't know how else to put it. She changed the subject.

'Whatever happened to Doris, Honor's pal?'

'Frightfully decorated and important now. But still the dearest ever. She managed to get a lot of people out of France before the Germans arrived. Now she's somewhere near Milton Keynes, doing something secret. Honor sees her as much as she can.'

'And that funny old Elizabeth Ponsonby? Do you remember that visit to Kelvedon, and all she had with her were clothes she borrowed from Honor? How she simply drank and drank, one cocktail after another, saying the most paralysing things.'

'Poor Elizabeth,' Brigid agreed. 'She died in the first year of the war.'

'Bomb?'

'No. I rather think she drank too much. No one told me, but Maureen said, "Trust Elizabeth to wait until there's a war on, and then kill *herself*," and Debo agreed and said, "She should at least have made the Germans waste a bullet on her."'

'Debo said that?'

'Yes. It seemed rather cruel of her. Have you seen her yet?'

'No. I told you, I haven't seen anyone. But she wrote me that she's married now. Andrew, Billy's brother.'

'Yes.' Brigid gave her a wry look. 'I wonder what she'll make of you, coming back to marry Billy and maybe being Duchess of Devonshire, when she picked the younger son?'

'Who cares about stuff like that?'

'Debo would.'

'Anyway, why aren't you married?' Kick asked. 'Or even engaged? Seems like everyone else is.'

'War does that,' Brigid agreed. 'People make up their minds in an awful hurry. But honestly, darling, I'm having far too interesting a time. I know one shouldn't say it, and of course I'm desperately sorry for the ones who die and have their houses destroyed, which might be any of us at any time, but when I think back to before and the dreadful boredom of nothing, ever, to do, I wouldn't swap.'

'Doesn't it sicken you, the work? So many injured, and worse?' Kick asked. She had tried to imagine what it must be like, to clean and tend wounds, staunch bleeding, but she found she couldn't. Not really.

'It doesn't. I wondered if it would. But there's something . . . clear about it, whether it's burns, broken limbs, crushed hands.' She must have seen Kick's face because she added gently, 'So many are dug out of collapsed buildings . . . But whatever it is, there are precise things to be done. A pattern to follow before and after the doctor arrives. And now that I know it, it's like something else takes over. I know what to reach for, what gauze to apply, what solution, what bandage. If you must know, I adore it. Having somewhere to go so that I can say no to Chips when he tries to bundle me in with his schemes, or to Mama when she tries to make me trot behind her to her charitable institution meetings – having something to do that I can understand and see the point of, it's rather wonderful.'

'I just hope I'm half as good at doughnuts and coffee,' Kick said. 'Now, I turn off here, don't I?'

'Yes, and down to the end of the street. Later at the Ritz bar?'

'Maybe.'

'Or come to Belgrave Square for tea first? There's a girl from Ireland coming, Sissy Something.'

Kick waved once at Brigid and, at the end of the street, turned into Hans Crescent. The door to the officers' club was open – it always was – and she went in. Already, even though it was only just after nine, the rec room was full. Edie was pouring coffee for a thin man whose uniform fitted him badly, smiling cheerfully at something he'd said. So many of their duties involved smiling cheerfully, even while they danced, baked, played cards and ping-pong. She waved as Kick came in.

'Where did you get to?' she asked, when Kick crossed the room. 'You were gone so early.'

'A visit,' Kick said evasively.

'I thought you said you didn't know anyone here?'

'I didn't say that. You asked me, and I didn't say anything because you don't let a girl get a word in edgeways.' Kick laughed.

'Well, go on then, who'd you visit?'

'I'll tell you on our break.' What to tell was the question. Only a small handful of the Dollies had been called for London. Most went to the mobile clubs that were stationed around the country. Kick's had been the first name called for London. Along with the twinge of relief, she had felt guilt. Undoubtedly her father's doing. Edie's name was called next and she had come to stand with Kick, muttering, 'If they'd said Yorkshire, like poor Maria there, I was going to get on that boat and go straight home. Let's stick together, you and me. We can figure it out together, this England place.' Kick had said yes, of course she had, but she hadn't yet told Edie how much she had already figured out.

Some hours later, when she finished her shift making dough and frying blobs of it to crisp deliciousness, she went back upstairs. It was time to tell Edie something of her former life here. She wished she hadn't left it so long. She tried to think of what she would say: 'As it happens, I do know London . . . quite well . . .'

She got back to the rec room and a great shout went up. 'Here she is, Queen Kathleen,' the thin GI in the badly fitting uniform called. Kick was popular – she was always popular. 'It's a gift you have,' her mother had said, 'to be liked' – but even so, she thought, this was strange. The GI was shaking a newspaper at her and his hand steadied for a moment. Long enough for Kick to see her face in black-and-white, smiling merrily with her father – arm about her shoulders – beside her. Underneath, she read, *We take our hats off to Miss Kathleen Kennedy of the sparkling Irish eyes and unquenchable zest for life.*

Her breath seemed to cut itself short so that she gasped. 'May I see that?' she asked. The room had gone silent. She reached out a hand and the thin GI passed her the newspaper, quite meekly, she thought. She scanned it quickly: a paragraph, under the photo, about her 'unhesitating response' to her country's need, how she had sacrificed 'a brilliant newspaper career' – that bit made her grin, remembering the hours spent filing papers in Frank Waldrop's office – and some awful stuff about her 'sweeping shoulder-length bob and the radiant colouring of her Irish ancestors'.

The room had stayed silent while she read. And now everyone was staring at her. She folded the newspaper. She hoped her mother was right – that she had indeed the gift of being liked. Because she certainly needed that now.

'Today's?' she asked.

The thin GI nodded. 'Just arrived. That is you, isn't it?'

'It is,' she agreed. 'But not written by anyone who's actually seen me recently. No kind of "radiant colouring" could stand up to an English summer. I must have had three blankets on my bed last night.' There was laughter at that. She had hoped there would be. So far, every GI she'd met had complained about the damp climate. 'And as for all the doughnuts I've been eating . . .' More laughter. Some whistled and even clapped.

But over the heads of the laughing men, Kick saw Edie staring at her. She caught Kick's eye, and raised an eyebrow, then turned away. Again, the breath Kick tried to take fell short so that she had to struggle for it.

Damn.

She remembered the *Washington Times-Herald*. How long had she been just plain Kick Kennedy there before anyone realised? Months, she thought now. Months of being just Frank Waldrop's secretary. Of living in a modest apartment – even if Jack did tease her that it was 'like the tenth day of Christmas, with English lords-a-leaping in every photograph on the wall' – and eating lunch in small diners with the other reporters and secretaries of the *Times-Herald*.

And she had loved it. It had felt like being weightless, she had thought. No looking up to find her mother's eyes on her, always considering. No being criticised by her father for 'bumming rides on other people's opinions'. Mostly, no being A Kennedy at every moment of every day. That was the real relief. Just being herself rather than being, always, *all* of them. Being singular, not many. Nothing to reflect well or badly on the others, only on herself.

The work was easy – very easy for someone who was a 'quick study', as her father called her. The friendships were easy too, complaining about the long hours and low pay with the other girls. She wore her plainest clothes and sympathised over the difficulties of darning stockings, quite as though she didn't own a dozen pairs that could be replaced in a morning.

And then came a day that her father was visiting Washington. He arranged to take her to lunch and Kick asked for the day off. Knowing her father's need to see all his children perfectly turned out, she dressed carefully, throwing on the mink coat he'd given her for Christmas as she left her apartment. It was February and there was still snow on the ground. She pulled the coat tight around her. As she passed the offices of the *Times-Herald*, she remembered she had forgotten to write an appointment into Waldrop's diary. It would take a minute, she reasoned. She ducked into the building and took the lift. As the doors were about to close, a voice called, 'Hold that elevator, Kick.' Obligingly, she put out a hand to keep the doors from closing, and in piled a mixed group of secretaries and reporters, back from an early lunch.

'My, don't you look nice,' said one of the girls, taking in Kick's carefully curled hair.

'Very nice,' added another, slyly, looking at Kick's coat. Then, 'Is that real alligator?'

'A gift,' Kick said awkwardly, looking at her too-smart, too-shiny purse with the gold clasp and chain. 'And the coat.'

'I see. A *gift*,' the girl repeated.

'I suppose the pearls were a gift too?' the first girl asked. The three men – reporters – were following the exchange as though it were a tennis match, Kick thought, heads turning one way and then the other.

'Yes,' she said miserably.

There was silence then, and when they got to their floor, one of the men said kindly, as they all got out, 'I think you look real nice.'

By the next day it was all over the building: Kick Kennedy had a rich sugar daddy who bought her expensive things.

'I don't,' Kick had protested, when someone finally told her. 'I wouldn't . . .' She was genuinely shocked that anyone could think such a thing of her. But what could she say? Which was the least of the two bad things? That she had a sugar daddy or that she had a rich papa? She remembered her father: 'Be proud of who you are.'

'He's not a sugar daddy.' She had choked a little on the words. 'He's my father. Joe Kennedy. I'm his daughter.'

From then she was 'one of *those* Kennedys'. The truth lost her a couple of friends, and gained her many more. And after a while, she thought the whole thing was forgotten. But it never was, not entirely. The other girls didn't gossip with her so much any more. They certainly didn't complain about the price of stockings. Or, worse, if they did, one would invariably turn to her and say, 'Not that you'd understand.' Mostly, this was spoken without bitterness – after all, wasn't that what they all hoped for and believed in? To create the kind of riches that meant their children didn't have to worry about the price of stockings?

But there were those who felt strongly, and said loudly, that she had no business taking a job from someone who actually needed it. Those voices suggested that being a Kennedy was to imagine yourself better than others.

That, too, was why she had wanted to come to England. To show that Kennedys played their part. They didn't step back into their privilege and money and let others take their turn at the hard things. They stepped up to the plate, like any good ball player, and took their turn.

Now here she was in this new place, only to see the same expression in Edie's eyes. Kick felt tired suddenly. Tired and *familiar*, she thought. Not the familiarity of something nice. No, it was a weary familiarity. Like a recurring bad dream that started up again just when you thought you were finished with it.

Who had told the newspapers she was here? She'd seen hardly anyone. Kick thought back over the newspaper story, her 'unhesitating response' to her country's need. Something about that phrase . . . She'd heard it before. And then she got it. Her father.

Of course.

As always, his children were pieces to be used in his game. Not pawns, she thought, better than that: knights, maybe bishops, even a rook. Sources of great pride, but also opportunities. Kick in England, dusting doughnuts with icing sugar, was a chance for him, same as Joe Junior and Jack in the navy. Well, that was Pa, she thought. What of it?

'So, unquenchable zest for life?' Edie said laconically, coming up behind her with two mugs of coffee. She handed one to Kick. 'They should see you first thing in the morning after a night of air-raid sirens.'

'Are you raging?'

'Dollie, I couldn't care less. You're here, ain't you? You took the same risk, the same leap, as the rest of us. I don't care who your pops is, or how sparkling your Irish eyes.' Edie grinned and tugged at one of Kick's curls that had escaped the neat hat. 'You're hard-working and you don't complain, and I like that.' Kick was about to thank her, when Edie added, 'But I do want to hear about your brilliant newspaper career.'

'That!' Kick laughed in relief. 'You can't imagine – not at all brilliant!'

'So, you lived here before?'

'I did. Pa was ambassador before the war. And I was here for over a year.'

'So you know a few people?'

'I do. A few.'

'A few, eh? I'm glad I decided to stick with you, Kathleen Kennedy.'

'Only my mother calls me that. If you promise never to do it again, I'll tell you something.'

'What?'

'We're going to the Ritz tonight.'

'The Ritz!' Edie's eyes shone. 'Really? Us? What'll I wear?'

Chapter Ten

Sissy

This house, Sissy thought, as she followed Brigid up a staircase so wide her brother could have driven one of his model cars right down it and never touched the sides. If the girls at school could see it, well, that would give them something to say 'stuck-up' about.

'Do you live here?' she asked Brigid. She was still unsure it wasn't a museum.

'I do, but only for now. My sister is away but she lives here, with her husband.'

'The man from the drawing room?'

'Yes.' The man had appeared just a few moments after Sissy had been shown in, and had looked through her as though she were a not-very-interesting picture, when Brigid had introduced her.

'What are you in London for?' Brigid asked now. 'It seems an odd time to visit . . .'

'You mean the war?' Sissy asked.

Brigid laughed a little. 'I do.'

'Yes. No one thinks it's good timing,' Sissy confided, 'but I had to get away and there didn't seem anywhere else to go. They talked of Cork, but . . .' she shrugged. 'And they thought I could be useful.'

'They?'

'Well, Mother, mostly. Father does what she says. She's related to your mother, Lady Iveagh . . .'

'So we're cousins?' Brigid said, in a teasing sort of way.

Sissy knew the teasing was because of her untidy hair and ill-fitting dress – one of Mother's, let out at the back where Sissy was bigger – but she said, 'Yes, somehow.'

'And can you be useful?' Brigid continued.

'I can try. I'm strong, and fast on my bicycle. I'm good with children. And I speak a little German.'

'German?'

'Yes.' Sissy gave a spurt of laughter. 'Mother thought the Germans might win, so she sent me for German lessons. *Just in case*, as she said. A little old German lady in a flat at the top of a house on Fitzwilliam Square. *Ich bin, du bist, er ist . . .*'

'Very . . . resourceful,' Brigid said doubtfully. 'So why did you have to get away?'

Sissy thought back to those last weeks at the house in Wicklow, as letters were written, telephone calls made, despite the expense, plans talked over that she wasn't told about, not until the last had been made: *You will go to London. To Lady Iveagh.* How the house, cheerless when she'd had the run of it was even more so when she was told to stay entirely in her bedroom. She couldn't even go to school.

'You seem to be rather beyond school,' her mother had said icily, when she asked.

Sissy thought back further, to the other side of those last weeks. To the moment she had looked over Tom's shoulder, even as she felt his thick arms around her, his mouth clumsily on hers, and seen Mother come into the stables to find why the horse and cart hadn't been sent round. The look on her face – the disgust that took in every aspect of what she saw. Not just Sissy, and Tom's bare arms, but the dirty straw, the badly whitewashed stable wall, Tom's ancient jacket, Sissy's skinned elbow from where she had come off her bike the day before, ambushed by one of the potholes in the drive.

That night, Sissy had crept down the gloomy stairs, skipping the ones that creaked badly, and sat in shadow where she could just see light spilling from the small sitting room, whose door was too warped to close snugly. Through the gap she heard her parents' voices, rising, falling, rumbling. It was hard to make out most of what they said, especially her father, who always spoke quietly, but then, clear as a bell, her mother: 'You didn't see them. I did. She was so horribly . . . *assured.*' There was a quiver to her voice. A flicker of the disgust Sissy had seen on her face in the stables. 'It's not Tom who needs to go,' her mother continued. 'I almost felt sorry for him. It's her.'

Sissy had crept back upstairs. For once, she didn't want to hear more. What had her mother meant, 'assured'? And why was that a bad thing?

The quiver, the completeness of Mother's disgust, had shaken Sissy out of her early defiance. At first her thoughts had run around like a clockwork train: *So what if I let Tom kiss me? It was nice, kissing Tom, feeling his arms around me. Even if he did smell like horses and blush terribly afterwards. What was so very bad about that?* But then she began to understand that it wasn't just the kiss or that Tom worked in the stables. It was the *assured* that was bad. And that was not something she'd done but something she was. She tried to imagine ways she could root it out. But she didn't even understand it.

She couldn't say any of that to Brigid who, although only a few years older than her – twenty-two, apparently, to Sissy's eighteen – was so crisp and clean and calm that she seemed far more than that. So: 'It was time,' she said simply. 'And I wanted to help. There's a war on.' God would forgive her that lie. It was what everyone said – *There's a war on*. Surely He wouldn't notice one more or dig too much into it?

'Well, I'm sure you'll be very useful,' Brigid said encouragingly. Then, 'This is your bedroom.' She opened a door.

'This?' Sissy looked around in wonder. The bed with its pale green canopy was twice – at least – the size of her narrow one at home. It was piled with pillows, and a sheet with an embroidered edge was turned down over the green counterpane. It did not seem to sag in the middle, as her own did. Beside it, on a small inlaid table, there was a lamp, a jug of water, and a vase of flowers. Real flowers too, she thought, a rose, some peonies – not the daisies and montbretia, hedge flowers, that would have been all she could pick at home. Beyond the bed, a window with a pale green curtain looped back, and outside a small garden. The wooden floor was varnished to a thick shine, with a large Turkish rug of woven pinks. 'Really this?'

'Yes. I'm sorry it doesn't look out at the front. Far more interesting than the back. But noisier. Now, I'll leave you to it.

You'll want to unpack.' She eyed Sissy's small case, all she had. 'Better get on.'

'Yes of course,' Sissy said automatically. She had no idea what, now she was here, she would do. Especially given that Lady Honor was away, although Brigid had said she would be back 'some time'. But she mustn't be a bore, or clingy. She squared her shoulders, wondering how long she could spend taking a couple of jerseys and skirts, some underthings and one dress – Mother's again, from several seasons ago – out of her case. And what she would do when that excuse was taken from her. There was a pause. Brigid stood with her hand on the door, half out, and Sissy wondered if she could ask for a book, maybe a magazine to read. Or was there, in this house the size of a museum, a library she could explore?

Just as she felt her lip start to tremble, tears threatening for the first time since all this happened, Brigid smiled at her. 'Come down to the drawing room when you're ready,' she said. 'You can say hello to Caroline. If you really do like children, that is. Not that Caroline is a child exactly, but . . .' She trailed off, perhaps distracted by the look of gratitude on Sissy's face.

'I would love that,' Sissy said solemnly. 'Thank you.'

'It's only tea,' Brigid said. But she smiled again.

Chapter Eleven

Brigid

Why had she asked her? Brigid wondered. Usually, she made certain to avoid Mama's waifs, lest they cling. And this one looked very much as though she might. She obviously had no idea what to do with herself, or even why she was in London. She was a queer little thing, Brigid thought. That unruly hair and large mouth, eyes too small and close together, for all that they were lively. Not pretty, not at all, but it was almost as if she didn't know it. Or, at least, wasn't self-conscious about it, as most of the girls Brigid knew were, rating themselves in the same ways society did. It was as though they carried around the descriptions the *Tatler*, or the *Express*, might attach to them – 'delightful', 'elegant', or perhaps just 'comely'.

Brigid was usually described as the 'charming youngest

daughter of the Earl and Countess of Iveagh' and that, too, was part of how she thought of herself. But this girl, well, if she knew she was no beauty, she seemed . . . maybe not indifferent but certainly impatient about it. In that, Brigid realised suddenly, she was like Kick, who brimmed over with so much energy and impetuosity that she had no time for minutely considering her appearance – 'You be beautiful,' she'd say, with a laugh, to Brigid. 'You're so good at it. I'll just have fun.'

And maybe it was the feeling of familiarity with Kick that had made her invite Sissy down for tea. Because Kick would be there too. And she hoped Sissy's presence might stop Chips match-making.

'I do think it's a bit much of Lady Iveagh,' Chips said peevishly. 'She knows I'd gladly do anything for her and, of course, with a war on one must do one's bit, but filling my house with strays at a moment's notice, well, I don't see how that's helping anyone. Where does she get them from?'

'This one seems to be the daughter of a friend from Ireland. And all I really know is that she needed to leave.'

'You don't think she's . . .' Chips made a rounded, swooping gesture with his hand placed at mid-height so that it hovered in the air next to his stomach.

'Goodness, no. Not even Mama would take that on. Anyway, see how skinny she is . . . No. Not that. But I don't know what.'

'Well, you'll have to find her something to do. I can't have her simply hanging around here. Especially now that your sister is gone again.' This was said even more peevishly. It was true, Brigid thought, that Honor was very often away, these days; mostly to various parts of the countryside. There seemed to be endless moving of people, preparing of hospitals, lodgings, camps

– but even when Honor was in London, she spent far less time at home. But it wasn't that that made Chips peevish, she thought. It was Honor's cheerful refusals that bothered him.

'I'm afraid I simply can't,' she would say, almost without pause, when he suggested a dinner, a small party, any one of a dozen entertainments he wished to get up. Before, she might have complained, or lamented, or sulked, but usually she would have given in and stood by his side, silent, perhaps, but present, as he welcomed guests.

Now, she said, 'No,' and was gone, without a backward glance. 'Yes, of course you must host Emerald and Lady Furness for cards,' she might say. 'I won't attend, but you hardly need me for such a thing.' If she was at home, Brigid would often see her disappearing upstairs to her room with a tray. Again, that wasn't so unusual – Honor had always been inclined to withdraw. It was the cheerfulness with which she did it that was new and strange.

'I think it's only for a few days. She said she was good with children,' Brigid said now, to Chips. 'And I rather think she might be.' She nodded to where Sissy and Caroline were chatting by the fire. Or, at least, Sissy was chatting, but Caroline was nodding along and smiling. Maybe Sissy would bring Caroline out of herself, Brigid thought. Something had to, and none of them seemed able.

'Caroline is a beauty. And a Guinness,' Chips said comfortably. 'She'll be all right.' How foolish he could be about people, Brigid thought. How clever, but how foolish too. Maureen, he could see with stark, almost cruel, clarity: her desire for power and position, her desire for her husband's unadulterated love, to be shared with no one, not even their children. But he had never understood Honor, although Brigid barely did either, and now looked to make the same mistake with Caroline. Distracted by her beauty and the possibilities this offered her, he was unable to see that she had no interest in these things.

And Brigid, for all he watched her and quizzed her about where she had been and who with, he couldn't see either. Again, it was the possibilities that blinded him. The things he himself would do with the advantages of looks, position and a fortune that dazzled him.

But that was good, she thought. It kept him distracted.

'Miss Kennedy,' Andrews announced, standing back to let Kick pass. In she came, with her usual rush of energy. She was already laughing, Brigid saw, even though there was nothing, yet, to laugh at.

'Do not offer me tea,' she said, grabbing Brigid's hands. 'I swear I smell exactly like a doughnut stall at a county fair. I'm so dusted in icing sugar I'm sticky all over. And if I see another cup of coffee, I'll yell.'

'Hard day?' Brigid sympathised. 'Don't sit yet.' Chips had drawn out a chair and was patting it invitingly. Brigid suspected he wanted to quiz Kick on her 'intentions' regarding Billy. 'I want you to come and meet someone, but first, did you find everything you need at the flat?'

'Oh, it's perfect,' Kick assured her. 'I mean, I wouldn't want Mother to see it . . .'

'No,' Brigid agreed.

'. . . but for us it's perfect. Edie thinks so too. Thank you,' she said, turning to Chips. 'This morning I had nowhere to go, and now I have a flat.' She beamed.

'No trouble at all.' He waved his hands expansively at her. 'Let me know if you need any repairs.'

'Come and meet Sissy,' Brigid said. She led Kick to where

Sissy and Caroline sat. They were playing Snap and Caroline looked more animated than Brigid was used to seeing her.

'Sissy's house sounds just like Clandeboye,' Caroline said to Brigid. 'We've been competing as to how far wallpaper can bulge with damp before it splits and starts to peel. Sissy says the drawing room at Ballycorry – that's where she lives – has a bubble the size of a grapefruit, still not peeled off.' For Caroline, this was a marathon speech, Brigid thought. Kick looked startled.

'Our nanny,' Caroline continued, speaking mostly to Sissy, 'Miss Allie, is so massively stout, her arms so giant, that she's like a slab of beef. A slap from Miss Allie is like being kicked by a horse.' She sounded almost admiring.

'Our nannies were poor creatures,' Sissy countered, 'barely better educated than the maids. Mother used to find them among the unmarried relations. They would teach us a bit of geography, the kings and queens of England, and how to accept a lunch invitation. When I went to school, I was shocked to realise that other girls had learned mathematics and even a smattering of science. I didn't know those subjects existed.'

'Before Miss Allie we had a nanny who put cushions into buckets under leaks, so the drips made less noise.'

Kick looked even more startled. 'Irish houses seem to be very . . .' She trailed off.

'Hopeless,' Chips agreed, coming to join them. 'It's the climate. Goes right through roof tiles and window frames, rotting everything it touches.' He looked comfortably around the snug splendour of the drawing room. 'I don't know how they bear it.'

'Sissy is visiting from Ireland,' Brigid explained to Kick.

'We might be cousins,' Kick said eagerly. 'My people are all Irish. Wexford and Limerick. And then Boston.' She laughed.

'Yours will be Catholics,' Sissy said. 'Most of the Irish are. Certainly the American ones. But not our lot. Proud Protestants. And we don't mix very well. My mother sent me to school with Catholic girls, then had a fit any time I did anything she thought was popish. Even saying, "Bless you," if someone sneezed was too Roman for her.'

'Oh,' said Kick, 'I thought . . .'

'You thought all the Irish were Catholic. Everyone does.' Chips tried to reassure her.

'We're like a secret society,' Sissy added. 'Hardly anyone knows we exist. And when they find out, they don't like us much. We don't fit.'

'Where I live, at Clandeboye, they won't drink out of a glass if a Catholic has used it,' Caroline said. 'They say the glass must be broken immediately.'

She spoke as she so often did – without much emphasis. Brigid wondered why she'd said it. Was it merely an observation, or to make a point? Impossible to say. But Kick, she saw, looked stricken. 'Sissy's mother made her learn German,' Brigid blurted. Anything to change the conversation. 'In case they win.'

'That's just the sort of thing my pa would do,' Kick said. 'And he wouldn't even see there was anything so very wrong with it.'

'Snap!' Sissy said. '*As well to be prepared.* That's what my mother said.' They laughed.

'Let me tell you what my father did today,' Kick said then. She told them a story about an item in the newspaper, about her, that was unexpected, embarrassing. 'It never would have occurred to him that I might not like it. Or if it did occur, he wouldn't weigh that up in his decision. All he will have seen is how much this helps him. How it makes him look patriotic, when people say he isn't. It's not enough for him to have two sons in the war. He needs me to make the Kennedys look good too.' It was the angriest Brigid had ever heard her. And certainly the angriest against her father.

'Two brothers in the war?' Sissy asked.

'Joe's in the navy, Jack too. And Bobby says he'll join up in a couple of months, as soon as he's eighteen.'

'How many in your family?

'Nine.'

'Nine! Well, you don't seem like a Catholic – too well dressed – but I guess you are after all,' Sissy said.

At that Kick laughed properly. So it seemed the most natural thing in the world, half an hour later, for her to say, 'You'll come too,' to Sissy, when they made plans to meet later that evening at the Ritz bar. Brigid, who still felt sorry for the girl, smiled gratefully at her.

'I would,' Sissy said. 'But I don't know what I'd wear. I don't have anything.'

'And I have far too much,' Kick said. 'My trunks have arrived. Come and see the flat and I can lend you something. I've got so much fatter since being here that half my clothes will fit you better than me anyway.'

'I'll see you both at the Ritz,' Brigid said.

When they were gone, she went to her bedroom and took out the letter Andrews had given her that morning, the one that had caused Chips to raise his eyebrows and say *another letter . . .* All day she had been conscious of it in her pocket, even as she dressed wounds, rolled bandages and scrubbed the wards. She had itched to read it, but knew that she would no sooner start than she would be interrupted – asked to fetch something, or be quizzed archly by one of the other nurses: 'Letter from a sweetheart?'

No, better to wait and read it properly.

My dearest it began. When had they moved to 'dearest'? And then she wondered at how much she liked the warm feeling of that word inside her: *dearest*.

It was the usual sort of letter. The rain had been bad; he did not know when he would get the hay in. The herd had been unsettled. Really, she thought with a snort of laughter, he should be writing to her father. Lord Iveagh had strong views on cows, and how to get the best from them.

Nothing about the letter was more than friendly; nothing spoke of love or even affection. If anything, it was dutiful, stilted, ending precisely at the bottom of the page. She imagined a matron standing over Fritzi, telling him to finish now as the post was going. But that was always how Fritzi had been. It didn't mean there wasn't feeling behind the words. And certainly didn't mean that she felt constrained in her replies.

She took out a piece of writing paper with *5 Belgrave Square* at the top in gold lettering. Always, she told him a lot about her life at the hospital, and about Will. Will who was painfully real where George Mansfield was not. The things he suffered were tangible – the wound that would not heal, the leg that would not work, the edges of infection that increased like an army on the march. Telling these things to George helped her to bear them. Indeed, sometimes she wrote to George the things she wanted to say to Will: '*When this is over, we will all be different, although I don't know how . . .*' To Will, she rarely spoke about 'after' or when this would be 'over'. She didn't dare.

At least this time she could tell Fritzi something different, that Kick was here, she thought, as she began to write. That was new.

Chapter Twelve

Sissy

Outside on Belgrave Square, tea over, Kick said, 'This way, it's only five minutes,' and set off at a brisk pace.

'It's less bad than I expected,' Sissy said, looking around as she kicked a piece of brick out of her way, then skipped to catch up. 'In Ireland, we only have the Emergency, as we call it. The way everyone talked about London, I expected there would be nothing but bomb craters. Instead, it looks perfectly all right to me.' She turned her head eagerly, this way and that. 'Interesting, at least.'

'I guess you were told more than we were,' Kick said wryly. 'I was real shocked at first to see it all so torn up.'

'I had no idea what to expect. I've never seen a city any bigger than Dublin,' Sissy said cheerfully. 'And even bombed, London is less broken-up looking. Dublin has even more houses that have fallen down all of their own accord. Heaps of them. So, you see, this doesn't look too bad at all.'

Kick laughed. 'I should think most things look good to you. You seem to have that sort of personality.'

'Especially anything that isn't home and familiar,' Sissy agreed.

'This is mine,' Kick said, stopping in front of a shabby brown door. 'Home. Though I only saw it for the first time a few hours ago. We're at the very top.' They climbed a broad but scuffed staircase, past hallways lit by bare bulbs. 'Edie's there now. She came over on *Queen Mary* with me and is Red Cross too.'

They reached the top floor and Kick put a key into the lock and pushed open the door, straight into a sitting room that had a battered brown sofa and an armchair with a high, carved wooden back and thin, carved arms arranged in front of an empty fireplace. A long sideboard stood against one wall. It was too high for the room and made that end top-heavy, as though everything must slide towards it. At the far end there was a doorway, and opposite the sideboard two more doors.

'You can see all of London,' Sissy said, going straight to the big window and looking out.

'If the windows were clean, you'd see a lot more,' said a girl who must be Edie, drily. 'I guess you could rub them with vinegar and old newspaper, but there's so much dust and rubble on the streets it hardly seems worth it.'

'But what bliss to look out and see buildings everywhere,' Sissy said. 'Churches, cathedrals, even a palace, and not a field or hedge in sight,' she ended with satisfaction. 'Barely any birds even.'

'You really are ready to be entertained, aren't you?' Kick said, amused.

'How do I look?' Edie asked Kick, turning in a circle, like a dog trying to reach its own tail, Sissy thought. 'The Ritz,' she said, by way of explanation to Sissy.

'Absolutely,' Sissy agreed.

'You look great,' Kick said. 'Ritzy.' She did, Sissy thought. Edie was the tallest of them, elegant in a black crepe dress. 'That reminds me . . .' Kick disappeared through the far door and came back with an armful of dresses. 'Let's see . . . Try this?' She held out a green silk to Sissy. 'You're taller than me, but we look to be about the same around, and the dress is too long for me anyway. My brother Joe says I'm like a plant being choked by ivy when I wear it.'

'Shall I go . . .?' Sissy, now holding the green dress, gestured towards the room Kick had just come out of.

'Oh, just change here. It's only us.'

Sissy began taking off her things and wriggling into the green dress.

Edie crossed to the sideboard and picked something up. 'A telegram arrived for you.'

Kick made a face. 'Probably my mother, making sure I haven't forgotten to go to mass.' But when she sliced open the envelope and read the telegram, Sissy saw immediately that it wasn't her mother. Or mass. It couldn't be.

'It's from Billy!' Kick said, eyes shining. 'He knows I'm here. He says he'll be in London on Saturday two weeks from now, and can I keep it free. Oh, but can I.'

'Who's Billy?' Sissy asked.

'Billy's her boyfriend,' Edie said. 'He's in something called the Coldstream Guards, based somewhere called Eastbourne.'

'So why didn't she just ring him up and tell him she was here?' Sissy asked, looking from one to the other.

'Because, he's not my boyfriend,' Kick said. 'He's . . .' She stalled. 'He's a friend, and we went around together a great deal when I lived here last. But I don't know what that makes him now.'

'I've never seen anyone so excited for a not-boyfriend,' Edie said, looking to Sissy for agreement. 'Have you?'

'I don't know,' Sissy said. 'I've never really known anyone who had a boyfriend. I mean, in Ireland, we don't. Or not anyone I know.'

'What do you do?' Edie asked. 'Just get married without knowing each other?'

'No. But not boyfriends either. I mean, one might meet a chap at a tennis party, or hunting, and he might call and take one out, but . . .' She shrugged. '*Boyfriend*. It sounds, I don't know. Daring.'

Edie burst out laughing. 'Where is Ireland?' she asked, when she was calmer. 'In the past?'

'Probably,' Sissy agreed, pulling the green dress over her head. 'So Kick has a not-boyfriend, who is sending telegrams to ask if he can take her out?' She tried not to let them see how dazzled she was, in case they thought her hopelessly provincial. More than anything, she wanted to impress these American girls. She had never met girls like them; it was as though they blew ahead of her, fast and sure, sails filled by a different wind.

'I wonder how he even knew I was here,' Kick said.

'Everyone knows you're here,' Edie said. 'Of all the hundreds of American girls working their fingers to the bone and wearing those scratchy uniforms, the only one the English press show any interest in is you. No wonder this Billy is sending telegrams. He must think you'll be snapped up a thousand times over.'

Kick looked mortified. And strained. 'I hoped and hoped he'd ask me out, but now he has and I . . . Well, suddenly I feel all *jittery*. Like before a race or a recital.' She was tapping her fingers against her collarbone as she spoke.

'Seems to me you're as much scared as excited,' Sissy said.

'I guess I am. Which is odd because normally I never am,' Kick said. 'Not about anything. But I've thought and thought about seeing Billy since I left here, and especially since I knew I was coming back. And now . . .' She drummed her fingers against her collarbone again, a rolling tap-tap-tap that was faint but agitated.

'And now he's coming in two weeks. So he must be just as excited as you. And maybe just as scared,' Sissy said.

'Maybe,' Kick said. 'That dress suits you.' It was an obvious bid to change the subject.

And the dress did suit her, Sissy thought, looking into the dusty mirror that stood against the wall. The way it clung made her seem better proportioned – usually, her head was too big for her thin body, but the dress gave her curves. Or, at least, the illusion of curves so her head seemed the right size. She swept back her hair, wondering if she could pin it so that it was less unruly. She mouthed the words *I hoped and hoped he'd ask me out*, just like Kick had said, even giving them an American accent in her head. She turned her head at an angle as she whispered them, and wondered would she ever be able to utter such a sentence as though she actually believed it.

'It does.' Edie gave her a critical look, eyes narrowed. 'It suits you real well.'

Sissy blushed and hoped Edie hadn't noticed her whispering to herself. 'Anyway, who are all these?' She picked up a photograph in a silver frame that stood on the sideboard, a group posing in the shade of a tree, white clapboard house behind them, all in crisp white clothes, men and women alike. 'Well, I see who one of them is – it's you, Kick, isn't it?'

'Yes, and that's my family,' Kick said, coming over to her. 'Taken the year before last, at Hyannis Port.'

'Aren't you a handsome lot!' Sissy said.

'I told you the Kennedys were a big deal,' Edie said. 'You didn't believe me, did you? That photograph was in a magazine my mother spent three days reading.'

'A magazine? Goodness, how odd,' Sissy said. 'Are these all your brothers and sisters?'

'That's Eunice,' Kick said, starting on the outside and pointing. 'She's a year younger than me. She's at home in New York. Beside her is Joe, with Jack on the other side . . .' She carried on, details about everyone tumbling out as she spoke, their ages, what they liked to do.

'She's always talking about them,' Edie said affectionately. 'I feel I knew all about them even though I didn't know they were *Kennedys*.'

'And her?' Sissy interrupted, pointing to the girl at the far edge of the photo, of whom Kick had said nothing so far. She wore a sailor dress and looked straight into the camera, hands clasped behind her back. 'She's terribly pretty, but the only one of you not smiling. Why is that? Does she not have the same perfect teeth as the rest of you?'

She was joking, but immediately there came a queer little silence that told her she'd said something wrong.

'That's Rosemary,' Kick said, after the tiniest pause. 'Rosie. She's the sister older than me. Rosie is a dear.' She took the photo from Sissy and put it back on the sideboard. 'You're going to need shoes with that dress.'

Sissy, bewildered by the change in topic, didn't know what to say.

'Her feet look about my size,' Edie said quickly. 'Come see what I've got, Sissy.'

Once they were in her bedroom – small and dark and stuffy – she whispered, 'She doesn't talk so much about Rosie. I get the feeling there's . . . something.' She shrugged. Sissy had got the feeling there was *something* too, but what?

By the time they came out, a pair of silver shoes on Sissy's feet that she was sure would trip her, Kick had Billy's telegram in her hand again. 'He must have sent this the minute he knew I was back,' she said, excited again.

'Maybe he read that newspaper,' Edie said.

'I'm sure he didn't,' Kick said. 'I can't see Billy paying attention to that.'

She sounded like Billy not paying attention to the newspaper mattered to her, and so Sissy was quick to say 'If he's at training camp, he'll hardly be reading newspapers,' and was rewarded by Kick's smile.

Chapter Thirteen

Kick

That photo, Kick thought, as she powdered her face, blurring her freckles; the one Sissy had picked up. Taken in the summer of 1942. All of them together. The Last Summer of Rosie, as she sometimes thought of it.

Sissy, in her blunt and blundering way, had landed on a truth Kick had never really thought about before: Rosie's teeth. That wasn't why she wasn't smiling in the photo – normally Rosie smiled, same as any of them. But it was true that she hadn't been sent to the dentist anything like as often as the rest.

'You're lucky,' Kick used to say glumly, aged maybe ten, setting out in the car for yet another trip to Dr Fenster. 'No one to go poking about in your mouth and making you say, "Ah!" even though he's got a fistful of screwdrivers in there.' And Rosie had laughed, same as she laughed at everything back then. If

Kick had thought about it at all, she realised, she would have imagined Rosie didn't need the dentist as much.

Now Kick understood. Rosie's teeth didn't matter as much. The perfection of her smile wasn't given the same priority.

How far back did that go? At what age had they decided Rosie was less worth bothering about than the rest of them? When she was fourteen and Kick was twelve and it was obvious that Kick was quicker and ahead in everything that counted in the family – lessons, catechism, tennis, touch football, the nightly debates, sailing . . . Or earlier, even? When Rosie was eight? Five? She didn't know. And didn't want to think too hard about the answer, because the younger Rosie had been, the more it hurt.

She had thought the operation was new, a way to stop Rosie's moods, the anger that had grown over the last summer they were all at Hyannis Port together. But what if it had been decided before that? What if Rosie was already less a Kennedy when she was a child so that they didn't bother with her teeth?

Kick had always believed that no one in the family had thought of Rosie as anything other than Rosie – even Mother, for all that she was strict with her – until that last summer. But maybe the teeth told another story. A story in which the terrible end was written much earlier. In which Rosie had never been the same as the rest of them.

Not now, she told herself, picking up a lipstick and applying a slash of red to her mouth. *Not before the Ritz. Not when Billy's telegram was sitting out there on the mantelpiece and Billy himself was coming on Saturday.*

'How does she look?' Edie appeared in the doorway, pushing Sissy in front of her. Sissy's hair was carefully pinned back behind her ears on either side, then coaxed into smooth waves to her shoulders.

'Aren't you clever!' Kick said admiringly. Already, the waves threatened to spring back into more unruly curls, but the effect was charming. 'Lipstick?' she asked Sissy.

The girl shook her head. 'I never know what to do with my mouth if I wear it,' she said. 'Anyway, Mother says no girl should till she's at least twenty.'

'No doubt Mother is right,' Kick said. 'My mother says the same sort of thing.' Rose said so many things about how to be, how to behave, what was suitable. How many times had Rosie flouted those things? *Not now*, she told herself again. Then, to Edie, 'Where did you learn to do hair?'

'My sister. She made me practise and practise on my dolls until she trusted me to do hers. If I messed up, she'd hold the hot curling tongs against my arm. Only for a second, mind, but it was enough to be sure I learned quick. By the time I was twelve, I was a dab hand.'

'I imagine one would be,' Sissy said. 'Do you think there'll be Champagne? I've never had it.'

'It's the *Ritz*,' Edie said.

The doorbell sounded feebly, followed by a few hearty thumps on the door. 'Brigid,' Kick said.

Out in the streets it was still light enough that they could walk without fear of bumping into a lamppost, or of the sirens going off. So light that Brigid said, 'We can go through Hyde Park and save ourselves a few minutes, but we must be quick – it's blacker than ink once the sun's gone fully down.'

Even so, they were the only ones, Kick thought, who walked with ease. Everyone they encountered seemed to hurry, to be rushed and strained. They were mostly women, with string bags of shopping. She imagined they must be trying to get home, make dinner, and get ready for whatever the night might bring. She had heard that children still slept mostly in their clothes although the raids had eased, even with a coat on, because no matter how warm the night, the shelters were damp and cold.

No wonder those women looked tired and pinched, she thought. No wonder their eyes were rimmed with red and their children's faces pale under the sticky residue left by the dirty air. 'Goodnight, good luck.' They saluted each other quietly on street corners.

'Isn't it fun!' Sissy skipped along beside her.

'It's more fun than it was,' Brigid said. 'The tide of war has turned. Or, at least, that's what we say, now that the Americans are in. It's to cheer ourselves up because, really, everything is just as awful as ever. Only now it's awful and we think we have a chance of winning, when before it was awful and we thought we must lose.'

At the Ritz, all was dark. By the time they arrived the grey of the sky had turned the same colour as the façade, solid grey brick melting into wet evening air. It was hard to see it as something corporeal: rather, it seemed a bank of thicker cloud, a mass of intention beside Green Park.

'Is this it?' Edie asked, looking up at the dull exterior with its blacked-out windows.

'Don't worry,' Brigid said. 'It's better inside.' She walked to the door, which was opened by a man wearing white gloves. Kick wondered how often he must change them in an evening.

'Good evening, Lady Brigid,' the doorman said. 'You'll find a few in the upstairs bar. Miss Kennedy.' He nodded at her. How on earth did he know? Kick wondered.

'Thank you, Thomas,' Brigid said. Inside, they stood in a tiny vestibule, created by the heavy draping of blackout curtains around the door, taking off coats and hats. It was nothing like the Ritz she remembered. Then they stepped beyond the curtains into the lobby.

'This is more like it,' Sissy said softly. The lobby was lit by two chandeliers that glowed softly. Along the wall, more lights, set in pairs behind crystal shades, picked out the soft pink and gold of the furnishings so that the place, with its branching doors and staircases, was as warm and glowing as it had ever been.

'We'll take our things up with us,' Brigid said, switching her coat to the other arm. 'The ladies' cloakroom is now a private bomb shelter for the Albanian royal family, who have taken an entire floor of the hotel for themselves.'

'Selfish,' Sissy remarked cheerfully.

'Oh, very,' Brigid agreed. 'I mean, can you imagine . . .?' It was, Kick thought guiltily, exactly what her father would have done for his family.

Upstairs, the bar was full. 'You'll find a few . . .' must be characteristic English understatement, Kick thought, looking at the crowd. There were people sitting, standing, leaning. One girl in a tight pink dress sat on a man's knee, his hat on her head. Music came from somewhere, although she couldn't see any musicians, but could scarcely be heard above the chatter and laughter. She could smell cigarette smoke, mingled perfumes and a good-natured hint of perspiration.

They had hardly gone more than a few paces when 'Kick!' A hand reached out and grabbed her arm. It was Debo. 'I knew you'd be here,' she said, smiling and standing up quickly from the high stool where she was sitting. 'Once word got out, and all this afternoon it simply *flew* about – like swallows in a barn – Andrew wanted to hunt for you, but I said no need, she will simply *appear* at the Ritz, like the most perfect vision. And here you are.'

'The perfect vision is you,' Kick said, laughing. 'Marriage has made you more beautiful than ever.'

'Isn't it nice for you to say such things and they be true?' Debo agreed, with a laugh. Sissy looked startled at the conceit, but to Kick it was nothing strange, just Debo. 'It's divine,' she continued. Then, slyly, 'You should try it.' She gave Kick a sideways look.

'Debo, darling, don't fish.' That was Andrew, in the uniform of the Coldstream Guards. Billy's brother. Billy's regiment. Kick felt a second of dizziness at the almost-ness of it. He came forward and embraced her. 'Lovely you're back.' He was being polite, of course, no more than that, but she allowed herself to believe it.

'Thank you.' He would tell Billy he had seen her. The thought made her glow inside. She was truly one step closer now, barely a step away. After the years of being thousands of miles away, it was intoxicating. 'I can't believe you're all here. It's like a secret society. Outside, the streets are so empty and half the buildings too, so it seems like hardly anyone's in London. But here you are, tucked away, having a swell time.'

'Yes, when on leave,' he said, rather stiffly, so that Kick felt rebuked. She had forgotten this trick of the Devonshires – Billy did it too: just when you thought they were determined never to be serious, to be casual and insouciant about everything, they would switch and be momentarily grave. Always, it threw her.

'So, back to cause trouble?' he said then. He spoke lightly, as though joking, but was he?

'To help,' Kick said firmly. 'As an American. It's our war too.'

She hoped he would remember she had always stood up for England.

'To help, then,' he agreed. 'Jolly good. Though I wonder if my father will think so.' He laughed a little at his joke. But Kick was stung by the thought that somewhere in England, perhaps even here in London, there were people who did not greet her return with joy. And not even with the scepticism of those who remembered her father's unpopular politics – no, people who thought of her with personal reservations: Billy's parents. Who might this very minute be groaning at the news. The idea took some of the sparkle from the evening.

'Don't be horrid, Andrew, darling,' Debo said. 'Now, let's find somewhere to sit. I want you to tell me everything. Andrew, bring some Champagne, the proper stuff, not that swill Bob keeps for the Americans. I say, sorry.' She peeped at Kick from under her lashes. 'Was that frightfully rude?' Kick didn't know how to reply.

'Real accurate, I'd say.' That was Edie. 'I can't believe you can sit and drink Champagne in the Ritz in the middle of a war,' she said.

'Well, what else would you do? Don't you love the idea that in Paris, right now, the Ritz is filled with filthy Germans? And here we are, having the jolliest time? Even Farv doesn't disapprove.' The Mitfords' terrifying father was given to violent rages about anything he considered unBritish.

They pushed their way to the back of the room where a small table was free. 'Go and steal some chairs,' Debo said to Edie. To Kick's surprise, Edie smiled and went off to do as she was bade.

'How's Diana?' Kick asked. Debo's sister, with her husband Sir Oswald Mosley, had been imprisoned once war was declared.

His years as leader of the fascist Blackshirts had made him a threat to security.

'Having the most marvellous time,' Debo said defiantly.

'In prison?'

'Yes, but thanks to Churchill – who really is a dear – she and Mosley are now together, so she's perfectly happy. The sweetest little house in Holloway . . .'

'The prison?' Kick repeated. She'd said the word twice, probably once too many times. And, indeed, a faint crease between Debo's eyebrows suggested the same.

'Yes,' she said patiently, 'but quite away from the other prisoners, who in any case are all women. They grow vegetables, listen to records and sunbathe in the garden. It's tiny, but has the perfect aspect, Diana says. She couldn't be happier.'

Beside her, Brigid's face held sympathy. Sissy's eyes were round with wonder, and Kick, who knew the Mitford itch to make everything – even, perhaps especially, the worst things – into something wonderful, felt Debo was protesting too much.

'What about the boys?' she asked.

'With Pamela.' She was the second oldest Mitford sister, the one Kick knew least. 'In Berkshire. Perfectly happy, I'm sure.'

'How old are the boys?' Sissy asked.

'Alexander is five and Max was born the month before Diana went to prison.'

'They put her in jail a month after she had a baby?' Edie, back with another chair, asked.

'I'm sure it was a frightful nuisance for them too,' Debo said. It was valiant, Kick thought, but it chilled her a little when Debo added, 'Though Diana is furious about her dog, Jacob. Pamela had him put down, with Diana's favourite mare, because she said Diana's future was too uncertain and she couldn't be expected to look after the animals as well as the boys.' The noise of the room seemed to die down as they all took this in.

Didn't war do *a lot*, Kick thought. Not just the obvious things – battles, air raids – but so many other disruptions. Diana had always been terrifying, somehow repellent, despite her beauty, and even though Kick could imagine her exactly as Debo described – perfectly happy in the 'sweetest little house' with Mosley, despite the separation from her boys – she felt a chill at the way things could change in an instant. The last time she had been in England, Diana had been adored, even by those who despised her husband, but the war had made them enemies overnight, to be contained within prison walls. What might war do to her and Billy? To her and Billy's parents?

'Champagne!' Andrew arrived with a bucket and a bottle, glasses thrust into the ice. He poured for Kick first, perhaps to make amends for the sting of his remark. A glass of Champagne wasn't enough to wash away the smart, but she smiled. They drank, finishing the bottle, and another, then a third sent over by a fellow called Hugh, whom Kick used to go about with and who, when he saw her, caught her up in his arms and twirled her around, saying, 'Of all the unexpected things war has brought, you are by far the nicest.' Everyone laughed.

'Let's go on,' said Debo, when the bar had emptied around them. 'The 400 Club?'

Kick still felt the barb of Andrew's joke – worse, it brought back sharp memories of all the ways she had been told she was 'impossible' for Billy. But she looked at Sissy's huge eyes, Edie's flushed face, Brigid laughing with her head thrown back, and said yes.

Chapter Fourteen

Sissy

Outside the Ritz, Sissy was shocked to see that the streets were completely dark. Dark like the countryside was dark, where the lack of light was a presence, almost as much as an absence. People moved about slowly and furtively. One man with a lantern scuttled past, his hand over the light as though he thought German bombers would see and be guided by its feeble flicker. Inside had been so gay and bright. And the Champagne she had drunk, she who had never drunk anything more than plum wine, had helped her forget that not all the world laughed, chattered and was merry. She had forgotten that war meant anything except herding tightly together into small spaces, gleaning comfort from proximity to other warm bodies, and telling stories to make each other laugh.

'Stay here and I'll get us a taxi,' Debo said. 'It's too dark to walk. Takes hours to go even a short distance without street-lights.' She disappeared around the corner.

'Is she quite mad?' Edie asked in a loud whisper, leaning towards Kick.

'Probably.' Kick laughed. 'But also much less mad than you might think. Isn't that right, Brigid?'

'Oh, yes,' Brigid assured them. 'Exactly.'

Sissy tried to slow her racing mind enough to think about Debo. Mad? Maybe. At least, she thought, she could see why Edie had said it. But mad wasn't what she had felt about Debo. That story about the sister in prison, and the two little boys being cared for by another sister. Even through the defiance, Sissy had seen sadness. Worry, too, beneath the insistence that no one must feel sorry for them. Sissy understood that. Her mother had a strong measure of it too, in the brittle way she disdained to care about the damp walls and bulging wallpaper at Ballycorry. The careless assertion that there was 'nothing' for families like theirs. She thought of the agonised calculations her parents made – would there be enough to send her brother to university after school? Which men might there be for Sissy and where might she meet them? And, without men, what could a girl of Sissy's background do?

As she listened to these conversations – Sissy had to piece together bits from a thousand others and try to shape them – what was most obvious to her was that her parents had no faith in her. In their eyes, she was nothing except what they gave her.

It was interesting, she thought then, how very little they saw her. Until the kissing in the barn. Then her mother had noticed her – *You didn't see them. I did. She was so horribly . . . assured.* And didn't like what she had seen. She had always felt a calculation in the way her mother looked at her – a question. But after the barn it had been different. The question had been answered. And Sissy was lacking. In what way she didn't know, only that she was. She wanted to ask, did these girls too have mothers who looked at them in a way that asked them to disprove some sly allegation never made out loud? But she couldn't begin to think how she might do so, so she said nothing.

Brigid was still talking, mostly to Kick: 'For all that the Mitfords are mad,' she said, 'no one blinked at her and Andrew marrying. I know he's a younger son and it's not the same as with Billy who will inherit, but all the same, I think it's mean, don't you?'

Kick murmured something noncommittal. She had gone rather quiet, Sissy realised. She wondered what Brigid had meant, but just then Andrew appeared with Debo's coat, which he had politely stayed to gather, and around the corner came a taxi with black paint over its headlamps so that it cast a streaky light that dipped almost to nothing. It was a light scared to be seen, and the taxi reminded Sissy of the voles and shrews at home that would poke out at dusk, noses questing into the air, venturing cautiously across dangerous ground.

'Get in,' Debo called, leaning out the window. 'Quick.'

They piled in, Andrew last, all squashing into the back seat. 'Leicester Square,' Debo said. 'Now, as an old married lady,' she smirked at Andrew, 'I feel I need to warn you that there will be any number of young men trying the old "I'm off to war tomorrow and may never come back" routine. I expect you'll see through it but, just in case, you should know that the war effort does not extend to being *too* kind to these chaps.'

'Or even kind at all,' Edie said, rolling her eyes. 'They do it at the club too. As if me going out with them could make a difference to anything that happens.'

Edie spoke so scornfully that Andrew murmured, 'I say . . .' and Sissy understood that the harshness in Edie's voice had upset him.

Their cab driver filled them in on the night's violence – no bombs but a badly bomb-damaged house in Mayfair had collapsed, taking half its neighbour with it. The damaged house had been empty, but next door had had a family of five living in it. They now joined the ranks of those with nowhere to go.

'What happens to them?' Sissy asked.

'I don't know,' Debo said. She sounded surprised to be asked. As though she had never thought about it. 'I suppose they move in with family or friends.'

'If they can,' their cab driver said. 'Or they stay in shelters. Some live in schools. Sometimes they just move back into their own houses and live around the wreckage if it's not too bad.'

'Goodness,' Brigid said vaguely. Then, 'I suppose that's what Chips is doing really. Belgrave Square has had its windows broken several times. And each time he insists they be replaced. Mama thinks he should just board them up and wait till it's all over, but he simply won't. He says that's tantamount to giving in.'

Sissy thought back to the house she had seen for the first time – was it really only that afternoon? – to the opulence and lavishness, the deep carpets, the sheen of brocade sofas and the wink of crystal. 'I wonder if it's quite the same,' she said, and heard Debo stifle a giggle.

At the entrance to the nightclub they tumbled out, and found their way blocked by a small woman with an improbable amount of hair piled on top of her head, dressed in a mannish jacket and tight skirt. She took their names – nodding recognition at Debo – and read them the rules: 'No fighting, no whoring.'

Andrew flinched, Sissy saw, which made her laugh even though she had only the vaguest idea of what whoring might be. 'No bothering the band, and no stumbling out when you feel like it.' The blackout curtains were carefully arranged and she didn't want trouble with the police, thank you, because fools wandered into the street leaving light spilling out behind them.

They agreed meekly, and were allowed through the curtains, behind which two large glass doors were crisscrossed with solid brass strips, then down a flight of steep dark stairs into music and the smell of bodies packed into a hot space.

'Careful,' Edie muttered, as Sissy stumbled against her. 'You'll have us all down.'

More doors, wooden this time, then a room in which the music seemed to hang, suspended by drifting wreaths of cigarette smoke. Wooden floorboards were alternately scuffed and shiny and on a tiny stage, sheltered by giant fringed plants, there was an improbably large orchestra. Sissy counted eighteen men.

'How clever they must be with their elbows,' she whispered to Edie.

Idly, she wondered how the plants stayed alive, down there in all that airless gloom. Lights hung in clusters from the ceiling, but were too high and too dim to make much of an impression. This, she understood immediately, was deliberate. The dark was protective.

Round tables with white cloths and spindly chairs crowded around a patch of dance-floor, and the room was full of people. Every chair, every table, every bit of space. She recognised faces she had seen only an hour before at the Ritz. A girl in a tomato-red dress with flushed cheeks and wide black eyes. A man with curly hair and a knowing smile.

As they pushed through the crowd, Sissy saw couples pressed

Emily Hourican

close together, some dancing, or swaying, others seated or even standing. She realised, with a hot feeling in her cheeks, that she had never seen men and women so close together before. *What a rustic I am.* The idea made her determined to be sophisticated. When a man asked her to dance, she said yes, waving Brigid away when she raised an enquiring eyebrow. He was swaying slightly and smelt strongly of beer but Sissy ignored that. On the dance-floor he held her tightly, too tightly, his arms wrapped around her as though she were an unruly bolster he hoped to subdue. At first she didn't mind – there was too much to look at: women with beautifully coiffed hair and satin evening dresses, men in uniform who held them as though they were something rare and precious, who lit their cigarettes and refilled their glasses. The band played music that was dreamy and slow, then quick and urgent. A group of men threw a rolled-up napkin between them as though it were a rugby ball, laughing immoderately.

Everything, she thought, was beautiful. Everything sparkled and glittered and murmured, rippling like dune grass on a windy day. The band played something familiar – she caught occasional words – and she allowed herself to be pushed this way and that by the soldier. But then she became conscious that he was stumbling more now, and in a way that seemed to pull her closer towards him. That his arms were so tight around her that she could hardly take a full breath. That she didn't like it. She looked around for the others but saw no faces she knew.

There was a sour smell. It was her soldier. She took a step back, trying to dislodge his arms. But he closed them tighter and pressed himself forward. The buttons of his jacket were cutting into her through the thin silk of Kick's green dress. She was conscious suddenly of her bare arms and the scratch of his

-136-

coarse khaki against them. She pulled away again but he didn't give an inch.

'I should think that's enough,' a man in evening dress, rather than uniform, said briskly, tapping the soldier on the shoulder. 'My turn now.'

The soldier looked bewildered, but didn't resist. He allowed the man to unravel his arms from Sissy, then turn him lightly on the spot and give him a gentle push. It was enough to get him moving, lurching clumsily, in the other direction.

Sissy and her rescuer stood and looked at one another, still and silent within the press of movement. The man was older than her in a way that felt comforting, but not enough for him to be 'old'. He was thin, tall, with a face all angles and sharp bones.

'How did you know?' Sissy asked.

'You looked like a cat on a windowsill on a wet day. Insulted and eager and canny, all at once.'

'I was,' she agreed. 'That's exactly how I felt. Aren't you clever, to see that?'

'I'm used to looking closely at faces,' he said.

'Why? Are you a spy?' What could be more likely, in such a place, she thought. But he burst out laughing.

'No!'

'Not that you'd tell if you were,' she reflected.

'Indeed. But I'm not. I'm a painter. Portraits. I spend my time drawing people's faces.'

Sissy turned hers upwards to the light – such light as there was – waiting. But he just laughed again. 'You're too young,' he said. 'There's nothing in that face yet, just an awful lot of hope.' He smiled, but Sissy felt vaguely insulted.

'I've had some very lowering experiences,' she assured him.

'Perhaps. But they aren't written there yet. Now, where's your party? Or did you come alone?'

'Over there somewhere.' She gestured towards the other side of the room.

'Let's find them.' He led the way, pushing through the crowd, weaving between tables with a confidence that impressed Sissy. She felt certain that, had she not been following him, indeed, had he not taken her hand in his to lead her, she would have bumped into everything, knocking over glasses and bottles. Yes, she was clumsy, she knew it – and had constant bruises on her shins and arms to prove it – but even so, why must everything be so crowded and spindly and rickety, she thought, as she brushed against a table and set four glasses on slender stems wobbling? This man seemed to feel no such apprehension, simply ploughed along until she cried, 'There!' spotting a table where Debo and Kick sat. Brigid and Edie were nowhere to be seen.

He stopped dead so she bumped into the back of him. 'Well, here we are,' he said. Then, head on one side as he looked at her, 'You don't have to dance with every soldier who asks, just because he tells you he's off to war tomorrow.'

Sissy giggled. 'That's exactly what my friend said . . . But what if I told you that it was *I* who was off to war tomorrow?' She lowered her lashes. 'Would you dance with me?'

'I might. Come and find me if you decide to.' He released her then and made a little mocking bow. 'You'll be all right from here, I take it?'

'Oh yes,' she assured him. He turned and moved away. The crowd closed around him almost immediately. But his black jacket was easy to spot among the sea of grey and khaki uniforms, at least at first, and she watched which way he went.

'Who was that?' She turned to find Debo standing beside her. 'Why isn't he in uniform?'

'I don't know. Should he be?'

'Everyone else is.' Then, 'There aren't any chairs. You'll have to find one. Wait,' as Sissy set off obligingly, 'you'll never manage. Stay there.' She walked to a nearby table where a couple were embracing heavily and tipped an evening bag off the chair beside them. Sissy watched it fall to the floor, chain slithering like a live thing. 'Here, sit.' Debo pushed the chair beside Kick's and Sissy sat.

'So?' Kick asked.

'He's an artist,' Sissy continued. 'He draws people's portraits.'

'Artists can fight too,' Debo said, lighting a cigarette with the snap of a square gold lighter.

'Probably a CO,' Kick said wisely.

'CO?' Sissy asked.

'Conscientious objector. Men who won't fight because they're pacifists.'

'Farv says they're cowards,' Debo said, exhaling smoke. But she didn't say it as though she believed it.

'They do other work,' Kick said gently. 'NCC, that sort of thing.'

'NCC?' Sissy wondered if she would spend the rest of the evening asking people to translate things, letters, that they all understood and she didn't.

'Non-combatant corps. They do a lot of the clearing up after bombs. Rebuilding. That kind of thing. Perfectly honourable. Otherwise they're in jail, if they really won't do anything.'

A girl blundered over to them. She wore a shiny peacock-blue dress that shimmered in the low light. Her hair was in fat curls but dishevelled, half pinned up, half tumbling down. In one hand she carried something furry. Sissy thought she clutched a small animal and worried about it, pressed so tight like that, before realising it was a fur stole.

'Kathleen Kennedy,' the girl cried. 'So it's true what they say, you *are* back.' She leaned in and kissed Kick clumsily on the cheek.

'Meredith,' Kick said, without much enthusiasm that Sissy could see.

'Me,' Meredith agreed. 'They all said you were here, but I didn't believe it. I said, "There's no way Kick Kennedy would come to London and not look me up."' She smiled round at them all. Her eyes, Sissy saw, were small and blue and hard.

'I only arrived a few days ago,' Kick said evasively. She clearly hoped Meredith would leave them.

'Well,' Meredith said, 'I suppose late is better than never.'

'What do you mean?'

'The Kennedy Retreat – isn't that what everyone said? The ambassador's yellow belly.'

'You'll have to take that up with him,' Kick said. 'He's big enough to fight his own battles.'

'Is it true what else they say?' Meredith asked.

'Which is?'

'That you're back to become a duchess?'

'I . . .' Kick seemed lost for words in a way Sissy hadn't yet seen her.

'Just because America has joined the war doesn't mean you can come over here and help yourself to anything you want.'

'Actually, it means exactly that,' Debo said, on a giggle. 'Haven't you seen the GIs in action? It's like duck-shooting with the Prince of Wales used to be – him bagging every single bird because everyone else was too frightened to have a go. That's the GIs now with English girls, who are simply silly about them. Or about their cigarettes and nylons,' she added. 'Our poor English boys can't get a look-in.' She paused. 'Your little friend seems thirsty.' She waved towards the fur stole, now drooping from Meredith's hand so that the end trailed in a glass of something orange that had a bright red cherry floating in it. 'What is it? A rat? Unity used to have a pet one. She says they make delightful companions.'

'Damn!' Meredith snatched it up but it was too late. A sticky liquid coated the fur. Sissy smelt aniseed.

'How *is* Unity?' Meredith asked angrily.

'Still funnier and livelier than anyone else,' Debo said defiantly. Meredith opened her mouth, hard blue eyes screwed up spitefully, and Sissy wondered what was coming.

But before she could speak, Brigid returned. 'Don't you think you've made enough friends here, Meredith?'

Something about her tone, her near indifference, seemed to shake Meredith, who muttered, 'People who don't know what's friendly . . .' and walked away, trailing the sticky fur. As Sissy watched, she stuffed it angrily into a pot with a giant fern.

'What was that?' she asked, turning back to look at her friends. 'Who's Unity?' No one spoke for a minute, but Brigid and Kick both turned to Debo.

'Unity is my sister,' Debo said eventually.

'Another sister?'

'Yes. She tried to kill herself when war broke out. She shot herself.'

'But she didn't die?'

'She survived, and I wasn't lying when I said she's funnier and livelier than ever. But there's a great deal she can no longer do for herself. She lives with Muv.'

'Debo's mother,' Kick supplied.

'Most people think it would have been far less awkward of her if she *had* died. But I don't. I'm glad she didn't and I shall go on being glad, even though she's getting odder, and people like Meredith think I should hang my head and be ashamed.'

'Why?' Sissy said. 'Why did she try to kill herself? Does she hate war so very much?'

'The thing is, she was rather in love with Hitler – still is, actually – but frightfully patriotic too, so with England and Germany at war . . .' Debo trailed off.

'Well, I say . . .' Sissy said. *She was rather in love with Hitler* . . . What on earth had Debo meant? How could someone be in love with Hitler? Not only was he the enemy, but they had all been told, again and again, how ridiculous he was with his small moustache and his puppeteer arms. What company had she found herself in that there were girls who knew and loved the man who was responsible for all their woes? She was silent, trying to take it in. Trying, too, to disguise the pure thrill she felt at knowing people who were so sophisticated, so rackety. Imagine Theresa Molloy's face now!

'Except you don't,' Debo said kindly. Correctly. 'Of course you don't. No one does. They don't know what *to* say. Anyway,' she turned to Kick, 'what *about* Billy? Have you heard from him?'

'He sent a telegram,' Kick said. 'It arrived this evening. He's taking me out Saturday two weeks.' If it hadn't been so dark, Sissy was pretty sure she would have been blushing.

'Well, that was fast,' Debo said. Andrew came back, with more drinks, and pulled her up to dance. A group of young men in uniform hailed Brigid, and then, when they realised who she was, Kick, and loud conversation of the 'When did you . . .?' variety began.

Sissy decided to go and look for her rescuer of earlier. She walked back through the crowd, past the dance-floor on the other side. She passed Edie with a couple of GIs. One had a foot up on a chair and they seemed to be counting how fast he could lace his boots. Sissy heard Edie shout, 'I win!' as he pushed the lace through the last eyehole. 'I told you it couldn't be done in less than twenty . . .' She looked up as Sissy passed and winked at her, jerking her head to say, 'Join us?' Sissy smiled and shook her head.

She had almost reached the very back of the room, when she spotted the man. He was sitting at a table with two others, also not in uniform. Now that she was primed by Debo, she noticed immediately. This part of the room was a bit quieter and emptier than the rest, and suddenly Sissy felt shy. What was she doing, following this man back here? What had she imagined she would say to him? She was about to turn and slide away, back to Edie, back to Kick, when he saw her.

'Coming to tell me you're off to war, are you?' he said.

His friends looked up too, so Sissy felt even shyer. But also pleased that he had remembered her joke of earlier. 'Maybe I'd be believable if I said Land Girl.'

'More believable, but far less pathos,' he said. 'Come and sit with us?'

'Yes, please.'

'We're drinking whisky, but I can get you Champagne?'

'Whisky is lovely.' She'd never had it. But she'd never had Champagne either until a few hours ago. She wished someone from home could see her now. Not Mother, of course, but maybe one of the maids. They'd be impressed. Shocked, too, of course. That was the point. 'I don't know your name,' she said, shy again.

'Yes, I know,' he sounded amused, 'because I didn't tell you.' Was he mocking her? He might have been. 'It's Peter.' He stuck out his hand and she shook it solemnly, even though she was pretty certain he was mocking her now.

'He rescued me,' she said to the other men.

'Hardly. I simply reminded a dull-witted and rather clumsy soldier that he can't hog all the nicest girls even if he is off to war.' Now she was glad the light was bad so they couldn't see her blushing: *the nicest girls* . . . He introduced his friends – Jim and Dylan – who turned out to be another painter and a poet.

'We're whatever the opposite of heroes are,' Jim said.

'Most people?' she volunteered. 'Most people are the opposite of heroes, otherwise heroes wouldn't *be* heroes.' They laughed at that and Dylan offered her a cigarette. She took it, allowed him to light it for her and breathed in carefully. The only time she'd tried smoking – one stolen from Mother's neat gold cigarette case – she'd coughed so much she'd almost been sick.

'And what about you, what do you do, now that all girls do something?' Peter asked.

'I don't know yet,' she answered. 'I'm here to do something, but I don't yet know what it will be. Or even where,' she put out her cigarette in a heavy glass ashtray already filled with butts. 'No one has told me yet.'

'Well, why don't you decide for yourself?' Peter said patiently, as though to a child. 'Then you get to choose where you'll be.'

'Could I?' she asked him, genuinely astonished at such an idea. And then, 'I could, couldn't I?'

'Of course you could.' The knowledge thrummed through her, hazy and without specifics. She didn't know what sort of things she could do – Brigid was a nurse, but she didn't know anything about that; Kick worked for the Red Cross, Edie too, but they were American. There must be many jobs that needed little more than willingness. And some of them at least must be in London. She'd find one.

Peter asked her questions then, about where she was from, what she thought of London. He listened carefully to her answers, and added bits of information of his own, so she learned that he had a flat in a place called Soho, and that he and Jim were indeed NCCs, but not because they were COs – she felt proud of how quickly she had learned the abbreviations. Peter had asthma and Jim 'something up' with his heart.

'We're the duds,' Jim said. 'Funny thing to be, a dud during wartime. We're like the bombs that don't explode when dropped, UXOs.'

'Hardly,' Peter said. 'UXOs are urgent threats that must be assessed and dismantled. There's a big kerfuffle over them. We're more like phoney bombs. Turnips painted to look like incendiaries.'

'How lowering,' Dylan said. He talked less than the others, Sissy noted. Maybe because he was more drunk.

'You're not such a dud,' Peter said to him. 'In fact, I dare say if you did try to join up – Dylan's sickly too, though not as sickly as us – they wouldn't let you. All those morale-boosting broadcasts.'

'Is that what you do?' Sissy asked, impressed. 'Broadcast?'

'I do. For radio. And the odd propaganda film.' He waved an arm modestly, knocking over a glass that was mostly empty. What whisky there was landed on his trouser leg and he rubbed the stain absentmindedly with a sleeve.

'What about you?' she asked the others. Jim said he drove an ambulance and Peter that he did 'clerical work' at the War

Office. He said it with a sneer and Sissy felt certain he was sneering first, in case she did.

'Someone has to,' she said kindly.

'That,' Peter said, 'is exactly what everyone says. *All war work is valuable,*' he parroted. '*An army marches on many things.*' He finished his glass, throwing his head back, and slapped it down on the table. Not quite a slam, but close. Sissy saw the humiliation in his face that he covered with an indifferent smile. She knew that was what it was because she did the same thing. The same kind of smile, used when Mother said something cruel, or hit her especially hard. Knowing that about Peter made her feel as though he had told her something secret about himself. Even though, if she thought about it, he hadn't. He had carefully not told her. He had, in fact, tried to hide the thing.

'There you are!' It was Kick. 'We've been looking for you. Wondered where on earth you'd got to.' She sounded tired and cross. 'We're leaving.'

'We thought you'd run away with a soldier,' Brigid said, joining Kick. 'Instead we find you tucked away in a discreet corner with this lot.' She gave the men a curious look. Sissy introduced them and everyone nodded at each other. Without, she noticed, much enthusiasm on either side.

'Well, thanks again,' she said to Peter. He looked momentarily surprised. Had clearly forgotten what she was thanking him for. She stood there awkwardly, wanting to say something else, ask something that would have an answer that meant they met again, but she couldn't think of anything.

'You should come to the King's Anchor some time,' Jim said kindly. 'We're there most evenings. Pub on the corner of Tottenham Court Road.'

'I will,' Sissy said. 'We will.' She looked at her friends. 'Won't we?'

'Come along,' Kick said. Debo and Edie were waiting in the doorway, ready to go up the stairs together and co-ordinate their exit through the front door, as they had been instructed.

'Although I bet it's bright outside by now,' Edie said. 'No need for blackout curtains and elaborate escape plans.'

'We're still doing what Ma Merrick told us,' Debo said, leading them up the dark stairs. 'Otherwise she'll turn us away next time.' Then, 'You can't let strange men pick you up like that,' she said to Sissy. 'It really was the limit, having to crawl into corners, looking for you.'

'Sorry,' Sissy said. 'Although if I'm very honest, I think I picked them up, not the other way around. I'm sure they weren't terribly interested in talking to me, only being polite.'

Edie started giggling. 'You're funny.'

'And I don't know why you picked a bunch of COs when all those men in uniform were simply dying to dance with a nice girl,' Debo continued. 'You really need to be more careful.' At that Edie went into a fit of laughter that she tried to disguise. Sissy could see her shoulders shaking when she turned on the narrow staircase.

'That reminds me,' Brigid said. 'Mama telephoned before I left Belgrave Square and has found work for you in Dorset. There's an aircraft factory. You can start immediately.' They had reached the top now, and Ma arranged them in twos, Brigid and Kick, followed by Sissy and Debo, Edie and Andrew behind them.

'Off you go.' She gave Debo a push and twitched aside the heavy black curtains. Out they went. Sure enough, it was dawn. The sun had struggled up and was casting a bleary light that fought with the dark and did not, yet, look as though victory was certain. A truck went past, tyres heavy on the pock-marked road.

'Dorset!' Sissy repeated in horror. 'How can I leave London, after this?' She swept an arm expansively about, to take in the greyish street, the houses and buildings slowly emerging from the dark around them as though they were being conjured with difficulty. A group of men in air-raid precautions uniform went past, chatting about the night's doings. 'Another quiet one,' they assured the girls cheerily, as they went by. 'Gerry's back to boring us into submission.'

'Well, come and volunteer with me, then,' Debo said idly. 'The YMCA canteen. It's disgusting – yes, you may feel sorry for me,' she said to Kick, with a grin. 'And not just disgusting, they all mock me terribly for the way I talk.'

'Hard to resist,' Brigid murmured.

'But you're very welcome to join me,' Debo finished, ignoring Brigid.

Quite as though she were inviting me to a party, Sissy thought, with a giggle. 'I'd love to,' she said. 'I'll work harder than anyone.'

'If you start to spoil things for the rest of us by being too eager, the other girls will hate you,' Debo said. 'They'll do far worse than mock the way you talk. One girl, well, they didn't take to her, and after a while she found all sorts of strange things in her tea. Sawdust. At least she thought it was sawdust . . .' She opened her eyes very wide.

Sissy laughed. 'Then I'll be as slow as a donkey,' she said. 'Whatever is required, I will be, if only I don't have to leave London now that I have discovered it.'

'You've been to the Ritz,' Brigid said, 'and the 400 Club. That is not London.'

'It's all the London I need,' Sissy said.

'The King's Anchor?' Brigid asked, head on one side.

'Now I shall need somewhere to live,' Sissy said, ignoring her.

'With us,' Edie said. 'Right, Kick? There's loads of space.'

'There isn't,' Kick said, 'but OK.'

'See me,' Sissy said happily, 'only a day in London and already I have a job, two places to say, and more friends than I've ever had. Isn't war *fun?*'

'What a baby you are,' Debo said. But she said it fondly, and when Sissy grabbed her arm and linked her, with Edie on the other side, Debo let her.

Chapter Fifteen

Kick

In the first minutes of struggling awake, Kick knew she hadn't had enough sleep. She also knew she had to get up. Her shift started at eleven. She checked the little travel clock beside her bed and groaned. She sat up, pushing her hair out of her eyes. The flat was silent. Edie, as she had reminded Kick smugly as she wiped cold cream around her face, had a later shift and wouldn't be needed till the afternoon.

Her hair felt dirty and smelt of cigarettes, but there would be no chance to wash it. No one to complain about it either, though. That was the glorious thing.

She still couldn't get over the freedom of London. Washington had been intoxicating, but this was even more so. There, people knew about her family, and that had meant trying so hard to be someone who didn't think too much of herself. Especially once the news of Rosie got out, and the whispers started; so too then did Kick's sense of responsibility, her wish to be proof that the whispers were wrong. To show them all that whatever they said about the Kennedys, well, they knew nothing.

Instinctively, she tilted her chin defiantly, then caught herself doing it in the blurred mirror over the bathroom basin, and dropped it. She wiped the glass with a corner of the towel and looked at her reflection. What was it her father had said? 'Your type fades fast . . .' Other fathers, she thought ruefully, called their daughters 'My Little Princess' or 'The Prettiest Girl in the World'. Not Joe Kennedy.

She decided that anyone would look dreadful after a late night and in the dull light of another grey English summer's day. What did they do with the sun here that they had so little of it? Did they put it away and keep it for best, the way some people did with their good china? She felt suddenly deflated, her memory of Andrew's remark of the night before too sharp: *I wonder if my father will think so . . .* Why, when so much of the evening was hazy, must she remember this so clearly? And why did it suddenly seem to spoil seeing Billy? Why couldn't she just look forward to being in his company, without the edges of that being pinched and squeezed by his parents and what they might think? Without the nagging little voice that asked her, *What are you doing, Kick Kennedy, coming halfway around the world for a man you can't ever marry?* She shook her head – literally shook it – to clear the thought. She must hurry.

She washed in water that wasn't cold, but certainly wasn't hot, dipping quickly in and out and drying herself on a threadbare towel. The flat was mostly furnished with cast-offs from Belgrave Square, and it seemed that anything Chips had been ready to pass on was well and truly past its best. She longed for a proper soak, in hot water up to her neck, then to wrap herself in a large, soft, clean towel. Maybe she'd ask Brigid if she could get dressed at Belgrave Square before Billy took her out. She couldn't see Chips putting up with thin towels and tepid water.

Dressed, Kick dithered. If she was quick, she could dash off a letter home before going to the club. But that would mean breakfast here – tea and bread with margarine was as much as their kitchen would yield – rather than at the club where she could have coffee, and doughnuts, or at least toast and jam. No, better write, she decided. They would send sharp telegrams if she didn't.

She made tea badly. She thought she might be someone who always made tea badly, no matter how often she was shown how, and sat down to write at the table by the window that had one leg shorter than the others. She shoved a wadded piece of paper under the short leg.

She looked out at the street. It had been brighter at dawn when they left the nightclub. That made her want to wake Edie so they could chat about the night: about Debo – Kick was dying to know what Edie, so American, so forthright, had made of this most English of her friends. But also to speculate about Sissy – where had she been half the night? Surely not with those strange men? And Brigid. There was a new reserve to Brigid that Kick had noticed immediately and that had become even more pronounced as the evening wore on. She spoke less than the others, seemed mostly immune to the giddy fun around them. Was it tiredness? The seriousness of her work at the hospital? Something more?

But she couldn't wake Edie, that wouldn't be fair, not when

Edie had said, 'You'll have to be gay and wholesome and American all on your own,' as she slid into bed and yawned luxuriously. 'I plan on being dead to the world until after lunch at least.'

She took a sip of tea – why did it have that thin layer of something greasy on top? – and began writing. A letter full of cheery news:

If I closed my eyes to the holes where houses were, and ignored the wail of air-raid sirens. I'd almost not know there was a war. And, boy, am I glad I brought a few evening dresses because I'm going to need them. I simply can't get over how nice everyone is. The newspapers are very friendly and even flattering but I'm sure you've seen that. Now, love to all and eat extra ice cream for me on Sunday!

She sealed the envelope and stuffed it into the pocket of her coat. Why hadn't she written the truth, she wondered, as she raced down the stairs, late now, and out onto the street? Why had she written about ice cream and evening dresses rather than about Rosie? Why hadn't she said, *A newspaper here has written of my arrival and I am furious* . . . Maybe because it would sound like she was complaining, and Kennedys never complained. But she was too tired to puzzle it all out.

Andrew's comment had crashed in on her sense of herself. It reminded her that there were those for whom the idea of her was unwelcome. And even though she tried to shake that off, it clung.

At the club there were new GIs, in London on relief, homesick and discontented just like the last lot. Their complaints were as

Kick had learned to expect: petty. Warm beer, unfamiliar food, unfriendly girls or, worse, calculating girls. 'It's just nice to talk to an American girl,' a GI, whose name was Charlie, said to her. 'You know where you are with an American girl. Why, I don't know if I haven't said the wrong thing half the time with these English girls. The way they look at you, so cold.' He seemed more upset by this, Kick thought, than any of the army privations.

'Let's get you another cup of coffee,' she said soothingly, 'and see if you can't beat me at ping-pong.' At first, she had tried to talk them into seeing the England she saw – a land where bravery hid behind indifference, where something funny was never more than moments away – but she rarely succeeded.

'The club is where they come to complain. Leave 'em be,' had been Edie's advice.

'You might let a fellow win!' Charlie said, after the third game of ping-pong, when she had again thrashed him. But he said it merrily. Clearly her refusal to be beaten didn't upset and confuse him as the coldness of the English girls did.

'She can't.' That was Edie, on her way through the door. 'Actually can't. Like some people can't sing. Kick can't let anyone win at anything.'

'Unless they're really better than me,' Kick agreed.

'They never are,' Edie assured Charlie. 'At least, not at any of the things we do here. Don't play bridge with her for money, that's my advice.' Then, untying the belt of her coat and hanging it on the stand behind the door, 'Do you think we'll ever be able to go out without a coat? If this is summer, what do they call winter?'

'That's it,' Charlie agreed. 'Exactly it. And if "friendly" is the word they use for the way they treat a fellow and it seems like they despise us, what on earth do they call it when they actually like us?'

'A proposal?' Edie asked, making Charlie laugh heartily.

'You're a pistol,' he said admiringly. Edie went to the kitchen while Kick and Charlie played another few games of ping-pong. He proposed going to the West End to see *The Lisbon Story* just as Edie returned. 'We could get up a party,' he said eagerly. 'Couldn't we, fellas?' Around them, men came and went. Some nodded.

'I say,' Sissy appeared in the doorway, hair wispy and damp from the drizzle, 'can I come in?' They assured her she could, and soon she was sitting on a table, swinging her legs as she bit into a doughnut. She rolled her eyes slowly up to Heaven. 'Blissful,' she said, through a mouthful of sugar. 'Never did I think anything so delicious existed.'

Charlie looked at her with approval. 'You could be in the party, Miss,' he said, 'for *The Lisbon Story*. Couldn't she?' he appealed to Edie.

'She could,' Edie agreed.

And Kick began to understand that although Sissy wore a very dull jersey and skirt, and wasn't pretty at all really, she was appealing. 'So what brings you here?' she asked.

'I woke up this morning, well, nearly lunchtime, and I thought maybe I dreamed everything,' Sissy said. 'I never went to bed so late in my life.'

'You're, what, eighteen?' Edie asked. 'I wouldn't consider yourself a lost cause just yet.'

'Brigid had gone to the hospital,' Sissy continued, 'and I was too scared to stay in that house by myself. I couldn't remember any of the places anyone said they worked, except this one. I thought I'd come and find you before the butler, Andrews, gave me a duster and made me do the stairs.' By now Edie and Charlie were laughing so hard that Charlie made snorting noises. Sissy, unperturbed – even, Kick thought, pleased – continued: 'I wanted to see if I did really do all those things last night, and if Debo did really say I could work in the canteen with her,' she finished.

'I can't imagine anyone will turn you away if you offer to work in the kitchens of the Y,' Edie said, still laughing.

'The Why?' Sissy asked.

'The YMCA,' Kick explained. 'I think it's probably pretty hard work. I'm surprised Debo sticks it . . . Maybe you want to try for something easier.'

'I don't mind at all,' Sissy said. 'Like I said last night, I just want to stay in London. If that means the Y,' she pronounced it carefully, 'then let it be the Y.'

'That's it,' agreed Charlie. He was bouncing a ball energetically on his ping-pong bat – rather more skilfully than he played, Kick thought.

'In the meantime,' Sissy said, looking sideways at them from under her lashes, 'does anyone know how I might find Tottenham Court Road? I thought I might take a stroll down there.'

'Sissy!' Kick said, laughing. 'Is that really why you're here?'

'No . . . A bit, maybe. But I will call to the Y as I go and tell them I'm strong and willing and have simply tons of energy. Mother says I'm positively unladylike because I never get tired.'

'Never mind Mother,' Charlie said, 'and never mind "ladylike". You're a pistol!'

'I have a map of the city,' said Edie. 'Let's look it up. What did you say it's called?'

'Tottenham Court Road.'

After Sissy had gone, blowing out as she had blown in – all noise and eager good humour – Kick went to the kitchens, which were in the basement and, as Edie drily observed, clearly built by people who never intended to spend any time in them. Two rooms, cold and dark, even at the height of the day, with rough wooden countertops and a big stone sink. She kneaded dough and fried it, dusting the finished doughnuts with sugar. Back upstairs, she played cards with Charlie and a GI from Texas, who hated England so much he said he couldn't wait until they were sent on active duty to France.

'I don't usually hold with such talk,' Charlie responded, 'but this little island is about the limit.'

Kick tried to cheer them both with packets of Lucky Strike and Hershey bars, but found she wasn't getting very far. She was surprised at how seriously she took her duties. She hadn't thought about them before she'd left the US, except in as much as they were the means of getting back to London. But now that she was here, she found she wanted to do what she had been sent to do – cheer these big, raw farm boys and tough city opportunists who were so far from home and familiarity. She decided she would suggest darts, or a walk to Buckingham Palace – she felt that the sight of the flag, showing that the King was in residence, might cheer them. And if they saw the bits of the Palace that had been damaged by bombs, they might be impressed. But before she could do so, 'Another for you, Kick,' Edie said, adding, 'Seems like you might need your own separate entrance.'

'Tony!' Kick stood up and went to greet the young man standing behind Edie, a bottle of Champagne in one hand.

'They told me you were here,' he said. 'Thought I'd come and welcome you. Jolly good you're back, you know.'

'Do you really mean it?' Kick asked. She found she was almost crying at the happy way he was smiling at her. He was the perfect antidote to Andrew's joke, Meredith's cattiness of the night before when she'd heard her family described as 'the colour of the season, Kennedy-yellow'. So now, to see Tony, one of the very same 'ten lords a-leaping' – now Earl of Rosslyn – whose photo Jack had laughed at on her Washington flat wall, was like a warm embrace. 'How nice you are,' she said, hugging him.

'This is for you,' he thrust the Champagne at her, 'and I've something far better outside.'

'Well, let's go and look at "something better",' Kick said, taking the Champagne and tucking her arm through his.

It was a bicycle, with a bell attached to one of the handlebars. 'By far the best way to get about,' Tony said. 'Even at night. Funny how much one can see by the light of a single lamp. 'Course, you'll have to paint over it, but even so . . .' Kick thanked him, already calculating how rapidly a bicycle would shrink the distance between the flat on Portland Street, the officers' club, Belgrave Square and Eaton Square, where Andrew and Debo lived.

'Well, aren't you smart!' Kick said. 'And right. I was just thinking I'd better get myself one, and here you are.'

'I don't suppose that means you'd come out with me next time I'm on leave?' he said, bashful suddenly. 'Saturday two weeks?'

'I can't. As it happens I'm busy . . .'

'Busy already,' he said, 'Well, that's no surprise.' He looked crestfallen. 'I was so sure I was first,' he continued, 'but I suppose first was already taken.'

First was already taken. First had long been taken, Kick thought, even as she smiled at him. So much so that it wasn't even first – couldn't be, because there was no second, no third. There was only Billy.

Chapter Sixteen

Brigid

'**M**aureen is on her way,' Chips said, as Brigid belted her raincoat against the morning's drizzle. 'Duff is threatening to join up again, and she wants to persuade him not to. She won't stay in Hans Crescent because she can't get enough servants to open it, so she has asked to stay here. It's like I'm running a guesthouse,' he complained, but Brigid could see that he was pleased at the idea of company.

'When does she arrive?'

'Late tonight. The boat train. And I've invited Tony Rosslyn for dinner. Cook's got hold of a side of beef, goodness knows how.' Brigid knew very well that Chips was responsible for the black-market triumph. He was as busy about bolstering the ration book as he was about everything, but always careful to attribute his 'successes' to his cook: *She's a wonder*, he would say. *I don't know how she does it. I simply daren't ask . . .* 'He'll be here at eight. And I know very well you don't have a late shift at the hospital, Brigid darling, so don't bother trying to tell me you do.'

'Why Tony? Surely there are others more deserving of Cook's brilliance.' Brigid turned up her collar against the rain. But she knew very well why Tony: he was young, and an earl, and not yet married.

'I saw him at the club the other day, on leave from the Rifle Corps, and he looked like he could do with feeding. It's our duty, you know, to keep up morale among fighting men.'

Brigid sighed. 'You know he called to see Kick a couple of weeks ago?' she said maliciously. 'At the officers' club. He brought her a bicycle. And asked her out.'

'Kick can't marry everyone,' Chips said composedly. 'Or, at least, not all at once. And if Tony is disappointed that she won't go out with him, all the more reason to invite the poor fellow and see if we can cheer him up.'

'I hope Sissy's coming?'

'So disappointing for her,' Chips said seriously, 'but she can't. They work terribly odd hours at the Y.'

'Odder than anywhere else, it seems,' Brigid said drily. She had been amused to see Sissy so speedily refuse the factory job Lady Iveagh had found for her and insinuate herself into something just as menial but more convenient – clearly the girl was more capable than she first seemed.

Sissy had moved into the flat the day after the night at the Ritz, taking her very small suitcase with her. 'Where's the rest of your things?' Kick had asked.

'This is all I have,' Sissy said. 'It's not very much, is it?' She had looked wonderingly at her little case. 'Though it seemed enough when I packed in my bedroom at Ballycorry.'

'I suppose your winter things can follow,' Kick said. 'You won't need them for a few months.'

'I don't have any winter things,' Sissy had said, making Brigid laugh.

Nevertheless, Sissy continued to spend many hours at Belgrave Square – 'The food's better. Nothing much to eat at the flat except bread and margarine' – coming and going in a way that seemed deliberate in its very casualness.

In fact, Brigid had a fairly good idea of what she was up to. The girl had been three weeks in London by now, and the constant moving, Brigid understood, was so that no one really knew what she was doing, or learned her rhythms and routines so that they might begin to expect her or ask where she had been. She had a bicycle, an old one of Honor's, that she used, and simply appeared and disappeared without much notice. This worried Brigid. Sissy might be more capable than she first seemed, but she was also far less capable than she herself thought.

She had become a great pet of Chips, whom she treated like a large, friendly, sometimes annoying dog, to be petted and fed and chatted to, then pushed down off chairs and beds when it became too obstreperous. At first he had found her beneath notice, but quickly decided she was 'wonderful fun', insisted on keeping a bedroom made up for her at Belgrave Square and tried hard to persuade her to join his card parties and lunches.

'You don't need to go to the Y,' he would say, cajoling. 'Come to lunch and let me introduce you to people who can give you much more interesting, and important, work.' But Sissy wouldn't.

'No, thanks,' she said blithely. 'I like the old Y. The first week was rather terrible but now I know just what I'm doing. The other workers, as Debo said, are terrifying but funny. Anyway

I daren't do anything really important – I'll only make a mess of it. Best keep me away from Lady Cunard and Lady Astor, I'll only shame you.'

'Really, she's as bright as a button,' Chips said to Brigid now, 'For all that she has no style—'

'No *clothes*,' Brigid corrected him. 'There's a difference.'

'Is there?' He sounded surprised. 'Anyway, I don't know why she chooses to waste her time down there among the boiled peas and turnip soup. Whatever can she be thinking? Sometimes she comes here smelling terribly strange . . .' Then, 'So you will be here for dinner with Tony?' he asked.

'If I must,' Brigid said, resigned. 'Though I don't have time. There's so much to do.' Mostly, she wanted time to write to Fritzi, a proper letter, not the hastily dashed off notes of recent weeks when she was never at home long enough to set down all the things she had been doing since Kick's return. She wanted to tell him about Will and the look that crossed the doctor's face now when he examined him – a sort of pinching-in look that Brigid didn't like.

'This war is a frightful bore,' Chips said. 'All the young ladies are so busy now. So hard to get together any kind of gathering. Lunch is almost a thing of the past. People can barely spare an hour. Lady Cunard said she could manage a "quick bowl of soup" last week. A "quick bowl of soup",' he repeated. 'What an idea!'

'We must all make sacrifices,' Brigid murmured, trying not to laugh. Poor Chips, she almost felt sorry for him. His duties at the House of Commons weren't enough to keep a mind as energetic as his busy, and his extra-curricular political intriguing no longer found many takers, now that there was the national interest to consider. He was very often alone, he who had been so careful to surround himself with company, from morning till night. 'Where *is* everyone?' he had taken to saying, almost sadly.

And Brigid had begun to understand that whatever was keeping Honor away so much, it wasn't just war work. Chips clearly knew it. One evening, coming home earlier than usual, Brigid had heard him on the telephone in the library: 'I'm willing to let it all go by, if you will only come home, Honor. You cannot imagine how everyone is talking. I have tried saying that, with Paul in America, you feel obliged to put in double the effort of others . . .' Was there a note of malice in his voice? '. . . but it won't be possible to stop the gossip for much longer.'

She had gone hastily upstairs, unwilling to hear any more. But whatever Honor might have said or agreed to, she wasn't often found at Belgrave Square. No wonder Chips had persuaded Maureen to let Caroline stay, and go to private lessons with a retired headmistress who lived in a small garden flat on Wilton Street. 'She learns watercolours, French, and the art of conversation,' Chips had said with a sly laugh; 'we both agreed Maureen should pay extra for that.' Caroline might be silent – eerily so at times – but she was company, of a kind.

'I must get on,' Brigid said now.

'Dinner at eight,' Chips reiterated. 'And do dress.'

Before leaving, Brigid went to tell Caroline the news. She was in her bedroom, reading. She wore a tweed skirt and a jumper with holes at the elbows. 'Can I come in?' Brigid asked, tapping at the door.

'Of course.' Caroline moved her legs so Brigid could sit at the end of the bed.

'Your mother is on her way. She arrives tonight.'

'Is she bringing Perdita and Sheridan?' Caroline asked eagerly.

'No.'

Caroline's face fell. 'I don't imagine I'll see her,' she said. 'She's here for Daddy, isn't she?'

'Yes.'

'So I won't see him either. Not while she's in London.'

'I'm sure your father will call as usual.' Duff visited often. Usually he stayed no more than fifteen or twenty minutes, but Brigid had seen how Caroline's face lit up when he arrived. Every time. How she almost chattered, so much more talkative when he was the one asking questions – always funny, silly questions, Brigid noted, not frightful ones like 'How's school?'

'Not if Mummie's at Hans Crescent,' Caroline said. 'She doesn't like him to pay attention to anyone but her.'

'But she's staying here.' Brigid thought that would make Caroline happy – knowing that her father would continue to visit. But she looked almost frightened.

'Here?'

'Yes. She says it makes more sense.'

'Does she?' She bent her head to her book again. *The Death of the Heart*, the cover said, and underneath that 'Elizabeth Bowen'.

'Is it good?' Brigid asked.

'What?' Caroline looked up. 'Oh, this. Yes. It's good.'

'You read a lot, don't you?'

'I suppose.' Caroline shrugged.

'You must be frightfully clever.' Brigid felt idiotic even as the words came out of her mouth.

'I'm not,' Caroline said flatly, making Brigid feel even more idiotic. 'It's a way of escaping, that's all.'

'Escaping what?'

'Everything.'

Tony was charming and funny at dinner, telling the kinds of war stories that were acceptable – tales of mix-ups and blunders, in which the enemy might have been a bunch of bungling schoolboys rather than lethal military divisions. He was polite to Chips, attentive to her, but even while Brigid smiled and pressed him to eat more, she found herself distracted, even bored. It wasn't that Tony was dull, she told herself, it was the familiarity of it all that bored her, people sitting around a beautifully laid table, passing silver dishes across a starched white tablecloth, speaking carefully, elegantly, so as to draw no attention to the chaos and disruption outside. Framing their remarks skilfully to avoid talking about anything unpleasant, no matter how close the unpleasantness came. And all the while, underneath, the current of Chips's scheming, and the possibility of Tony's collusion, ran on.

She had spent all her life in this sort of company, so much so that it was only recently, talking to Will, writing to Fritzi, that she had learned just how artificial it was. Such was her irritation with it that it was a relief when Tony left and Maureen arrived, with Pugsy and a set of matching pigskin luggage that was unloaded by the last remaining footman, too old for war, whom Andrews bossed around as though he were three men. 'How long do you plan on staying?' Chips asked, eyeing the cases being carried up to the room Brigid had had prepared.

'That depends,' Maureen said, peeling off a pair of soiled white gloves.

'On what?'

'This and that. Duff, mainly.' She marched through the hallway, heels clacking smartly on the tiled floor. She carried Pugsy in her arms, his pink tongue lolling from his mouth.

'On Eddie Cavendish?' Chips asked slyly, following her. Brigid watched Maureen scowl. 'He telephoned for you an hour ago.

Now why is that?' Why indeed? Brigid wondered. Why would Billy's father be ringing Maureen?

'Always an unpleasant explanation with you, Chips,' Maureen said.

'Oh, yes,' he agreed. 'And isn't it interesting how often I'm right?'

'Go away, Chips. Fetch a drink or something. Don't just stand there. Now, where does one sit in this mausoleum?'

Brigid stifled a laugh. Only Maureen could make the might of Belgrave Square seem somehow absurd. Chips scowled and she rushed to interrupt. 'Here's Caroline now,' she said, hearing her on the stairs. The girl came in. It was only when Brigid looked at her with Maureen beside her that she realised just how badly Caroline was growing out of everything she had. She looked like a scarecrow. And her hair – thick, curly enough to be hard to manage at the best of times – seemed especially stiff and dull. Seeing the irritation on Maureen's face, Brigid wondered if Caroline had done it on purpose. Surely she hadn't looked this bad all the time she had been staying?

'Hello, Mummie.' Caroline stood stiffly in the doorway, hands twisted behind her back, then moved closer to her mother, as though unsure whether to kiss her or not. Maureen put out a hand – to stop her, it seemed to Brigid – and patted the top of her arm once, quickly. After that, Caroline remained standing by the side of Maureen's chair while she quizzed her. How were her studies? What had she learned? Had she seen her father? Caroline answered every question without looking at her mother. She kept her eyes on the floor and spoke almost in monosyllables. Any of Caroline's funny side – the biting wit that was black as pitch – was hidden. Damped by Maureen's presence as surely as water will quench fire.

'Come over here,' Chips said, after a few moments, patting the seat beside him.

Caroline went gratefully and sat with her hands in her lap as Maureen, taking another cup of tea, leaned back and said, 'Now, Chips, I want all the news . . .'

Brigid tuned out the back-and-forth of 'news'. The two were like birds building a nest, she thought, trading twigs and bits of fluff that were really secrets and scandals, darting in and out to bring something fresh or pick up a scrap let fall by the other, together creating something ugly but intricate. She tuned back in when Caroline said goodnight and went up to her room, and Chips leaned in to Maureen to ask, 'What exactly is your plan?'

'To talk Duff out of joining up.'

'Surely his mind is made up.'

'Then he can unmake it. He's far more useful in the Ministry than on a battlefield where he's just another hand to hold a gun. Only foolish, stubborn pride prevents him from seeing that and I will not let him go to war because of it.'

Maureen might be 'frightful', as indeed they all agreed she was – 'though so very amusing with it' – but she was, Brigid thought, definite and resolute in a way almost no one else was. Like a pair of scissors or a sharp knife, she simply sliced through everything that stood between her and what she wanted. Ask Maureen what her plan for anything was and the answer was swift and sure.

Chapter Seventeen

Maureen

'Now that you're here, you must help me with Brigid,' Chips said, coming into the morning room where Honor usually wrote her letters and that Maureen had taken over as her own.

'Why?'

'Because you're here,' Chips said patiently. 'Because you're in my house, my guest, and I ask it of you.' He rang the bell. When Andrews appeared, he asked the butler to bring the cocktail tray.

'I'm here for Duff, as you well know,' Maureen said, 'but if I have time, I might. What is it you need my help with?'

'Brigid must be persuaded to marry someone, rather sooner than later. She turned twenty-three last week.'

He moved about the room, straightening things, twitching at

the curtains, touching things, stroking them, picking them up and putting them down again. He was, Maureen thought, like someone reassuring themselves that everything they saw was indeed real and tangible. 'Twenty-three is not so very old,' she said, watching him gently rub a silver snuff box with his handkerchief to bring up the shine.

'Not so very young either.' He placed the snuff box back, then turned it ever-so-slightly to an angle.

'The exact age I married Duff,' Maureen mused.

'*Quite* the best age to be married,' Chips said politely.

Maureen laughed. 'Very well, then. I'll help. What about Tony Rosslyn?'

'I thought of him,' Chips said eagerly, sitting beside her, 'but after dinner last night, I'm not so certain . . .'

They talked of young men, of titles and fortunes and families, for a good half-hour, throwing out ideas and possibilities, until Maureen said, 'There is one name we haven't yet mentioned . . .'

'No,' Chips agreed. 'But I rather think that ship has sailed.'

'I rather think it has not.' Maureen hesitated. 'The duke may invite Brigid to Chatsworth for Billy's next leave.'

'So that's why he telephoned for you? He thinks you'll help him?'

'That,' Maureen waved her hands airily in a way she hoped would distract Chips, 'and other things . . . But I feel he's right to try.'

'I do not,' Chips said. 'It won't work, Maureen, and you'd do well not to meddle there. If nothing else, Brigid wouldn't go. She would never do something she considered unfair to Kick.'

'Why must young girls these days be so friendly with one another?' Maureen was peeved. 'That's not how we were in my day. Other girls were to be bested in marriage, same as on the tennis court, or at croquet or anywhere else. Now they have fanciful ideas around eternal friendship.' She made an expression of distaste.

'I think some always did have those ideas . . .' Chips said. Andrews came with the cocktail tray and Chips began to busy himself with the bottles.

Maureen laughed. 'You needn't be so careful,' she said. 'I won't bite.'

'Actually, you've been a tremendous help,' he said, pouring gin into a gold-rimmed jug and adding a hefty dash of bitters. 'I'm glad you feel as I do, that Brigid really ought to get a move on. And that you'll help me.'

'I didn't say I would, I said I might. Although I suppose I may consider it practice,' Maureen said ruefully. 'Something I'm going to need a lot of.'

'Caroline?' He handed her a drink.

'Yes.'

'But she's a dear.'

'Is she?' Maureen gave him a wintry stare. 'Hard to know what she is when she never opens her mouth.'

'Not *never*,' Chips said, sitting back beside her. 'Maybe not often, with you . . .'

'I know you think I'm a terrible mother –' when he began to interrupt, she shook her head at him '– no, I see that you do. You aren't alone.' She tried, failed, to sound indifferent. She knew Chips would have heeded the hesitation in her voice, of course he would, but she was determined to deny him any more. 'But it isn't the same with Perdita and Sheridan. I don't know why, but it isn't. With them, well, it's easier. There's something . . . I don't know . . . *off* about Caroline. Something almost cruel in the way she looks at one . . .' It was more than she had ever yet said out loud, and she stopped herself saying the rest of what she felt – that it was only her Caroline looked at like that.

'Try to be kind to her,' Chips said. 'You'll find it rewarding, I assure you.' He took a long sip of his cocktail. 'This is nice,' he said. 'I feel as though we're village elders, with the gathered insight of generations between us.'

Maureen stiffened. 'I am not an elder of this village or any other. What rubbish you do talk.'

'I don't mean elder,' he said hastily, 'only that you have such wisdom.' It was a view of herself that Maureen liked, and so, when Chips had gone and Caroline came in with Pugsy, she took the dog and patted the seat beside her on the sofa. Caroline sat at the edge, her back straight, hands clasped in front of her.

'We must think of getting you home,' Maureen said. 'Back to Clandeboye.'

'Daddy said I could stay here as long as he's back and forth to London.'

'But what will you do?'

'The same as I usually do,' the girl shrugged, 'drawing, French, conversation . . .'

Maureen bit back a harsh laugh. 'And when Daddy isn't in London? Will you go back to Clandeboye then?'

'When he isn't in London he will be at the front, so it won't much matter where I go. To another boarding school, I suppose.'

'He will not be at the front,' Maureen said. Her teeth felt sore, so hard did she clench them. 'Who told you that? Chips?'

'Daddy did.'

'What?' Maureen's voice was so sharp and loud that Pugsy let out a yelp. 'He talked to you about this?'

'Yes. He said why he wanted to go – that he believes it's his duty to be where he's most needed, and for a while that was here, in London, at the Ministry, but now he thinks it's in uniform.'

'You are far too young for such conversations.'

'Not really.' Caroline lifted her eyes to stare straight into Maureen's face. There it was, the look that had always disconcerted Maureen, ever since Caroline was tiny. The eyes were too big, too defenceless, but with something calculating in them. As though she was considering Maureen and thought private things about her that weren't kind, were harsh and cruel and horribly clear. 'I understood perfectly,' she continued. 'I don't think it's particularly difficult. He no longer feels he wants to be here so he is making plans to go.'

'It is very unbecoming when you pretend to knowledge far greater than any you could possibly have.' Maureen spoke as coldly as she could. She fought the urge to push the girl physically from her. 'If that is what all your reading has given you, then perhaps it's time we looked at limiting it.'

'Pugsy needs a walk,' Caroline said, scooping up the dog and standing. 'I'll take him round the square.'

After she had left, Maureen poured herself another drink from Chips's jug. Her hands were shaking. What had the girl meant, that Duff talked to her? Why would he tell her such things? And how dare she say them back to Maureen as though she alone were in her father's confidence.

Try to be kind to her, Chips had said. But how was kindness possible when the girl herself was so strange, so withdrawn, seemed to carry so much silent hostility towards her mother?

Maureen had meant what she'd said. It was different with Perdita and especially Sheridan. She would never be the sort of mother her sister Oonagh was – always with her children, keeping them about her constantly so that she seemed to need the physical affection of their hands in hers, their kisses and embraces. Maureen looked for affection from no one except Duff, couldn't abide being 'pawed', as she thought of it. But she found some enjoyment in Perdita and Sheridan's arrival in the drawing room for the hour before dinner, neatly washed and brushed. She liked watching Duff question them about their day, hear their tales of ponies and puppies.

With Caroline, there had never been even that much harmony. The girl stirred something in her. Memories of dark nights, forlorn cries and a kind of emptiness that had seemed to pull the whole world into itself. Between them, cold and unfamiliar depths had never been bridged, had been deepened by all the ways Caroline annoyed her – the girl's heavy silences, the awkward twisting of her hands, the slow way in which she spoke as though the words must be physically pulled from her. Maureen felt inadequate as the mother of this painful creature. She couldn't abide failure – never had been able to – but she had to admit, as Caroline's mother, she was a failure.

She stood up quickly. She must go out. She would go to Duff. He could take her to lunch, talk to her, touch her hand, her arm, her hair. Take away this chill, grey feeling.

Chapter Eighteen

Brigid

The next afternoon, Brigid met Sissy coming in as she left Belgrave Square. 'Just visiting us?' she asked.

'I thought I might stay a night or two. If I may?'

'If you can put up with Maureen, Caroline's mother, you're very welcome. But why?'

'Just, you know . . . comfort, food, hot water.'

'I'm to believe you're so terribly spoiled, you can't make do without?' Brigid laughed. 'Don't think I can't see what you're doing.'

'What am I doing?' Sissy asked.

'Throwing dust, or blowing smoke, whatever it is. Aren't you? What I mean is, you're covering your tracks.'

'Me?' Sissy opened her eyes wide. 'How sneaky you make me sound.'

'Not an answer,' Brigid said sternly. The girl was far too good at evading direct questions.

'I'm not hiding anything. It's just such Heaven, never needing to tell anyone where I am or where I'm going or who I'm with,' Sissy admitted.

But was there something more? Brigid wondered. Something in the way she'd said, *I'm not hiding anything* . . . that was defensive.

'You do know we're not going to start giving you a curfew, and asking who you go about with,' she said, amused.

'I know. At least, I hope you wouldn't. But, even so, it's such perfect bliss to have places to go to. People to go with. I never did, you know, at home. Only school, and church on Sundays, sometimes the horse show in the summer. Other than that, there was nothing – nothing! – to do. I used to think it was a treat if the cook let me peel apples or roll pastry. Such bliss to be in a city, so full of *everything*. I don't know how I'll ever see it all and do it all.'

'You don't have to see and do everything.' Even though she remembered, a little sadly, that exact feeling of wanting to.

'Oh, but I do. I want to. It's so exciting, knowing it's all out there.' She gestured wide, arm sweeping to take in all the wonderful things she imagined. 'That GI at the officers' club, Charlie, took me to see *The Man Who Came to Dinner* the other night,' Sissy continued. She clasped her hands together.

Brigid hadn't the heart to tell her that the play had been on for two years, more even, and was generally considered very tired. 'Well, don't fall between too many stools,' she cautioned. 'It's not really the thing to be off so much that no one knows where you are if anyone needed you.'

'Why would anyone need me?' Sissy asked. 'I'm not like you,

Brigid. My job is just chopping carrots and onions, not saving lives.'

'I don't really save lives,' Brigid said scrupulously. 'I scrub floors and roll bandages and take temperatures. But I'd better get on. I swapped my shift for the evening.'

She sometimes did this for one of the girls with responsibilities at home. This time it was Mary, who had to mind her little brothers and sisters while her mother worked late at the factory. Conscious that she had no real reason to say no, Brigid had agreed, and received Mary's heartfelt thanks – 'You're a brick, Brigid.'

It wasn't just being a brick, though. Brigid wanted a chance to sit with Will for longer than the half-hour or so she snatched during the days. Nights were quieter, recently anyway, since the bombing raids had all but stopped. She would bring a flask of coffee and some slices of fruitcake – was there any other kind, these days? – and they would be left alone together.

Will had recently been moved to his own room. The fight against the infection in his leg wasn't going well, and the doctor wanted him isolated. 'It's a dubious honour,' he'd said, when he told her about the move. 'Those whom the gods wish to destroy first get their own rooms.' She had laughed and complimented his classical education, but mostly to distract herself from the truth of what he'd said.

'I brought you another book,' she said, putting a copy of *Silas Marner* on the bedside locker. 'And coffee and cake for both of us. Plus I have lots to tell you.' She had learned that asking him questions yielded very little. He didn't much like talking about himself and definitely not about his family. His lack of family. So instead Brigid told him about her work, the people who came and went in Belgrave Square, about Sissy, Kick and Edie.

It made her feel older, being there with him. Knowing about the infection, how worried the doctor was, and that Will knew as much as she did, gave her what her mother would have called perspective. Finally, Brigid understood that that meant being able to see from a distance, not always close up, so that you could understand what was happening without wondering how it affected you.

He asked had she been back to the Ritz, or the 400 Club – she had told him all about the night with Kick and Sissy. 'The Ritz,' she answered, 'but only for tea. Not at all the same.'

'I've never been,' he said, 'though I've passed it.'

'When you're better, we'll go,' she promised. Promised herself as much as him.

'I'd like that. You in a silk dress, me in a suit, if one can still buy such things now.' He was curious about the city outside the hospital – how it had changed, what was and wasn't to be found in the shops. 'It's so long since I've been out in it,' he said wistfully. Since moving to his own room, no one talked about Will going home as a possibility.

'It's not so very different,' she said. 'You'll see. We'll drink Manhattans – that's a new cocktail – and dance.'

'I hope the dances haven't changed too much or I'll never keep up.'

'Nothing much has changed,' she reassured him. 'There's still waltzes played.'

'But not at the 400 Club, I bet. Tell me more about it.' So she told him. The tiny dance-floor. The loud music that was all sorts of songs one knew, but played fast or slow depending on the mood of the orchestra. The heat, the bodies pressed together.

Ma Merrick and her insistence on carefully paced two-by-two departures. 'It's always a surprise,' she explained, 'because in there you forget entirely about what's outside. When she makes you leave through the blackout curtains, so quick and cautious, it's like being shoved out of a lovely dream.'

'How lucky, to forget for a while.'

'Yes,' she agreed. 'Do you ever manage to forget?' She meant all of it – the hospital, the doctors' visits, the constant murmur of voices and sound of subdued footsteps back and forth outside his room.

'No. The pain makes sure of that. But sometimes when I'm reading or when you visit, it fades into the background.'

She told him about Tony; 'Chips cannot allow that I don't want or need him to plot for me.'

'Was he so terrible, this Tony?'

'No. Not at all. Even rather sweet. But I don't want him as a husband. Or any husband.' Even talking about it made her irritable. She was grateful when he changed the subject.

'Tell me more about Sissy.'

'That girl!' Brigid laughed. 'She is both the slyest and the most artless creature I've met . . . Up to something, no doubt about it, but also as foolish as a kitten . . .'

'Something or someone?' Will asked.

'Probably someone,' Brigid agreed. 'Though goodness knows who. She won't allow Chips to make plans for her, much as he's longing to. She slides out of that just as she slides out of anyone knowing where she's meant to be. And so cunningly that Chips doesn't see what she's doing.'

Brigid knew she sounded cross, even envious. Why couldn't she say, *You're kind, Chips, and another time I'd love to, just not this time* . . . and wriggle out of his schemes the way Sissy did, without any argument, without Chips realising that the wriggling was happening. But Brigid hadn't found the right formula. Or else Chips was too determined: willing to let Sissy wriggle, but not Brigid.

'Chips is your brother-in-law?' Will asked.

'Yes.' She knew he knew that.

'Not your father?'

'No.' She was confused.

'But he makes plans for you?'

'He does.'

'And do you have to go along with them?'

'Well, no, not exactly, but it's just . . . Oh, you don't really mean that as a question, do you?' And when he said nothing, she added, 'How clever you are. I see what you're getting at.'

'I'm not exactly getting at anything,' he said. 'Only you have such a sense of duty.' She tried to protest, but he shook his head and continued, 'You do. You wouldn't wear that uniform if you didn't or turn up here day after day to see how I am when we both know the answer to that. And I admire it awfully in you. Only sometimes it might be your duty not to be so dutiful, if you see what I mean?' He looked suddenly anxious, as though worried she might misinterpret him.

'I do see,' she said. 'At least, I think I do. I have spent such a long time doing what I was told it simply never occurred to me not to. Nanny, the governesses, Mama, Papa, Honor, even Arthur and Patsy.' She giggled. 'I'm the youngest so, really, everyone had a turn. And then war came along, and no one had as much time for telling me what to do, and, well, I found I rather liked that. So now they've started up again . . .' She faltered. How to explain the mulish feeling that came over her now when Chips tried to order her life?

'You no longer have the habit of agreeing so easily?'

'Exactly.' She smiled at him. 'I no longer have the habit and I don't want to get it back.'

Chapter Nineteen

Sissy

Sissy felt bad, being so slippery. She wasn't lying, not exactly, but she wasn't telling either. And that was what made her feel bad. Brigid wasn't the sort of person with whom she was happy to be slippery, but Sissy wasn't ready to give a full account of her time. Not yet.

She thought back to her first trip to find Peter at the King's Anchor. She had found it by diligently following Edie's map, and asking anyone she could persuade to stop and talk to her. The pub had small windows with neat diamond-shaped glass panes. On one side of the red-painted front door, they had been blown out and wooden boards nailed over the gaps.

Because of the wooden boards, it had looked closed. Even so, Sissy was surprised to find that in fact it *was* closed. So she had gone to the Y and got signed up, but late that afternoon she went back. And this time, it was open. A man came out as she stood watching, and went off down the street, whistling. The door was left ajar behind him. Now that she was here, she didn't know how she could go in, all alone as she was. She had a dim understanding of the things girls were and weren't supposed to do – there hadn't been much time to learn, she supposed, before she was caught with Tom in the stables and sent packing, but neither had her mother ever shown much inclination for that sort of teaching.

Even so, Sissy was pretty sure that going to pubs alone, to meet men – if she was lucky, she reminded herself – probably wasn't done.

'We're there most evenings,' Jim had said. What did *most* mean? Did tonight, a Thursday, count as *most*? And what did *evening* mean? It was six o'clock. She had thought that was most definitely evening, but now she wasn't sure. And if they weren't there, what would she do? Stay or leave? And if they were there . . . She took a breath to stop her hands shaking, and pushed open the door.

She didn't know what she had expected, but not this. The light inside was bad – how would it be otherwise, with the boarded-up windows? It took her a moment to make out much more than a strong smell of stale beer. A red carpet was worn in many places; newer squares of a different red carpet had been cut and placed over what were presumably actual holes. Sissy thought immediately of the likelihood that she would catch her foot in one and trip.

Small round tables were clustered in the corners. They looked more pushed out of the way than arranged to entice. And, indeed, most were empty. But groups of men, and a few women, she noted with relief, were standing or sitting at the bar. The sound of a radio turned too low to make out the words was in the background, a kind of soothing hum to the chatter of the groups. She stood in the doorway until a man behind the bar, his shirtsleeves rolled up, yelled at her, 'Come in or get out.' That made everyone turn and stare. Sissy felt hot and large and untidy. She was about to turn and leave when someone said, 'Sissy?' One of the men in the group furthest from her stood up from his bar stool and came towards her. 'It is Sissy, isn't it?' he said.

'Jim.' She twisted her hands together in the way that annoyed her mother. 'Yes.' Now she was standing on one leg, the other tucked behind her awkwardly. Why couldn't she stand still and poised, like Brigid? 'It's me.'

'What are you doing here?'

'You said to pop in if I was passing.'

'And were you? Passing?' But he said it kindly. Kindly enough, anyway, so that when he followed with 'Well, now that you're here, come and have a drink,' she said, 'Yes, please.'

He turned back to the group he'd been with and Sissy followed him, a pace behind. She was far too confused and shy to make out any of the faces of the people she passed, only noting that there seemed a lot of them, and they stared at her with open curiosity. The carpet was sticky by the bar, thousands of slopped drinks she imagined, and the stools were worn, their velvet seats rubbed bare, like the skin of newborn mice. Jim's group included Peter, she saw. Peter, who looked at her without curiosity, almost as though he'd never seen her before, and nodded just as anyone might when Jim, introducing her to everyone, said, 'You know Peter, of course.'

'Why "of course"?' demanded a woman with red hair, tied up tightly, and wide brown eyes.

'We met,' Sissy said, as much to Peter as to the woman, 'at the 400 Club.' Did she imagine a faint look of irritation crossing his face? And if she was right, why? Was it her?

'What on earth were you doing there?' the woman asked Peter. 'I thought you couldn't stand the place.' Perhaps that was why he looked irritated, being caught out going somewhere he'd said he couldn't stand. Sissy wished she hadn't said anything.

'Well, I can't,' Peter said, 'but one does sometimes find something amusing there.' He looked at Sissy as he spoke. He seemed less annoyed now, and she wondered, with a little thrill, if she was the something amusing.

'You said you couldn't stand it,' the woman repeated firmly. Then, 'Aurora,' she said to Sissy, putting out her hand.

Sissy shook it. 'Sissy.'

'I know,' Aurora said patiently. 'Jim just said.'

After the introductions, and once she had told them she had a job and would be staying in London, Peter mostly ignored her. Jim was much nicer, chatting to her, lighting her cigarette, then putting it out when she left it smouldering in the ashtray.

Soon Sissy realised that everyone there was older than her, often by as much as ten years, and they all 'did' something, but not the sort of things she was used to. They didn't talk about their war work – hospitals, canteens, ambulance services – or about hunting and horses, as her parents' friends did. They talked about art and writing as their 'work'. She discovered this when the woman with the red hair asked her, 'What do you do?' and laughed at Sissy's response. 'Volunteering at the Y isn't *doing* something,' she explained. 'That's just what you have to do, while this goes on; same as I am an ARP warden – Air Raid Precaution,' she explained, seeing Sissy's face. She spread her hand expansively, gesturing towards the pub door and, presumably, what lay beyond it. Sissy saw that her hands were thin and white and the nails painfully short. 'But really, I write, or try to. Peter paints. Jim paints. Selina . . .' she gestured towards the other woman in the group, who had short black hair that was shiny and bluish, like a magpie's wing, 'Selina is a poet.'

'Like Dylan?' Sissy asked.

'You know Dylan?'

'I met him.'

That seemed to reassure Aurora, because she nodded and repeated, 'You know Dylan.'

They drank more, beer mostly, although Jim bought her a sherry when he saw the face she made after her first cautious sip of beer, and Sissy was content to sit and listen to what the others said. At first she expected the conversation would be terrifyingly high-brow, an intense discussion of art and literature that she wouldn't be able to follow, but quickly she realised that they talked a great deal about other people they knew and she didn't. Peter was clearly a brilliant mimic, taking off voices and mannerisms in a way that had the rest roaring with laughter.

Where she was delighted by what he said, more even by the way he said it, he seemed scarcely to hear her. He might nod as she spoke, even smile once or twice, but she felt he did these things mechanically, rather than in response to what she said. Certainly he didn't ask her anything about herself. He showed no curiosity at all about her, and after a while turned all his attention to Selina.

'Do you really come here every night?' Sissy asked Jim.

'Most nights. Sometimes there's food to be had. The landlord makes a kind of Anything Stew, stretching the meat ration with what the regulars might bring – pheasant, usually, or rabbit. But bits of offal too. You wouldn't want to look too hard.'

'What about bombs?' Sissy hoped she didn't sound cowardly.

'It's not as bad as it was. You missed the really bad times.'

'Not on purpose,' she assured him. That made him laugh. He was nice, Sissy thought. Nice in the way her brother's friends were nice. Not interesting, the way Peter was. She looked covertly at him, and found that he was looking at her, although he turned away as soon as he saw her noticing.

'You'd better come with me,' Aurora said, after a couple of hours.

'Come where?'

'You'll see.' Sissy followed her behind the bar and through a narrow doorway to a cramped, dark hall, with a flight of carpeted stairs so narrow that Sissy almost had to turn sideways. Up they went, Aurora leading the way, to the floor above. A tight landing with three doors off it. 'It's Harry's flat. He's the barman. There's no WC downstairs any of us could possibly use, just a privy out the back for the men, so Harry lets us come up here if we're quick.' She opened the door at the far end and showed Sissy a bathroom with stained lino on the floor. 'Wait here.' Aurora went in first and Sissy listened to the pipes gurgle after she'd flushed, then turned on taps. There was nothing to look at except a picture of a horse that seemed to have been torn from a magazine and pinned to the wall.

The door opened again. 'Your turn.'

Sissy went in, shutting the door carefully behind her. The lavatory chain had been broken at some stage, and a heavy iron screw was attached to it, rather than the usual wooden handle. Afterwards, she washed her hands with a piece of cracked Pears soap and dried them on a worn towel, then wished she hadn't. It made them feel dirty again.

'Thanks,' she said to Aurora, when she came out. 'I don't know what I would have done.'

'Doesn't bear thinking about,' Aurora said. 'So you're here for Peter?'

'Not for Peter but because of Peter, I suppose you could say.'

'Not for him? You sure?'

'Certain,' Sissy confirmed. She wouldn't admit that she *was* there for Peter. Not when he'd been so dismissive. 'I don't know anyone in London, except the girls I live with. I thought it would be good to get about and meet some people. That's all.'

'Jim,' Aurora said firmly, 'is a dear.'

By closing time, Sissy had decided that Aurora was right. Jim *was* a dear, and Peter wasn't. He hadn't been pleased to see her or taken much trouble to talk to her. Twice more she had looked up to find him staring at her. Each time he had glanced away immediately.

Yet he was the one who asked, 'Which way are you walking?' as they all stood outside the pub.

'Back towards Belgrave Square, I suppose,' she said, not at all sure which way that was and how she might get there.

'I'll walk part of the way with you,' he said, switching on his bicycle lamp but angling it carefully towards the ground.

They waved to the others and walked along in silence. Sissy could feel every inch of the thick darkness, unleavened by anything except his cycle lamp and the occasional warden with a lantern.

'Why did you come?' he asked.

'You said to.'

'I didn't.'

'Well, Jim did. I thought it was the same thing.'

'It isn't.'

'I suppose not.' She was so mortified that when he stopped pushing his bicycle and leaned in to kiss her, she assumed he had stumbled and ducked out of his way. He lurched and had to steady himself.

'Let's try that again,' he murmured. He leaned his bike carefully against the wall of a house and this time, when he went to kiss her, she understood what he was doing and stayed still. He kissed her for a minute or so, then stopped just as she was starting to enjoy kissing him back. It wasn't like it had been with Tom, she thought. It was more, well, *exciting*. Tom's mouth on hers had been heavy and solid, almost immobile. Peter's lips were thinner, and the way he kissed her more playful. She felt him almost break into a smile at one point, and wondered what was so funny about kissing her.

'That's enough for now,' he said.

She wondered if there was something not nice about kissing her that he was so quick to stop. She wished he hadn't. If this was the kind of thing Kick felt when Billy kissed her, Sissy decided she understood why the American girl had come all the way to London.

She assumed that, after the kiss, he would walk all the way to Belgrave Square with her, but she was wrong. A minute later he had said, 'I'm that way,' gesturing into the darkness, and 'I suppose I'll see you.' He got onto his bicycle and pushed off, disappearing into the night with a wave, moving far faster than Sissy thought was wise, given the state of the roads and the lack of visibility.

She walked the last streets to Belgrave Square quick and light. He must like her, to kiss her like that. Which meant she could like him as much as she wanted to. Or admit how much she already liked him. She'd never really known any men, she reflected. Except Tom. And Father. Her brother was too young to count. But even so, she felt certain Peter was superior to others. He must be. There was stillness about him, an economy of movement that made her want to move closer to him. To feel some part of her – hand, elbow, knee – touch some part of him. 'Goodnight,' she called loudly, to an ARP warden at the corner of Belgrave Square. He shushed her irritably.

Since then she had been twice more to the King's Anchor. Each time she had found Peter, Jim, Aurora, sometimes Dylan, others whose names she was learning. They had begun to hail her with familiarity, making room for her without surprise.

Look how much everything had changed in just a few short weeks, she thought gleefully now, as she approached the pub. She had a flat, a bicycle, she was part of the 'war effort'. And now she had a boyfriend too.

She remembered the conversation with Edie, that first evening before the Ritz: *I've never really known anyone who had a boyfriend . . .* Well, now *she* was someone who had a boyfriend. She must be: he had kissed her, hadn't he? Several times now.

She pushed open the red-painted front door and went in, looking around for the faces she felt certain would be looking for her.

Chapter Twenty

Kick

Saturday came and Kick finished her shift with several hours to go before Billy arrived to take her out. She had planned this carefully, knowing she wouldn't be able to concentrate on talking about golf with GIs while her stomach turned cartwheels at the idea of seeing him. He had suggested dinner at the Mirabelle, then dancing.

'Can I come to you?' She telephoned Brigid. 'I'm filthy and there's no way I'm going to get cleaned up with the trickle of warm water we call a bath.'

'Of course. Come and let us help get you dressed. Caroline will adore that. I remember, with Honor, how much Patsy and I used to love watching her dressing for an evening out. We thought she was the most glamorous creature alive because she was our big sister, had a few silk evening dresses, a string of pearls, and a young man to collect her in an open-topped car.'

'How is Patsy?'

'Wonderful. Three little boys now.'

'And where's Honor, these days?' Kick asked cautiously. Was it odd, she wondered, that she was never home?

'Still away. Essex now, I think. Kelvedon,' she said. Kelvedon was Chips's country house.

'Isn't it shut up?'

'It is, but she's got a few rooms and a local woman who can cook a bit, Welsh rarebit, scrambled eggs. Honor says it's all she needs and that she can't believe all the years she spent eating rich, disgusting food with dreadful bores.'

'I see. Ouch.'

'Yes, rather. She put it in a letter. Chips looked green around the gills as he read it.'

'What's she doing?' Kick asked.

'I don't know. Refugees, I think. Some chaps from Czechoslovakia who escaped just in time before Hitler took over. Now they want to help in our war effort. Pilots, so they're jolly useful. Some of them have families – I think Honor is helping to settle them.' Brigid spoke vaguely and Kick didn't ask any more. The vagueness might be deliberate. So much was these days. The British had never been much for questions, but now her English friends were positively sphinx-like, avoiding asking anything in case it might be *sensitive* or, worse, *classified*.

She arrived at Belgrave Square with three dresses. Billy had said he would take her to dinner and then a nightclub. 'You can help me choose which to wear,' she said to Caroline, who was hanging about in the hallway when Andrews opened the door.

The girl looked indifferent. 'If you like,' she said. 'Brigid's upstairs.'

Kick couldn't see any of the enthusiasm Brigid had spoken of, but Caroline followed her up and hung around while she bathed and then dressed. Brigid kept up a stream of chatter, sitting on the bed while Kick was in the bath, door open between them, and then while she did her hair.

'I've got a brooch that would look simply lovely with that dress,' Brigid said. 'Let me run and get it.' That left Kick and the silent Caroline. The girl didn't even fidget, Kick saw. Simply sat on a small footstool by the end of the bed, hands at her sides, staring at the floor in front of her.

'How are your lessons?' Kick asked her eventually. 'Do you like them?'

'No,' Caroline said.

'Are you homesick?'

'No. Although I miss Perdie and Sheridan.' Then, after a pause that Kick found thoroughly awkward, 'You're the one who wants to marry Billy, aren't you? I wasn't sure if it was you or Sissy at first. I hope you do. He's nice. And it would serve them all right to lose for once.'

'Who? Lose what?'

'All of them. They think they can make everything into whatever way they want it. That they can do whatever they like and the rest of us have to do as we're told.'

She spoke with the bitterness of someone much older and Kick could think of nothing to say. Luckily Brigid came back with the brooch, and Caroline left soon after, getting up silently and walking out.

'Do you like having her to stay?' Kick asked.

'Caroline? Oh, she's a darling.' Kick couldn't see how Caroline was anything of the sort, but maybe you had to be a Guinness. 'Are you excited,' Brigid asked then, 'to see Billy?'

'Oh, yes.' She turned back towards the mirror, brushing her fringe to one side, pretending to decide if it looked better like that. Was she excited? Now that the moment had all but arrived, what was it she felt? Slightly sick, keyed-up and apprehensive, yes. But was that excited? And if so, about what? It had been so long since she had seen him, she worried that she remembered him wrong. In the weeks since she had been in England, she had thought more than ever about him – reminded everywhere she went of places they had been together, things they had done, conversations they'd had.

So what did she feel now? Terrified, if she was truthful. Terrified that she had got it wrong, and had come all this way only to see in front of her a man who was just the shadowy outline of the person she remembered. As though time and distance had coloured him far more vividly than he was. And yet impelled all the same to come and see for herself.

'All the time I was home, and he wrote to me, all I could think about was seeing him again,' she said now to Brigid, putting down the hairbrush and standing up to try to see her dress at the back.

'Nervous?' Brigid asked sympathetically.

'Yes. But also I know it will be OK. It's Billy.' She shrugged a little, repeated, 'It's Billy.'

And then, finally, it was Billy. Standing in front of her, back in the dingy flat, looking curiously around him at the accumulated mess of three girls living together. She had wondered how this moment would be. Would he rush to her, catch her up in his arms? Kiss her – try to, anyway? Would he say how much he had missed her?

'Jolly good to see you,' he said, keeping an awkward distance from her, closer than an acquaintance would ever stand, but too far for them easily to touch one another. He put out a hand and clasped hers sideways, in a way that was a shade warmer than a handshake, but hardly a demonstration of affection. She thought of the American boys she knew, who would pick her up in their arms and swing her around.

'It's jolly good to see you too,' she said. He laughed at that. He knew she was mocking him, and he liked it.

Edie came in from the club and he greeted her politely. 'Kick tells me you're from Virginia. Are you finding all this . . .' he nodded vaguely towards the window '. . . frightfully tedious?'

'I wouldn't say *tedious*,' Edie said. 'You do know I'm not here for a holiday, don't you? I mean, if I was, I'd be disappointed as hell.' He laughed, and Kick watched Edie's expression turn from dubious to certain.

He looked thinner, but that was no surprise. They were all thinner. The crisp newness of his uniform was gone, but so, too, was the way in which it had seemed to wear him, to stuff him in behind the rows of buttons and stiff pockets, hidden behind epaulettes and belt buckle. He was so clearly older, but in a way that suited him. He had always seemed older than the American boys of her acquaintance, and now he looked it. Where before he had been slightly stooped, as though apologising for too many things to name – now that was gone. He stood straight and tall.

She felt so awkward that it was a while before she noticed that he did too. Only when they were opposite one another in the Mirabelle did she register that his silences were as sharp as hers, his questions just as rushed. It made her like him more. Suddenly, Kick knew it was going to be all right. 'You stopped writing to me,' she said.

'Not stopped, suspended.'

'But why?' She knew why, but she wanted to hear him say it.

'What was I to do? Write to you for the rest of my life and never see you again?'

It was halfway to the answer she wanted. Yet seeing him made her sad – because of all that had happened since the last time they were in the same room together. War, yes, but other things too. Things that were far harder for her to bear. Her father's disgrace, her mother's rush to insist that everything was exactly as it should be. Jack and Joe's efforts to stand against the shame by enlisting, defiance written in their naval uniforms. Most of all Rosie and the space where her name was no longer spoken.

'How is your sister, Rosemary?' Billy asked, as though he had caught her thoughts.

'She hasn't been well. She lives very quietly now.'

'I'm sorry to hear that. I always thought she had a great deal of spark to her.'

'She surely did,' Kick said. She paused. 'Do you think we're the same?' she asked, as Billy lit a cigarette. She saw that he smoked a stubby Turkish brand. The kind his men in the regiment might smoke, she thought.

'I smoke more than I used to,' he said. 'So I smoke these. Easier to get. The same as what?'

'As we were. Do you remember the day you joined up? How you came to Prince's Gate in your brand-new uniform?'

'And you saluted me and told me, "At ease, soldier."' He laughed.

Kick grimaced. 'Pa heard and was mad as hell at the joke, because he said war was no laughing matter.'

'Did he ever change his mind?'

'He did, a little. He's an American. Now that America's in the war, he's full of patriotism, even though it terrifies him to see Jack and Joe in uniform.'

'I suppose you can't view war the way he does – all the horror and carnage, none of the play for glory – and not be terrified.' Billy spoke judiciously, although Kick knew how instinctively he recoiled from her father's way of seeing the world, which was shaded, complex, pragmatic, subject to so many things at once. So unlike Billy, who saw the world in the straightforward way he had been shown it – a place of right, of wrong. 'Since Dunkirk, I suppose I understand his view a little better,' he said then as he stubbed out his cigarette, adding, 'although I agree with it rather less.'

Kick remembered Brigid telling her how humiliated Billy had felt, his conviction that they should have fought to the death rather than retreat. Knowing that, she understood his efforts to be fair to her father meant his feelings for her hadn't changed. But what of hers for him? Seeing him again, after so long in which he had been the constant drum roll in her head – *Billy, Billy, Billy* – what did she feel now?

'You didn't answer my question,' she said.

'Do I think we're the same people? No, of course I don't. We aren't. How could we be? But we're the same in the way that matters.'

'And what is that?'

'We're still two people who care for one another.' He spoke stiffly.

'Are we?'

'I am.' He took her hand. 'I am, Kick.'

'What about Sally Norton?'

'I had to try, darling.'

'Try what?'

'To forget you. Everything and everyone said it was useless, and war made it seem all the more so. And I tried. With Sally. Who is a dear girl.'

'But it was no good?' Kick said happily.

'It was no good.' As though relieved to have said even that much, he talked then of his regiment, their training camp at Eastbourne and how frustrated he was to be still there, rather than at the front. 'I know I must be patient, but it's jolly hard when I see others being deployed, and we are back to playing at war.' He described the hours they spent in physical training: 'Up at six to run miles before breakfast, like being at school again,' weapons, what he called 'fieldcraft' – camouflage, orienteering, movement in strange terrain – as well as his officer training.

'Learning how to hold a knife and fork?' she joked.

'More like making decisions under pressure. They fire a barrage of weapons close to us, while we scrabble to make complicated decisions with no time to consider the consequences,' he said ruefully. 'And it's realistic – all the noise, the explosions, the yelling. Except for the most important thing.'

'What's that?'

'If we make the wrong decision, no one dies.'

After dinner, they went to the 400 Club, and Kick relearned the rhythm of being seen with Billy. Whatever she was alone, she was far more with him. Even Meredith made a penitent detour by their table to say hello, as though she hadn't yet seen Kick. They danced and talked and were silent, and afterwards they walked back, hand in hand, through a delicate dawn. It was warm, although the sun was barely up, and even the bomb-damaged streets seemed tidier and more benign.

'Will I see you tomorrow?' Kick asked. 'Lunch?'

'I must visit my parents while they are in London.'

'Will you tell them you've seen me?' Surely now things would be different. How could the rules of the old world – the world of Billy's parents, in which being Catholic was shameful, mortifying – matter anymore?

'Not tomorrow.' He was uneasy now.

She felt tired, the hours of dancing, drinking, talking only now landing upon her. 'Why did you take me out, Billy?'

'I wanted to see you.'

'And now that you have?'

'I want to see you again.' Kick almost held her breath, afraid that if she spoke, it would be to lead the conversation in the wrong direction. 'Actually, I thought you might come to Compton Place with me,' he continued. 'Just for one night. We could drive down tomorrow, in the afternoon.' Compton Place, she remembered, was the large, ivy-covered house in Eastbourne owned by Billy's family – large, that was, until one saw Chatsworth, their Derbyshire estate with its three hundred rooms.

'Your parents . . .'

'Will be going back to Chatsworth.'

'Will you tell them we're going?' she asked again.

'I will, but when it's time.'

'You're sure you want me to come?' She needed him to be sure. To tell her again that he wanted her to go with him, despite what they both knew his father would think.

'Yes, really.'

'I'll have to pack some things,' Kick said, excitement sending her voice high. 'Will I need an evening dress?'

'It'll be very quiet. There's no one but us and half the house is bombed. It's not like before, Kick. I hope you won't be disappointed.' Now he sounded uncertain.

'How could I be?'

Chapter Twenty-One

Sissy

They might all be dead in a year, Sissy thought as she half walked, half skipped along Tottenham Court Road. Or living under the Nazis. People said the war was turning in the Allies' favour, but it had taken a long time and might swing back at any moment, for all she knew. And who was to say the people she overheard even knew what they were talking about? Maybe there were other people, hidden away in the War Office or the Houses of Parliament, who knew a different tale, which they carefully didn't broadcast because of that delicate thing *morale*.

Maybe Peter knew more. After all, he worked at the War Office. That was a jolly good reason to keep seeing him, she decided. If anyone asked, and she knew the others were starting to wonder where she spent her time, she could say exactly that.

They wouldn't believe her, she thought, but it would be something to say.

She paused outside the door of the pub. She wore another dress of Kick's – this one was plain yellow cotton with embroidery around the neckline and hem. It suited her. Edie and Kick had both said so. They had advised her to leave her hair loose, and she fidgeted nervously at it now with her fingers, trying to comb it neatly behind her ears when it wanted to spring upwards in tufty curls.

As she raised her arms, she detected a faint smell of grease. She had spent the afternoon frying carrots and onions, to turn into huge vats of what they called 'soup', though often it was so thin as to be more like gruel. Better keep her arms down, she thought.

She pushed open the door and walked into a room that was far busier than it had been on previous visits. It was Friday evening. That must be why. The tables were placed around the room now, not pushed into corners, and all were full. There was a roar of voices, of laughter, mixed with music from a man with an accordion near the door.

'Sissy!' a voice called. Aurora was waving her over to the corner furthest from the door.

'We're trying to keep out of the accordion's way,' Aurora said, when Sissy reached the table. 'He only knows a handful of songs so he plays them in a loop. Makes you feel you're going mad to hear "Every Time You're Near" again and again.' Sissy laughed. 'Sit down,' Aurora said, moving up to make space for her. 'Jim will be along in a bit. Someone will get you a drink in the meantime.'

Sissy still didn't dare ask if Peter would be along too, just hoped for the best. The pub continued to fill so that soon it was thronged and she wondered how Jim – Peter if he came – would ever find them. Someone bought her a drink – she remembered to ask for sherry – and she tried to return the gesture, but Aurora told her the barman wouldn't serve women, only men. 'If you really want, you can slip a few shillings into his pocket,' she said, nodding towards the man who had bought Sissy's drink, 'but, honestly, I wouldn't bother. Save it for something to eat later. You're jolly thin.'

'Am I?' Sissy said eagerly. 'I suppose it's because, these last weeks, working at the Y, I hardly eat at all.' It was true. There was food if she wanted it – in fact, that was half the problem: there was food everywhere, in such quantities. After a morning chopping mountains of carrots, of celery, cutting up bits of gristly meat to make it go further, the last thing she wanted at lunchtime was to eat any of it. She loved having a job, which made staying in London possible, even commendable, but the work was back-breaking and monotonous. The good nature of her co-workers helped pass the time, but there were still long, dull hours that, more and more, Sissy filled with thoughts of Peter.

In the evenings, unless she went to Belgrave Square, there wasn't anything to eat except bread and margarine. Neither she nor Kick nor Edie was good about their ration books, and even when they did buy the weekly allocation of two and a half pints of milk, a shilling's worth of meat, a few rashers of bacon and so on, none of them was clever about making the various bits into tempting meals. 'It's like being given three magic beans,' Sissy would complain, surveying the spoils of a morning spent queuing outside the greengrocer or butcher.

'Just put it all in a pan and cook it,' was Edie's advice. So they did, but the results were hardly delicious. 'Like the messes

Pat and Eunice used to make in the kitchen when Cook would let them,' Kick said, poking at the brown heap. 'Mother used to go mad. She said it was wasteful, and that was a sin. Once, she made them eat it instead of lunch.'

Edie made a face. 'Your mother sounds quite the ticket,' she said. 'I'm starting to learn her rules. No being late for meals or you go without, no complaining, always being appropriate – competitive in sport, gracious in victory, beautifully turned out at parties.'

'That's about it,' Kick agreed. 'Oh, and no crying.'

'Not even the little ones?'

'Not anyone,' Kick had repeated. 'Ever.' It sounded, Sissy realised with surprise, not unlike Ballycorry. No one had spoken rules the way the Kennedys did, but certainly crying was not permitted. Or rather, it was not acknowledged. If one cried, one did it entirely alone, and as silently as possibly, hidden away in the laundry room or linen cupboard. Funny, she had thought, this similarity when everything else about the Americans seemed so shiningly different.

'I didn't say it was a good thing,' Aurora said now. 'You being thinner. Only that you are. Look,' she nudged Sissy, 'here's Jim.' Sissy looked up as he came towards the table, a pint of beer in his hand. Sure enough, Peter was behind him. Jim gave her a cheery wave. Peter glanced at her and gave a half-smile, but he didn't try to sit beside her, or talk to her. He talked to the man beside him and was generally more subdued than usual. No impersonations, no stories to have everyone in fits of laughter.

Sissy went to the lavatory, slipping up the narrow staircase to the flat above. On her return, she made sure to squeeze in beside Jim, who gave her shoulder a kindly pat when she sat down. 'Is he annoyed I'm here?' she asked him quietly. Peter never made much effort to greet her, but he seemed more than usually distant that evening.

'Peter? No. That sort of thing doesn't annoy him.'

What sort of thing? Sissy wondered. Were lots of girls coming to find him at the King's Anchor? Or, indeed, other pubs he might frequent? 'If he's annoyed, it's work,' Jim continued. 'Means it must be going badly.'

Sissy felt relief. If it was only work . . . 'He's in the War Office, isn't he?'

Jim gave a shout of laughter that made Peter turn and stare at them both. 'Not that work,' he said, more quietly. 'He doesn't care a bit for that work. No, it's his painting that's going badly. Or, rather, not at all. He can't buy brushes, or paint, or canvas. So he's not painting.'

'How dreadful for him.' She said it vaguely, because she felt she should. But knowing Peter wasn't angry with her gave her confidence to shift nearer him when the man between them got up.

'Hello,' she said, beaming. 'I hoped I'd see you.' There was, she had decided, no point in pretending not to be keen. That sort of thing was for girls who weren't her.

'Did you now?' he said. But he was smiling, his thin lips curving upwards. 'And are you glad you have?'

'Oh, yes.' She lit a cigarette and took a shallow puff. She kept expecting to like them – everyone else seemed to – but they still made her feel sick. 'Jim tells me you're not painting.' She felt very sophisticated as she said it, but his smile dropped immediately and his face scrunched in annoyance.

'The hell he did.'

'Only because I asked him,' she said, in a rush, in case he decided to be angry with Jim. 'I thought I could help. There are paints lying around in the house where I live. Well, I don't live there, exactly, but I visit an awful lot, and I'm sure they'd let me take them.'

'I suppose you mean children's watercolours,' he said dismissively.

'No, proper paint, in tubes, called things like Cadmium Red and Burnt Umber and that sort of thing. I've seen them just lying around. No one uses them and I'm sure they wouldn't mind if I asked for them.' It was true. She had seen a beautiful rosewood box lined with crimson leather in Chips's study. Opening it idly one day she had found it filled with tubes of paint and sticks of oily colour. The tubes were barely squeezed, the sticks barely used.

'And why would they let you take them?'

'The house is full of things, all sorts of things, so I think Chips – he's the man who owns it – doesn't buy them so much because he wants them as because he likes buying things. I've seen him come home with a new lamp or a snuff box or something from the antiques shops he visits, and he's always so full of excitement, making you look at it and admire it. A day or so later, it'll be as though he's forgotten all about it.'

'Dilettante.' His lip curled in scorn. 'If he's idiotic enough to fill his house with things he doesn't need, I suppose I'm happy to help him by taking some of it off his hands.'

'You would be helping,' she assured him humbly. She could see that was important to him. 'I'll ask, next time I'm there, and I'm sure he'll say yes.'

'You said you lived there?'

'Well, more like I half live there . . .' She explained about the flat, and Belgrave Square, and how she went between the two, 'So this way, I can go where I like and no one can ask where I've been and say I should have been home or that sort of thing.'

'Well, aren't you a resourceful little thing?' he said.

'I just want to do the things I want to do,' she said.

'And what things are those?'

'I don't always know, but I know them when I see them.' She held his gaze when she said that, even though she was trembling so hard she was sure he could feel her vibrate through the inch or so of space between them. She wished she could be cool and icy, like Brigid, or magnificently indifferent like Edie, but she couldn't. She wasn't cool or indifferent. Instead of icy she felt she burned below the skin, so much so that if he put his hand on her, he would be forced back by the scorching contact.

When it came to chucking out, he cycled all the way to Portland Street with her, and would have come to the front door of the flat, only Sissy was afraid one of the others would spot them. 'You can leave me here,' she said, shifting her bicycle behind her in case he wanted to kiss her again. He did.

Afterwards, he got onto his bicycle and pedalled away. She began to push hers towards the flat, then paused when he was halfway down the street and watched as he cycled around the corner. She waited for him to look back. When he didn't, she resumed walking and pushing along the deadened street, which was dark and silent except for the faint squeak of her tyres.

Chapter Twenty-Two

Brigid

Being surrounded by friends in the throes of exciting love affairs was rather trying, Brigid decided. It wasn't that she was jealous – not exactly, or at least not of their boyfriends – but she could see that the shimmer of an affair, laid over the hard work and late nights of wartime London, was a kind of magic that she was outside.

Since the first night she had gone out with Billy, Kick saw him as often as she could. Every leave, either he would come to London from Eastbourne, or she would travel to meet him. Half of London was taking bets on the announcement of their engagement. The other half was adamant it would never, could never, happen. They pointed out that his parents still remained aloof, and insisted that Billy would 'come to his senses'. Kick vacillated from elation to despair, from 'It has to be' to 'It can never be,' in a way that was exhausting for those around her.

Meanwhile Sissy, although she tried to hide it, was clearly pursuing an affair of her own. Even amid the fractured to-and-fro of their lives, between hospital, home, the Y and nights out at the 400 Club, Brigid could tell that Sissy was often unaccounted for. And she was vague when questioned. 'Out,' she might say, in response to a question as to where she was going. 'With some people . . .' Vague, but no outright lies.

All around Brigid, girls were skipping from duties in hospitals and canteens to meet young men, stopping only to change their clothes and wash their faces on the way. It didn't help that late in August a run of sunny days finally came, and everyone who wasn't on duty seemed to be sitting in pairs in the parks and other green spaces, picnicking among the torn-up railings and deep-dug trenches.

Maureen was worse – conducting a blatant wartime love affair with her husband. Duff remained at his club, but every day she would get dressed up and meet him for lunch. Then they would spend the afternoon together at Hans Crescent. 'What on earth do you do there?' Brigid had asked, then immediately wished she hadn't.

'Wouldn't you like to know?' Maureen had said, smirking. 'There are *some* advantages to a whole house with no one in it.' Brigid had blushed.

Even Caroline was busy. Not with friends – she still didn't have any – but 'With writing,' she said, when Brigid enquired.

'Writing what?' Brigid had asked.

'Nothing much,' Caroline had said evasively. But whatever it was, it was enough to keep her up in her room.

How was it possible that she felt old? Brigid wondered. Older than Sissy, of course, but older than Kick, Edie too. Older than Maureen, absurdly, and even Honor, who these days – when she appeared – seemed almost young and gay. Something inside her felt so worn, so overused. *It's this war*, she told herself. *It drains one.* But it wasn't that. Or not just that. Others weren't drained.

She would go to the flat, she decided. Take them some elder-flower cordial Cook had made. Maybe there she would feel more herself. Or at least less unlike herself.

She rang the bell at the street door, and waited while Sissy threw down the key in a sock. She let herself in and climbed the stairs. She found Sissy sitting on the sofa reading one of Kick's American magazines and eating bread with jam.

'How lovely,' she said, as Brigid came in. 'I was afraid no one would come back and I'd be stuck here all alone.'

'Well, if anyone knew to expect you, I'm sure they'd have left a note. But your comings and goings are as mysterious as the weather.'

'There's nothing mysterious about English weather.' Sissy licked jam off a spoon. 'Until now it's been grey nearly every day.'

Edie arrived from her shift and flopped down on the sofa, pushing at Sissy to budge up. 'Where's Kick?' Sissy asked.

'Gone somewhere with Billy. Compton . . .?'

'Compton Place,' Brigid said thoughtfully. 'Again? I wonder what that means. I must ask Chips.'

'Must it mean something?' Edie asked. 'Isn't it close to his training camp?'

'Yes, but even so . . . Billy's parents will know she's been. There may not be many servants now but the few there are will tell tales as much as ever. So if Billy hasn't yet brought Kick to see his parents, but he's bringing her to Compton Place and knows his parents will find out . . .'

'How exhausting you all are,' Edie said. 'In America, we just do things.'

'Let's go out,' Brigid said suddenly. 'I am sick, sick, sick of nothing but hospital and bedpans and carbolic soap and sleep. I feel like one of those mechanical toys that just does one thing, again and again, when you wind it up. Either it's in motion, doing always the same thing, or it's mute and immobile. And eventually it breaks through overdoing that one thing, and everyone is terribly surprised.'

'Seems like you feel real bad,' Edie said. 'That almost sounds like complaining.'

'I'm not. It isn't. Just, you know . . .' Brigid shrugged, too tired to explain further when she didn't understand herself.

'I stink of onions and my hands are raw from chopping, but we're here and why not?' Sissy agreed. Then, as she went next door, 'I hope Kick hasn't taken the yellow dress with her.'

Brigid laughed. 'What a grasping little thing you are, Sissy. For all that you seem as innocent as a kitten, you're jolly quick to snuffle out what you want.'

At the 400 Club, Ma Merrick barked, 'You lot, usual drill,' at them. The people coming up behind looked envious as they slipped through the heavily curtained doors.

It was early enough that the underground room was only half full and they found a table near the door, half surrounded by palms in large pots. 'We can see everyone coming in and out,' Sissy said happily. 'Isn't it lucky nightclubs are so often in basements? War means nothing to them. They just carry on as ever.'

'Since when are you so wise in the ways of nightclubs?' Brigid asked.

'I'm learning,' Sissy said, with dignity. 'I know you think I'm the most perfect fool, but I'm finding my way.'

'And what way would that be?' Brigid teased.

'I have plans,' Sissy said, lighting a cigarette and taking a tentative drag.

'What kinds of plans? You sound like someone's match-making mama.'

'Perhaps I'm my own matchmaking mama.' She tilted her head back and blew smoke into the air.

'Good for you,' Edie said.

'What are your requirements?' Brigid asked. 'If one is a title, I'm sure Chips would help. He's very fond of you and no one knows more than he does about who's in line to inherit an obscure peerage if an elderly uncle pops off. Why, in three moves he could probably have you a baroness, I'm sure.' She laughed and took one of Sissy's cigarettes. 'Since when do you smoke Chesterfield? Are you a working man?'

'A friend gave them to me,' Sissy said. 'I don't mind about titles. Though it would be nice to go back to Ballycorry as a baroness.' She looked wistful. 'Wouldn't Mother be impressed! But no. Not that. I want to do my own choosing.' A man passing their table stumbled and lurched against one of the potted palms. The pot tipped and would have fallen if Edie hadn't leaped up and blocked it. Brigid began to wish they hadn't come. The room was filling and soon their table of three would be jostled on all sides. The music was too loud, she decided, and, as the potted palm tilted again, the crowd too boisterous. Whatever she had been hoping for in coming here, she had been wrong, and would be better off at home in Belgrave Square. What had she been hoping for? Some excitement, she supposed, something to break up the dreariness around her that she suspected was really within her.

A crowd of young men in uniform came in. 'Brigid, there you are!' one called. 'Ma said you were skulking down here!'

'Tony, how sweet!' Brigid said, standing to greet him. Within a moment, their table was surrounded, chairs pulled up and then a second table for the overflow. Brigid had Tony on one side of her and a man in the uniform of the Irish Guards on the other.

Tony asked her up to dance, and they jitterbugged energetically to 'In The Mood'. Around them, the tiny dance-floor cleared. 'Must be Americans!' Brigid heard one girl say snootily.

'Jealous!' Tony murmured in her ear, as he spun her around. Then the music switched to something slow and he drew her close. Brigid, who was tired, let her head rest against his shoulder, thinking he was just the right height for her to do that. He held her close and moved them carefully in and around the other dancing couples. 'I say,' he said after a while, into her ear, 'I wonder if I might ask you something.'

Brigid drew back to look at his face. What she saw there – a shyness she hadn't expected – surprised her. He had the look of a man nerving himself up to something, she thought, as he blinked rapidly. But what? Surely . . . She thought briefly about what it might be. And then what it might be like to say yes. How happy Chips would be. Even her mother, although she wouldn't say so. The Earl of Rosslyn. Tony – a dear fellow, someone she knew well, whom she liked and respected. Saying yes would mean the end of so much that was making her . . . 'unhappy' was the wrong word, she decided, but certainly discontented. The perpetual nagging sense of life passing her by as she toiled in the hospital. Of sitting by the bedside of a man she had no skill to heal, whose pain and discomfort she could barely ease. Of writing to a man she never saw and could only construct in her imagination through half-remembered conversations and whatever he put on the pages he wrote back to her.

Saying yes, now, to Tony, would be one way to push past all of that and give herself new certainties: a wedding, a house – a castle, actually, she remembered – maybe later a family.

But it was no good. It wasn't what she wanted. He wasn't whom she wanted. And she had spent too long trying to understand what she did want – almost, she thought, she had it clear. She couldn't abandon that now for the ease of saying yes to Tony.

'You can ask me anything you like,' she said gently to him, 'but I should tell you, it's probably no good. Unless I am being thoroughly conceited,' with a small smile, 'in which case you may mock me as much as you wish.'

'I would never mock you,' he said. 'You're jolly good to be so straight.'

She rested her forehead lightly against his shoulder for a second. 'I'm sorry,' she muttered. And she was.

'Don't be.'

'Shall we?' She gestured behind her.

Back at the table, Debo had arrived, without Andrew but with a friend she introduced as Louie. Louie's eyes were red and she wore too much powder, almost as though she had tried to obscure herself, Brigid thought. 'Louie had a telegram today,' Debo said, when the friend had gone to the powder room. She said it loudly but in a way that was meant to be a whisper. The table looked sympathetically after her. Everyone knew what a telegram meant. Someone missing, maybe dead.

'Husband?' Edie asked quietly.

'Brother,' Debo said.

Would that be worse or better? Brigid wondered. She thought

of Arthur, and the way his eyes crinkled when he smiled. Worse, she decided. Wasn't it strange, the way they dipped in and out of war? Sometimes days went by when it was just noise in the background, a hum in the distance that never let up but caused no personal trouble. Then suddenly it would draw close, horribly close, clutching at them. It hadn't got her yet, not really, but it had got Louie and so many others. How much longer could she evade it?

'I hear Kick and Billy . . .' a girl at the other end of the table said. The table leaned in closer.

'Do tell . . .' a woman in dark blue silk urged. Brigid was careful not to listen. She didn't want to hear what these people had to say, when they knew Billy so well and Kick not at all.

Sissy was talking to a man who had a balled-up napkin in his hand and was recreating the fence his horse had jumped. Edie had found some of the more adventurous GIs from the officers' club and was urging one – he was called Charlie, Brigid thought – to ask the woman in dark blue to dance.

She thought of telling them she was leaving, then decided just to slip out. She got up and wove through the crowd to the heavy curtain covering the door to the stairs. At the door she looked back. Only Edie had noticed her leave. She gave Brigid a brisk nod and a smile.

'Work,' Brigid mouthed at her. And, indeed, if she left now she would get a few hours' sleep before her shift.

That evening at the hospital Brigid was more than usually worried about Will. His temperature went up and down as fevers gripped him. The wound was ulcerated now and the pain terrible. There seemed no plan to get rid of the infection, only to keep fighting it as it appeared and reappeared.

She had written to Fritzi how frightened she was, how strong the infection had grown. *At the camp in Canada,* he wrote back, *the army doctor used leeches. He learned it in the Great War, he said. And when there wasn't enough medicine to go round, that's what he tried. An older trick. I recall it worked. It could be tried?* Brigid hadn't dared raise this with Dr Carr yet, but she promised herself she would.

'I'm just like the war,' Will joked feebly, when she called in to see him before going home. The room was hot and stuffy. Unexpected sunny weather was no gift to the sick. She wished he was still in the basement ward where at least it would be cool. 'The thing has opened so many fronts now that I can't keep fighting them all. I haven't the resources.'

'Don't say that,' she said. 'You must keep heart.' What she didn't say was how much she needed him to do that. She remembered her thought of the night before – war, in the distance, reaching for her but not yet touching. That clutching grasp seemed closer now.

'I can't see that it makes any difference,' he said wearily. 'I had so much heart for so long and I couldn't beat it. And now I have less heart – not none,' he said, as she began to interrupt, 'but less. And I don't see that I'm any worse.'

But he was worse. Brigid could see it. He was thinner, paler but, more than that, he was quieter. Some days he said almost nothing, although she might sit beside him for half an hour at a time. The books she brought him piled up unread and she had long since stopped bringing food. When he did talk, he liked her to keep telling him stories of Kick and Sissy, Edie and Caroline.

'Will she marry him, do you think?' he asked now, of Kick and Billy.

'I honestly don't know. Everything says no, but those two . . . her especially . . . maybe.'

'I hope they do.'

'You're a romantic,' she teased him.

'I am,' he agreed. 'I used to be, anyway. But it's not just the romance. It's other things too. Like, how much change has the war really brought? I know everything looks different, but beneath that, perhaps it rumbles on in the same way. Kick and Billy will be a good test of that.' He smiled. 'What's it like outside?' he asked then. 'One of those rare late summer evenings? I think I can smell it.'

'Yes, at last.' She told him how the afternoon had been the brash blue and gold of a packet of Sunlight soap, and how that had softened even as she walked to the hospital, blending and blurring. How the air was heavy with an abundance of roses as though the bushes had kept this in reserve, hidden and secret, until the sun loosed it. Talking, she was horribly conscious of making him feel too acutely everything he was missing. Almost, she wished it was raining and grey so that she could say he was better off, tucked up indoors. But she couldn't lie. Even here, a tale of heat and sun had travelled, invisible and unquantifiable but definite. 'Autumn will be lovely,' she said instead. 'That's how it goes after a summer like this one. Autumn will be lovely, and you will be stronger. Perhaps we can go out then. To the banks of the river?'

'Perhaps,' he said politely.

The doctor came in. He called twice every day now. He asked Brigid the usual questions – mood, temperature, pulse, appearance of the wound – and put his hand on Will's forehead for a moment. He took out his stethoscope and Brigid unbuttoned Will's plaid pyjama top, exposing his thin chest, the blue-white colour of buttermilk. The doctor leaned in and listened. He frowned and Brigid hoped Will hadn't seen.

When the doctor had gone she leaned forward and gently adjusted Will's fringe where it had been left sticking up. 'Are you all right?'

'Yes,' Will murmured. He was exhausted, his eyes closing. Brigid folded the sheet below his shoulders, whispered, 'See you tomorrow,' and slipped out. She went to look for the doctor, to ask if he'd thought of leeches. To ask if there was nothing else they could try, because what they were doing wasn't working. But she couldn't find him.

As she made her way home, she passed a soldier and his girl walking together. He was whistling and she had one of his arms clasped in both of hers. They walked so close together, you couldn't have slid a piece of paper between them, Brigid thought, with a pang. She half recognised the tune he whistled, and tried to find it in her mind. She used to know it, she thought, but had forgotten.

Having Maureen around meant the clearing up of small mysteries, Brigid had discovered. Nothing could remain unspoken, or elusive, once she took an interest in it. 'Where is Honor, really?' she asked, over cocktails that evening, looking around as though she thought her cousin might pop out from behind a chair or sofa.

'Essex, I believe,' Chips said.

'Why?' Maureen took a cigarette from a gold case and fitted it into a long ivory holder. She was the only person Brigid knew who still smoked like that. Everyone else had dispensed with holders now, women smoking like men.

'Some kind of war work,' Chips said evasively. It was what

he'd said to Brigid. But Maureen, unlike Brigid, kept up the attack.

'What kind of war work? No one else is doing anything that keeps them away from home for so long. Honor is nothing like Lady Iveagh and you cannot persuade me she is. I've been here nearly six weeks and she hasn't been here at all. No,' she concluded, 'doesn't sound very convincing to me.' And she fixed Chips with her large seagull-egg eyes, staring silently at him until he broke.

'If you must know,' he said with dignity, 'she is conducting a love affair.' Brigid was too surprised to react.

'I rather thought she might be,' Maureen said, in satisfaction. She sat back in her chair and exhaled sharply. 'Who with?'

'Well, that's the problem,' Chips said, leaning forward eagerly. It seemed to Brigid that he was actually relieved to unburden himself. 'Not at all the sort of chap you'd expect. Some Czechoslovak pilot. Funny little chap who came to join the RAF when Hitler took Czechoslovakia.'

'Sounds wonderfully brave,' Maureen drawled. 'And Honor is providing respite and comfort? How patriotic of her.'

'Don't be silly, Maureen.' Chips was nettled. 'It's not at all the thing.'

'Cross that she didn't consult you?' Maureen asked.

'You know exactly what I mean,' Chips said irritably. 'You clearly keep your own activities *quite* confined, if it is indeed Eddie Cavendish.'

'I don't know what you mean,' Maureen said coolly.

'Very well,' Chips said. 'If you insist. But Honor has taken up with this chap we know nothing about. They met at a dance in a village hall.' He sounded baffled.

'Poor Chips.' Maureen laughed. 'Your wife's lover hasn't

thought to provide you with his *Debrett's* entry. How unfortunate.'

'Apparently they spend all their time together in the pub,' Chips said. 'The pub!'

'Oh dear,' Maureen agreed. 'That does sound like she's got it bad.'

'Very bad,' Chips said. 'She's talking of divorce. But you mustn't say it to anyone. I'm sure I can bring her to her senses.'

Brigid was shocked. She had begun to suspect there must be more to Honor's absence than being busy with Lady Iveagh – even though their mother had as much work as anyone would allow her to dispense: always another meeting to attend, another programme to administer, another relief effort to co-ordinate – but this? An affair, perhaps, but divorce?

It was true, she thought, that Honor had been unhappy in her marriage for a long time, something she had made no secret of. And, indeed, she had been noticeably happier over the last months, the few times Brigid had seen her, but Brigid had assumed it was down to being busy, and easy in her mind about Paul, safe in America. Not divorce.

No wonder Chips had been subdued of late. He must have been ruminating on the various ways in which his life must change if Honor – and her money, because Brigid knew how that would weigh with him – were to be removed from his reach.

The idea of Honor spending all day in a pub made Brigid want to laugh. It was so unlike her – what would she even do there? And yet, if that was indeed what she was doing, there was something curiously encouraging about it. If even Honor – so correct, even timid – could step outside the tightly woven limits of expectation, could set off on a new path with all the joy Brigid had recently seen in her, why on earth was she herself still stuck, heavy like someone drugged, in the hard amber of her own life?

'Speaking of the Devonshires,' Maureen asked, eyes bright with mischief, turning to Brigid, 'how is dear little Kick getting on?'

'She's kept terribly busy by the GIs,' Brigid said. 'They seem quite dependent, almost childish really, for all that they're grown men and soldiers. Unable to do anything much for themselves so Kick and her friend Edie are in demand for everything. Every outing, every game of tennis, every hand of bridge. They make coffee, doughnuts, give them chocolate bars, take them to the theatre . . .' She grinned. 'It's like being Nanny to a gang of overgrown schoolboys.'

'Never mind the GIs,' Maureen said, as Brigid had known she would, 'what of Kick's romance with Billy? I presume that's why she's here?'

'I'm not sure she knows quite why she's here,' Brigid said. 'Billy, of course, mostly, but there's something else too . . .'

'How odd. I always know exactly what I want,' Maureen said.

'Yes, but that's not the same as getting it, is it?' Chips said, with delicate malice.

Maureen ignored him. 'How is it with her and Billy?'

'He's taken her out a few times,' Brigid said cautiously.

'Which, with Billy, is tantamount to an engagement. Except of course it isn't. And won't be. I don't know why she wastes her time.' Maureen sounded cross now. 'She'd do better to forget about him and find someone less fussy.'

'Maybe he'll become less fussy,' Brigid said.

'Impossible.' She said it matter-of-factly. 'There is no way to be a Cavendish and not dislike Catholics. It's second only to breathing with them.'

'But they don't dislike Kick.'

'Yes, that's the pity of it,' Chips said cheerfully. 'They rather adore her. But it won't be enough.'

'It might be,' Brigid said.

'It can't be,' Maureen, equally cheerful, said. 'Why, the duke has had his bedchamber moved to the other side of Devonshire House, so he no longer has to look out onto Westminster Cathedral or "hear those popish bells", as he puts it.'

Chips pounced. 'And how do you know where the duke's bedchamber is?' he asked.

Maureen stared at him and Brigid could see she was planning one of her most savage responses.

'I think I hear Caroline,' she said quickly. Sure enough, the girl slid into the room and perched on the arm of a chair. Sight of her daughter galvanised Maureen, as Brigid had known it would. It was increasingly obvious that Caroline had used up any possible benefit of lessons with the retired headmistress and was at a loose end, but Maureen had shown no interest in thinking about what she might do next.

'I must go.' She got up. 'I said I'd meet Duff at the Savoy.'

'Shall I come with you?' Caroline asked.

'Why would you do that?' Maureen asked. Caroline, head bowed, got up from her chair, moving clumsily through the drawing room so that it was a wonder she did no more than bump into a chair.

'Honestly, Maureen,' Chips said quietly, when Caroline had gone.

'Honestly, what?' Maureen asked, eyes opened to their widest as she stared at him. 'Honestly, *what*?' When he said nothing she drained her glass and stood up, stretching her arms showily. 'I must change. Chips, can you order the car round?'

'There's a war on, Maureen,' Chips said patiently. 'There are no cars to order.'

'I'll call you a taxi,' Brigid said.

Once Maureen had gone, Brigid went to her bedroom, stopping outside Caroline's on the way. She tapped at the door and opened it. Caroline was sitting at the little table by the window, writing furiously in an exercise book.

'Shall I come in?' Brigid said. 'We can chat?'

'No, thanks,' Caroline said. 'It's better if I keep writing.'

Brigid went to find Chips, who was in the library. 'Should we say something to Maureen?' she said. 'She can't know how unhappy she is making Caroline.'

'Why can't she know?'

'Well, if she did, she wouldn't do it.'

'Wouldn't she? I'm afraid you don't know Maureen as well as you think. Tremendous fun, I grant you. Quite the most entertaining companion, when she wants to be. But as a mother . . .' He shuddered. 'I don't know why Nature allowed it.' He had always, Brigid remembered then, been the one little Paul went to when he was hurt or upset, running to his father, rather than his mother. It had been Chips who had soothed bumped heads and gently bandaged bloodied knees.

'Then we must tell Duff,' Brigid insisted. 'He could say something to her.

'That would be the very worst thing we could do,' Chips said. 'Don't you see? Caroline's greatest crime is the amount of her father's affection she holds. Maureen cannot stand to share him with anyone, not even his children. Caroline will have to find her own way through this. I have no doubt she will.'

'But *she* . . . Maureen . . . well . . .' Brigid couldn't think how to put it. 'What about the Duke of Devonshire?' she finished.

'That's different. What Maureen allows herself and what she allows others, especially Duff, are very different things. In any case,' he grinned, 'I was only fishing. I know nothing for certain. She insists there is nothing to it.'

Brigid went to her room and sat down. She was upset by what had gone on between Maureen and Caroline, by the child's evident misery and, even more, by her resigned acceptance of it. But Caroline didn't want to talk, and Chips wouldn't. She pulled out a piece of writing paper and began to do what increasingly brought her comfort – writing an account of the whole thing to Fritzi.

You must be terribly bored by all these long tales of people and things you hardly know . . . she had written in her last letter. But no, he had insisted, when he wrote back,

Not at all. It makes me feel that I am in some way still part of the world you are in. Not simply abandoned to this life of rural routine although, truth be told, I am surprised at how much I enjoy it. It has a simplicity that is almost that of the internment camp, but without the privations. Each day, I know exactly what I must do, and there are barely hours in which to do it so that I am never at a loss. At the end of each day, there is the satisfaction of knowing I have contributed, in however small a way, to the efforts of this country against the country that was once mine. And then there is the hour before bed, when I re-read your letters and, if I am especially lucky, read a new one that has arrived. I write to you, sometimes on paper and sometimes in my head, and I go to sleep, content in a way I would once have found impossible to imagine. The days when my thoughts were taken up with fevered considerations of my inheritance, my standing, my ambitions to edge closer to my grandfather's crown, all of that seems laughable now . . .

As Brigid poured out her concerns over Caroline and Maureen, and Will, she thought how strange it was that she should have no one to voice them to except a man she barely remembered.

He was a place to send her most troublesome thoughts. A way to have those thoughts ordered and returned to her in a shape she could understand. He seemed to welcome everything she told him, no matter how trivial or troublesome, and devoted time to puzzling out their implications. At times, Brigid felt that she was like the miller's daughter from the fairytale, sending out heaps of unruly straw, only to have it returned to her neatly spun into gold.

What was it Caroline had said? *It makes it more bearable if I write them down . . .* Brigid realised that the contents of her own letters had changed. Where she had been vague – at first she had been scared to tell him more than the most basic details of her work – now she told him everything. And the more she told him, the more she read his responses, the more solid Fritzi became. She realised she now needed his advice, his impressions of the things she wrote about. Needed these things to make sense of what she saw and felt.

Chapter Twenty-Three

Kick

'Joe's coming!' Kick said, holding out the telegram to Edie as if it was a religious offering. 'Read it!'

'POSTED TO YOU STOP ARRIVE SOONEST STOP PFGT', Edie read. 'What does that mean? He's posted what to you?'

'It means he's been posted to London, but doesn't want to say so in case the telegram is intercepted.'

'And what's PFGT?' Edie asked.

'Plan for Good Times. It's what Joe, Jack and I used to say to each other when we were younger, during the summers at Hyannis Port, once Joe was allowed to take the car and drive us to picnics and parties. We always said "PFGT" so Mother wouldn't know what we meant. She wouldn't have liked it.'

'And were they? Good times?'

'Oh, the best! Those summers, when I think about them now, they seem like they went on for ever. Every day was a perfect day.' How to describe the excitement? Salt wind in your face, trying to get the knots out of your hair after a day of sailing, then changing into a grown-up dress and going to a party on the beach or at someone's house . . . The heady mix of freedom and protection that came with being taken about by her brothers? It was like being at the very centre of the gravitational pull.

There were other pictures too, when she thought of those summers. Her mother's cool gaze the first day she put on her bathing suit. The eyes that missed nothing, raking up and down, followed by 'No potatoes for you, Kathleen. Not for a few weeks anyway. Luckily you get slim as quickly as you get fat.' Rosie ate twice the amount of potatoes in defiance, until Mother told the cook not to prepare any for her.

'Plan for Good Times,' she repeated now. 'I certainly will.'

'So what's he like, this brother of yours?'

'Joe? He's the serious one, not like Jack. Jack's a kidder. Joe is responsible and takes things to heart more. He likes to do well at everything, whether it's football or school and college. I imagine he's exactly the same in the navy. Everyone falls in love with him, so you'd better watch out!'

'My, you Kennedys are conceited. You think the rest of us just have to meet you and we'll fall in love?'

'It's not that,' Kick protested, 'but girls do. Some of them my friends. And sometimes they aren't so much my friends after.'

'I promise I'll be just as careful as can be,' Edie said. 'The way you talk about your family . . .' She shook her head. 'I can't wait to meet more of you and see if you're all just as nuts.'

'We're Kennedys,' Kick said. 'This is how we are.'

'What does "soonest" mean, do you think? This month? Next?'

It was almost September, the dog days of summer replaced by crisp hints of autumn in the mornings and evenings.

'I don't know but I'll ask Billy. He's calling for me in an hour. He'll know how things work.'

'More leave?' Edie asked. 'He seems to get away an awful lot.'

'He's an officer,' she explained proudly. Then, 'but always short passes; a day, a night, rarely more. So it doesn't seem like that to me,' Kick said. 'Now that I see him sometimes, I think I miss him more than I did when I never saw him at all. Isn't that strange?'

'And have you seen his parents yet?' Kick could hear the caution in Edie's voice. She knew – because Kick had told her – that they had been careful not to see her. It had upset Kick, who recognised it for what it was.

'Not yet,' she admitted. 'But Billy promises me I shall the next time they're in London.' She ducked her head to avoid Edie's sympathetic face. She knew what it looked like, Kick Kennedy waiting around, hoping to be acknowledged. What it looked like and what it felt like.

And then, that very evening, Billy asked her to lunch with his parents the next day. 'They'd be so pleased to see you,' he said. Kick had to force herself not to point out that the duke and duchess could have seen her at any time over the past month and more. Instead she smiled and said how nice that would be, and was furious that her stomach lurched with apprehension.

He called for her on a borrowed bicycle so they could cycle together to the restaurant in Covent Garden. There, they leaned their bicycles against one of the heavy beams reinforcing the entrance and Billy wedged a stray brick by the back wheels to stop them falling over. Kick took a powder compact out of her coat pocket and dabbed at her face. In the bright daylight the powder seemed too pale, as though she were colouring herself with chalk.

'Do I look all right?' she asked Billy.

'You look beautiful,' he said. 'You always do.' It was the way he said it, she thought: head bent as he pulled his trouser leg out of his sock, not even looking at her. Anyone else would have tried to make something of the compliment, even tried to kiss her. Billy just said it as he might have said, 'It's going to rain' or 'Your shoelace is untied.'

By the front door, a shabby man in a worn grey jacket shook a tin cup at passers-by. 'War Wounded' read the sign he held, white letters painted on a piece of plywood.

'Which war?' Billy asked, as they reached him.

'The other one,' the man said. 'The Great War.'

'Nothing great about war,' Billy muttered, putting a shilling into the cup. The man thanked and blessed him, then blessed Kick. The head waiter opened the door for them, bowing briefly at the waist and assuring 'Lord Hartington' that it was good to see him. Once they were past him, he went outside and Kick heard him say sharply to the man with the tin cup, 'Further down the street. I told you. Not here.'

The restaurant was elaborately dressed with heavy linen table-cloths, silver covers and sparkling glasses. Kick wondered if it was deliberate, to distract from the sparse amount of food on offer. If so, it was clever, she decided. *Nothing has changed*, the tablecloths and silver cutlery insisted, even though everything had changed.

Billy's mother, the duchess, was seated at a round table set back from the window. 'There's grouse,' she said, by way of greeting. 'Makes a change from rabbit.' Billy kissed her cheek.

Kick went to shake hands but the duchess presented her cheek so Kick, too, kissed her. 'After all this time,' she said warmly, making it sound as if there hadn't been nearly enough. 'You look wonderful.' She'd taken in Kick's appearance with a swift glance. 'You must be the only girl in London who has nice things any more.' Kick blushed. She had deliberately worn a plain dress of light brown tweed, but plain wasn't enough to fool the duchess.

'My mother sends me things,' she offered, as excuse.

'*Of course* she does,' the duchess said. Kick blushed again and Billy threw her a sympathetic look. She picked up the menu even though she knew exactly what would be on it. The same dishes that were on every menu in London: fish and potato pie, meat and potato pie, roast lamb and mint sauce. Theirs was the only table occupied in the room so waiters vied to pour water, offer wine, ask whether they wanted the one permitted slice of bread now or later. 'How are your parents?' the duchess continued.

Kick told her the public version. Everyone was well; her father was considering writing his memoirs; her mother was busy supporting Red Cross fundraising efforts and getting Ted ready for boarding school. She spoke quickly, closing gaps before they could widen enough to allow questions. It was a relief when the duchess turned to Billy.

Outside the window, Kick watched the beggarman walking back towards the restaurant. He moved more briskly now: was his limp faked? The man drew closer and she realised it was the duke, wearing a grey jacket just as old – older – than the beggar's. He approached the door and the head waiter leaped forward. He hadn't recognised the duke either, Kick thought, and was about to order him further down the street. She twisted in her chair, wondering how she could prevent what must surely be a most mortifying scene.

'Your Grace,' the waiter was bowing low, ushering Edward Cavendish, 10th Duke of Devonshire, through the door he held open, and to their table. *Of course*, Kick thought.

'There's grouse,' the duchess greeted her husband.

'Makes a change from rabbit,' he said. Kick stifled a laugh.

They ordered: grouse with bread sauce for Billy and his parents, plain for Kick who hated bread sauce, and even more the wartime version. The duke quizzed Billy on the news from Europe – Allied troops in Sicily, Germans evacuating for mainland Italy at a rate of a thousand a day, American forces moving inexorably up. 'You may never see more action at this rate,' the duke said. The surge of hope he tried to hide made Kick pity him desperately.

'Don't,' Billy halted him. 'Don't say it. Tell me about Andrew.'

'You must tell me everything you've been up to,' the duchess said brightly, turning to Kick. So Kick told her stories of the club and the GIs. She had discovered that English people enjoyed hearing how hard Americans found life in England – especially when the hardship was due to privations the British took for granted: lack of hot water, cold beds, limited food.

'They must never come to Chatsworth,' the duchess said happily. 'I don't imagine they could stand it for a moment. Why is it that you are so very different, Kick?'

'I think it's because I'm Catholic,' Kick blurted out, then wanted to slide under the table at the look on the duchess's face. Why had she said that? The truth was that she had wondered the same thing: why did all the scarcity the GIs complained about mean so little to her? 'It means I don't mind hardship,' she rushed to say. 'I was brought up to it, in the convent.' Again, that look on the duchess's face. 'We learned to be hardy about cold water and thin blankets,' she continued. 'It meant that when I first came to England, I was already used to those things.'

'I see. But I think it's more than that. The rest of your family aren't like you. They didn't settle in the same way, did they?'

'No, I guess not . . . I just always felt at home here.'

'I imagine that's true,' the duchess said. 'You know, I'm happy you came back. Billy has been far more cheerful. Don't think I haven't noticed.' Kick began to beam at the idea that Billy's good humour might be laid at her door, but his mother hadn't finished. With a troubled look on her face, she continued, in a lower voice, 'But please don't think that this means things are any different. Or easier. The differences are as great as they ever were, Kick. It's not what anyone would want, because we're very fond of you, but there we are . . .' She pulled her cardigan up around her shoulders. Outside, the day had darkened towards rain.

'I don't think you'd like to live here,' she continued. 'It wouldn't agree with you, I'm certain of it. And think how much your family would miss you. Your sister – Rosemary, isn't it?' Did she know? Kick wondered. Could she have heard the rumours? But there was nothing malicious in the duchess's face, just the honest hope that her son would fall out of love and that Kick would help him do it. 'Young people never understand how very difficult it all is,' she finished.

The duke, when he turned to her, was even blunter. 'I wasn't at all pleased to hear you were back,' he said. Billy twitched, but said nothing. Kick almost apologised. His voice softened. 'But that doesn't mean I'm not pleased to see you. It's the devil of a situation. Hard to see Billy so happy and know it can't be.' She would hear only that Billy was happy, Kick decided, clenching her hands under the table. Then, 'I believe your brother made his First Communion in the Vatican,' the duke said. 'The Pope himself?'

'Teddy? Why, yes,' Kick said. She thought back to the day, three years ago. Teddy in his double-breasted wool coat, self-conscious and delighted because for once it was him they all looked at and spoke to, not his older brothers. Her father, politics set aside for a few hours. The echo of the choir as they sang the *Kyrie*. How she had turned to glance at her mother and seen tears in Rose's eyes. 'It was a really nice day,' she said, unable to convey any of it.

'Traitors,' the duke said bitterly.

'The Vatican claims neutrality,' Billy reminded his father, leaning towards her. Grateful, she shifted a little so their shoulders were touching.

'No such thing,' the duke snapped. Then, 'One hears you spend a lot of time with Brigid Guinness,' he said to his son. 'Charming girl.' He glanced at Billy, who kept a straight face as he took Kick's hand and agreed politely that Brigid was 'charming'.

'Maureen Guinness tells me she's invaluable to that hospital. That they can't do without her.' Kick tried to imagine Maureen saying any such thing. She failed.

'What's this about Maureen Guinness?' the duchess said sharply, looking up from whatever she was rummaging for in her handbag.

'Nothing,' the duke said hurriedly.

'Nothing,' Billy echoed.

Outside the restaurant it was raining and they split up quickly, the duke and duchess to Devonshire House, Billy and Kick to her flat.

'Goodbye, Kick darling,' the duchess said. 'My love to your parents.' Kick promised she would pass it on, even though she knew *love* was not what the duchess felt.

'If he means what I think he means to you, you won't pursue this,' the duke said quietly, as he shook her hand. 'The funny thing is, I rather think I can trust you not to tell him I said that.'

As they cycled back towards the flat, Kick forced herself not to think about what the duke had said – especially the bit about trusting her. Instead, she asked Billy what he thought about Joe's unit, and what 'soonest' meant, in military terms?

'I'm not sure it means anything much,' he said. 'Plans change and change again. How many times have we been told to be ready to ship out within a week, only to have the order postponed? Don't get your hopes too high. Now, I'll pick you up later, for the Ritz.'

And she said yes, even though, after that lunch, she knew she should say no. Billy might not have heard his father, but he certainly knew his father's thoughts. His mother's too. All that about Brigid . . . Kick would have been a fool not to understand. She understood perfectly, and the thought of how unwanted she was made her miserable. So Billy certainly knew, yet he did nothing. Or nothing much. He continued to see her every chance he got, but made no plans other than 'my next leave' and only ever for small things: 'We might see that play/ take a horse out and go for a ride on Rotten Row . . .'

'Billy, darling, what are we doing?' she said, when they reached the flat and he was about to leave.

'What do you mean?'

'What are we doing?' she repeated. 'You and I?'

'I don't know,' he said miserably. 'I only know that I can't stop seeing you. And I believe, somehow, this will all come good.'

It was a terrible answer. No answer at all really. But what else was there?

Billy was wrong, and 'soonest' turned out to mean two days later. Kick was at the officers' club, pretending to learn to sew – 'Wouldn't it be nice if we could stitch a button onto their shirts?' one of the other Dollies had said. Kick thought it wouldn't be at all nice, but was too good-natured to say so – when a warm, familiar voice in the doorway said 'I have a jacket that's all out at the elbows. I wonder if I could bring it to be mended?'

And there he was, Joe; handsome in his uniform, his face as tanned as though he'd spent the summer sailing. There were more angles to his face than before, emphasising the slight downward turn to his blue eyes, but his expression was pure celebration. He laughed, showing even white teeth, and came towards her as she rushed at him, so that they met in a tangle of chairs, in the middle of the room.

'You look wonderful,' she said, when she could step back far enough to look at him.

'So do you. I guess the reports of the gay time you're having haven't been exaggerated at all.' Joe smiled down at her and Kick basked in the warmth of that familiar blue gaze.

'It's like the sun coming out, you being here,' she said. 'I don't think I even knew how lonely I was for home till this very moment. How long are you on leave?'

'Only a week, but I'll be back often. I'll be stationed here from now on, in Cornwall; I'm on loan to the RAF – Bomber Squadron 110, Special Air Unit.' He saluted her smartly. 'I've volunteered for a new kind of operational duty, and I'll be in and out of London for a while until it gets up and running.'

'What kind of operation, exactly?'

'You know I can't tell you.'

'Have you told Pa?'

'No. I can't tell him either. Which he doesn't understand. No matter how much I explain that "top secret" means top secret to everyone, he still thinks I can tell him. Truth is, he's not at all pleased that I won't.'

'I imagine he wouldn't be. I don't much like it either. Where are you staying?'

'Right here, at the club.'

'That I do like. Let me introduce you around.' And she took his arm and brought him through the room with its ping-pong and card tables, dragging him from group to group and forcing everyone to stop what they were doing to say hello.

'I see why they're called Doughboys,' he muttered in her ear, after the first round of introductions.

'Stop that!' But she couldn't help laughing. And indeed, she thought, beside Joe, with his crisply pressed uniform, his clean features and those dazzling blue eyes, everyone looked shabby. Blurred round the edges. Vague. She felt they knew it too, the way they looked at him, how quickly they took in his sheer vitality.

'It's my fault,' she whispered with a laugh. 'Mine and Edie's. We're supposed to be looking after them.'

'Looking after them far too well,' he whispered back. And, when they had finished the rounds, 'Every one of them's in love with you, exactly as I expected.'

'They are not,' she said amiably. 'Oh, sometimes they pretend to be, because they're lonely and away from their own girls, but they surely aren't.'

'And you? In love with any of these nice American boys? Must be one among all that lot has made your pulse race?'

'Not a one,' she said gaily. 'I think I'm immune. It must be growing up with boys just like that. They're awfully sweet and nice, but my pulse isn't racing at all.'

'Still Billy?' he asked then. 'Jack said yes, but I said it couldn't be.'

'Well, maybe,' she admitted. 'But don't tell Mother. Or Pa. There isn't any point.'

'Why not?'

'Because nothing can come of it. He takes me out when he's on leave. I even had lunch with his parents. But all the old objections are still there. Truth is, I don't even know why we do it, and neither does he. Mostly because it's too hard not to. But he won't ask me to marry him, and that's that.'

He squeezed her arm. 'You sure about that?'

'Absolutely certain, poor me.' She pulled a face, mostly to disguise how upset she was. With every bit of her, she hoped Billy would ask her to marry him, even while she told herself that he would not.

It was a mess. After the lunch with his parents, when he walked away, pushing his borrowed bicycle, she had run up the stairs to the flat and over to the window that looked onto the street. She had thrown open the shutters and then the window. Leaning out, she had watched him along the street and round the corner. She had thought of calling him back, saying, 'Why don't you come up?' Edie was out, Sissy too. The flat was empty and no one would ever have known. Not that anyone in England would have cared. But she didn't.

'Yes, poor me,' she said lightly now. 'Sometimes it seems like he's the only man who doesn't want to marry me, and yet he's the one I want.'

'It's often the way,' Joe said wisely.

'Anyway, enough of me. I want to hear all about home. But, first, there's someone else I want you to meet.' She took him to the kitchen to say hello to Edie who was vigorously pounding dough, hair scraped back into the tight hats they had to wear while they baked. Her face was flushed from the heat in the airless basement and the effort of kneading. Any other girl, Kick thought, confronted by an officer as handsome as Joe, would have been self-conscious – she would have whipped off the hat and tried to smooth her hair or made an excuse to go and 'tidy up' as quickly as she could. Not Edie.

'So, Lieutenant Joe Kennedy,' she said, slapping the dough down hard on the countertop, 'I won't shake your hand because I'm dusted in sugar, but I can order your sister to make you a cup of very bad tea, as that's the only kind she can make, if you like?'

'I do like,' Joe said, 'and I'm not a lieutenant. Not yet.'

'A Not-yet-enant,' Edie said, with a laugh. 'They're the best kind, I hear.'

'You hear right,' said Joe, hoisting himself up to sit on the counter where she was shaping star cookies with a steel cutter. Edie shifted up a bit to make room for him, and warned him about getting butter on his trousers. 'I'm not a tidy baker,' she said, 'but I make up for that with effort. I must have made two hundred of these this morning. We serve them to the GIs with their coffee. It makes them feel less like they're in England. Most of them hate being here, but the ones who love it,' she cast a sly look at Kick, 'well, they *really* love it.'

Joe laughed. 'I forgot to say, Kick, Mother's sent you a parcel. Ham, eggs, cookies, candy, oranges, lemons, apples . . . All the way across the Atlantic, I've been balancing it on my knees, trying to make sure the eggs don't break.'

'Oranges!' Kick said. 'Actual lemons! The luxury! We must have a dinner party. Right, Edie?'

'If it's a small one,' Edie said. 'And we don't give out the candy. I want to keep that. I might let you have some,' she added, to Joe.

Kick watched Joe take the cut-out stars and arrange them on a baking tray beside Edie's. She moved in towards him so that her arm almost touched his.

Had her warning about love been enough, Kick wondered now, watching her brother and her friend laugh over the dough as though they'd known one another for ever.

Chapter Twenty-Four

Sissy

When Harry, the barman, threw them out of the King's Anchor that night, Sissy hoped Peter might walk her home again. But instead he said, 'Why don't you come back for a drink? My place is close.' When Jim and Aurora said, 'Terrific idea,' he shook his head at them and said, 'No, you're too noisy and my neighbours complain. Sissy will be quiet, won't you, Sissy?'

'Oh, I will,' she assured him, blushing even though she didn't know why.

'I can walk back with Sissy,' Aurora said. 'Come along with me, girl, and we'll walk together.' There was a queer sort of pause. No one said anything, Sissy because she didn't want to walk back with Aurora, much as she liked her, but didn't know how to say so.

Peter watched her, and when she didn't respond, he broke the silence. 'Sissy's coming with me, aren't you?'

'I am. But thank you.' She turned to Aurora, who shrugged and leaned down to pull her bicycle up from where it lay slumped against the pub wall.

'Suit yourself,' she said, swinging her leg over it and ringing the bell, which sounded shrill in the night. 'Tally-ho.' She pushed off, cycling up the street with one hand raised in farewell. 'Goodnight and good luck,' she called back sarcastically.

Jim walked them some of the way, then said, 'I suppose I'll leave you here,' but in a pausing, dawdling kind of way.

'You will,' Peter said firmly, 'because your place is that way,' giving him a firm push.

When it was just the two of them, Sissy thought he would take her hand, but he didn't. 'No bicycle tonight?' she said.

'Puncture. There's so much broken glass on every street, I spend half of each week mending punctures. So much so that the inner tube must be replaced and I haven't the money to do it.'

His flat was in a block called King's Mansions, which ran the length of the street and was grander than she had expected, given his talk of being broke.

He must have seen the surprise on her face. 'Rent is cheap,' he explained. 'So many have evacuated by now that there are empty flats all over London. This place is a pound a week. But the lift is always broken.'

They walked four flights up to his two rooms. They weren't at all what Sissy had expected. The furniture was plentiful, but drab, as though one of her aunts had held an attic clear-out, she thought, looking at the stiff green velvet sofa and matching armchair set at an angle around a heavy teak coffee-table. There was a hob with two rings, a kettle and a small sink. The windows, from what she could see beyond the blackout curtains, were small. Through the door into the second room she could make out a single bed, with a too-high bedside table and a large ugly lamp on it.

'Not mine, any of it,' he said. He took off his jacket and threw it over the armchair. 'It came with the flat. And, yes, I know it's depressing. You can leave now, if you want.'

Always, he pushed first, she thought, as though anticipating some insult, some blow, determined to land his own before it came. 'I don't want,' she said. 'You promised me a drink.' She sat on the green sofa and pulled her cardigan tighter around her. It was cold.

'I did,' he agreed. He switched on a lamp and poured red wine into two mugs, gave her one and sat beside her. The sofa seat was narrow, and leaning back made her legs stick out awkwardly, so she remained perched on the edge. She felt like a bird on a too-thin twig: ill at ease, poised for flight.

'Where do you paint?' She looked around the room. There was no evidence of any painting, except for a stained rag on the coffee-table that might account for the smell of turpentine. 'Are those . . .' She gestured to the paintings on the wall, heavy, dark landscapes.

'Mine? Good God, no. In fact, if things get much worse, I'm thinking of using the canvas and just painting over them. Only I feel certain the ghosts of those gloomy trees and sullen mountains would somehow find their way into anything I did.' He smiled. 'No, there's a room on the roof, a shed really, and I paint there. Used to belong to the caretaker, but he's gone and hasn't been replaced, so no one uses it. I keep my stuff there. What stuff I still have.'

He put his mug down then, and Sissy did too. She had barely touched her wine, which smelt like vinegar. Peter reached out and pushed a strand of hair off her forehead. 'This is the moment you say you must be going,' he said softly. Sissy didn't speak. She held his gaze, even though she was shaking.

'Very well,' he said, and leaned forward to kiss her. 'You don't seem the bourgeois, prudish type,' he said, after a while, tugging gently at the neck of her dress so that it slipped down past her shoulder. And she supposed she mustn't be, because when he kissed her bare shoulder, then pulled her closer to him and began to undo her buttons at the back, she didn't stop him. She didn't think of stopping him. Instead, she wriggled closer again and kissed his neck while he unbuttoned and, when he fumbled, reached her arms around to help him.

She understood she should make more of a show of resistance, but *You're a long time dead*, she thought as, naked now, she let him lead her to the narrow bed in the other room where the iron springs twanged loudly at their combined weight.

Chapter Twenty-Five

Brigid

Joe's food parcel became the basis of what they called a dinner party until Sissy looked through the assortment of food he had brought and said, 'It's not dinner, more like a high tea, ham, eggs, pound cake . . .'

'High tea?' Kick said, turning the words over thoughtfully.

She looked at Edie, who shrugged. 'I don't know either,' she said.

'I remember high tea,' Brigid said, thinking back. 'We used to have it in the nursery on days when we went hunting. It's tea, but with something hearty, like ham and salad. That makes it "high".' She laughed. 'Funny of you to remember that, Sissy.'

'Well, I'm closer to the nursery than you are,' Sissy said. 'Although our high teas weren't so very high. A tin of sardines, sometimes just extra toast with dripping. I think it was more about what we called them . . .'

It was a Sunday morning, a few days after Joe's arrival. Kick was back from mass, which was always Edie's cue to get up. 'You were late last night,' she said to Sissy, pouring a cup of tea from the big brown pot. 'Or should I say, early this morning,' she continued, flashing a look at Sissy that was, Brigid thought, sharper than usual.

'Was I?' Sissy asked, seeming deliberately vague.

'You were and you know you were,' Edie said. 'Who were you out with?'

'Some girls from the Y.'

'Debo?' Kick asked.

'No, other girls. Less grand than Debo. You know what they call her at the Y?' Was Sissy trying to divert attention? Brigid wondered.

'What?'

'The Duchess! Isn't that screamingly funny? They say she's so grand, exactly like they imagine a duchess must be.'

'Funny!' Kick echoed.

'Especially given that, if you marry Billy, it's you who'll be the duchess,' Edie said.

'I wonder what that would do to a friendship?' Sissy asked thoughtfully. 'When one person is a duchess and the other isn't?'

'Why should it do anything?' Kick asked.

And so it became 'high tea' to which they invited Debo, Joe, Billy and Andrew. As well as Joe's food parcel, Sissy made soup. She was turning out to be cleverer at the coupons than Kick or Edie, maybe because she didn't have the luxury of eating at the officers' club where the food was better than it was anywhere else in London. She had begun to learn which butchers would give you a bit extra, which greengrocer kept onions under the counter and would add a few to your bag if he liked you, and how to put the stray ingredients together so they were almost appetising.

'I do it by remembering what the cook at Ballycorry did, then trying to do the opposite,' she explained. 'Mrs O'Shea used to boil entire cabbage leaves in water for hours so that the whole house stank of it and the leaves were like *poultices*.' She shuddered. 'All fibrous and flabby, soft and stinking. So instead I slice it thinly and put it into boiling water for just a few minutes until it's crisp but not hard.'

'And it's delicious. Well, as delicious as cabbage is ever going to be,' said Edie, loyally.

By the time their guests were due, the room looked very pretty, with the table pulled over by the window and laid with plates of food and a vase of flowers Sissy had picked surreptitiously from gardens round about. 'Not easy at all,' she had complained, coming back with a handful of dog roses and marigolds, 'when everyone has dug up their gardens and planted rows of vegetables. Endless overblown marrows,' she said. 'I even saw a pig in one garden, in a sty made out of bricks and an old bedhead.' The rest of the furniture had been pushed back against the walls and Kick had draped a silk scarf over the one lamp so it gave a dim rosy glow. She picked up her little wood-and-gold icon of Mary and the infant Jesus from the side table under the lamp and stood with it in her hands, then moved to her bedroom.

'For safe-keeping?' Brigid asked, following her.

'More for discretion,' Kick said, 'although it feels a bit cowardly,' she grimaced at the word, 'but also like it might be the smart move, now that Andrew and Billy are both coming.

Pa always taught us never to run from a fight, and I guess I never would. But I don't see that I have to start one, either.'

'No point in rubbing their noses in it,' Brigid agreed. Then, as she watched Kick put the icon carefully into a drawer, 'Don't you sometimes feel as though we do an awful lot of anticipating trouble? Like, I don't know, deer or . . . or grouse, or something; all us girls, forever with our heads up, scenting the wind for danger.'

Kick laughed. 'Oh, I know what you mean all right. I don't see my brothers doing much of that . . .'

'Nor mine,' Brigid agreed. 'Arthur does whatever he wants, when he wants, and always as though he expects a round of applause.'

'And even though this is England, where even in wartime danger mostly just means "unpleasantness", it's real tiring,' Kick reflected.

'The thing about unpleasantness is that it's unpleasant,' Brigid agreed.

It was the drowsy hour, when the business of the day was nearly done, but before the blackout blinds went up, before the night shift of ARP wardens and fire patrols. It was the time when London was at its quietest, especially on a Sunday. It felt empty and sleepy.

'Apparently it was never like this,' Edie said. She leaned out of the open window, both hands on the sill, staring out over the rooftops towards St Paul's. 'Before the war, they say there was never a time in the day or the week when it wasn't busy and noisy. I guess Washington was like that,' she said to Kick. 'Richmond, Virginia, wasn't. We have whole days where barely anything stirs. I like this,' she said, 'although there is something real nice about those long hot drowsy afternoons too . . .' Her words reminded Brigid of quiet summers at Elveden, nothing to do all day except listen to the drone of bees, the distant lowing of cattle, the river bumbling over stones. How long had it been, she thought, since she had felt anything like that kind of boundless peace?

Billy was the first to arrive, punctual to the minute. He had with him a brown-paper bag with five peaches. 'From Eastbourne,' he said, giving them to Kick. 'Compton Place greenhouses. These aren't for the high tea, they're to put away and eat later, for you girls.'

'Peaches!' Kick cried. She stuck her nose into the bag and inhaled deeply. 'Ned Bolton's farm, the Fourth of July . . .'

'I promised I'd bring you some when they were ripe, and here they are. Now hide them before the others get here. Andrew will think they're for him and there aren't enough to go round.'

'They'll smell them,' Kick said. 'No matter where I put them, that delicious scent will waft out and madden everyone. It'll be the smell of guilt and deceit.'

Joe arrived next, followed by Debo and Andrew. 'All one's favourite foods together,' Debo said, surveying the table approvingly. 'I can't think why we don't put ham and apples and jam and hard-boiled eggs together more often.'

When tea was finished and the table cleared, as dusk deepened outside and a dusty wind picked up, they sat listening to records on Kick's gramophone and smoking. There was more silence than talk, the chatter of earlier worn out, a mood of stillness on them. On the gramophone, Glenn Miller sang about black magic.

'How nice not to have any grown-ups,' Sissy said lazily.

Kick leaned against Billy; he had his arm tight around her

and she put her head on his shoulder. Debo and Andrew sat close together too, whispering about something and giggling. 'Grown-ups spoil everything,' she agreed.

Joe said he'd take a walk about the streets before heading back to the club. 'I leave for Cornwall tomorrow.'

'So it's your last chance to get some good city air,' Edie joked. She said she'd go with him and pulled on a brown beret.

'What about that?' Debo asked, when they'd left. Brigid, who had wondered too, turned to look at Kick.

'I don't know . . .' Kick said. 'I worry about it,' she confessed. 'Joe isn't – well, he isn't the steady sort. Not yet. And even if he were . . .'

'It won't do, will it?' Debo said sympathetically.

'Why will it not do?' Sissy asked, looking from one to the other. 'Edie's a dear.'

'Yes, but Kennedys are almost as bad as Cavendishes,' Debo said, with a mocking look at Andrew and Billy. 'They think a great deal about who and what are fitting.'

'How can anyone still bother with that now?' Sissy asked. 'I mean—'

'*There's a war on!*' everyone chorused.

'It's true, I know,' Brigid said, when they had finished laughing. 'But some people carry on caring about the old ways even while they're being torn down in front of their eyes.'

'It's hard to stop,' Kick said. 'Hard to break habits that are laid down so early.'

'It is,' Brigid agreed. 'Which, when you think about it, is rather terrible. Like, I don't know, never wearing your own clothes – oh, not you, Sissy. I mean . . .'

'Always agreeing and never making your own argument?' Kick said.

'Exactly,' Brigid agreed. 'Hard sometimes even to see what's habit and what one truly cares for. But I think I'm getting cleverer at it.'

'Me too,' said Kick. 'I know I want to.'

No one else, Brigid realised, looking at the confusion on Debo's face, knew what they were talking about. And suddenly she felt as if she and Kick were just as they had been when they first met. Before Edie, before Sissy, before Billy even, and Fritzi. She had missed that, she realised. The way they spoke to and understood one another. Like no one else could or did.

'As it happens,' Billy said then, 'I don't think this country will look anything like it used to, when we get out of this.'

'We're not out of it yet,' Andrew said. A glance passed between him and his brother. A kind of warning, Brigid thought.

'No,' Billy agreed. 'But eventually we will be. Not all of us, naturally . . .' Again that look between him and Andrew. 'But things feel different since the invasion of Sicily and Musso falling; your lot joining in –' he winked at Kick and she touched her forehead in mock salute. 'It will end. A year ago it didn't feel like that, but now it does. And what will be left afterwards will look quite different.'

'Different, how?' Brigid asked. She had heard other people say the same sorts of things, but hadn't really understood what they meant.

'Lots of ways,' he said. 'I don't think places like Chatsworth or Compton will carry on as they have been. The idea that one family would own half a dozen large houses, well, I can't see that lasting.' Brigid was momentarily stunned at the idea. She saw Elveden, the vastness of its domed interior and endless corridors, not simply as her childhood home but as an oddity; an affront.

'Quite the socialist, aren't you?' Andrew said. 'I'm glad it'll be you in the firing line, as it were,' he flushed a little at the unfortunate choice of words, 'when the time comes to make those sorts of choices. The "Eleventh and Final Duke",' he teased. 'It'll end on your watch?'

'God, not that! There will still be dukes, but maybe in somewhat reduced circumstances,' Billy said.

'I wonder if the reduced circumstances include being allowed to marry Catholics.' Andrew laughed loudly. He passed it off as a joke, Brigid could see, or tried to, but somehow it didn't come off and there was a sharp pause.

'Don't be absurd, Andrew. We English love our dukes and our stately homes,' she said lightly, to turn the conversation and disguise the mortification she could see Kick felt.

'We do,' Billy said, responding quickly, gratefully. 'But perhaps there's a limit, even for us. A staff of sixty, cooking, cleaning, laying fires, serving food, tending gardens, horses and hounds all for one family? I can't see that continuing.' He sounded solemn, so that Brigid could see he had thought these things before. Was it being in love with Kick that had showed him his world anew? And was that what she, too, was finding, as she wrote and talked to Fritzi and Will? As though their eyes were hers, and what she looked at became unfamiliar, things to be questioned and considered, rather than the almost-invisibility of the familiar?

'Rather you than me,' Andrew said again, stretching his arms above his head. But he sounded uncomfortable and added, 'Better get on, darling. Ready?' Debo said she was, and Billy said he would go too, and asked if he could walk Brigid as far as Belgrave Square.

'Perhaps I'll stay a while longer,' she said, looking at Kick.

'Do,' Kick said. 'Do.'

Chapter Twenty-Six

Kick

Brigid was newly quiet these days, Kick thought. Today was the most talkative she had been in ages. So much of her former dash and curiosity now seemed squashed, almost out of sight. Kick thought back to her arrival, two months ago. Brigid had been more subdued then, yes, but she had been quieter again over the last few weeks. Until this afternoon when somehow, between the moving of the icon and the funny remark about old habits, Kick had seen a spark of the other Brigid – the impish, stubborn creature she had first known.

'What's the news of Honor?' she asked now when Billy, Andrew and Debo had gone.

'I rather think she might feel like Billy does,' Brigid said, 'that the old ways are ready to be dynamited.' She smiled as she said it, although there was concern in her voice too. She sounded, Kick thought, more affectionate towards her sister than before. Billy and Andrew, she thought, were closer and fonder of each other, too. When Kick had last been in England, the gap of more than two years between them had seemed great; the gulf between the elder and the younger, the heir and the 'spare', as unkind teasing had it, had seemed large. They had had different interests, different friends, different outlooks. A certain lofty dismissal on Billy's part, met by a touch of petulance on Andrew's. They had never been as outwardly competitive as Joe and Jack but, then, no one could be, she thought.

Eunice had written to Kick just days ago, with news of the family celebration after Jack's heroics in the Pacific – he had helped to rescue his crew members after the Japanese torpedoed their boat, and led them to safety on a tiny island, then swum to other islands, searching for food and water. As Eunice wrote, it was '*just the most Jack-like thing to do. He may as well have been on a jaunt at Hyannis Port.*' Naturally, Eunice wrote only about the family joy at Jack's success, nothing at all about their fears for him in the terrible days he was missing.

When she and Joe had talked about Jack's heroics, his medal, Kick had seen Joe's face screw up almost in pain. 'He's OK,' she had reassured him. 'His back is bad but they say he'll be perfectly fine.'

'It's not that,' Joe had said. 'I just can't bear that he's been given the Navy Medal and I haven't.' Even allowing for exaggeration, Kick saw a kernel of truth in what he'd said.

Billy and Andrew were nothing like that – mostly because Andrew seemed ready to concede everything to his older brother – but theirs had been a sometimes-fractious relationship. Not any longer. Now, she saw only affection between the two. A fondness that expressed itself in awkward pats on the back and clumsy jokes, and was all the more endearing for that.

Could Joe and Jack ever be like that? It would be wonderful if they could show the kinder things they felt for one another. But that wasn't how they had been brought up. And Pa wouldn't like it, she thought, with an inner laugh. He'd hate to watch his sons behave in a brotherly way, celebrating one another's successes rather than each being fired by the urge to do better. She felt her lips twitch and wished Joe were there so she could tell him what she was thinking and see him laugh at the idea of Joseph P. Kennedy appreciating demonstrations of kindness and brotherly love.

Maybe Sissy read her thoughts, because she said, 'Having Joe here must be wonderful.'

'Oh, it is. That's the thing about big families, I guess. You spend so much time in company with your brothers and sisters that when you're not with them you feel like something's missing. I've always felt we were "we" not just "me",' Kick said. 'When I learned to walk, I did it at the same time as Rosie. There's fifteen months between us, and she was slow to start and I was quick, so we toddled around together at the same time. When I learned to swim, it was with Jack. He's older, but he was sickly as a child. When I learned to ride, it was with Eunice. You see? Always there was me and someone else. And now, here, it's just me.'

'Until now,' Sissy said.

'Until now,' she agreed happily. 'And you've no idea what it means to have Joe especially, all to myself, for once. He's the one everyone always wants to be with, the one Pa has the highest hopes for, and Mother expects the most from, "not just because you're the eldest, but because of your natural qualities that inspire others".' She mimicked her mother's voice. 'And now I get to hog him, completely hog him,' she said, with glee. 'Even Pa, I guess, is jealous.'

'Does she really say such things? Your mother?' Sissy asked.

'Oh, yes. All the time. There is a plan for everyone. Joe is to be the President. Jack will be the first man to walk on the moon.'

'You?' Brigid asked.

'It's a bit vaguer for me. Because I'm a girl. Lots about my moral qualities and setting a good example through prayer and going to mass.'

Brigid winced a little at that. 'Always religion,' she murmured.

'I guess my plans have a deal to do with whom I marry, too,' Kick continued.

'I guess everyone's plans do, only they're not so blunt about it,' said Brigid.

'And Rosie?' That was Sissy.

'It's different with Rosie. The plans for her are changing.' Kick didn't know how to say more. Or less. Sissy looked like she was about to ask what she meant, when to Kick's relief Edie came back.

'Had fun?' Kick asked, somewhat archly.

'We had a walk, if that's what you mean,' Edie said, throwing off the beret and heading for the tiny kitchen.

'What do you talk about?' Kick asked, curious.

'This and that,' Edie said. 'I told him he needn't bother being all attentive and charming to me.'

'Why not?' Kick asked.

'Because I'm never going to be in love with him.'

'Why not?' Kick asked again. She felt almost insulted at Edie's certainty.

'I told him I'm immune to the Kennedy charm. It comes of knowing you so well.' She smiled and Kick grinned back.

'And how did Joe take it?'

'He said it was kind of a relief.'

'I can't believe you said that,' Brigid said.

'I don't do things by halves,' Edie said, 'and I felt he'd want to know, so he could spare himself the trying.'

'I know just what you mean,' Brigid said. 'The trying is just too much. If only one could say to every young man, *Please, you mustn't bother*, wouldn't that be divine? You are brave, Edie.'

'Not brave,' Edie protested. 'I'm not going into a bombed-out building, just telling a handsome young man not to waste his time.'

'The kind of bravery no one appreciates,' Brigid said, resignedly.

'I don't want to do things by halves either,' Sissy declared then. 'I want to do them completely.'

'How very young you are,' Edie said. She made it sound like something Sissy could have chosen not to be, Kick thought.

'What has that to do with it?'

'You know nothing of life, yet.'

'I'm finding out, though, aren't I?' Sissy said. She lit a cigarette and inhaled carefully, then blew out a cloud of smoke. 'I want to find out everything, feel everything. Even the bad stuff,' she said, with relish. 'Even when it makes me unhappy, I still want to feel it.'

'What a baby you are,' Edie said. 'Don't look for bad things because you're curious. Plenty will find you whether you want them or not.'

'You think I don't know that,' Sissy said, 'but I do. And I'm learning pretty fast about all sorts of other things.'

'What other things?' Brigid asked.

'Oh, art and food. And men.'

'What men?'

'Mostly one called Peter. He's a painter.'

'The one you met that night at the 400 Club?'

'Yes.'

'Have you seen him since?'

'Yes.'

'Where?'

'At the King's Anchor. I found him,' she said, with pride.

'And saw him last night, I bet. Not those girls from the Y, like you told us,' Kick said.

'You'd only fuss,' Sissy said, 'and there's no need to.'

'Did you really chase that man from the 400 Club all the way to a pub on Tottenham Court Road?' Brigid asked.

'I suppose I did.'

'But why?'

'He was nice. Or, not *nice* exactly . . . Interesting.'

'And you've been seeing him ever since? All on your own? So that's all the sneaking around,' Brigid said.

'Not sneaking.'

'Sneaking,' Brigid said firmly. 'Do be careful, Sissy. You have no idea – not the slightest – what you're doing.'

'I have,' Sissy insisted.

But, Kick thought, how could she? A girl who had never left an isolated country home until two months ago. A girl who had very little education, no connections, just an abundance of energy and curiosity. 'Please be careful, Sissy,' she added her voice to Brigid's.

'And could you please stop trying to smoke?' Edie leaned forward and took the cigarette from her. 'You clearly hate it. So why bother?'

'It seemed sophisticated.'

'Not the way you do it.'

Chapter Twenty-Seven

Brigid

Because Maureen was visiting, because Joe had arrived and Billy had more leave, 'though that will surely stop soon'; perhaps inspired by the high tea – to which he was very cross not to have been invited – a week later Chips insisted on a dinner party for them all at Belgrave Square.

'It won't be like the old days,' he said, cornering Brigid before she set off for her shift, 'but it'll be better than whatever they're eating. Sissy looks positively scrawny. I don't know what Lady Iveagh is going to say.'

'Nothing,' Brigid said. 'You know she won't notice. Mama sees only one's moral qualities, rarely the physical ones. Unless one has something especially disfiguring, like a stye or a cold sore.'

But even as she said it, she thought of Sissy, blundering about

London, meeting men in secret, men whom no one knew the slightest thing about – how had none of them noticed? There seemed something rather wrong about it. She considered telling Chips. He would know if it was actually bad, or if Brigid was just being fussy. *Old maid-ish . . .* The phrase leaped at her, like something feral. Where had it come from? Was that what she really thought of herself, deep down? Or was it because she lived now between the heat of Kick and Billy, Sissy and this Peter fellow, maybe even Edie and Joe, no matter what Edie said? She had no one. Only Will, who was less every time she saw him, and Fritzi who was more each time she wrote to him, but still a secret.

As if he had seen something in her face, Chips said, 'I worry about you too, Brigid. You seem to be slipping from sight.'

'What nonsense you talk.'

'Either you're aware of it, and dissembling, or you're unaware and therefore need telling. You're half of who you were, and I worry that, if this goes on, you'll disappear entirely. Fold yourself up smaller and smaller.' He smiled at her in a way that was kindly. 'What is it?' he asked.

That did it. Chips was so rarely kind. Mostly he was demanding, conceited, self-centred, boastful and inclined to view everything in terms of how it affected him. His kindness was unexpected, and therefore hard to reckon with. Would she tell him about Fritzi? No, she couldn't. Not yet.

Instead she began trying to talk about Will, who was worse. Recently he had begun to confuse the things she told him.

'Is Caroline the one who wants to marry the duke?' he had asked only yesterday.

'No, that's . . .' Brigid had stopped, because she couldn't bring herself to addle his poor brain any more when already it was clear that there were more and more things he didn't under-stand.

'Where am I?' he murmured a little later. 'Has the bell gone yet?' She understood that he thought himself back at boarding school. 'Not yet,' she had said, putting a gentle hand on his chest to calm the agitation. 'Not yet.'

'Ah, the hospital,' Chips said now, in relief. 'Of course. Awful for you, when at your age you should be out having fun.' He spoke energetically, like one who had it all worked out, and so she changed her mind about telling him any of it.

'I'm perfectly all right, truly,' she said. 'Perhaps a little peaky, but aren't we all?'

It was the right thing to say. Chips's mind turned immediately to himself. 'My doctor, Lowe, says he's never seen me so run down,' he said enthusiastically. 'All one's usual diversions – Switzerland for skiing, a few weeks in the South of France for the sun, Paris, Rome, everything's suspended. I don't recall the last time I had a holiday. And one does feel it.' He looked beadily at her. 'Lowe says my liver isn't behaving at all as it should. I do hope this war doesn't go on much longer or the damage will be irreversible.'

Brigid bit off a laugh. She wished Maureen were there to hear him. 'It's only a matter of time,' she said soothingly. It was what they all said: that victory was only a matter of time, now that Hitler was so stretched on the eastern front and the Luftwaffe rained death elsewhere. *What else does he have to throw at us?* they asked one another cheerily, as they queued.

'So everyone says,' Chips responded tartly. 'I don't know what made the man in the street such an expert. They can't all be field marshals. And they are fatally underestimating Hitler, if you ask me. No,' he said, putting up a hand. 'Don't. I'm as loyal as anyone. More, even' – *Of course you are*, thought Brigid, stifling another laugh – 'but underestimating one's enemy is foolish, and particularly this enemy. I can't believe he'd pull all his bombers off and divert them east if he hadn't something else up his sleeve.'

'Is that what's being said in government?' Brigid asked.

'No. Or not openly. No one wants to admit the possibility that anything like the Blitz could happen again. Morale would collapse completely and everyone knows it. So we say nothing. Not overtly, anyway.'

'Maybe don't bring it up at dinner, either. You'll only make everyone nervous. Who's coming?'

'Well, Maureen and Duff, Kick and Billy, Debo, but not Andrew, who is with his regiment, Kick's brother Joe, Sissy, and I've rather had to invite that American girl, Edie.'

'She and Joe are inseparable.'

'Not so inseparable that he isn't already going about with Cara Smithson, whose husband is far away, fighting in Africa.' Brigid was astonished, all over again, at Chips's ability to know everything, even about near strangers. 'But that is absolutely under lock and key,' he added. 'You mustn't breathe a word.'

'Not a word,' she promised, even though she knew very well that Chips would tell everyone he met, exhorting them to keep it to themselves.

'Now, I must go to the House. But I haven't forgotten, Brigid.'

'Forgotten what?'

'That you haven't answered me. Something's wrong with you. I see it. And when the time is right, perhaps you'll tell me.'

'Nothing's wrong,' she insisted. But Chips was right, she thought, as she walked wearily up to her room to change. She had faded. She could feel it. She was less herself than formerly.

Where girls like Kick and Sissy relished the freedom of war, the unsupervised, chaotic nature of the days – as she had too, she reminded herself, even until quite recently – she felt increasingly defeated by all of that. She was stretched too thin. The hospital hours were long, the Ritz and the 400 Club less appealing than they had been. She was tired, always tired. She disliked hiding Fritzi's letters; being unable to say, 'there is already someone,' to Chips when he tried to set her up with Tony, with Hugh Fraser, with any of the young men of their acquaintance. Mostly, she disliked being the sort of person who hid things. And she worried about Will constantly, even though she knew it was useless. Worrying would change nothing.

Brigid had too much experience by then not to know that the infection was winning. Will was dying. Only a certain quiet stubbornness now kept him with them. But it was the stubbornness of a man who had decided to choose the time of his going, not of a man who believed he would live. She had been trained to deal with this, she thought now. Trained to maintain a kindly indifference and until now she had, almost. But Will was different.

At the hospital, she changed and went to his room first. These days, he was better in the mornings, stronger of speech and clearer in his mind.

'I'm glad you're here,' he said.

'Do you need water?'

'No. I want to talk to you.' His voice was soft, but his words distinct.

'What is it?' Her heart beat a little faster.

'I want you not to keep visiting,' he said. It wasn't – not at all – what she'd expected. She had wondered if he would tell her he loved her. And, if so, would she tell him? She would. Of course she would. To a dying man there was only one answer. Was it true? She didn't know. It had been, she thought, at least a little. But as he became sicker, love had changed, shrinking to concern. And at the same time as Will had begun, oh so gently, to fade, Fritzi had grown sharper, more vivid. Were those things connected? Perhaps. But she couldn't think about them. And maybe, she thought, the very opposite was true for him. That friendship, once death entered the room, became confused with love.

'But why?' she asked.

'Because it isn't any good.'

'You don't know that. You must make an effort,' she said. 'You must *try*.'

'I can't,' he said. 'I know I can't. And I can't because, for such a long time, that's what I did. I tried.' He was silent and so was she. There were too many things to say and they all led away from what he was trying to tell her. Into a future that didn't exist for them and that felt wrong for her to talk about. Or into a past that might be better left unparsed.

'You remember why I ended up here?' he continued.

'I do. The wall of a house fell on you. You were trapped under it.'

'Under that wall,' he said, 'I had hours to think, and mostly what I thought was, *why did I try so hard?* After the first injury, I was a model patient.' He laughed, though it was more like a sigh. 'Even though no one much believed I would walk again, I did. I did every exercise they showed me again and again until I mastered it. And then again and again until I perfected it. I forced myself, and I succeeded. I walked sooner and better – for all that I limped – than anyone expected. I was so proud. I felt I had taken *life by the horns*,' he smiled without heart, 'just as we were always taught to do. And it seemed my efforts were worthwhile. I liked working as a clerk, a cog in the great machine of the Foreign Office. First a soldier, then a sort of secretary. But that night, when I was trapped, I thought about it all, and I couldn't understand why I'd bothered. Why I'd made all that effort. For what? It made no sense. Such effort.' His voice was hoarse now, the words harder to make out. 'So much effort,' he whispered. 'All I could think was, how futile. All that, to end up under the remains of a house on Mayfield Road. And when they found me and dug me out, brought me here, cleaned me up and I woke, I found I felt the same. *Why all the effort?*'

'But that was just the weariness of infection. I've seen it before. It saps all a chap's energy . . .'

He smiled gently. 'Maybe. But as long as the infection won't let up – and it won't – I can't find another way to look at it. I've tried. Mostly because of you. All your kindness . . .'

She tried to tell him it wasn't kindness, but his efforts were still in speaking, not listening. 'I can't try any longer, and I don't want you to see me not trying.'

'But I want to see you,' she said, in a small voice that barely made its way out past the lump that blocked it.

'I know you do. But please, I beg you, I can't. I want you to promise me because I won't be strong enough to ask you again. And something else,' he murmured, exhausted now. He didn't wait for her to agree. 'I know I'm less each time you see me . . .' he gave the ghost of a smile and shook his head a little (to stop her wasting time disagreeing with him, she suspected) '. . . but you are too, Brigid. You bury yourself in work and duty. And it's admirable, but there won't be much of you left if you continue. I wish you'd be more selfish. More yourself.'

'For you?' She tried to smile back at him, make a joke of what he'd said.

'No, for you.' He closed his eyes and turned his head away. She waited, and when he said nothing more, she left the room.

Halfway along the corridor, Matron fell into step beside her. 'Mary will take over from you,' she said, the soles of her rubber shoes squeaking. She must have been waiting, Brigid thought. 'It's for the best,' Matron said, not unkindly. She speeded up, the squeaks coming closer together, and passed Brigid. Had she known Brigid would turn off to the locker room and sit for a few moments while she beat back the tears that threatened? Probably. And that was why she had been sure not to see.

It was what they did. A relay of hope and despair, batons passed seamlessly back and forth, *Now you, now me*, as time, circumstances and energy demanded.

She would write to Fritzi, Brigid decided, in the empty locker room. She would tell him all of it and ask what he thought she should do. Stay away, as Will had asked her? Or keep visiting, as she wanted?

Chapter Twenty-Eight

Brigid

On the evening of the party, Caroline came down to the drawing room where they gathered before dinner. Chips offered her a drink, ignoring Brigid when she hissed, 'She's only twelve, for goodness' sake.'

In any case, Caroline refused. She took a glass of water and went to sit by Sissy, as far away from her mother as she could get. Maureen took up one side of the sofa. She was wearing a rose-pink silk evening dress, and smoking long black cigarettes tipped with gold. The dress was old – everything was old now – but Maureen wore it with the mix of casual and smug she had perfected, and that made whatever she put on seem perfect. Beside her, Kick and Edie were squeezed into what was left of the sofa. Duff stood at Maureen's end, arm resting across the marble chimneypiece, talking to Joe Kennedy and Billy. Before,

Brigid thought, those men, together, would almost certainly have talked of war. Of when and how it might come, showing off what they knew, what they dared. Now they talked about cricket.

Brigid had met Joe several times, but never for very long. Her impression of him – which she kept to herself – was that he thought rather too much of himself. But maybe she was just miffed because he didn't pay her any extra attention, she thought. He was polite, considerate, interested, but that was all. Not as he was with Edie, forever laughing at some private joke between them. He didn't flirt with Brigid or behave as though he was awed by her. Which was unusual enough that she noticed.

For all his conceit, though, she saw that he gave off a kind of joy at life, an interest in everything, a confidence that it would all prove amusing, that made her envious. Watching him made her more conscious than ever of her own exhaustion. Where did the wellspring come from that made him – Kick too – seem about to bubble over with energy? Was it being American? Being Kennedys? Something else?

'It's plain to see you don't have to rely on clothing coupons,' she said to Kick, who was wearing a glorious turquoise dress that was clearly brand new.

'Isn't it beautiful?' Kick agreed. 'Mother sent it, in the parcel Joe brought.'

'No wonder half of London hates you,' Brigid said.

'The girl half, obviously.' Joe laughed.

'They don't really, do they?' Kick asked. She sounded honestly put out, in a way that Brigid would not have been if she'd thought 'the girl half' of London hated *her*.

'You're too nice, Kick,' she said. 'Why should you care what they think?'

'You give them a run for their money,' Joe agreed. 'It's to be expected.'

Brigid went to Caroline and Sissy who sat on two spindly chairs. It was a rare warm autumn evening and the sun was only beginning to drop out of sight. The windows of the drawing room were open to the garden. Through them came the smell of late-flowering jasmine and damp grass.

Sissy and Caroline were giggling together, which Caroline did with no one, not even Duff, other than Sissy. Somehow Sissy had tapped into whatever lay beyond Caroline's frozen silences, the brittle awkwardness of her hunched shoulders and twisting hands. Watching them, Brigid thought suddenly how little they must remember from before the war. Neither had any real experience of grown-up life. The strange rhythm of hostilities – boredom mixed with fear, freedom with constraint – was all they knew.

The thought made her feel so much older than they were.

'What are you two talking about?' she asked. 'Whatever it is, it can't be worse than cricket.'

'We're swapping more stories of cruel nannies,' Sissy said. 'Caroline wins on every count. Tell Brigid what you told me about the eggs,' she said to Caroline.

'You tell her,' Caroline said, shy again.

'Miss Allie – that's their nanny – orders an egg every morning for each of the children in the nursery. Even in wartime, they can do that, because they're in the country, and in Ireland. So that's one egg for Caroline, when she's there, one for Perdita, one for Sheridan,' she had all their names, Brigid noticed, 'and when their cousins are staying, as they often are, she orders one for each of them too. And then she eats every single egg, starting with her own! That's five or six eggs, all to herself. Every morning. The children eat bread and butter.'

'What monstrous story are you telling?' Maureen called. 'I heard only the end. Who is this dreadful person?'

'She's the nanny of a family we know,' Caroline said after a moment, and before Brigid could stop her, she had told the whole story again, only this time without names. 'What would you do with a nanny like that?' she asked her mother when she had finished. Brigid was too appalled to think of any way to stop her.

'She should be horse-whipped,' Maureen said. 'Who is this person? And the family? They should be warned.' She looked from Caroline to Sissy, who looked terrified now.

'It's us, Mummie,' Caroline piped up, in clear tones. 'It's Miss Allie, and the children are me, Perdita, Sheridan.'

There was a horrible silence. Duff, Joe and Billy had stopped their cricket talk to listen to the story too. Brigid watched Duff's face turn a furious dark red. He was too well-mannered to shout, but he moved closer to Maureen and, bending down to her, hissed, 'What is the meaning of that fantastical tale?'

'I have no idea,' Maureen said icily. 'I can only assume some frightful piece of malicious invention by Caroline. Perhaps you should speak to her about that unpleasant imagination of hers?'

'Caro?' Duff asked, turning to his daughter.

'Sheridan has rickets,' Caroline said, in the same cool tone as her mother had used. 'The doctor came and I heard him say it to Mummie.'

Duff turned back to Maureen.

'He's getting cod liver oil,' she said, with rather less bravado now. 'He'll be perfectly fine. It's very hard, with rationing.'

'Clandeboye produces enough food to feed an army,' he said, teeth gritted. 'And every other child in England seems to manage perfectly well on rations.'

'Caroline, perhaps it's time for bed now,' Chips said. Brigid didn't know if he was saying it to spare her or get rid of her. Both, she assumed. 'And, Sissy, you'd better come over here and help me with these drinks.'

'Yes of course.' Caroline stood up immediately and walked from the room, the obedient child once more. 'Goodnight, Mummie. Goodnight, Daddy.'

Once she was gone, Chips sent more drinks round, and started a conversation about a new book he had read. Maureen questioned him eagerly, kicking dirt over the incident with Caroline, and Joe joined in politely, asking questions. Something about the determined way in which they all avoided anything serious, anything 'unpleasant', began to itch at Brigid. It was like watching someone fumble at a keyhole, the right key, the right lock, yet they were unable to turn it. Fidgeting and jiggling, all in the wrong way. The urge to intervene was too strong to resist. 'I have a question for you all,' she said. They turned to her.

'Ask away,' Chips said expansively, twinkling at her. 'Although, if the question is *Tony*, well the answer is surely yes . . .' How much has he had to drink? Brigid wondered.

She ignored him. 'It's a patient, at the hospital,' she began. She saw that Duff sat up a little straighter. 'I've nursed him for a long time now, longer than anyone else who is there.'

'Him?' Maureen asked archly.

Duff glared at her. 'Go on, Brigid,' he said.

'The reason I've nursed him for so long is because he has not got better. For a long time, it seemed as though he might. Now it seems certain that he will not.' There was silence. They all listened. 'He has asked me to stop visiting him.'

'Surely your responsibilities mean you can't stop.' That was Joe.

'I can. He can be given into someone else's care. Quite easily. But I don't know if I can bear that.'

'He's asked you to stay away?' Duff asked.

'He has.'

'Then I rather think . . .'

'I know,' she said, 'I know. But I feel I cannot.'

'Maybe he'll rally,' Sissy said hopefully, looking around at them all. 'People do. One hears of it . . .'

'There won't be a miracle,' Brigid said. 'It's childish to think there will.' When she saw Sissy flush, she added, 'I don't mean you, darling. I mean me. I believed exactly that for so long – that he would rally, grow stronger, be given up by the doctors only to shake off the infection . . . But nothing like that has happened and I see now that it was silly of me to hope like that.'

'Why don't you want to stay away?' Kick asked. 'Do you think there's something more you can do for him?'

'No. I know there's nothing, but I don't want not to see him.'

'He has asked you not to,' Duff said again.

'It's not really up to you, then, is it?' Maureen said briskly. 'You simply have to do what he's asked.'

'But what if he is asking for me, not for himself?'

'For you, how?'

'To spare me. What if he wants me to visit but is saying he doesn't for my sake?' Her voice sounded strained and she saw Kick shoot her a sympathetic glance.

'I don't think there's any way you can know that,' Edie said. 'I think . . .' slowly '. . . if you start trying to guess what people want, even when you're guessing against what they tell you, it's not going to work.'

'Maybe you just need to do what you want,' Kick said. She sounded uncertain. 'Once you know what you want, that is. In the end, it might be that it's the best way.' She spoke in answer to Brigid's question, but it was Billy she looked at.

'I don't know what I want,' Brigid said. She spoke almost wonderingly. 'I don't know if I want to be with him at the end, or see no more of his slipping away. I hoped you would tell me.'

'I think perhaps you have to make up your own mind on this,' Edie said.

'But—'

'You should keep visiting him,' Sissy said stoutly. 'No matter what he said. He couldn't want you to stop. He couldn't.'

Before Brigid could say anything, the door opened abruptly. Instead of Andrews with another tray, it was Honor, in a fur coat that was far too warm for the evening, unbuttoned over a grey travelling dress. Behind her, at the bottom of the stairs, Brigid could see a pile of luggage. 'Well,' she said, far more expansive than she usually was, 'you must have guessed I was coming. All my favourite people gathered in one room.'

'We had no idea, my dear. We do this every night, hoping you might deign to show your face,' Chips said, with a great show of humour. He went to kiss her.

She leaned back, out of reach. 'Not you, Chips. My really favourite people.' He looked hurt and surprised. As though one of his precious *bibelots* – a china snuff bottle or a glass paperweight – had slipped through his fingers and broken at his feet.

'You've quite thrown out the *placement*,' he said, taking refuge in irritability. 'We're too many women now.'

But Honor, rather than being insulted or irritated, just smiled and took Brigid's arm. 'Darling, how lovely you look,' she said. But she hardly glanced at Brigid, who knew she didn't look as good as usual. Instead Honor was looking around with a pleased expression on her face. 'I hardly remembered what this place was like,' she said. 'Isn't that funny? How one forgets?' Even though she had been away only a few weeks, she spoke as though she had returned to a childhood spot, something feared – a deep well, a high wall – only to find it reduced and diminished, not the alarming place of memory.

Something about the way she spoke, and looked, settled quietly within Brigid.

Chapter Twenty-Nine

Kick

Honor's coming somehow loosened them up, after Caroline's little pantomime and the intensity of Brigid's question. Her arrival defused the tension that lingered – most of it, anyway, Kick thought. Some still remained in Duff's lowered eyebrows, his avoidance of his wife.

Honor knowing nothing of Caroline's joke meant they could all pretend to forget about it. Her arrival made it easy for everyone to move about, and Kick found herself by the fireplace with Debo. A fire had been lit, more for show than heat, and now, even though it was still light outside, they drew close to the flames.

Debo seemed sad, Kick thought. In fact, she had thought it from the moment Debo had arrived. Her perfectly symmetrical face and candid blue eyes were as arresting as ever, but she was pale and her collarbones in the thin evening dress stuck out sharp and high. And although her chatter was fast and cheery, it seemed forced. After a while, Kick tired of the effort of laughing when she didn't really feel Debo had the heart to be funny. 'What is it, Debo?' she asked. 'Is it Andrew?'

'It's Unity,' Debo said, drawing her winged eyebrows together.

'What about Unity? Is she worse?'

'No, a bit better.' Debo paused. 'It's Farv. He won't see her. Won't say why, though I can imagine. He never was much good if we were sick. But he won't go anywhere near Unity. She's in the gate lodge – she lives there now. Muv goes every day, but Farv won't, and he doesn't allow Unity into the house.'

'How does Unity feel about it?'

'Never mentions it. Hard to know how much she's aware of . . .' She paused. Kick still didn't know the extent of the damage to Unity's brain. Unity had fired a bullet into it, but survived. What might that mean? Was she like Rosie? And what a strange coincidence that she and Debo should both have sisters so damaged . . . But how could she tell Debo about Rosie when she hadn't even told Billy?

'Maybe your father just needs time,' she said, thinking of her own father and how he had never once been to see his eldest daughter, not since the operation he had authorised. Did *he* need time? At least Lord Redesdale hadn't been responsible for Unity's injury, Kick thought, with a sudden, painful flash of anger. It wasn't his hand that had held the gun, or his confident assurance that it was 'for the best' that had set the thing in motion.

'Maybe.' Debo sounded doubtful.

'What does Andrew say?'

'I can't mention Unity to Andrew, not a word. In fact, you might be the only person in England who can bear to hear me say her name. To everyone else, she is simply a disgrace, and must never be mentioned. And you mustn't tell Billy I've been talking about her. I should think, if that family dislike anything more than Catholics, which I'm not sure they do' – she flashed a grin that was more like the old Debo – 'it's traitors. And that's what they say Unity is.' She looked sad again. 'They don't understand that she tried to blow her brains out for the very reason that she couldn't stand being a traitor either. Her loyalties were impossibly divided, and she chose death rather than betray either of them. Except it didn't work . . . You'd think they'd be impressed with her but no one sees it like that except me and Diana.'

'I'm sorry,' was all Kick could bear to say. She couldn't talk about Rosie, not even to someone who might know what she meant. In any case, how to explain what she didn't understand?

Maureen was on her best behaviour at dinner. Charming and witty as only Maureen knew how. Clearly, she was mortified. Though not as deeply as she should have been, Kick thought. About Caroline, she obviously didn't care. All the effort Maureen made was directed towards her husband but Duff would barely look at her. He answered her questions and observations with quiet monosyllables. Mostly, he talked to Brigid on his left and Billy, opposite him, while Maureen dominated the other end of the table.

Joe, beside her, was an enthusiastic foil for her efforts and after a few minutes Kick caught him looking across at her with raised eyebrows. She had assured him the dinner would be very dull, 'lots of people being polite and correct. That's how they do it in England at this type of thing,' and could see that he was mocking her warning, as Maureen launched into a scandalous story about her dashing uncle Walter, who had a pet monkey, and his volatile mistress, Ida Rubenstein, who had a pet tiger and a panther, 'although neither animal is any more tame than Ida, who is *entirely* savage . . .' she said to Joe, but loudly enough for everyone to hear.

'Really, Maureen,' Chips said. 'Must you?' He nodded at Sissy, whose eyes were wide.

'Oh, don't mind me,' Sissy said. 'I assure you, I've grown up no end since coming to London. Why, I'm positively bored of everything at this stage.' That made everyone laugh – anyone less bored than Sissy, Kick couldn't imagine.

Chips had put Honor at the end of the table, opposite him, with Debo to one side of her and Maureen to the other. 'Too many women,' Kick heard him muttering again, casting cross looks at his wife. But during dinner he tried repeatedly to engage her in conversation, asking her questions of the 'do you remember . . .' type that Honor mostly disdained to answer. If she spoke at all, she returned answers that couldn't have been satisfactory: *If you say so. I don't recall. I can't have been there.*

Once she saw that Duff wasn't to be charmed out of his anger with her, Maureen's mood switched. She drank more and faster, and soon, rather than charming, she was rude and sneering. She teased Duff about being too old for active service, of trying to show off by insisting on going to the front rather than staying usefully at the Ministry of Information, 'where you might do some good rather than getting in the way. Don't you think you might be under the feet of younger men? Slowing things down?' Duff ignored her. Joe and Billy looked shocked.

Kick knew why Maureen did it – she was terrified at the prospect of Duff going to war so she mocked him. Kick could see it in her face. But, clearly, not everyone could.

'Shut up, Maureen,' Debo said. 'It isn't a joke, you know.' Debo, to whom everything was a joke.

Kick watched them all: Duff, so angry; Maureen, desperate for his approval but too proud to admit it, instead spiky and cruel; Chips, unable to tell Honor that he was happy to see her and wanted her to stay; Honor, quietly triumphant at Chips's discomfort, serene in the upper hand for once.

'Let's never be like them when we're old,' she whispered to Billy, beside her.

'Certainly not,' he whispered back. Under the table, he took her hand in his. 'We'll be entirely different. They are a warped generation. Filled with prejudice, veins frozen by it. We could never be like that.' He ducked his head and, lifting her hand, kissed the inside of her wrist where her blood pounded hot and quick. Kick flushed at the touch of his lips, then looked up and found Maureen staring at her, a gleam of amusement in her pale blue eyes.

After dinner, Chips insisted the men stay at the table for port while the women withdrew. Joe rolled his eyes at Kick in mock panic, mouthing, 'Help me,' as Chips moved to a seat beside him. She gave him a reassuring wave as she left.

In the drawing room, she made for where Debo sat with Sissy, but Maureen blocked her path. 'Do sit with me a moment,' she said, patting the sofa beside her. Kick looked longingly at Debo and Sissy, but had to sit down.

'So what are your intentions with Billy? Or, rather, his with you? Because that's how it works, isn't it? For all that you are young and modern and American, that's still how it works?' Maureen looked so pleased with herself that Kick wondered if she had heard as well as seen them at dinner. Had her sharp ears caught the drift of their conversation? Their dismissal of her and her generation? And was she now taking her revenge? With Maureen, anything was possible. And everything was personal.

'We don't have intentions,' she tried to say. 'We're just happy to spend our time together when he's on leave. It's not really a time for making plans, is it?' She hoped to divert Maureen, but of course she couldn't.

'Nonsense. Plans must still be made. You don't have any? No, of course you don't. If you did, all of London would know it. It would be a matter for a great many people, not just you and Billy. That's what you young people don't understand,' she said peevishly. 'It isn't about you two at all, really. It's a matter of families, of traditions, of precedents and honouring – or not – ancient traditions. I do not expect you to understand. You couldn't possibly.'

'I do know some things,' Kick said sharply.

'No doubt. But nothing very useful. No, what I wonder,' she stared at Kick, 'is where all this leaves you.'

'It leaves me where I am.'

'No, it doesn't. You can't see that either, can you? Poor thing. No, if Billy is simply "spending time" with you when he's on leave, with no marriage to follow, it leaves you somewhere much worse than where you are. It leaves you humiliated,' she finished, with satisfaction.

'How?'

'Because then you are a diversion. A temporary one. If he has circled for as long as he has, but you haven't landed him – don't bother telling me I'm vulgar,' she said, patting Kick's hand, 'let's assume Chips, or someone, has already done that, and I couldn't care less – you are simply the girl Billy Cavendish didn't marry.'

'Maybe he won't marry anyone,' Kick said with spirit. She

thought of Billy kissing her wrist. *We will be entirely different.* Maybe that was how they would be different: Together for ever, never marrying.

'Of course he'll marry someone.' Maureen looked at her with pity. 'He absolutely will, because he must. And if it isn't you, there's a stain, a mark you can't see but everyone else can, right here.' She reached out the hand that had been patting Kick's and touched her in the centre of her forehead. Her fingers were cold and Kick drew back.

'It's not the olden days,' she said. 'These are modern times.'

'In such matters, no times are modern,' Maureen said. Kick saw that the men had joined them. Joe had drawn near to her and Maureen and was listening. Probably he had come to see what more outrageous things Maureen might come out with, but now he stayed, thoughtfully hooked to what she said.

'Go on,' he said now. Kick saw him cast a considering look at Billy, who was turning the pages of a book of sketches with Brigid. She wanted to do something violent, to silence Maureen, distract her, stop her saying such terrible things. But she did nothing. Nothing that anyone could see. Inside her, something shifted. Keen and hard.

'It's a question of value,' Maureen said, speaking mostly to Joe now. 'I think you'll understand. Something that someone else wants has more value. It's as simple as that. If that person loses interest, the thing has less value, simply because he's walked away from it.'

'Billy isn't losing interest,' Kick said, flushing red.

'Maybe not, but it'll look like he is if he doesn't propose.' The something inside Kick shifted again. She saw Billy dutifully married to someone suitable, perhaps still in love with her but silent, far away from her, in a way that no one could see and that Kick could never again be certain of. She shook her head from side to side.

Joe, however, nodded.

Despite Honor's unexpected arrival, the pall cast by Caroline's joke never fully went away and the party broke up early. As they left, Joe said firmly, 'I'll walk the girls back, Billy. You'd better take a taxi with Debo.' And when Billy tried to demur, Joe held fast. 'No, I'll walk them.'

Sissy and Edie went ahead, arm in arm, giggling noisily so that an ARP warden shushed them as he went past with his lantern, quite as though the Germans might be listening and be guided by the sound of laughter. How like a troll or goblin he was, as all the wardens were, bundled up in their bulky regulation-issue coats, with their little lanterns bobbing around in the dark city street.

Joe tucked Kick's arm into his. 'You know,' he said, 'she might just have a point.'

'Who?' Kick asked, unnecessarily.

'Maureen. She's a livewire, but she's not stupid.'

'She's old-fashioned. She thinks like all that generation does. We won't be anything like them.' She thought again of her whispered conversation with Billy at dinner.

'I'm not sure people change as fast as you think. Men don't, anyway. If Billy ditches you—'

'Billy isn't going to ditch me.'

'Well, not ditch, then, but say he doesn't marry you. Say he can't. How's that going to look?'

'It's going to look terribly sad, which is exactly what it would be.'

'And to the rest of the world, it'll look like he didn't want you enough.'

'But everyone knows it isn't that. Oh, I know he'll never give in about religion, and he knows I never would either. But he is very, very fond of me, and as long as I'm about he'll never marry. Even if that means neither of us ever does.'

'That,' Joe said, rather as Maureen had said, though less cruelly, 'is just impractical and you know it. Of course you'll marry. What else would you do? A girl like you.' He sounded shocked. Kick imagined her mother Rose's blue eyes bulging a little in the way they did, 'But, Kathleen, whatever is this nonsense?' and how Kick's efforts to explain would falter before that look. 'You'll marry, and have a family,' Joe continued, speaking with certainty. 'And so will Billy. He'll have to. The only question is, who?'

At the idea of there being someone for him who wasn't her, Kick felt again the anger Maureen had stirred in her. 'You don't know him like I do,' she said.

'Maybe not. But I do know the world, kid.' They reached the door to the flat, where Sissy and Edie waited for them. 'I'll see you at mass tomorrow morning. Church of the Immaculate Conception in Mayfair?'

'Aren't you coming up?' Kick asked.

'No, thanks.'

'Joe's got plans,' Edie said slyly. 'Big plans.'

'I've got plans too,' Sissy said.

'Your plans should be bed,' said Edie. 'You've black circles under your eyes as heavy as coal smudges. You need rest.'

'She's right,' Kick said. 'You look beat.'

'I'll rest later,' Sissy said. 'Right now, I'm going out.' She said it with such vigour that Kick envied her youthful certainty, the cheery belief in better around each corner that sent her out into the night so willingly.

The next morning Billy rang her, as he usually did, before going back to base. Kick pulled the cord of the telephone as far over as it would go and curled up on the sofa. 'When will I see you next?' she asked, dragging a rug over her bare feet.

'I don't know.'

'Leave cancelled?' she asked sympathetically. Hopefully. She watched Sissy come in – at this hour! – quietly, as though she hoped no one would notice her. When she saw Kick, she grinned and put her finger to her lips, before walking softly to her bedroom.

'It's not that,' Billy was saying. 'It's . . . Look, you know I like going about with you, don't you? I think you are the most wonderful girl I've ever met. But this isn't fair. Not on you.'

'Or you.' She couldn't bear to be the only one it wasn't fair on.

'No, I suppose not. But, in any case, I have to be the one who puts an end to it.'

'An end . . .'

'Yes. We can't keep going on like this, when there's no way to make it come out.' Like they were a hand of patience, she thought. 'It isn't fair on you,' he said again.

'Did Joe talk to you?'

'No.'

'Maureen, then?'

'Well, yes, but she only said what I was thinking and have been thinking for a jolly long time. It's impossible.' He sounded miserable. 'What a thoroughly *Romeo and Juliet* situation this is.'

How typical, she thought, that solid, unemotional Billy should suddenly show himself as a romantic at the very moment she needed him to be his most practical. 'So what are you saying?'

she asked, although she knew. Of course she knew. He was saying what his parents wanted him to say, what Maureen had said he would say, what even Joe knew he would say. She wanted to talk fast and long to stop him, prevent his words with a million of her own so that he couldn't ever articulate the thing that would break her heart. But nothing would come. And into her silence, he spoke.

'I don't know when I may see you again.'

Chapter Thirty

Brigid

The day after the dinner party was a Sunday. A day when no letter could arrive. Brigid disliked thinking of Saturdays and Sundays like this – days of absence, days of lack. She had volunteered to do a double shift at the hospital. She often did now. If she couldn't see Will, and if there couldn't be a letter from Fritzi, she wanted to have some way to occupy her day. And offering like that made her popular with the girls who had boyfriends, and the married women who had families.

She opened her bedroom window and leaned out. The autumn morning was fresh, if not sunny. Fresher than she felt. It had been a strange night, she thought, looking back. Certain moments stood out. Caroline, and her odd, cruel prank. Maureen's face when she realised Duff had heard what their daughter had said. Her own question about Will, and the differing responses.

It wasn't that they were wrong, any of them, she thought, as she closed the window. Even Maureen, for all that she had sounded so cold. Maybe they were right. But, Brigid realised, her mistake had been thinking they could guide her, give her the certainty she lacked. Because, after all, she knew what she would do. Those who had advised something different, maybe they were right, but that didn't mean she had to listen to them. They could be right and she could still do something different. The idea was like a rush of ice-cold air, crisp and exhilarating.

She dressed quickly, in a jersey and skirt, and went downstairs to the morning room that looked out onto the small, quiet back garden, with no view of the torn-up spaces where the iron railings around Belgrave Square had been, and no sight of the half-bombed house on the corner. A small escape from war.

She didn't expect to see anyone. But Maureen was sitting with a plate of toast and marmalade in front of her. 'Andrews was pretty shocked too,' Maureen said, seeing her surprise. 'I think he'd counted on at least an hour alone with the newspapers before anyone emerged.' She gestured at the paper lying beside her plate. It hadn't yet been ironed and the front page was crumpled: *Dunkirk Germans Hide in Beach Caves. Broken and beaten, the panzer troops pour to the coast and embark on the desperate dash for Italy.*

'Some good news,' Brigid observed.

'Yes,' Maureen agreed, but dully.

'At this rate, there won't be a war for Duff to join,' Brigid said, trying to cheer her.

'Yes,' Maureen said again, just as dully.

'Isn't that what you want?' Brigid asked. She knew she was being blunt – far more so than Maureen might have expected from her. She helped herself to kidneys from a dish on the side-board. She sat down opposite Maureen.

'It is, but it isn't what he wants. And now, by mocking him, I've rather put myself in a fix.'

'How so?'

'If the war ends before he joins up, he'll resent me because I didn't encourage him. Even though I haven't done anything to stop him. Why must it be so complicated?' she asked irritably. 'There's Chips, with no more intention of putting on a uniform than I have.' Brigid ducked her head to hide a smile. It was true that Maureen had shown no interest in service, not even the most informal kind. Lady Iveagh had tried to persuade her to join any number of committees, or even just volunteer for a few hours, but each time Maureen had said she couldn't find time. 'He's content to go to the House every day and do whatever he does there. Why can't Duff be the same?' She crumbled a piece of toast between her fingers, raining sticky crumbs onto her plate, then wiped the tips of her fingers with her napkin.

'Because he isn't the same,' Brigid said patiently. 'That's not what Duff is like.' She would have thought Maureen knew this. 'I'm sure it's been torture for him, standing by.'

'It's not all about fighting and *Boy's Own* adventures,' Maureen said sulkily.

Brigid was thoroughly sick of the dissembling. Sick of Maureen's way – everyone's way – of hiding everything they really felt behind a joke, a sneering remark, an insistence on the triviality of important things. 'Don't you think it would make more sense to tell him you're frightened at the idea of him leaving? Rather than jeering at him and hoping he understands that something else lies behind that?'

'And what would you know about it?' Maureen asked, hostile

as ever when she felt attacked or even disagreed with. She pushed her plate away and lit a cigarette, blowing smoke across the table at Brigid.

It was the closest Brigid had ever come to a quarrel with her terrifying cousin, and she chose to veer away. 'Where's Caroline?' she asked.

'I don't know. In her room? Out? You seem to know rather more than I do about her comings and goings.'

Brigid was about to ask, *And whose fault is that?* when the door opened, and Sissy put her head around it. 'May I come in? Andrews said you were here. But if I'm interrupting, I'll go away again.'

'Sissy! No, do come,' Brigid said with relief. 'You're out early.'

'Sundays in the flat are simply impossible,' Sissy observed cheerfully, going to the sideboard and taking a plate. 'Kick is up for mass at the most unfriendly hour. She gets ready by making a great deal of noise. Even singing hymns; "Nearer My God To Thee" at the crack of dawn . . . It's like she *wants* to go to mass. Catholics, I suppose.' She lifted large domed silver covers off dishes, contemplating what lay underneath. 'So much offal,' she complained, looking at the kidneys. 'It seems to be all that's left to eat these days . . . Anyway, Edie yells at her to keep it down from her bedroom, and between the two of them, it's impossible to sleep.

'But this morning Kick was worse than ever at first. I came in and heard her on the telephone to Billy, early as you like, but then, well, silence. Which was strange and somehow worse than "Nearer My God To Thee". So I got up, to see what the matter was, but she said, "Nothing," and went off to church, but she looked most peculiar.'

'Peculiar, how?'

'Like she was trying not to cry, but without believing she would manage it, if you see what I mean. Can you pass me the milk?' She poured herself a cup of tea.

'So oddly specific, it seems hard to imagine anyone could *not* know what you mean,' Maureen said witheringly. But there was a thoughtful crease between her eyebrows. 'I wonder if he broke it off. I may have rather suggested he should, last night . . .'

'Maureen, why would you do that?' Brigid stared at her.

'Because someone had to,' Maureen said with spirit. 'It has become perfectly absurd. Every leave, he comes to London to take her out. Brings her to Compton Place, and all for what? They cannot be married. There isn't any possibility of it. His parents are at their wits' end. Every eligible girl in London is tearing her hair out. No, they are simply wasting one another's time, and it's foolish and frankly boring to continue in this way.'

'So you took it upon yourself?' Brigid asked. Maureen's certainty that *they cannot be married* irritated her. After all, she thought, why ever not, when really there is nothing to stop it? Nothing concrete anyway.

'Acting on orders,' Maureen countered. 'Well, somewhat . . .'

'Did his parents ask you to say something?' Brigid asked. Again, she saw surprise in Maureen's face at her bluntness.

'Not his parents . . . his father, the duke. We had a little chat and it seemed a good idea. Moucher is too fond of the girl and, in any case, not the sort of person one can trust to be properly *clear*.'

'Whereas you can be relied upon to be just that?'

'I said I'd try to help, that's all.'

'I wonder if you have,' Brigid said. She poured herself a cup of coffee. 'So, Sissy, why *are* you here so early?'

Sissy was now eating toast spread with marmalade. 'Actually, I wanted to ask a favour.'

'Ask away.'

'Well, it's a favour of Chips, really. They're his.'

'What are his? He isn't down yet.'

'And won't be for some time,' Maureen said. 'We sat up after you'd gone to bed, Chips, Honor and I. When I went up they were embarking on what seemed like it would be a very long talk . . .'

'Oh dear,' Brigid said. 'Well, what is it you wanted to ask him? Maybe I can help.'

'It's his paints,' Sissy said.

'His paints?' Brigid had been expecting a question about . . . well, about anything except that.

'Yes. You see, I noticed in his study that he has a box of paints, hardly used.'

'A short-lived enthusiasm for landscapes,' Brigid explained to Maureen.

'And I have a – a friend who is a painter, and because of the war he can't buy paints so he can't work. Which means he isn't a painter, just a clerk in the War Office, which is making him thoroughly bad-tempered. He's used sheets stretched tight as canvases, and squeezed every drop out of his paint tubes, even mixed dried paint on old palettes with turps to make it usable. But that's run out now too.'

'Who is this friend?' Maureen asked.

'Just a friend.'

'Has anyone ever met him, this friend?'

'Brigid has.'

'Peter? Oh, Sissy, is this wise?'

'Very, very wise,' she said, eyes lighting up.

'Surprising little thing, aren't you?' Maureen said.

'So now you want to give him some paints?' Brigid continued.

'I do.'

'Well, go and look in Chips's study. If you can find the box, I'm sure you can take it. He abandoned that fad a long time ago.'

Sissy put the last piece of toast and marmalade into her mouth and jumped up. 'Thank you,' she said, still chewing. 'You are a sport!'

'I rather think she might need an eye kept on her,' Maureen said, after Sissy had left the room, the door banging behind her. 'That girl, charming, no doubt, is altogether as foolish as a fledgling.'

'You may be right,' Brigid said, thinking that when Maureen wasn't being completely impossible, even downright unpleasant, and when there was no risk to herself, she was capable, almost, of kindness.

She would put that in her letter to Fritzi, she decided. She had set aside an hour before her shift to write to him. If she couldn't receive a letter, she could at least write one. She would tell him about Maureen, about Sissy, about her own impatience – new as it was – with their way of *carrying on*, as she called it to herself: saying one thing, meaning another; saying no to things that were perfectly reasonable because they *weren't done*. About how she found, quite suddenly, that she cared far less than she'd thought for what was and wasn't done.

She would tell him about Will too. How she had decided to go and see him for what she knew might be the last time. Even though he had asked her not to. Not because she guessed he didn't mean what he said but because she wanted to so very much.

She felt certain Fritzi would understand. His letters told her of his own losses – men he had been close to in the internment camps who had been transferred elsewhere, or who remained while he was set free. Some had died of disease, or whatever it was that plagued men's hearts when they were held captive too long. He knew about loss. He had told her so.

Chapter Thirty-One

Maureen

'You seem to have *quite* taken possession,' Honor said, coming upon Maureen in the little sitting room later that morning where she sat at Honor's desk, writing a letter. 'I'm almost surprised to find you haven't been through my things.'

'What would I do with them?' Maureen asked. 'Give them to the Women's Institute? I'm not sure they'd take them. Anyway, if you will leave it all so unattended, what can you expect?' She finished the letter, signing her name with a flourish.

'Maybe now you'll let me sit at my desk,' Honor said. 'I too have letters to write.'

'Of course,' Maureen said, with excessive politeness. 'Shall I order us some coffee? It's no trouble.'

Honor burst out laughing. 'Do. Ring for Andrews. I'm not

sure he recognised me when I arrived last night. Which reminds me, *what* a strange party . . .'

'Never mind that now. Darling, have you really thought about what you're doing? It isn't "The Raggle-Taggle Gypsy-O", you know. You can continue to meet your Czech pilot without chucking everything else on a bonfire.'

'Yes, but I don't want to. I think you understand that.'

'I suppose I do. If I met Duff and wasn't married to him, nothing on earth could stop me.'

'How is that going?'

'Not well,' Maureen admitted. 'Oh, being in London, like this – me here, him at his club – is divine. You cannot imagine—'

'No, and I don't want you to tell me,' Honor said hurriedly.

'Very well. But persuading him to stay at the Ministry, not well. He won't discuss it and every time I bring it up he changes the subject, makes a joke, or tells me not to worry. Only,' she spoke faster now, not her usual drawl, 'what else am I to do but worry? He's too old for the army and there's no need – no need at all – for him to go.'

'Perhaps it isn't about need. Or, rather, perhaps it isn't about the army's need so much as his . . .'

'And why on earth would Duff *need* to go into the army?' Maureen asked, voice low and hard.

'No reason at all,' Honor said swiftly. 'And, anyway, he hasn't resigned from the government yet, has he?'

'No. And if I can just stall him a little longer, perhaps the war will end and this will all blow over.'

'Perhaps.' She sounded far from certain.

Andrews appeared with the coffee. They sat in silence while he poured it and passed them cups. Then, when he had left, Honor said, 'Were we like that, as young girls?'

'Like what?'

'Like Brigid, Kick, the American—'

'Edie?'

'Edie. That Sissy child . . . All of them, running around London on their own, making plans, no one to watch or question them. Do you ever think what we would have been like with such freedom as they have? As I recall it, we weren't allowed do anything much. The lending library, Hyde Park . . .'

'Don't tell me you weren't allowed to go to balls and parties. In fact, I seem to remember it was quite the opposite – like getting a reluctant horse into an unfamiliar stall, persuading you to a party.'

'Don't tell me you've forgotten how terrifying it all was,' Honor said, with a wry smile. 'The hours spent hiding in powder rooms, afraid to go down in case no one asked us to dance . . .'

'Someone always asked me to dance,' Maureen said. Then, with an answering grin, 'But the Season was alarming, I grant you.'

'Rather. But that's not what I meant. I mean all the other things – the way they have jobs now, do their own shopping, even cooking—'

'Badly, from what I hear.'

'Perhaps. But they do it. They have the freedom of married women. No one quizzes them.'

'They quiz each other.'

'It's not the same. Aren't you envious?'

'Of Brigid, scrubbing floors and sluicing walls? Sissy, chopping mountains of vegetables? Hardly. Even the Americans work hard at cheering those GIs who are positively *morbid*.' Never would Maureen admit that she barely saw those things when she looked at the girls – saw only what they had, the intoxication of it, so that the burden of what they did was nothing in comparison. Of course she was envious; how could Honor even ask it?

'I wonder if we'd have been any good at it,' Honor mused.

'I wonder if they're any good at it,' Maureen said sharply. 'That Sissy child is quite ridiculous. No more armour than a duckling, yet goes about as though she were something with teeth and claws to defend itself. Brigid, so sensible and good, suddenly far less either of those things. And Kick, blind to anything that isn't Billy, blinder again to how impossible that is.'

'I rather think you might have set her straight on that last night.'

'I rather hope I have.' She remembered the hurt on Kick's face, the way she had tried to claw back belief in a future with Billy even as Maureen took it from her. It had all been more unpleasant than expected. And yet, something about the younger woman's blind belief that love would be enough to bring her and Billy through a storm of objections had annoyed Maureen. The girl's ignorance of things Maureen had learned – love alone was not enough to cut through misunderstandings, not always – had made her cruelly glad to be the one to wield the axe. She changed the subject. 'What will you do now?'

'Immediately, nothing much. Gather a few of my things to take back to Essex with me.'

'And Chips?'

'After last night, Chips knows it's hopeless. He just won't yet admit it. Keeps plotting and planning, offering me all sorts of deals if only I'll take them.'

'Poor Chips,' Maureen said lightly.

'Certainly he thinks so.'

'Well, aren't you harsh?' But she spoke almost admiringly. She had always despised Honor for the subdued way she accepted the unhappiness of her circumstances. Often, seeing her cousin's bowed shoulders and silent performance of duty, Maureen had wanted to shake her. Well, now Honor had shaken herself.

Chapter Thirty-Two

Sissy

Chips's study bore traces of his many short-lived enthusiasms. One of these had been painting: an expensive mahogany case, rows of neat tubes, some barely touched, with exotic names: Raw Sienna, Gold Ochre, Venetian Red. They gave her a thrill, as though in knowing them she spied into a corner of Peter's life that he didn't know she could see. Maybe this would make him happy, she thought. Take away the impatience that she turned too surely to anger. Once he could paint, he would be pleased with her. Kind to her.

She hugged the case to her as she walked briskly back to his flat. She thought back to early that morning when she had left. There had been just enough light – the colour of the dirty water on washing day – to see by. 'You don't need me to come with you,' Peter had said sleepily, from the twanging bed.

'No,' she assured him, even though it hadn't been a question. 'It doesn't make any sense.'

'That's what I thought,' he agreed. She had leaned over to kiss him, then spent longer than necessary putting on her coat in case he said something else. He didn't.

Arriving at his building, she politely held the door for a man carrying an old whiskery dog in his arms. Then she ducked inside and climbed to the fourth floor.

At Peter's door she took a deep breath. There was, she knew, a chance that he would not be pleased to see her, would feel she was intruding. And he would be right, but she had such a prize that surely he would forgive her. She knocked hard.

'Who is it?' His voice through the door was impatient.

'Sissy.' Almost – because even after the nights she had spent with him she still didn't have any faith that her name would be enough – she added, *From the King's Anchor . . .*

The door opened. 'Sissy,' he said politely, as one would welcome an acquaintance. 'Come in. What have you got there?'

'It's for you.' She was excited again. 'Look.' She thrust the case at him. 'Open it.' Her fingers twitched to open it herself but she waited while he walked, so slowly, to the table by the window, placed the case on it, drew up a chair and sat down. Only then did he lean forward to click open the two hinged clasps and lift the lid.

'Paints!' she said.

'Paints,' he echoed.

'Are they the right kind? The kind you use?' she asked anxiously.

'They are.' He ran his finger along the many tubes. 'Where did you get them?'

Did he sound snappy? Angry, even? 'I told you, the house I –'

'– don't live in,' he supplied.

'Yes.' She smiled. 'The man who owns it used to paint and now he doesn't and has no use for them, so I took them.' He lifted the top tray from the case – Sissy hadn't realised there was a top and a bottom – and below was another row of paints, untouched it looked like, a bottle of turps, more paint brushes, and a stained rag that Chips must have used to wipe the brushes.

'He took good care of these,' Peter said. He lifted out the rag and sniffed it. Released from the box, the sharp, oily smell came to Sissy like a reminder of something. Again, she wondered if he sounded angry. 'But I don't understand why you've brought them here.'

He definitely sounded angry. Her stomach lurched. 'You said you needed paints.' Her voice sounded tinny and faraway to her, as if it had come from the other end of a long-distance telephone call. 'You said you'd take them off his hands,' she tried to remind him. 'And he doesn't use them, so . . .'

He was silent, running a finger along the untouched bottom layer. Sissy wondered if he would make her take them back. 'So you thought you'd give them to your *poor friend*?'

He was angry. She understood that he was proud – the way he talked about the 'feeble' work he did at the War Office, his scorn of men in uniform told her that. She saw she had wounded him with what looked like charity.

Quickly, she rushed to make it all right. 'You'd be doing him a favour,' she said hastily. How to explain that wasn't how she thought of him? And that no one knew more about charity than she did, in Kick's borrowed dresses, Edie's hair grips, with Lady Iveagh's patronage. 'The paints are a reproach to him. A reminder of what he didn't succeed at.'

It worked. He laughed. A little. 'I can guess exactly what sort of painter he was, just by looking at these.' He pointed to the tubes that were used – greens, blues and browns mostly – and the untouched ones, scarlet, crimson and yellow. 'Landscapes. Big, heavy renderings of fields and woodland. Maybe a mountain in the distance . . .' he picked up a squeezed tube of Prussian Blue '. . . always on a clear sunny day.'

'Exactly,' Sissy agreed, even though she'd never seen any of Chips's paintings. 'That's it.' She wanted Peter to be right, because she could tell that if he was he would be happier with her gift.

'I knew it.' And then he was all right. He thanked her, packed the paints carefully away and said that, if she gave him time to finish dressing, they would go to the pub and be there in time to get something to eat before the hordes arrived. 'Unless you've got something in your pockets,' he said, patting her down affectionately.

'Like bringing a carrot to the stables?' she said. 'I'm afraid not.'

They went to the King's Anchor and were sitting over bowls of stew at one of the little tables by the time the others came in. Sissy saw the look of surprise, maybe a trace of disappointment, in Jim's face. And a flash of something else in Aurora's. Afterwards she seemed to avoid Sissy. So it was a surprise to find her waiting outside the door when she came out of the upstairs lavatory.

'When you came here first, you said you were here for Jim,' Aurora said, abrupt.

'I didn't. You asked if I was here for Peter, and I said no, only *because* of Peter, so I suppose you presumed I was there for Jim.'

Aurora flushed angrily. 'You knew perfectly well what I meant so you answered dishonestly, pretending not to. I despise that kind of thing.'

'Please don't despise me,' Sissy begged. 'I know it was dreadful but, honestly, I didn't know, that day, if there was any point, coming here for Peter. So I didn't say it. I so want us to be friends.'

'Friends?'

'Yes.'

'Friends,' Aurora repeated, thoughtful. Then she turned in the dank passage and walked off down the cramped stairs. Left behind, Sissy watched her disappear around the turn. Aurora's perfume lingered, heavy in the sour air of the upstairs flat. Sissy felt the sting of rejection, but also the secret thrill of knowing that Peter was ready to be seen with her, known to go about with her. And the even more secret thrill of having something – someone – that someone else wanted. Like a tiny poison-tipped dart, she felt it burrow into her and spread a hot little glow.

Chapter Thirty-Three

Kick

There'll be no crying in this house, Kick said to herself. She said it to herself so often, now, that it had become like a constant drumbeat – *no crying in this house, no crying in this house* – albeit one that often changed its tone. Sometimes it was mournful, sometimes resolute, almost comforting. Other times it was mocking, like a lone bird: *no crying, no crying, no crying.*

But it was effective. She didn't cry. Not even when Billy had hung up after his terrible words – *I don't know when I may see you again.* She had got ready for mass, quietly, putting her rosary beads into her handbag, and walked alone and silently to the Church of the Immaculate Conception in Mayfair. There she had met Joe, and listened quietly to him when he told her about his visit to the Dorchester and Mrs Smithson. She had stood and knelt and sat as directed by the priest, and even found comfort, momentarily, in the familiarity of Our Father and the Credo. Only afterwards, as they walked back to the flat, did she tell Joe, 'You don't need to worry any more about me and Billy. It's done.'

'What's done?'

'He's given me up. Just as everyone wanted.'

'When?'

'This morning, on the telephone.'

'Must have been awful early. It's only gone ten now.'

'It was.'

'Must have been up all night, wrestling with it,' Joe said. Then, 'I gotta say, I admire that.'

'I'm glad. Not that it really matters any more.'

'What will you do?'

'Make the best of it. What else is there?'

It was when he said, 'Kick, you are the very best person I know,' and took her arm and squeezed it, that the tears almost came. But only almost. Just like that time with Rosie, she found herself wondering if they would finally spill out. Would she abandon herself to sobbing and hiccuping, the way she had seen others do? Her eyes prickled and her throat closed with a hard lump.

She shook her head, sharply, to clear both, and said, 'I've got a long shift today at the club.'

'Maybe just as well.' Joe squeezed her arm once more, then let it go.

And that was that. She told Edie, Sissy and Brigid swiftly, with the kind of resignation she wished she felt: *What else is he to do? It's just crazy to go on pretending this can come right. Much better for us both it ends now.*

'Are you sorry now that you came back to England?' Sissy blurted out.

'No,' Kick said. And found it was the truth. 'Not one bit sorry.'

She went to work that day, and all the following days, and did as she had always done. She played ping-pong and made doughnuts and found stationery and stamps for GIs to write to their parents, their sweethearts. She listened to their news from home – babies born, cars bought, exams taken – congratulated and sympathised as required. When news of the break-up got around, the GIs and the other Dollies were briskly sympathetic. 'Hard luck,' the one called Charlie said. 'I'm sorry for sure because I could see you thought a great deal of him, but you'll be all right, Miss Kathleen. You're a pistol.'

And so she was. She was a pistol. She was her father's Great Girl. She would be all right, just as Charlie said. And if in the meantime she moved through the days as though something clung to her and tried to drag her backwards, well, that was only for a little while, she was sure. 'Anything done for Our Lord will be rewarded a thousand-fold,' her mother wrote to her when Joe told them the news. Kick had begged him to do it for her – 'At least someone may as well be happy,' she had said, with an attempt at a laugh.

And indeed her mother was. She wrote words of comfort that were nothing of the sort because her relief was all too obvious. As was her conviction that Kick would quickly throw off any unhappiness – Kick realised that in this her mother didn't know her at all. Her words of charity were hollow, her reminder of the comfort of prayer useless, because she didn't understand that, for Kick, there was no *soon*, or *later*, or *after*. There was only now.

Lady Astor, calling to see her at Hans Crescent, looked around the recreation room and said, 'You don't work in a Red Cross club, you work in a lunatic asylum.' Kick smiled and thought of how happy she had been to be among the restrained chaos of so many young men and women. Now, she found it tiring, the constant noise, the long hours, the demands on her to be cheerful. The days came and she squared her shoulders to meet them, gritting her teeth to get through. At the end of each one, she went quietly home to bed, exhausted, promising herself that the next day would be easier. Knowing it would not.

Chapter Thirty-Four

Brigid

Autumn advanced and the days got colder. To the dullness of blacked-out nights was added the thick air and acrid smell of many coal fires. Kick spent more time at Belgrave Square. Brigid could hardly blame her. The flat was cold and, while she lacked most of her usual exuberance, cheerless. Sissy and Edie were often out, and Kick took to walking round to Number Five and knocking at the door like some kind of stray. 'Come and stay properly,' Brigid urged her.

'Thanks, but no. It's enough to come when I do. Like this, it's a way to feel different from my dismal self for a while.'

'That bad?'

'Everyone tells me I'll forget him, find someone else,' Kick said dully.

'Already?'

'Oh, yes. Lady Astor came all the way to the club to tell me, the very day she heard the news. Seems some people are real excited at the idea of me forgetting him. But I won't. I know I won't. If I could, I would have already. I don't know why they don't understand.'

'I see that . . . You know that people will always say something?'

'What?'

'There will always be someone to tell you what you should do and who you should marry and why you should do this and that.' Brigid spoke with the certainty of a thing seen clearly at last.

'Certainly feels like it,' Kick agreed.

'But the thing is,' Brigid said eagerly, 'you don't have to listen to them.' She shrugged. 'I don't. You don't either.'

The next day, Brigid went to see Will. She knew he was unconscious. Mary had told her that he had last shown any awareness two days earlier, and that now it was 'just a matter of time'. She said it briskly, patting Brigid's arm in a way that was kind but impatient. Brigid thanked her. She went straight to Will's room. There, she met Matron on her way out. 'May I go in? For a moment?' she asked.

'You may. But best be quick,' Matron said, holding the door for her. 'You have rounds to do.'

Brigid slipped into a room that already felt empty. She stayed only a moment. Not because of Matron, but because there was no reason to linger. Everything had already happened. Everything important, anyway. Yes, there was the final going, but that was simply the dot at the end of a sentence already written.

She stood, gazing down at him, listening to the quiet rasp of his breath. She tried to find, in her mind, an idea of where he was: somewhere grey and dim and muffled, she thought, with the clamour of the hospital now far behind him, and in front, getting closer, a light that drew him. There must be a light, she thought, mustn't there? Soon he would be at the light, would be within it and then he would be gone from them.

His arms lay flat by his sides, outside the sheet. She put a hand lightly over one of his. 'Goodnight and good luck,' she whispered. As she left, she picked up the book that lay on his bedside table. It was one of hers but that wasn't why she took it.

In the empty corridor she flicked through it. She didn't know what she was looking for – some underlined passage, perhaps? A page turned down with a line or two that would have shown her what Will had been drawn to when he read it? But there was nothing. Things should mean something, she thought. Death should mean something. There was so much of it now, and what was the point if it didn't mean anything?

'*I feel as though I have let him down,*' she wrote that night to Fritzi. '*But I don't know how, or what I could have done differently.*'

'*It's natural,*' was his answer when it came. '*You felt he was yours to care for and you couldn't save him. I felt the same about the men in the camps who died. That I had let them down.*'

He understands, she thought. It must be because he knew death. He had seen it.

Her friends didn't. Not really. Sissy's eyes filled with tears when Brigid told them. 'I'm sorry!' She threw her arms around Brigid's neck and hugged her. 'How rotten for you.'

Edie told Sissy to stop crowding Brigid. 'Let her breathe,' she said, and when Sissy had stepped back, added, 'You did everything you could have done.' Brigid nodded, because it was true, and didn't say, *There should have been more. There must have been more.*

Kick took Brigid's hand and held it for a few moments, then gently let it go. 'I was thinking this morning, we've been so lucky that it scares me. I guess maybe the luck has to run thin sometime.'

'Just a little longer,' Sissy murmured. 'That's what they all say now.' It was true. All around, the talk was cautious but hopeful: there was an end they all believed in. A time when the war would be over. Brigid believed it too, but the idea didn't spark excitement in her as it did in others. Yes, the war would end – of course it would: nothing lasted for ever, not even the terrible things. It would end and there would be peace and they would all have to learn what that meant. But whatever it meant it would not include Will.

Part Three

1944

Chapter Thirty-Five

Brigid, Clandeboye, Northern Ireland

Brigid went to her parents at Elvedon for Christmas, alone of her siblings, and spent the days pretending to be interested – in the progress of the war, improvements to the herds and farm acres, Mama's relief work – when really she was absorbed in her private grief at Will's death, and confusion over Fritzi. She didn't speak of either to her parents. It wasn't that she felt afraid to – not any more: she just didn't see what good it would do. They couldn't console her for Will and they wouldn't accept Fritzi so she stayed quiet, and was amused and a little upset when her mother congratulated her on being 'so full of repose'.

She was pleased when Maureen telephoned shortly after Christmas to invite her to Clandeboye. 'I know you don't shoot,' Maureen said, voice high and snappy on the crackling line, 'but you might like to come anyway.' Brigid had missed Caroline since the child had gone home at the start of December, when the fiction of useful lessons with the retired headmistress had come to an end at last and Maureen had ordered her back to Ireland. She said she would.

'It'll be the last of the season,' Maureen continued. 'Impossible to shoot in England now. Some busybody will report you to the Ministry for wasting shot. But in Ireland no one cares a bit.'

Brigid made the journey by boat and train. She got down with her case at St Helen's Bay station where a pony and trap was waiting to take her up the sunken avenue that led to the house. Caroline was at the back door. 'I knew you'd be brought round here,' she said, reaching for Brigid's case. 'And I knew Mummie would neglect to send anyone to help with your things.'

She had forgotten, Brigid thought wryly the next morning, looking out her bedroom window, just how inhospitable Clandeboye was in winter. How damp the place got, how the fires smoked, how the wind crept through the ill-fitting windows. And how few, and surly, the servants were. If you rang to ask for a hot-water bottle, it might be half an hour before anyone came, and at least that before they returned with a lukewarm offering. If they came back at all.

But also how beautiful it was, she thought, looking at the fields and woodlands that lay beyond the raddled old house, greens and browns lightly brushed with the cold silver of early-morning frost.

She finished dressing, laced her stoutest shoes, and went down-stairs. There was no point in accepting the offer of breakfast in one's room at Clandeboye. Better to take pot luck in the morning room with the others.

Duff was sitting at the head of the table with a bowl of

porridge. Caroline was beside him, a book open in front of her. She looked up and smiled as Brigid came in. Opposite her, on Duff's other side, two friends of his whom Brigid had met at dinner the night before and whose names she had already forgotten. She had an idea one of them was in the Ministry with Duff, and the other was a friend from Oxford.

'I'd have the porridge,' Duff said, as she went to the sideboard. 'It's pretty reliable. I can't speak for the rest.'

'I wouldn't be in a rush for the kedgeree,' one of the men said, with a diffident smile. 'Hard to know what some of the things here are . . .' He picked through the contents of his plate.

'We'll set off at ten,' Duff said. Which meant five to ten, Brigid knew, and also meant Maureen wouldn't be joining them. Not at that hour.

'We're short a couple of gun-dogs,' Duff continued. 'The gamekeepers will have to do some of the fetching.'

'Let me, Daddy. I'll do it,' Caroline said, lifting her head to look at him. 'I'll be quick and keen, just like a hound.'

'I'm not sure your mother would like it,' Duff said.

'She doesn't have to know. She won't be up for hours, and even then she won't venture out.' Caroline was right, Brigid thought. Maureen would spend the time in the drawing room, playing records and smoking, drinking cocktails and waiting for them to come back. 'Please!'

'Well, all right. But don't tell your sister or brother or they'll want to and I can't have that.'

'I won't tell a soul,' Caroline promised. 'I'll be at the back door, ready, before you even think to look for me.' She ran out of the room, eyes shining with excitement.

'Peculiar child,' the other man said.

'Do you have children?' Brigid asked him.

'No.'

'Well, then, how would you know what's peculiar and what isn't?'

He flushed. 'I suppose I wouldn't,' he agreed, so crestfallen that Brigid immediately felt bad. She did this more and more, slapped people down. Especially men. Especially young men. She seemed unable to stop herself saying snappish, cutting things that were partly a joke, but only partly.

'You've gotten awful mean,' Kick had said to her only a couple of weeks ago, half admiring but also not. They had been at the Dorchester, a tea dance with a handful of GIs from the club. A young man had stumbled into their table, knocking over all the glasses. He had offered to replace them, adding hopefully to Brigid, 'Then maybe you'd give me the next dance.'

'Now that I've seen what you can do to a tableful of Champagne glasses, I think maybe I wouldn't,' she'd said.

The GIs seated around them had all roared laughing, and Brigid had been pleased by her wit. But she'd seen surprise on Sissy's face, and afterwards Kick had said, 'Poor guy, it's probably not easy for them always to have to ask us. Maybe if we had to do the asking sometimes, we'd be kinder.'

Brigid had felt bad. She had vowed to stop snapping. But now here she was again, with Duff's friend.

'Take it easy on the poor chap,' Duff said, under his breath, handing her a section of newspaper. 'Not everyone's been raised in the Guinness school of hard jokes.'

Brigid laughed. *The Guinness school of hard jokes.* She must remember to say that to Kick. She'd love it. As much as she loved anything.

Since the break with Billy, Kick had been like someone impersonating herself. Or that was how Edie described it. 'It's like her body remembers how to be Kick Kennedy, but her mind doesn't.' By which, Brigid supposed, Edie meant the way Kick seemed to be lost inside herself. She did all the things she was meant to do – went to the club, danced the Jitterbug, played table tennis and cards, threw darts, and mostly still won at these things. She went to dances and out to the Ritz, to nightclubs, but in everything there was a gap, a silence, a delay so that she was no longer the most vital person in any room.

It was sad, Brigid thought. More than that, it was wrong. Kick not being Kick was wrong.

'I say,' the man across the table asked, 'do you shoot?'

'No. I hunt, but shooting . . .' How to explain that she disliked even the idea of it? What chance had the poor birds? At least a fox, in its own territory, slim and wily and silent, might evade hounds and often did. And even when the poor fox was old, or unlucky, it was just one. A day's shooting might result in scores of dead birds, their limp bodies strung together in braces and brought home with a triumph she couldn't understand. A man holding a gun, a loader behind him ever ready with a fresh gun, need simply stand and blast, and if he was in any way a decent shot, the birds would fall before him, like autumn leaves from a well-shaken tree. It was unfair.

'But you'll come out with us?'

She had been rude to him, and now he was eager for her company. How strange men were. 'Yes.' After all, what else was there to do?

She arrived at the back door on time, to find Caroline already there. She had changed into shorts despite the cold, a brown jersey and a pair of white plimsolls. 'It's wonderful to have something to do for a change,' she said.

Imagine having so little, Brigid thought, that the idea of playing gun-dog on a pheasant shoot was appealing.

Duff and his friends arrived and were joined by a couple of neighbours, red-faced countrymen, and they tramped for half-an-hour through sparse woodland and out the other side to an expanse of bare fields. The guns took up position, dogs frothing at their feet. Far ahead, on the other side of a line of trees, the beaters moved, making their curious trilling noises and swiping at stubble with their flags.

Caroline crouched at the end of the line and they waited. And then came the moment that always took Brigid by surprise, no matter how many times she witnessed it. Out of the silent, sleepy and seemingly empty landscape, birds erupted, hurtling from the coarse cover of stubble and lurching skywards, trying desperately to gain height. Instantly the guns were loosed and some dropped abruptly, plummeting earthwards.

The dogs set off, barking hoarsely, Caroline with them. She was fast, even crouched low to the ground. Brigid saw her stoop and pick up a bird, then another, and run back with them. Even though Brigid knew there was no actual danger – the guns were turned firmly skywards – something about the sight of Caroline, running in a zigzag motion, stopping, picking up, doubling back, depositing the feathered bodies and running off again, worried her.

Around her the guns burst forth their small explosions. A smell of hot metal lay across the morning air, covering the wet earth and leaves. Already there were mounds of feathered carcasses, and Caroline was tiring. She ran slower now and her breath was ragged. Her white shoes were soaked and filthy.

Caroline plucking dead birds from the ground, bringing them back, piling them up, running off for more: it was a hateful image, and suddenly Brigid thought she understood why there were government orders for no shooting parties. It wasn't that shot was rationed, or not only that, it was that it was much too close to what was actually happening in the fields of Europe and deserts of Africa, in the air above England and Germany. More firing, more killing, more dying.

She got up from her shooting stick and went to where Caroline was. The girl's bare legs were bleeding, scratched by the stubble. Her hands were sticky with pheasant blood, to which a few downy feathers clung. There was blood on her face too – either from where she had wiped at the sweat that had sprung up on her forehead, or because she had scratched herself there too. She was trembling all over, from exhaustion, but also something else, and the light of excitement in those large pale blue eyes was gone, replaced with distress.

'Surely that's enough now,' Brigid said. 'Come and have a cup of tea.'

'Do you think that would be all right?' Caroline asked.

'I do.'

At the picnic basket, Brigid found a tea towel and rubbed at the girl's hands. But the blood was dry and hard to get off. She dampened a corner with water from a stone bottle and cleaned the worst of it off her face. 'Here.' She poured a cup of hot tea and gave it to her, then another for herself. They sat on the plaid blanket and Brigid asked, 'Are you hurt?' indicating the scratches on Caroline's bare legs.

'They're nothing.' She took a bite of fruitcake. 'It's harder work than it looks,' she said, perhaps to explain why her legs were shaking. Brigid didn't think it was the hard work that had got to her.

'I'm sure it is. There's a reason why they use dogs,' she said gently. 'Maybe call it a day for now.'

Caroline looked upset. 'I can't. Daddy will think I'm shirking.'

'I'm sure he won't. Why don't I tell him we're both needed back at the house?'

'I can't.' She set her mouth in a stubborn line. 'I said I'd be a hound for the day and I will be.' She swallowed the last of the cake and scrambled to her feet. The beaters had put up another scattering of birds and the guns were busily dropping them from the sky.

'Ready, Daddy!' Caroline called.

'Thank you, darling,' Duff said, as she ran past him. 'You're as handy as a small pot.' Despite everything, Caroline's face flushed with pleasure.

Brigid decided she'd had enough. All shoots were boring after a while but this one had become grotesque. 'I'm going,' she called to Duff. She trudged through the woods and back out to the gardens that were half tended, half wild, just as everything at Clandeboye was. At the house, she left her walking shoes with the jumble of riding boots, wellingtons and old galoshes that lay in the little boot room.

It was almost lunchtime so Brigid went to the small sitting room Maureen used in the mornings. Sure enough, she was up and in a good mood. With Maureen, it was always perfectly obvious. 'Come and have coffee. You must be frozen,' she said. 'How were the pheasants?'

'Numerous,' Brigid said. 'And perfectly stupid as always. Allowing themselves to be driven straight towards the guns. Impossible not to feel they could try a little harder to escape.'

'Well, don't say that to Duff. He prides himself on his sportsmanship.'

Manning, the butler, came in to say that 'Mr Channon' was on the telephone 'for Lady Brigid'.

Brigid took the call in the draughty hall.

'There's a telegram here for you. Would you like me to read it?' Chips said, barely able to let her say, 'Hello.'

'I wouldn't, but I suppose you'd better.' She waited, hearing Chips tearing open the envelope. Must he sound so eager? she thought. A telegram couldn't be good.

'It's from a George Mansfield,' he said.

Fritzi. 'Go on.'

'He's been in an accident. A tractor. He's hurt and cannot write.'

'What else?' She kept her voice as steady as she could. The important thing now was to find out what she could, not to let go, into the fear that grabbed at her.

'Nothing else. Just that. Brigid, who is George Mansfield? Is this whoever has been writing you all those letters from Hertfordshire? Not a *"school friend"*?'

'Yes.'

'But who is he? I've never heard of a George Mansfield.' And, when she said nothing, he added pompously, 'Brigid, you are living under my roof. I am answerable to Lord and Lady Iveagh. You must tell me who this man is, and why you are writing to him.'

'It's Fritzi.' The words shot out of her mouth so that she wondered at how she had contained them all this time. How long had she kept them choked in, afraid of everything that would be said to her, the storm that would break about her head? Now, she revelled in saying his name, ready to face whatever trouble came. If it was to be a gauntlet, as well to throw it down now.

'Fritzi?'

'Yes.'

'I had no idea.'

'No,' she agreed pleasantly.

'You were supposed not to see him.'

'I'm not. I haven't seen him. But he has written to me, and I have written back.'

'I thought he was in Canada.'

'He was, in an internment camp, but he's been back in England more than a year now. He was a Category A prisoner, because of his father and joining the Luftwaffe, but then, someone argued for him that he should be downgraded to Category B, because of his brother Wilhelm and the Oster conspiracy against Hitler. I thought it was you.'

'Not me, although I'm glad for Fritzi. So, he's back, and you've been writing to him? Even though we told you to forget all about him.'

'You do know I'm not a wind-up toy like Paul's monkey?' She was indignant now. 'To be turned on and then turned off, as it suits you?' How good the words sounded to her ears. Even better that they emerged solid, whole. She didn't stutter or falter. That, more than anything, told her she was right to speak.

'But you didn't even like him,' Chips said plaintively. 'I remember – well! – how difficult it was to persuade you even to be civil to him.'

'At first, yes. Mostly I was furious that you were plotting and scheming about me. But when I stopped wanting to box everyone's ears, I found him to be a rather sweet fellow. He asked if he could write to me once he was back at Cambridge, and I said yes, and he did. And then war, and you told me to stop corresponding with him, but it was too late. I found I couldn't. Especially once he was interned. It felt far too much like kicking a fellow when he was down.'

'It would. To you.'

'To anyone with any decency.'

'Well, what will you do now?'

'I'll go and see him. If he's hurt as badly as the telegram says, I can nurse him.' *You felt he was yours to care for . . .* Fritzi had written that about Will, but now it belonged to him. He was hers to care for.

And even though Chips said he was scandalised – Chips, who lived for scandal – and even though she knew her parents would be angry and uncomprehending, even though she scarcely knew herself what she was doing, Brigid held firm. She would go.

Chapter Thirty-Six

Kick

I t was, Kick thought, as though Billy, having made his decision and told her of it, then forgot to implement it. After the first weeks, when she had hardly gone out and had spent many nights with Brigid at Belgrave Square – it was a little easier there to force herself not to think of him – she now saw him almost as much as she had before he'd broken off with her.

London in wartime was a city of so few places to go that there was no way not to bump into people. They were animals at a shrinking waterhole, herded closer and closer together, lions drinking beside zebras. Even if she had wanted to avoid him, it wouldn't have been easy.

But she didn't want to avoid him. And when she did see him, it was almost as though nothing had changed between them. He still made a beeline for her, talked to her, asked her to dance.

Sometimes, if there were no taxis, he even walked her home. She thought perhaps she should prevent him, refuse him. But she couldn't.

'I don't think it's right,' Joe said, as they walked briskly in Hyde Park one cold morning in early February when he was on leave from Cornwall. 'The way he keeps buzzing about you. He said his piece, and now he should leave you alone.'

'That would be worse,' Kick said. 'If it's between seeing him and not seeing him, I want to see him.'

'You think that, but in the end it would be easier if you don't. If it can't be, you need to forget about him.'

'But I can't,' Kick said. 'If I could, I would.' Why did everyone think she had the ability to switch off what she felt, as she would a tap or a lamp? 'I want to see him, same as he wants to see me.' Joe continued to try to dissuade her, even saying, 'Jack thinks the same.' As he talked, Kick heard the unspoken – the weight of experience both he and Jack had in breaking off with girls and the best way to do this. She didn't know this like they did, Joe hinted but didn't say. And it was true, she knew that. But they didn't know her and Billy the way she did.

So she let Joe speak, and when he had done, she said, 'I know you mean it kindly, and most of the time I guess you must be right, but not with me. Not with Billy.' And when he still tried, 'You have to trust me, Kick,' she found herself remembering another time, another voice; her mother's: *You have to trust me on this, Kick . . .*

'You remember that summer at Hyannis, the summer you and Jack enlisted?'

'I do.'

'You know I think of that as the Last Summer . . .'

'Why the last? There will be more summers. Many more.' He spoke idly, with satisfaction.

Why indeed? All that summer, Rosie had been different. Always sad or angry – frustrated at all the things Kick and Eunice could do that she wasn't allowed to, a list that seemed longer every day. Most of all she was angry with the men who called to take Kick out, the parties they went to, the drives along the coast on hot days, the dances and nightclubs.

'Why?' she had demanded, stamping her foot. 'Why can't I go? I dance as well as she does. I'm prettier than her, I know I am. You all said so.' And it was true. She was, and they had. It was one of the things they used to say to Rosie, to cheer her up when her lessons went too slowly. *'You're the prettiest, Rosie, anyone can see it.'* And for a while it had been a comfort to all of them. And then, when Rosie tried to use it as a weapon, it wasn't a comfort. It was a worry.

'Looking like that, going around with God knows who . . .' Kick had heard her father say angrily, after yet another of Rosie's escapes.

By the end of those sun-filled weeks – light that moved constantly, dancing on waves, moving around the house from back to front as though chasing them – after Rosie's midnight flit to the bar, after Mike, Kick had known that change was coming. She just hadn't understood what.

It had felt like an ending at the time, but only an ending in the way they were all growing up and setting off on different paths. Not an ending as it turned out to be.

That autumn, just a few weeks after Kick had gone back to Washington, Pa had made his decision about Rosie, the operation that was to be 'for her own good'. It was the first time the word 'lobotomy' had been used, although he had continued to call it 'only a minor operation, no anaesthetic even needed. It will give her peace,' he had said. 'You can see how badly she needs that.'

But that was not what peace looked like, Kick thought now: Rosie's silence, her immobility. The slump of her shoulders and the way her tongue would no longer form clear words.

You have to trust me on this, Kathleen. The words, the voice, came back to Kick. First spoken in the clear air of a summer night, they now reverberated around the dingy walls of the homely London flat. *You'll look after her?* Kick had asked, after Rosie's escape.

Of course we will. Whatever do you think? You have to trust me . . . Rose had said. And Kick had trusted her. Trusted that home, indeed, was where Rosie should be. Was where she would be cared for. But her trust had been misplaced.

'That's what Mother told me,' she said now, to Joe.

'What?'

'She said I had to trust her. That night, when Rosie ran away to the bar and met that guy, Mike. You remember?'

'I remember.'

'I asked if Rosie would be all right, and Mother said I had to trust her. And I did. And you know what happened.' Joe shifted away from her, uneasy, as Pa had been when Kick talked about Rosie at the dock.

'They did what they needed to. For Rosie,' he said.

'You never saw her, did you?'

'Pa said not to.'

'I know he did. He said the same to me. But I went anyway.' Then, 'You know he says the operation was to blame? That something went wrong with it?'

'Yes?'

Emily Hourican

'I did some reading. Afterwards. Too late . . . But what I read, I think the operation mostly did what it was always going to do.'

'So?'

'I guess Pa meant the best,' she said, as firmly as she could, 'but if you'd seen her, Rosie . . . If you'd seen Rosie . . . Well, I guess you'd find it hard as I do to understand why he ever thought that could be best for her.'

All the things Kick tried never to think of came to her then in a rush. Rosie's blackened eyes, the bruising still fresh around her forehead, the small bloodied scabs at each side of her head that had proven how delicate it was, how little stood between her – anyone – and violent change.

Most of all, the tearing absence where her sister had been. The person in front of her that day had been a flesh-and-blood form surrounding an empty hole. Rosie's arms and legs were there, her face, even her eyes, blank behind the liquorice-coloured bruises, but those things were a lie because Rosie was nowhere in them. Her form was like a dress, taken off after a party and dropped, empty, to the floor.

Kick had sat with her, in George Washington Hospital, for more than an hour. She'd fed her sips of water, massaged her hands with lotion, and talked, endlessly talked, like someone rubbing sticks together, hoping to raise a spark: *Do you remember the ice-cream parlour in Hyannis and the way you'd get an extra scoop sometimes because Tam who owned it liked you best of all of us? Do you remember the way the sand felt under your feet the first day of every summer? Do you remember* . . . stories of wind, of waves, of picnics and baseball, hide-and-seek . . .

And when *do you remember* brought nothing, she tried a

−330−

different tack: 'When you're fully better . . .' *we'll go to my flat together and we'll look at photos of England and our friends there. When you're fully better, we'll have lunch at the 21 Club, just the two of us. When you're fully better you'll see me and talk to me again, and I'll gradually forget what it feels like to sit here and stare at your black-and-blue face, desperate for a flicker of you behind the damage.*

Rosie had said nothing at all, not the whole time. Once she made a noise that was like cattle lowing and a nurse wheeled her away, saying, 'I'll bring her right back. We'll just freshen her up.' That was when Kick understood that her sister couldn't do anything for herself any more. Restless, agile Rosie, with her long stride and swinging arms, her impatience when the things she wanted didn't happen fast enough, now reduced to an ungainly body in a chair. A body that didn't work.

She was, Kick thought now, like the bombed houses on London streets. A wall, a front door left standing, and behind them nothing but emptiness and rubble.

Her second, her last, visit had been more than a month later. Rosie was able to talk a little by then. Her words were slurred and indistinct but Kick could understand her. And that had been worse again. When Rosie could only sit and stare, it had been possible for Kick to believe what she was told, that Rosie was 'recovering' from the operation, and would improve. On that second visit, when Kick understood that Rosie scarcely knew who she was, she knew there would be no improvement. Their lives together had been cut out of her. Rosie didn't remember any of it. Not the bedrooms they had shared, the books they had passed between them, the jokes, the protective camouflage they lent one another: sisters.

As she realised this, Kick had known that she herself would

never again be certain that anything in her childhood had happened in the way she thought it had, now that the person she relied on to corroborate her recollections couldn't.

All over again, as she talked to Joe, she slipped into the thing that was a terrible sin: believing that Rosie would have been better off dead, even though their church told her that to wish such a thing was to scorn the greatest gift of the Almighty. She talked and talked, trying to tell Joe what she had seen, what she had found in Rosie's place.

Joe stayed quiet. He didn't look at her, not once.

When she had finished he still said nothing, and then, at last, in a voice that had none of his usual energy, 'I didn't know.' He made a motion with his hands, as though pushing something away. 'They didn't tell me. Pa said the operation had "some complications", but . . .'

'I guess it did, at that,' Kick said. 'But that was the operation he chose. He said yes to it. He signed the paper saying Rosie was to have it. Maybe if it hadn't had those complications she would have been better, but how much when they took out bits of her that were *her*?' And when Joe said nothing to that, she added, 'I just haven't felt so good about trusting what people say ever since.'

They walked in silence for a while, and Joe looked around the park as though for the first time. He kept his attention on the bare trees, on the emptied pond with its scattering of skeleton leaves, the sparse grass. Anything, she suspected, to avoid looking at her. She didn't mind. She understood. He needed time. She'd had so much more of it than he had. All he'd had was that word 'complications', which meant everything and nothing.

*

Much later that night, Billy walked her home from a disappointing party and told her he was resigning his commission in the army and standing for election as an MP in West Derbyshire.

'It's the family seat,' he said, in what she thought was a dispirited sort of way as they crossed an empty road. 'My father's uncle had it, my grandfather before him, going back two hundred years. Now apparently it's my turn.'

'But is this what you want?'

'Not really. I'd rather continue in the army. We are to be sent overseas soon now at last. But it's what the family have decided.' As he said it, Kick felt a silent excitement at the idea that Billy, after all, might not go to the front. She would never say it, but it was there. 'It seems it's my duty,' he continued.

Around them, London was waking up. It had been another quiet night. Everywhere there were signs of a new complacency. In basements and attics, lights were on, visible as thin streaks around and through ineptly drawn blackout blinds. A baker's van rattled past. Someone had scraped the black paint off its headlights so they cast a steady beam in the purple dawn. The kind of beam that would have been the object of an ARP warden's fury just six months ago when she had first arrived.

'Couldn't Andrew?' she asked, tucking her hand into Billy's arm. It was cold, yes, but mostly she liked to be close to him. A particular kind of quiet came upon her when she was able to touch him. A sense that her heartbeat slowed, steadied, under the silent influence of his. It was how some people were with horses, she thought, somehow imparting calm to them.

'After all, surely you'll have enough to do with being the Duke of Devonshire one day, without being an MP as well,' she continued.

'It doesn't work like that.' He drew her tight into his side.

'Well, maybe you won't win.' She meant to sound consoling, although the idea of not winning was awful to her.

They reached the flat. Kick opened the front door with her key, and stood back. Usually, Billy didn't come upstairs any more. Not since the break. But this time, almost without noticing what he did, he went past her and up the stairs.

'Oh, I'll win,' he said, somewhat bitterly. 'It's a pretty safe seat. Even someone with my poor public-speaking skill can't mess it up.'

'Maybe I can help with that,' she said, following him. 'I'm awfully used to it. Pa used to run his speeches by me, Joe and Jack from the time I was about ten. And the boys.' She was excited by the idea. 'I used to give them all sorts of advice. Why, Jack once told me I was easily as good as his Harvard classmen.'

In the flat she put the kettle on and began measuring out a spoonful of the powdered coffee Edie had taken from the officers' club. She hoped Billy wouldn't notice how much better it was than anything you could buy in the shops. He didn't approve of anything he said was 'unfair'.

'I don't think I'll need that,' he said, with a diffident smile, when she sat on the creaky sofa beside him. She handed him the cup. 'I rather think I just have to stand up and read what's in front of me. And Father will be sure to have that covered. But,' he said, putting the cup down and taking her hand, 'I'd like it if you'd come with me, to the hustings – the meetings? If you'd like to?'

'I would. I really would. You've no idea how sick I am of babying GIs and trying to cheer them up. Even when I try, I can't seem to lose to them at anything. A break would be the best thing. And you wait and see how good I am at speeches.'

'Really, you don't need to do anything except stand at the

back. In fact, it probably would be best if no one knows you're there. The press, I mean.' He shifted a bit, making the sofa creak more. 'Because of . . .'

'My father?'

'Yes, that. And because of . . .'

'Being Catholic?'

'Yes.'

Kick sighed and took her hand back. 'Don't worry, I won't give myself away,' she promised wearily. It was as if she had a disfigurement that everyone said didn't matter yet couldn't stop talking about. It had begun to irritate her. 'Maybe you'd rather I didn't come at all?' she asked snappily.

'No. I would very much like to know you're there.'

'What will your parents say?'

'I've already told them I intended to ask you. They think it a good idea. Well, Mother does. Father will, as long as I can promise him you'll be discreet.' Kick wished she could say, *To hell with all that. I'll only come if I can be myself.* But she didn't. She knew how it would play – if she did, in a few days, Billy would ring her up and stutter his way to saying perhaps it was better if she didn't come after all.

And she wanted to go with him. More than anything. So she said again, 'I'll be so discreet that not even you will know I'm there.'

'I'll know,' he said. 'I'll want to know.' He took her hand again, pressed it gratefully.

'Does that sound like a fellow who's broken up with you?' she asked Sissy and Edie. Billy was long gone, and she had slept for a few hours. They were having a late breakfast as none of them was on the morning shift. She had told them what Billy had said, how he had seemed while he said it. 'Does it?' she asked again.

'It doesn't,' Sissy said stoutly. 'It sounds like a fellow who simply can't break off with you.'

'But it also doesn't sound like a fellow who's exactly asking you out again,' Edie said drily. 'All that about standing at the back and not being seen?'

'If anyone but Billy had said it . . .' Kick muttered. 'I'm getting real tired of being the poor relation at everything.'

'Hardly poor,' Sissy said.

'OK, maybe not poor, but the one who did something scandalous – like, they have to be invited, but everyone whispers about them.' Kick spoke crossly.

'I think it's romantic that Billy wants you to be there but for no one else to know,' Sissy said. 'It's like a secret tryst.'

'And you know all about secret trysts, of course,' Edie said.

'The only reason I don't tell more is because I know you won't approve,' Sissy said. 'Peter's an artist, and he's talented but he hasn't any money, or any prospect of any. And not even like me when I say I don't have any money, because I told him about Ballycorry, how full of holes and cracks and damp it is, and instead of being sympathetic, all he could talk about was that it has, I don't know, thirty rooms or something. He said his house, where he grew up, had five rooms and one was a pantry too small to fit more than a mop and a pail.'

'Why should you think we'd care that he hasn't any money?' Edie asked.

'Well, it's the sort of thing people do care about, isn't it?' Sissy asked, looking from one to the other.

'*Some* people,' Edie said. 'But not us. At least, not me.'

'Not me either,' Kick said.

'Says the girl who was going to marry a duke with a castle in Ireland, one in Scotland, one in Derbyshire and one in Sussex,' said Edie, but kindly.

'Not "a duke", *Billy*,' Kick said. 'And, anyway, now I'm not. For all that he still telephones and takes me out, one of these days even he will realise that he's better not seeing me, and all that will stop,' she said sadly. 'I'm just glad he hasn't yet. He talks a lot about me being free to marry someone else, quite as though he never will, but of course he will. Joe's right. It's only a matter of time.' She hoped Sissy or Edie would contradict her, insist that Billy would never marry anyone. But they didn't.

And then Edie said, 'It's kind of his duty, isn't it? I mean, not marrying anyone and not having a son to pass the title to is almost as bad as marrying a Catholic, isn't it?'

'Maybe,' Kick said. She felt a surge of what at first she thought was misery. Until it itched at her in a different way and she saw that it was something else: anger. She hadn't recognised it because it wasn't familiar from the landscape she had grown up with. 'Don't get mad, get better,' she had always been told. Or 'Don't get mad, get ahead.' Time was not to be wasted on anger. Instead it was base metal to be spun into winning gold. But she began to see it wasn't completely unfamiliar either. She had felt like this when her mother had refused to let Rosie go to the party, and far more in the room with Rosie during her second and final visit. 'Anyway, since when are you such an expert on the duties of hereditary peers?' she snapped. Then apologised. After all, it wasn't Edie who had made her feel like something picked up in a shop, turned over, examined, then put down again.

Chapter Thirty-Seven

Brigid

Was she mad? Brigid wondered, as the slow train clacked its way towards east Hertfordshire and Little Hadham. She didn't even know exactly what she was doing. Answering a distress call, yes, but from whom? Her memories of Fritzi were so faint. Mostly, he was just a spidery hand on pale blue writing paper. He was the answer to all the questions she asked herself by writing them down and putting them into an envelope directed to George Mansfield: *Why do you think Honor never comes home? What must I do about Will? What does it mean that Maureen is so cruel to Caroline? How will Kick protect herself if Billy stays strong and refuses to marry her?*

Chips had been furious that she insisted on going, increasingly so as she had calmly withstood his efforts to change her mind. While she gathered rolls of bandages, compresses, disinfectant creams, and packed only the fewest cardigans and skirts, he had repeatedly tried to talk her out of it.

'He may be all alone in that house, without even female servants,' he had said. 'It isn't suitable.'

'No one cares about that sort of thing any more,' she had replied.

'They care more than you imagine.'

But Brigid had continued packing, and then, at the end, he had insisted on sparing her some of his petrol ration and driving with her to the train. 'I wish you wouldn't,' he said again in his green Rolls-Royce. 'There is no sense in it. Fritzi belongs to the past. There is no place for German princes now, not in Germany or anywhere else.'

'He is not his family,' Brigid said. 'Just because there is no place for German princes doesn't mean there is no place for Fritzi. He's a person, you know. And he's been farming valiantly, contributing food to the war effort, and has hurt himself. Anyone would go and help.'

'*Anyone* wouldn't,' Chips said. '*You* would.' He pressed her gloved hand with his. 'It makes me sad, you know.'

'What does?'

'Thinking of him.'

That, Brigid thought, would explain why he was so resistant to her going. It made *him* sad. Her lips twitched towards a rueful smile, but she stopped herself.

'I remember how very happy we all were, that last summer.'

By *that last summer* he meant 1938. They all did. Before Chamberlain and his announcement: *You can imagine what a bitter blow it is to me that all my long struggle to win peace has failed*, the prime minister had said that September day. Did men only ever consider themselves? she wondered briefly.

'How very happy,' he repeated. 'Only we didn't know it.'

'I think we did know it,' she said. 'Most of us, anyway. Only we didn't know that we knew it.'

'How wise you are.' And at the station he had bought her a copy of the *Tatler* and two buns in a brown-paper bag. 'For your journey. Now don't stay away too long, promise me?'

That was when she realised that loneliness, as much as anything, had driven his opposition. 'Ask Caroline to come back,' she had said. 'I don't like to think of her mouldering at Clandeboye. She should be at lessons.' *And away from Maureen,* but she didn't say it.

An official at the station carried her case and went to ask at the office for Little Hadham. There was no taxi, she was told, not any more, but she might be able to get a lift with someone going that way if she waited for the local train, due in ten minutes. So she sat in the first-class waiting room and ate one of the buns, and when the local train arrived, a Mrs Hardy, the vicar's wife, said of course she could give her a lift.

The lift turned out to be in a trap drawn by a solid chestnut pony. 'He was almost put out to pasture,' Mrs Hardy said fondly, 'until war gave him back his job.' Brigid was careful to ask only for George Mansfield, and to let it be known that she was 'family'.

The vicar's wife left her outside a pair of iron gates too rusted to be worth melting down, set in a wall of neat red bricks. Brigid walked the last quarter-mile or so up to the house, carrying her case, along a track that was heavily pitted and ran straight so that the house was in front of her the whole way: red brick, like the wall, with a pitched roof of russet slate. She wondered if anyone was watching her arrival.

She didn't even know how Fritzi was, and the thought caused

her stomach to lurch in fear. In response to the telegram she had dispatched, saying, 'ARRIVING SOONEST STOP WITHIN THE WEEK,' she had heard nothing. Perhaps he was too ill, in too much pain, to write, she thought anxiously. After Will, she could hardly bear it.

She rang the bell and heard it sound shrill within. She was about to ring again when the door was opened by a girl in a pair of brown overalls, hair tied back in a handkerchief. 'Sorry. No one uses the front door. We're all in the kitchen.'

Who were *we all*? Brigid wondered.

'Are you . . .?' The girl looked at her case.

'I'm looking for George,' Brigid said, stumbling a little over 'George' in case it was wrong; terrified lest the girl stare at her and say *'oh I'm so sorry . . .'* She wanted to ask how he was, but couldn't find the words.

'He's somewhere. Come to the kitchen.' That must mean something, Brigid thought; the casualness with which the girl spoke. It must mean he was all right.

So Brigid followed her, through a pleasant but untidy house that obviously had more than one person living in it. Overcoats and wellington boots, though not as hysterically numerous as at Clandeboye, told her that. The kitchen was at the back, past a large drawing room. As they went by the half-open door, Brigid saw it had at least three folding beds, maybe more, made up with sheets and blankets, a wooden chair beside the head of each. On the chairs were piles of clothes, some neatly folded, others bundled untidily.

'Four of us are in there,' the girl said, 'the rest upstairs.'

In the kitchen, the back door stood open to a cobbled court-yard. A smell of manure from outside mingled with the cloud of cigarette smoke around the table. Five girls, at least three smoking, a brown glazed teapot bigger than any Brigid had ever seen, mugs and a plate of rough-looking biscuits.

'Are you joining us?' the girl who had opened the door asked.

'May I?' She realised Fritzi had never told her, in all his letters, that an army of girls was living on the farm with him. She supposed she should have known. How else did work get done these days?

'Yes, of course. Here.' The girl poured tea into a mug and handed it to Brigid. One of the other girls pulled a chair forward and shunted up so there was space. They talked about clearing fields and digging in compost, good-natured complaining at how hard it was. They showed each other calloused palms and broken, dirty nails.

'Try disinfectant and carbolic soap,' Brigid said, showing them her own hands, red and rough and cracked.

'Nurse?' one of the girls asked, passing her a packet of cigarettes.

'Auxiliary,' Brigid said, taking a cigarette and lighting it. Still she resisted the urge to ask how he was. Be patient, she told herself.

That was how Fritzi found her when he came into the kitchen half an hour later with a tin pail of vegetable peelings in one hand, the other strapped across his chest in a dirty bandage.

'Lady Brigid,' he exclaimed.

The girls looked at her with sudden suspicion. 'You might have said,' one muttered.

'Brigid,' she said firmly. 'Nurse Brigid.' Then, 'Fr— George!' She stood up. Fritzi – George – set the pail on the table and came towards her. He wore the same colour overalls as the girls, with a checked shirt underneath. His hair was long, almost to his ears, and unbrushed. At first glance, he was unrecognisable as the stiff, polished young prince she had first met five years ago, the boy she and Kick had called King Midas's son.

She wondered if he would embrace her. He didn't. The hand he held out to shake hers, the one that had held the pail, was dirty, the nails ragged. There were calluses on his palm – she could feel them when she put her hand into his. So unlike the slender, soft hands of Prince Friedrich. The bandaged arm was in a rough sling made from a belt.

But then she looked again and the perfectly straight nose, the moulded mouth and even features were the same as they had been. But his complexion was rugged, even weather-beaten, with lines about his eyes and a new set to his mouth. He looked older – of course he did – but as if the five years that had passed were nothing like the twenty-seven that had gone before them.

'You're here,' he said now. 'You're really here.'

'I am,' she agreed. Relief made her want to laugh aloud. 'Just arrived.' She gestured to her case on the floor beside her. Around them, the girls were getting up from the table, rinsing mugs and tidying away plates. One retied the kerchief holding back her hair. They shrugged on overcoats and pulled on mucky welling-tons from a line standing beyond the back door.

'Back to work,' the one tying her kerchief said.

'I hope that isn't for compost, George,' the girl who had let Brigid in called, as she moved the pail to the floor. 'It looks like it would make good soup.'

'Not if George makes it,' another girl interjected, and they all laughed. Brigid liked the way they spoke to him. It suggested he was kind to them.

'You'll have a cup of tea with me?' he said to her, as the kitchen emptied.

'Of course.' She sat down again and watched as he filled a

kettle, one-handed, and put it on the hob. She resisted the urge to jump up and help him. 'You didn't answer my telegram, so I just came. I was worried you were unable to.'

'I'm sorry,' he said, sitting down opposite her. 'I was so over-joyed when your telegram came that when I realised the injury wasn't so very serious I put off telling you. Because I wanted so much for you to come.' His English was as carefully faultless as ever. She wondered how anyone could possibly believe he was George Mansfield.

'So what happened?'

'A tractor got away from me,' he said ruefully. 'The load was unbalanced and I overturned it.'

'May I look?' she asked.

'Nurse Brigid,' he said with a smile. 'You may.'

'Not here,' she said, looking around the kitchen. 'Where?'

He showed her to a small library at the front of the house with a lot of books that looked like no one read them, and a heavy square desk. This she pulled closer to the window where the light was better, and asked him to sit. She unbuckled the sling and untied the dirty bandage, relieved to see that the underneath layer of dressing was cleaner. He winced as she removed the gauze, revealing a quantity of vivid blue-and-black bruising around his upper arm and shoulder, and a deep cut that ran down the arm and had been stitched.

'Who?' she asked.

'The local doctor. But he hasn't been back. There are too many calls on his time. He told me to change the dressing and keep it clean. But it's difficult, working with only one hand. The wrong one.'

'It's not as clean as it should be,' Brigid said, pointing to the angry edges of the wound that were red and inflamed. 'This is very close to becoming infected.' Her throat closed on the word. 'And once that happens, with a gash this size, it's very hard to manage. We must halt this immediately.'

'How much you know,' he said.

'It's my job,' she said. 'That's why I'm here. Because I know about nursing.'

'Is that why you're here?' he asked, now looking at her face rather than at his arm.

His question caught her off-guard. Of course she had known they would have to have this conversation – strange and awkward as it must surely be – but she hadn't expected it so soon. 'Let me clean this,' she said, rather than answer him. 'Then we can go for a walk.' Easier to speak when in motion, some-where outdoors. He was too close to her, or she too close to him, to speak now. It was too sudden, the rush from the odd, almost impersonal intimacy of their letters, to this. She needed time to catch up.

'Stay here.' She fetched boiled water from the kitchen, and her case, taking out the things she had brought. She bathed the cut thoroughly, being especially careful at all the little stitches even though she felt him catch his breath at the pain, then re-dressed it in clean bandages. 'We need to do that twice a day for the next few days until we get the infection under control.'

'Yes, Nurse,' he said.

Outside, he walked her through the walled garden behind the kitchen and out to the fields beyond. The girls Brigid had met in the kitchen were dotted about the bare ground now, often in pairs, spreading manure, she thought, from the smell. Well, it was that time of year.

The sky was grey and flat and the earth was brown and flat, and she felt as if she was walking through a painting. She stretched out her arms and took a deep breath. With it she delighted at being once more in the country, away from London and its filthy air, filthy piles of rubble, filthy air-raid sirens. The constant noise, motion, rumble of the city had begun to make her sick, like being on a boat for too long.

'Thank you for coming,' he said.

'Chips didn't want me to.'

'No, I suppose he didn't. I asked him for help. At the start. When I was in the camp on the Isle of Man. I thought he could explain that I was a friend, not an enemy, but he told me he couldn't. At first, I was very angry, but I learned to be thankful.'

'Thankful? How?'

'I was angry the authorities wouldn't take my word for it. That they disbelieved me. Or, rather, didn't fully believe me. I wanted Chips to show them I had powerful, important friends who would speak for me. And when he wouldn't, when no one would, I felt humiliated.' He smiled ruefully. 'I had felt humiliation before – when my father made us stand and shout *Heil Hitler* with those thugs who meant it. But this was different. This was the humiliation of an ordinary man. That was hard.'

'I'm sure,' Brigid said, remembering how he used to talk to her about his grandfather, the Kaiser, and the heavy expectation he felt because of him.

'But those months on the Isle of Man, and later in Canada, showed me I wasn't so very different from any of the others in there,' he continued. 'Germans, Italians, dissidents, Communists, even some Jewish refugees from Germany ended up there, held alongside the devoted Nazis.' He curled his lip in disgust. 'And I saw that for most of them there was no more reason to be there than there was for me. For those Jewish refugees, far less reason. We were all just men, like other men, and if we were to do better than simply survive, we needed to think of each other and not just of ourselves.'

'Were the conditions so very terrible?'

'Not for anyone who has been to an English boarding school,' he said, with a laugh. 'Pretty soon I was used to the regime, and began to find ways to make all our lives a little easier. That's why I was elected camp leader.'

'Both times,' she said. 'On the Isle of Man and in Canada.'

'You remember?' he said.

'I do. I thought I'd never known you seem so proud of anything.'

'I was proud,' he admitted. 'Maybe prouder of that than I ever had been of my family's titles.'

After they had walked about the fields, he explained what the farm grew, and how much. Brigid, brought up listening to her father talk about the herd at Elvedon, had plenty of questions that she could see surprised him by their knowledge. She liked the feeling of having such topics as yield and pest resistance to discuss with him.

As it grew dark, he walked with her to the house. 'How long will you stay?' he asked, as they reached the back door, left open despite the chill of the day.

'I don't know. A few days. Until that cut is better, anyway.'

'I hope it will be a long time. Perhaps I will rub earth into the cut, to make sure it doesn't heal.' He took off his boots, lined them up neatly at the door. One of his socks was darned, a different blue from the original wool.

'Don't joke,' the words erupted from her. 'You've no idea how awful it is to see an infection take hold so that it cannot be contained.'

'I'm sorry,' he said. 'Will?' When she said nothing, 'Of course

Will. I made a clumsy joke before I thought . . . And I do know,'
he said. 'I saw it many times in the camps.' He pulled up a chair
for her to sit on while she undid her shoes. But she stayed
standing.

'Did you ever think we would have such a conversation, you
and I? Do you remember what we talked about before? Tennis?
Dancing?'

'We did. But we talked about other things too,' he reminded
her. 'About our parents and what they wanted for us. And from
us. And what we ourselves wanted.'

'I suppose we did.' But it was too late. She was too tired to
continue that conversation. 'Is there room for me?' she asked.
'I hadn't realised you would have so much company.'

'The land girls?' He laughed. 'They've been a cheerful addition.
At first it was just me and two old men. Sometimes I think the
girls work harder than all of us.' He didn't think that, she could
tell, just liked saying it. It was what men said these days: 'She
can strip an engine faster than I can'; 'She's handier behind the
wheel of a truck than I am.' They didn't mean it: it was something new and amusing to say. What would happen after the
war? she wondered. Would they still be so happy to live
surrounded by these newly able women?

That evening, after a noisy dinner in the kitchen with the girls,
Brigid and Fritzi went back to the library. He had lit a fire there
and it was much warmer than anywhere else in the house. The
kitchen door seemed never to be closed, with people coming in
and out constantly. As well as the girls, there were the two
elderly men, taciturn, there for food, not chat, and a number of
dogs that came and went.

He lit a cigarette and poured brandy for them. Brigid took

hers even though she had never drunk it before. It felt like the right thing to do. The grown-up thing. Suddenly she realised what she had been feeling all day – just that: grown-up. Like an adult. Someone in charge of themselves, with things to do and decisions to make that were hers alone. Not subject to the impressions of her mother, the fears of her father, the desires of Chips or Honor, worry about Will, not even the giddy considerations of her friends. Just hers. And not idle decisions, such as which invitation or which coat, serious ones that would play out into real lives.

She revelled in it. For the first time she felt like a complete version of herself. As though all the bits of her had been gathered tidily at last into one place, beside this man. It was a wonderful feeling, after being scattered, distracted, never fully whole for so long. She stretched her legs before the fire. She was still wearing the jersey and skirt she had travelled in, and thought how much she would like a bath.

As though he read her mind, Fritzi said, 'The best time for hot water is late at night. The girls go to bed early – they get up at dawn – so you should be able to have a bath in a bit.'

'Thank you . . . It's easier to call you George than I expected it would be. It rather suits you. Does no one know who you are?'

'They don't. They could, it's not exactly the stuff of the Official Secrets Act, but who is interested? No one. For now, certainly, my title is of no use to me or anyone. I am happy to exchange it for simple George Mansfield, farmer.'

'Do you remember how you were certain you would be dragged into some kind of plot against Hitler?'

'I do. I was terrified of it,' he admitted. 'Now, I rather wish I had been.'

'You do?'

'Yes. A plot that succeeded. Imagine if all this had been avoided.' They were silent then, imagining. But Brigid couldn't.

He reached out his good hand. She let him take hers and squeeze it. On the small mahogany table beside him, his glass of brandy poured a winking golden warmth into the room.

'You know,' she said, 'all those letters from Canada, you never wrote the slightest thing to make me feel you were writing to *me*. That you remembered me. Your letters could have been to any girl in the world – a sister, a cousin, anyone.'

'All our letters were read, and I was afraid if I wrote anything personal – about my family – they wouldn't get to you. But, also, that was the everyday existence and it was all I could bear to think of. I knew if I began remembering the smell of English grass on an English summer evening, you in a white evening dress, tennis and croquet, I would not be able to bear the cold, the drudgery, the ugliness of it all.

'I wrote to you in the same way that men navigate by the North Star,' he continued, drawing closer. 'Because it is constant, a fixed point to move by and find oneself. If I hadn't had that, I think I would have gone mad. And even though I never knew if my letters would reach you – I think many did not – it was a way to feel a thread, still, with that other life, in that other part of the world.

'When I got out, and came to England, to this farm, and wrote to you from here, at least I knew my letters would arrive. Knowing there were days, not weeks, between the writing and you reading, was like the coming of spring.'

He asked her more about Will, and listened silently as she told him everything, all of it, and then, as though he knew she had said enough, he asked about Honor, Kick and Sissy.

In the days that followed, Brigid found herself sleeping longer and better than she had in years, as she told Fritzi when she had cleaned and dressed the cut on his arm one morning. She saw with relief that it showed signs of healing. 'No one sleeps in London any more.' It was true. A new giddiness animated the quiet nights. To sleep seemed ungrateful, careless of the freedoms that were theirs, for the chance that saw them still alive when so many were dead or hurt.

Here, there was nothing like that. Just a too-soft feather bed, a household that retired by nine to rise at six, and outside, acres of silent fields and dark tranquil sky.

'You look better than you did when you arrived,' he said cautiously, no doubt wary of giving offence.

'So do you!' she retorted, with a laugh. 'A lot better. You're no longer in danger of losing an arm.' They winced as she said it. 'As long as you keep the cut clean, it will heal perfectly . . . I suppose I must think about going.' The idea of London filled her with dread she didn't fully understand.

'If you must,' he said. 'But I wish you would not.'

'I wish that too.'

'When it's over, will you marry me?' he asked, in such a way that she knew he had planned it. Maybe from the very moment she arrived. There was no hesitation in his voice. He didn't stumble over the words or show any nerves. *Will you marry me?* It might as easily have been *Will you walk with me? Will you have another cup of tea?*

'Why when it's over?'

'I need to know what happens. Remember, I am still German, even if I am English too. Until this war is fought, and finished, I cannot see my future or make plans.'

And even though she wondered if he really knew her, could

see her – actually *her* – or just the figure he had spoken of, who had guided him in his years in the camps, someone ideal and fixed and made of light, she said yes.

Perhaps he was in love with the person he had created from scraps of memory in the years when they were apart and he was far from any comfort or friendship, someone made up of things half remembered and half imagined. Perhaps she, too, felt close to an idealised creation of her own mind and not an actual person. But still she said yes.

It was the feeling of quiet she had, standing with him, the further layers of the quiet that lay around them, in the house and in the gardens and fields. It was all the letters they had written and the belief that, in this stiff and somewhat awkward man, she could detect the warm interest and wise counsel of those letters. It was also that he knew about Will and understood the sharp twist of failure she felt. Mostly, it was in the way he didn't pretend not to need her.

Chapter Thirty-Eight

Maureen

Spring came so late to Clandeboye that some years it was like the last guest to dinner, hustled straight in to table under cover of the first course. Which meant the early part of the year was so very dreary, Maureen thought looking out the windows at long grey fields giving way to long bare woods, under a flat grey sky. Duff was gone, to London, promising only that he would be back when he could.

'Don't come down,' he had said to her the night before. 'I leave at dawn and it's far too early for you.' But she had woken with the first grey light and decided to get up and wave him off. Hers was the last face he would see, she thought with a wave of sentimentality, standing on the steps with the vast bulk of Clandeboye behind her. It was an image she found pleasantly touching.

Except that when she got down, Caroline was there. Still in

her plaid wool dressing gown, the girl rushed about, fetching last things she thought her father might need. Did he have a newspaper? Would he like a flask of tea? So Maureen sat at the breakfast table and tried not to snap 'why would he want a flask when he can have tea on the train?'

'Be good to your little sister and brother,' Duff said to Caroline as he embraced her at the door. 'Be sure and mind them.' He pinched her chin gently.

Caroline promised she would, and Maureen had felt a sharp pang that it was his daughter he said this to, not his wife, their mother. 'Don't worry about the children,' she said, loudly. 'They will be perfectly all right.' And she stared defiantly as both he and her daughter turned to look at her, surprise carefully hidden in Duff's face, blazing impudently from Caroline's.

After he had gone, Caroline went to the stables. Maureen took another look at the day, and went back to bed. What else was there to do?

'No one will come and stay,' she complained to Chips that evening on the telephone. 'I have invited simply everyone, even people I barely like, and they all say they cannot travel or are too busy. Since Brigid left in such a tearing hurry, and now that Duff has gone back to the House, it's been deathly dull. Why don't you visit?'

'You know I can't.' He spoke with careful regret that didn't fool Maureen for an instant. Chips hated staying at Clandeboye; 'all that way, and for what?' she'd heard him say once to Honor. 'If one doesn't shoot, or hunt, or much care for the killing of wildlife in any of the half-dozen ways your family so enjoy, there isn't a single thing to do. Except marvel at the gruesome curios collected by Duff's grandfather, and wonder which bit of roof might fall in next.'

'All these young people to look out for,' he said now.

'I'm not sure what you think they need from you,' she said sharply.

'More than you might expect,' he said cosily. 'There's Brigid off in Hertfordshire—'

'Isn't she a dark horse. Positively sneaky, the way she kept all that so hidden. *An old school friend* . . . Isn't that what she said? And all the while letters simply pouring into Belgrave Square, under your nose . . .'

'I know you want me to feel frightful about it,' Chips said, 'but I don't. What was one meant to do? Censor her letters? There's quite enough of that going on already. No, I feel entirely blameless in this. And, after all . . .'

'After all, what?'

'Well, it is *Fritzi*. Not just any old somebody; some farm boy GI or handsome cad in uniform. Fritzi may be a little awkward at this time, but after all, we know him. And he is—'

'The Kaiser's grandson. Yes, Chips, I do remember.'

'Exactly. And then dear Kick . . .'

'What about dear Kick?' Maureen toyed with the telephone cord, curling it around and around her finger.

'Suddenly it rather looks as though she and Billy will make a go of it after all. Despite all your marvellous efforts at my dinner party.' He spoke with malicious enjoyment. She pulled the cord tight so the tip of her finger went white.

'I thought that was done with?'

'I think everyone did. Thought and hoped. But they do seem very determined, underneath all that guff about respecting their families' wishes and so on. They are like two little magnets, pulled back together again and again. It's rather sweet.'

'Don't be sentimental, Chips. It doesn't suit you.' But she

was surprised by what he said. She hadn't imagined Kick – energetic and hearty, yes, but also constrained by a piousness that had always annoyed Maureen – had that much rebellion in her. She had always seemed quite childishly under the sway of her mother – Maureen remembered Rose Kennedy with no affection but some respect – and not at all like someone who would dare, if she spoke the truth and wasn't exaggerating in that vulgar way of Catholics, risk her immortal soul. Almost, Maureen blushed at the absurd dramatics of such a notion. But after all, it was what Kick always said: that to marry without the blessing of her Church would be to jeopardise her place in Heaven.

Heaven wasn't anywhere Maureen thought much about. In fact, she had always been thankful for her own indifference to anything that wasn't here, now, in front of her; grateful for the way this allowed her stretch and reach openly for what she wanted. But Kick, well, she talked about her soul as though it were an extra arm or leg, a thing to be seen and considered. It made her, Maureen thought, fundamentally dull, despite the energy and high spirits.

So how was it that she and Brigid both had suddenly found steel where Maureen had till now seen only obedience and weakness?

'Those girls seem to be growing up jolly fast,' she said. 'It's really quite unbecoming.' It wasn't at all what she meant, and she suspected Chips knew it from the tactful way he changed the subject.

'How's Caroline?' he asked.

'Fine. How should she be?'

'If you're going to be so very spikey, Maureen, I'll tell Andrews to say I'm not at home next time you telephone.'

'Why does everyone ask me how Caroline is?' she retorted.

'Because you are her mother, Maureen,' Chips said patiently. 'It's entirely natural and not intended to tease.' She wondered was that true. Possibly. Then, 'How's the master plan coming along?' Chips continued. She heard the creak of leather as he settled himself more comfortably in his seat. She could picture him in that great green chair in the library at Belgrave Square. How she missed London, she thought, looking at the rain slide down the bumpy glass in the windows. Beyond them, the garden huddled in sodden defeat. 'Operation Keep Duff Home?'

'Rather well I think,' she said, lighting a cigarette. 'He hasn't mentioned anything about joining up for quite some time now. I think we've put paid to that notion.' She spoke with satisfaction, exhaling smoke in a long breath.

'Are you sure you don't think that because you want it to be true? He is most frightfully stubborn. And never more than when it comes to matters of Duty and Empire. You know how he gets.' Maureen did indeed know. Of all the things she doubted in her husband – his ability to live in harmony with her, to refrain from cruel words when they were angry or spiteful with one another – two things she never questioned. His love for her, and his love for his country.

'If he was still thinking of it, he would have said,' she insisted, knowing even before Chips spoke what he was going to say. Sure enough:

'I wonder if that isn't exactly what he wouldn't do . . .' he mused.

'I'd better get on,' she said sharply, ignoring Chips's protests. She knew he had settled in for a long and cosy chat, but she found she couldn't bear his dissections and speculations just then. Because what if he was right? What if Duff's silence on the subject was simply the stubborn belief that, having announced his intention, he need now only execute it.

She got up in a hurry, crushing her cigarette out on a saucer that lay beside the telephone. She must go back to London, she decided. He couldn't do anything drastic under her very nose, could he?

Chapter Thirty-Nine

Kick

Billy's campaign was to last three weeks, and Kick took leave from the officers' club for the first few days. 'I can cheer you off to a good start,' she told him.

He drove her to Chatsworth – although she had been to Compton Place with him, several times now, this was the first time she had been back to the family's Derbyshire estate since returning to England – and they arrived late in the afternoon on a day in February. The tide of day had turned so that, although the sky was still a silvery blue, the outlines of trees and bushes were etched in black. They swept through the fanciful wrought-iron gates. 'How come you were able to keep them, when every iron post and railing in the country seems to have been gathered by the salvage campaigns?' she asked idly.

'Works of national importance,' Billy said, somewhat stiffly.

'Made in 1690. I wouldn't mention them to Father. There have already been questions from locals. And if we're asked to have them collected, and melted down, of course we will. Only, so far, we have been asked by the heritage chaps *not* to.' He was wearing a tweed suit and Kick thought how strange it was to see him out of uniform, no longer a soldier.

'I didn't mean that,' Kick said hastily, 'but you bet I won't mention them.'

It was a short drive from the gates to the front door, and she watched the bulk of the vast house, built of honey-coloured stone, rising before them. The sun was setting and the front was lit by a final wash of gold that made it blaze against its surroundings.

The last few times she had been here before the war, it had been with the thought at the back of her mind – shoved away, but not buried, impossible to bury – that she might one day enter this magnificence as mistress rather than guest. The idea had been, at first, an amusing impossibility. But gradually, as she and Billy had become closer, it had settled, and grown almost comfortable. Once, she had even found herself thinking she might someday move a particularly smug-looking marble bust of Napoleon from the library, before sternly bidding herself stop – *For even if I do marry Billy and come here as duchess one day, the last thing he'll ever tolerate is me moving things around,* she had reminded herself.

But now she came to the house again as a guest. A friend. Someone who might visit over the years but would never belong. The thought made her feel tired, and again the flicker of anger, which she held back. It wasn't Billy's fault, she told herself.

She wanted to say something of what she was feeling to Billy, and started, 'I always did think this the most beautiful house in England when I came here before the war.'

'You'll hardly recognise it,' he said, steering carefully along the wet road. 'It's full of wounded soldiers, convalescing.'

'Do you mind seeing them there?' She meant did he mind these living, breathing, damaged reminders of the fate that might still be his, or Andrew's, or any of theirs. But that wasn't what he answered.

'Not in the slightest. The place is far too big. If we can't melt down the gates, the least we can do is provide a place for men injured in battle to regain their strength.'

'But do you mind seeing them; seeing what can happen?'

'I never let myself think of them like that. They are they and I am I. And perhaps, by the time this is all over, any of us would be jolly glad to be the chap missing a few fingers, or with a bit of shot in his leg.' It was macabre, even for Billy, who mostly held emotion a joke's length away.

'Don't say that!'

'Well, it's true. They are the lucky ones, many of them.' And for once, he was serious.

They drove past the South Front entrance that Kick knew, and round to the side, where Billy stopped beside a smaller door. 'Easier to come this way now,' he said. 'Mother and Father have moved into new rooms. It's not just soldiers, there are nurses, orderlies, extra kitchen staff, a regular chorus line in the main house. So the family have retreated to smaller apartments. I rather like them, I must say.'

Billy's family welcomed her with varying degrees of enthusiasm. The duchess embraced her warmly and told her she was 'too thin. You must be tired. I suppose everyone is by now.'

Billy's sister, Lady Elizabeth, greeted her with 'Good, you can help me canvass. We go door-to-door and it's the most frightful bore, but we'll get on much faster with two of us.'

The duke shook her hand and asked politely after her work at the officers' club, but he didn't say he was pleased to see her. At dinner, when Lady Elizabeth again brought up her plan for Kick to canvass with her, he said sharply, 'But she mustn't go as herself. You understand, I'm sure,' he said, turning to Kick. 'If the press get wind of you it'll bring no good to Billy's campaign.'

'I won't say a word,' she promised, and tried to keep her voice light. 'And if I do, I'll say it in my best English accent.' She put on the voice she used to affect for her friends in America, her impression of the English girls she knew. Everyone at the table laughed and she smiled back, as though their laughter was what she had intended.

'You sound like one of the girls from the village,' Lady Elizabeth said. 'In fact, I rather think that's what we'll say you are. Billy's opponent is the most frightful socialist, Charles White. It'll be good for the campaign to show that the village supports Billy.'

'She'll need a name,' Billy said. 'A new identity.'

'Rosemary Tonks,' Lady Elizabeth said. 'That's a combination of my old doll, Tonks, and Rosemary, my favourite of the nursery-maids.' They all nodded enthusiastically, and Kick, who couldn't think how to explain why she couldn't bear to be Rosemary, simply nodded with them.

'You won't wear your nicest things, will you?' the duchess said then.

'I will wear only my oldest and most darned,' she said dully. She had been wrong to come, she felt. How had she believed she could come here simply as a friend, an acquaintance? One to be kept firmly and politely in the place of acquaintances? To be told what to do, who to be? She could leave early, go back to London. But she had come for Billy, she reminded herself. To cheer him on.

It didn't take her long to see that Billy was a terrible speaker. You couldn't have grown up with Joe and Jack, even Eunice, and not see that. He was hesitant and diffident, as though he observed and doubted the words even as they came out of his mouth. Only when he talked about his years in the army did he sound as though he had any faith in himself. And it didn't take any of them long to see that his opponent, the 'frightful' Charles White, was more formidable and aggressive than anyone had expected.

'Perhaps not such a safe seat after all,' Billy muttered to her, after the first meeting. He had been heckled by the large crowd from the very start.

'Why aren't you at the front?' was the first shout, barely minutes after Billy had introduced himself.

'I've been in the army five years and have seen action overseas, including at Dunkirk,' Billy responded politely. Kick could see how much it cost him to mention what he still considered an ignoble defeat. He began to lay out his plans and promises, including projects for the 'relief of the working poor'.

'What do you know about being poor?' a lady in the front row asked loudly.

'Or working,' the man beside her added, to general hilarity.

It seemed not to matter what Billy said – the crowd was determined to mock him. 'Why isn't the park at Chatsworth ploughed up and planted?' was one question, but when Billy tried to explain that it was – the gardeners had kept some of the formal gardens and cleverly positioned rows of vegetables behind them – no one listened.

Kick burned with indignation for him. On all her previous visits to Chatsworth, she had believed that those living in the hamlets and villages round about the estate loved the family and accepted them as vital parts of local life. Everything Billy's parents had ever said about their lives there suggested they were firmly knotted into every bit of the place: summer fetes and the annual garden party, hunting, patronage of the local school and hospital, endless visiting of the sick, new mothers, tenant farmers . . . But that wasn't the tale told by the heckling.

When Billy had finished speaking, he sat down to a thin smattering of applause. Kick clapped till her hands were sore, and Lady Elizabeth hissed, 'I say, steady on.' Then Charles White got up, and Kick saw that here was a formidable opponent. Straight away he attacked the very idea of Billy standing for election. 'A young man' – emphasising 'young' as though it were something shameful – 'with no experience, who expects to take a place in the House of Commons because he thinks it belongs to him. Whatever will he do there? Play parlour games?'

The cheers, when he went to sit down, were thunderous.

Back at Chatsworth that evening, Kick listened as Billy gave his father, who hadn't been there, a brutally honest account of the meeting. He spared himself nothing, and many times Kick wanted to jump in and try to tell it differently. But she knew Billy would hate that.

She waited for the duke to swing into action, as her father would have done. To strategise and scheme, first asking an opinion of them all, then laying plans for victory. She had her ideas ready, but the duke didn't ask. He didn't ask anyone. Just listened to Billy and said, 'Yes, I see.'

'But how can you bear it?' she asked later, when the family

had gone to bed and it was just her and Billy by the fire in a small sitting room Kick had never seen before. Instead of answering, he went to poke the fire, which smoked. He handed her a brandy glass and sat down.

'It'll get a lot worse,' he said, with a very Billy-like grin, wry and patient and amused not only at the thing but at everything else around it.

'That man, White, seemed to hate the Cavendishes like poison.'

'It isn't personal,' Billy said. 'He knows exactly what people want to hear, and he gives it to them.'

'And what do they want to hear?'

'That families like ours, places like this,' he waved an arm, 'are finished. That they belong to the old ways and after the war there will be a new way. I'm not sure anyone is able to keep fighting without that belief. It isn't enough any more to defeat the Germans. We have to promise a new England too.'

It was then she realised that Billy was preparing not to win. Her father or brothers would have been moving Heaven and Earth, plotting, calling in favours, shouldering obstacles out of the way. He had made his peace with losing, swallowed the shame. He would go out there every day and do his best, entirely without the animation of hope.

She loved him so much in that moment that she jumped to her feet and said, 'I must go to bed,' lest she blurt it out and embarrass him.

And he was right. The next day was worse. A larger village, an even more packed hall. Billy spoke first and was heckled – the same sorts of heckles: 'Did you ever do a day's work?'; 'What do you know about the lives of working men?'; 'Why are you here?'

White did the same routine about the root-rot of hereditary

privilege, only this time, no doubt encouraged by his successes, he added a new goad: the Mosleys. 'What exactly is the relationship,' he began conversationally, quite as though he was one of her mother's friends, teasing out a tangle of family alliances, 'between my opponent and Oswald Mosley, a fascist, a traitor and a man imprisoned as an enemy of this country, with his wife, who is my opponent's sister-in-law?' Kick could feel silent despair from the duchess and Elizabeth.

In vain did Billy try to explain that Diana wasn't his sister-in-law but his brother's. 'I am not my brother's keeper,' he was reduced to saying, over a noisy crowd who showed no inclination to listen.

'I thought that was rather clever,' he said afterwards. Kick could see he was only saying it to appear cheerful.

'Pity the crowd didn't agree,' said his mother.

Kick loved him for how bad he was. The way he squared his thin shoulders and got up there each time, knowing he would be talked over and ridiculed. And the funny thing, Kick thought as she packed to go back to London, was that he had improved as a speaker. As the days wore on, despite the obvious hopelessness of it all, he had become more, not less, confident, more relaxed and cheerful in the face of the hostility.

'Can you even milk a cow?' was one of the heckles at the final meeting she attended.

'Yes,' Billy responded, with a grin. 'I can milk a cow, and I can spread muck. Something my opponent seems rather good at too.' That got him a genuine laugh.

Even so, White destroyed him day after day. It didn't much matter if Billy spoke well or badly, because as well as his 'muck-spreading', White had, Kick saw, something that Billy did not.

An actual plan. A manifesto: Labour's blueprint to create a new England.

Yet everything Kick saw showed her that Billy could have a real shot at a career in politics. He cared, that much was obvious, he was learning, and he was starting to think very differently about what Charles White kept throwing into his face: privilege and position.

'It's a pity we're not just starting,' she said to the duchess, who drove her to the station where she would take the train back to London.

'Surely you can't mean that?' the duchess asked. 'I long for it to be over.'

'Oh, no,' Kick assured her. 'Now that I see how good Billy can be, how much he's learned and the way he's thinking about the future, well, I just can't wait to see what he'll do next time.'

'You're a funny girl, Kick Kennedy,' the duchess said. 'In so many ways, you're perfect for my son. I've seen how much confidence he gets just from you being in the room with him.' It was the most anyone in Billy's family had ever done to acknowledge the possibility of a marriage, not just the impossibility.

It had been all Kick wanted to hear for so long, and now that it had come, she almost smiled at how hopeless it was. It was too little. Too thin, too inadequate. When all around them change was tearing up the old ways, tearing down the old walls, how could they, Billy's parents, sit in the rooms off the main wing of Chatsworth and cling to the idea that keeping their son from the girl who was 'perfect for him' was right?

'Thank you,' she made herself say. 'That means an awful lot.'

'Come back for the count,' the duchess said. 'It's in ten days. I think Billy will need you there.'

'I will,' Kick promised. She had already decided she would. 'But not as Rosemary Tonks. As myself.'

The duchess looked startled. 'As yourself?'

Kick straightened her shoulders. Behind her, the station master blew his whistle and she heard doors slamming. She didn't move. 'Very well,' the duchess said after a moment. 'As yourself.'

On the day of the vote, she was back. Billy rose at dawn to do some last-minute canvassing – 'more reminding people to vote' – and Kick went with him. They took a flask of coffee and went around the polling stations, handing out leaflets. 'How are you feeling?' she asked, much later, as they made their way to the town hall for the count.

'Fired by the prospect of utter defeat,' he said cheerfully.

'You can't mean it?'

'I do. My prediction? A massive swing to the left.'

He was right. Charles White beat him by more than five thousand votes. 'It won't just be Billy who's reeling,' the duchess said, 'the whole country will be.'

'I don't know what the people want,' the duke said peevishly.

'I do,' said Billy 'Or, rather, I know what they don't want – they don't want the Cavendishes.' He said it with grim relish.

Outside the town hall, he made a quick and graceful speech, conceding defeat and congratulating his opponent. 'It's been a fierce fight,' he said, turning back to the crowd after shaking White's hand. 'Now I'm going out to fight for you at the front.' It was the largest cheer of his campaign. And his face, as he spoke, was happier than Kick had yet seen it while on stage. He meant it, she thought. All the eagerness he showed – to rejoin the army, to be deployed, to be sent back to the front – he really meant it. There was to be no reprieve for Billy, no evading active service. He would go, and that was how he wanted it.

In the car, driving the half-hour or so back to Chatsworth, she complained about Charles White – 'His entire campaign was just tearing into you, and promising people what they wanted to hear.'

'It's not just what they want to hear,' Billy said. 'It's what they want to happen. Everything White spoke about – high taxation, nationalisation, the shift from the old way of patronage by families like ours to state responsibility – that's what the people want. And if they get it, well, I don't see how families such as ours can continue.'

'Are you just being a good loser?'

'No. I'm doing my best to read the signs that seem to be under my nose. Under all our noses. Unpalatable as they are.' He lapsed into silence, taking the bends in the twisty road carefully. Then, 'I want to be proud of what I am, even if that is something Charles White despises.'

'So do I,' Kick said. 'And I didn't feel very proud, hiding at the back of halls, pretending to be a girl from the village called Rosemary Tonks.'

'No,' he agreed. 'I see that. As a matter of fact, I was rather surprised you agreed.'

'I hope you know why I did?'

'I do. And thank you.' He drove in silence for a while. Then, 'But if all this' – he made a sweeping movement that took in the front and side windows of the car, through which the silhouette of Chatsworth was now visible – 'is doomed anyway, why am I trying so hard, and refusing myself the one thing I know will make me happy?'

Kick held her breath. He sounded as though he was talking

more to himself than to her. She feared what any interruption might do to a train of thought that seemed inclined, at last, to end where she wanted it to end.

'It seems idiotic,' he continued, 'when I think of it like that. To try so very hard to be unhappy . . . And because of that, darling Kick . . .' He took his hand off the steering wheel and, still wearing his leather driving glove, reached for hers. She gave it gladly. With his eyes still on the road, he continued, '. . . can we finally stop this messing about, and be married?'

'If mine is the yes you need, you have it,' she assured him. 'You've always had it.' She squeezed his hand in the glove. At the next space where he could pull in, he cut the engine and reached to put his arm round her. She found there were tears in her eyes when he kissed her.

'Don't cry,' he said, wiping her cheek with his handkerchief. 'It's surely not as bad as all that?'

'It's just the nicest thing ever,' she said, 'and I'd given up believing it could happen.'

'We've a long way to go still,' he said, kissing her again, then starting the car.

Chapter Forty

Kick

Kick's twenty-fourth birthday, February twentieth, was a week after polling day, and Billy invited her back to Chatsworth, this time with Sissy and Edie. There was a proper party, with cake and jelly and sandwiches. 'Cook's been saving the rations,' Billy told her, with a grin. 'Father was quite put out to get nothing but bread and dripping for the past two days.'

He gave her a pair of sheepskin gloves 'to keep your hands warm as you bicycle about London,' and the duchess presented her with a glorious brown-and-orange silk scarf. Sissy and Edie had clubbed together to buy her a tin of toffees, a large enveloping apron – 'because you complain that you get greasy from the doughnuts' – and a new murder mystery by Agatha Christie.

Just when Kick thought she had opened everything, the duke

solemnly handed her a gift wrapped in newspaper and tied with scarlet ribbon. She undid the ribbon and the newspaper slid onto her lap. Inside was an old and beautifully bound leather book. Kick opened it carefully. *The Book of Common Prayer of the Church of England.* She darted a laughing look at Billy, who was clearly as surprised as she was, then thanked the duke warmly. 'I love it,' she assured him. 'I will treasure it.'

'I hope it will bring a great deal to your life,' he said meaningfully. 'A very great deal.'

'I'm sure it will,' she said.

Later, when she and Sissy and Edie were preparing for bed – they were all to sleep in one room – Edie asked, 'What was that about? With the old book?'

'*The Book of Common Prayer?*' Kick said. 'It's the prayer book of the Anglican Church. Billy's prayer book.'

'Not yours?'

'No. Catholics don't use it.'

'So why would he give it to you?'

It was Sissy who answered: 'Because he wants it to be hers, silly,' she said. 'I would have thought that was obvious.'

'So does that mean . . .?' Edie asked.

Kick blushed. 'I think it does.'

'Does what?' Sissy asked, looking from one to the other.

'That Billy's asked her to marry him, *silly*,' Edie said.

'Does it? Really?' Sissy demanded.

'Yes. I wasn't sure if he'd told his family, so I didn't dare say anything. But yes.'

When they had finished their congratulations, and Sissy had thumped her enthusiastically on the back a couple of times, Edie said, 'I was watching you, Kick Kennedy, when we came in here today, and you weren't a bit surprised by this place.'

'I've been here before,' Kick responded. 'Plenty of times.'

'That's not the point,' Edie said severely. 'How is it possible you walk in here and don't even blink? This place . . .' She trailed off. 'For one family . . .' She trailed off again.

'But Chatsworth isn't just the family,' Kick tried to explain. 'It's all the people who work here as well. The maids and the cooks and the gardeners. Grooms, carpenters, electricians.'

'All the people Billy reckons won't want to work here after the war,' Edie said drily.

'Edie, you sound like the girl from school who came to Ballycorry for tea,' Sissy said. 'She went back and told everyone I lived in a mansion, and they all hated me. Even more. But she didn't see that it's like a sort of industry so that Father is more like a bank manager, who just happens to be in charge. And Ballycorry is nothing like Chatsworth. Here, it must be like being governor of the Bank of England.' She laughed. Kick did too. Edie didn't.

'The governor doesn't own the Bank of England,' she said witheringly. 'Billy's family own Chatsworth. It's nothing like the same thing. One family owns a house the size of a town? I'm surprised, Kick Kennedy, that you can't see what's wrong with that. You are the dearest person I know, but in this you're blind. And you an American.'

There was silence between them as they undressed. Kick wondered if Edie was really as censorious as she sounded, and tried to remember how she had felt the first time she'd seen Chatsworth. She couldn't remember, but by the time she'd been there, she had visited so many other houses like it that Chatsworth had seemed, well, almost normal, she realised with a faint glow of mortification. Those sorts of places had been all she knew of England then. And she an American!

She was about to try to explain this when Edie said sharply, 'Sissy, what's that on your arm?'

Sissy had lifted her dress – Kick's dress, the green one – over her head and stood in her underthings as she wrestled to turn her nightgown the right way out. Edie pointed to a dark purplish smudge on her upper arm.

'A bruise. From work,' Sissy said, turning her head to look at it. 'You've no idea how rough that canteen is.'

'It looks real painful,' Edie said. 'Have you put something on it?'

'Arnica,' Sissy said. 'It's what we use on the horses at home when they get swollen hocks from the carriage harness.'

'You've one on your other arm as well,' Edie said.

'Have I?' Sissy looked down. 'I didn't know. Don't worry, I'll put arnica on that too.'

'Be sure you do,' Edie said. 'And if you can't reach, I'll do it for you.'

'Shall I ring for cocoa?' Kick asked. 'Or will that make you despise me all the more, Edie?'

'If Chatsworth can provide cocoa as well as that cake earlier – real butter and eggs! – I might forgive it everything,' Edie said.

So Kick rang the bell and the maid came and said, 'Yes, miss,' and they each got into bed. Kick opened her new book: *An administration of the sacraments and other rites and ceremonies of the Church . . .*

It was easy to laugh, she thought. The book meant many things, yes, and not all of them easy to contemplate, but most of all it meant that the duke knew. Why else would he give her such a thing if he didn't know Billy had asked and she had said yes? That they were going to be married. *It's done*, she thought. *At last. It's done.*

Chapter Forty-One

Sissy

I t had been nice, Sissy thought, being at Chatsworth. Even though it had been only two nights, it had felt longer. She hadn't realised how much she had missed wet green air and damp brown earth until her nose and eyes were filled with them again. The heavy smell of clean rain and rotting leaves and, most of all, distance all around her, the feeling of space and openness that she had forgotten.

London had been so exciting, so vital, that she had felt no kind of homesickness at all. At Ballycorry she had longed and longed to get away. And then she had, and London had been heady from the start so she had never looked back, except with relief. And she still felt relief, she thought, settling back in her third-class carriage and watching the fields flash past. Opposite her sat Edie, deep in a book. Kick was driving back with Billy.

Sissy had watched her taking leave of everyone – not just Billy's family, but the servants too, the few who remained, and had had to stifle a laugh. Kick's manner said she was already imagining herself in a future role. 'I do hope that cold gets better,' Sissy heard her say to the elderly butler, brought out of retirement because the actual butler had joined the army. Sissy had had to hide her face by belting her coat very firmly at the waist.

'You were really cross with Kick last night, weren't you?' she said to Edie.

'Was I?'

'You were. About not seeing how absurd it is that Billy's family owns, I don't know, half the country or something. I've never heard you talk like that to her.'

'It was the first time I really got it,' Edie admitted. 'How rich that family really is. Oh, I know everyone says it, but to see it . . . It was different. And how easy Kick was with it just surprised me.'

'Kick and Billy, together, will do something good with it,' Sissy said. She spoke with certainty. There was something about Kick, about how earnest she was in wanting to do what was right, that told Sissy she was correct.

As they drew towards the sprawling outskirts of London, the devastation left by bombs was far more evident. Houses built in dense terraces, like so many dominoes lined up one against the other, had gone down like dominoes too, in hefty chunks, entire rows flattened to lumpy rubble. Sissy stretched and Edie looked back at her. 'Nearly there,' she said. 'Are you coming to the flat?'

'No. I have things to do,' Sissy said. 'But I'll come back later.'

'What things?' Edie demanded. 'The Y?'

'Yes, and other bits and pieces.' That was a lie. She wasn't going to the Y. She wanted to call and see Peter. She wasn't sure why she didn't just tell Edie, but she still preferred to keep most of Peter secret. She hadn't told him she was going to Chatsworth, and she hoped he would have missed her when she didn't show up for four full days. And she had some rhubarb the gardener at Chatsworth had given her that she planned to stew. She thought he would like that.

She hoped so much that he would be happy to see her. He wasn't always. She knew that her visits were an interruption sometimes, but he had no telephone so she couldn't ring in advance. He had suggested she leave a note at the King's Anchor, but that meant walking all the way down there, and even then – as she explained to Peter – there was no way for him to respond, except to leave another note, and that would mean two trips for Sissy, even if Peter's response was no.

'Easier if I just call in,' she said, 'and if you're there, you're there, and if you aren't, you aren't. And I won't mind if you're not. If you are there and busy, you don't even have to let me in,' she finished humbly. He had agreed, but grudgingly, and indeed there had been days that Sissy arrived and he was there but showed no pleasure at seeing her. He barely spoke, seemed morose and impatient. Those days, she stayed only a little while. She might cook something for him and leave it. Or, sometimes, by the time she finished cooking, he would be in a better mood and would tell her to stay. Once, she had arrived and knocked on the door and he had opened it, said, 'No,' and taking hold of her by the upper arms – hard, so hard he left bruises – had turned her around, sending her back down the dark hallway with a push, and shut the door firmly behind her. She'd hung around a bit outside the flat, but he hadn't emerged so she had gone home.

Those were the bruises Edie had noticed last night. Sissy had felt bad lying, but knew telling the truth would have been worse. And all Peter had really done was hold her too tight. Maybe she bruised easily, she thought, liking this idea of herself as delicate, fragile.

But other times – and she hoped this would be one – he was happy to see her. 'Another visit to the stables,' he would say, with a grin. 'Come in. What have you got?' and he would pat the pockets of her coat and bag until he found whatever jar or packet she had brought.

It was those times that kept her coming back. Because they were more frequent than the dismissive or surly times. In those moods he was more intoxicating than the sherry or brandy she'd learned to drink without screwing up her face. Unlike everyone else, he never talked about the war, except as the most remote inconvenience. Almost, he seemed indifferent to the relentless flow of news – this battle, that front, the advance. Instead he teased her and made her laugh, and talked about music, books and painting in a way she'd never heard, as if these were the most important things in the world, but not in a way that was reverential. As if they could be mocked, or criticised, or quizzed just like anything else. Now that she knew more of his friends, from being in the King's Anchor with him, his impressions were funnier than ever. In his company, hours went by that felt fleeting. And bed, well, bed was the best of all.

'You're born to this,' he'd said, after the second time she'd stayed at his flat. 'If I didn't know you better, I'd wonder . . .'

'Wonder what?'

'If you weren't a lot more experienced that you let on.'

'I suppose you mean that as an insult,' she said. 'I can hear that you do. But I'm not insulted. It's nice, being good at something.'

'No other girl I know would want me to say they were good at this.' He laughed. 'They'd be sure I'd despise them for it.'

'Why would you despise someone for being good at something?'

'Because people do,' he replied. 'Men do.'

'But you don't?'

'Oh, but I do.' She'd assumed he was joking, but afterwards she wasn't so sure. In his angry moods, she thought maybe he did, a little. But the strange thing was, it wasn't in bed he seemed to despise her, or afterwards when she lay in the crook of his arm, the sheet rumpled beneath them, while he smoked, the tip of his cigarette glowing urgently in the dark. It was at other times, when she was cooking for him, when they sat on the sofa together after eating whatever she had cooked. When she arrived at the door of his flat and – every time! – seemed to catch him unawares so that he looked at her for a second as though he didn't know her. That was when she felt despised.

This, too, was why she didn't talk to Edie and Kick about him. How to voice any of that? How to repeat what he'd said – *Oh, but I do* – in a way they would understand? They would think he meant it. Really meant it. Always meant it. Whereas Sissy knew that he didn't. Not really. Not always. Just in certain moods. And she was learning to clear out when he was in a mood like that.

At the flat, the old man with the wheezy dog was coming out at the front. Seeing Sissy with her armful of rhubarb, he held the door with a courteous inclination of his head. 'Fool,' he said, as she went by. Sissy whipped her head around. Why would he say that to her?

'Fool?' he said again, nodding at the rhubarb. This time she understood. It was a question.

'If I had cream, yes,' she said, 'but I don't. So stewed.'

'Very nice,' he said, and let the door close gently behind her. She didn't bother checking the lift any more but went straight to the stairs and up them to knock on Peter's door.

No answer. She knocked again, louder, in case he was asleep. Still no answer. She dithered there on the dark landing. Stay or go? He might have nipped out for cigarettes, and be back in a minute. But, then, he might have gone to the King's Anchor and not be back for hours. She could go to the pub, but then she'd miss him if he had just gone to the shops. She decided she would wait ten minutes. She sat on the floor with her back to the wall. She had no watch, so gauging ten minutes was hard. It was too dark in the hallway to read – and she had nothing except the newspaper the rhubarb was wrapped in. Instead, she listened, trying to work out the building from the sounds around her. There were few. It was early afternoon, a Sunday, and the block was quiet. A thump somewhere above her suggested a door slamming. She listened for the sound of footsteps that would tell her someone was walking along the landing above her, but the floor was too thick or too densely carpeted or no one walked. She heard nothing.

She sat there until her bottom was numb, then got up. At least ten minutes must have gone by. Maybe more. She couldn't keep sitting there in the gloom. She knocked again – just in case, she told herself, already wondering what she would do, what she would believe, if he now answered the door. But he didn't. That, anyway, was a relief. She walked back to the stairs and was ready to start down them when instead she looked up. Above her, the stairs climbed in a regular, angular progression. Up and up, towards, well, towards the roof, she supposed. And the shed Peter had talked about, his 'studio'.

She decided to leave the rhubarb behind. She balanced it upright in a corner. She climbed another two flights, at which point the stairs ended in front of a door. Would it be locked? It wasn't. Out on the flat roof, she saw that the day had turned dreary. It was almost dark even though it couldn't be more than half past three. The space was about the size of the walled garden at Ballycorry, and in one corner, just as Peter had said, there was an uncertain-looking shed made of corrugated metal. Must be tin, she decided. Iron would have been taken for the war effort.

It was windy, so high up, and the wall around the edge of the roof was low. She felt peculiar walking across the exposed middle. She supposed it would be nice on sunny days. Perhaps they could have a picnic here when it was summer. She began thinking of what they could eat – sandwiches of fish paste, tomatoes, imagine if Kick brought back more peaches from one of Billy's greenhouses.

There was a padlock on the shed door but it stood open, the shackle sprung wide. She tapped at the door but knew before she did so that no one was inside. Nothing had ever been as empty as that hut. The door yielded a little to her tap and she pushed it open.

The shed was small enough to see it in its entirety immediately. A window directly opposite the door through which she could see the rooftops below. She imagined what it would be like to stand there and watch lights come on in windows all around. The flicking on of a thousand illuminated squares, each a frame for the play of life going on inside.

But, of course, there would be no lights. Blackout blinds would see to that.

There was an easel and on it a painting. Canvases stacked

around the walls, leaning against one another at all sorts of angles, backs to the room, so she couldn't see what was on them. On a stool beside the easel, the paint box she had brought him. The sight made her swell with delight. The oily tang of paint, of linseed oil and turpentine was like Peter himself magnified a thousand times.

She went closer, to look at the painting on the easel. A series of lightly sketched lines in browns and yellows gave her little clue as to what it was meant to be. She went to turn the canvas nearest to her.

'There you are.'

She hadn't heard him behind her, and jumped. Only then did she realise that she knew she wasn't meant to be there. 'Peter. I was looking for you.' She felt it was important she say that quickly.

'I saw your rhubarb.'

'How did you know it was mine?'

'Only you would leave rhubarb on a fellow's stairs like that.' He sounded affectionate. 'What are you doing here?'

'I came to look for you.'

'And when you didn't find me, you decided to snoop around my studio. Even though I told you I don't want you up here.' There was no affection now. Possibly there had been no affection in the earlier remark either.

'You didn't say that. Not exactly. You said you wouldn't show me your work.' The distinction was important, but she felt she failed to convince him of it.

'So you thought you'd just come up and look for yourself.'

'I was looking for you,' she said again. He was right beside her now. The cramped space wasn't meant for two.

'And now you've found me. Or, rather, I've found you.' He

took hold of her arm, above the elbow, the sort of place a man would take your arm when he was politely showing you to your seat, or into a car. But Peter held hers much tighter. Squeezed it hard so that she could feel the grip of his thumb – a painter's thumb, mobile and dexterous, she thought – and was surprised by the pain he caused, digging it into the soft inside of her arm. *Another bruise*, Sissy thought. She was reminded of other grips, other pressure. The bruises left by a nanny who had brought her back up to the nursery after she had disgraced herself in the drawing room. Mummie, pinching her in mass because she wriggled in her seat, but pinching far harder than the wriggling deserved. She had been – what? Five or six? She was already expert, though, at calibrating the scale of offence and punishment. It wasn't that she minded being pinched, slapped, her hair pulled or scalp scraped by the hard bristles of a hairbrush – she didn't. She was used to it. But it mattered that it be proportionate. That was where her anger and resentment had lain and pooled – where she felt the punishment was more severe than the sin deserved.

This time, though, she didn't understand the gravity of her transgression. She was still learning Peter's rules, so she couldn't judge the fairness or otherwise of his pressing fingers.

'You're hurting me,' she said, in a small voice. In case he hadn't realised.

'I am,' he agreed. And he pressed harder. 'I did say I didn't want you in here, but here you are.' He almost sounded jolly. As though it might be a game.

'I didn't see anything.' She felt like Bluebeard's wife. Felt sure that poor woman must have said the very same thing: *I didn't see anything . . . Didn't notice those severed limbs in the pool of blood on the ground . . . Paid no heed to the stench of butchery in the air . . .*

'It's not really the point, is it?' he asked.

'I suppose not.' By now she was through the door, moved by him, and they were halfway across the roof, heading for the door to the stairs. He marched her along and she didn't resist. Couldn't have resisted. Her legs felt weak, the way they do after an illness when you haven't been out of bed for a few days. 'Now I know, I won't come up here again,' she said politely, as they reached the door that swung open to the evening air.

'No. I'd rather you didn't.' They were at the top of the stairs now. 'If I want you to see something, I'll show it to you. It isn't likely that I will, but the choice must be mine, you see.'

'I do,' she said. How irritating she must be. She could see it so clearly now.

He let go of her arm. He did it with what might have been a flourish, and might have been a push. She wasn't sure. Even as she lost her footing and fell, she wasn't sure. Perhaps it was just a letting-go kind of gesture, not a push, and she was merely clumsy and off-balance. It was the sort of thing she usually told herself: an accident, a misjudgement of distance, of strength. *Mummie didn't mean it*, when the curtain rod had been wielded harder than usual, that time the poker was hot. *Of course she didn't mean it.* Now she said the same, only about Peter.

She didn't fall very far, maybe five steps down. She'd had worse falls from horses. Many. Quickly she picked herself up. 'I'm fine,' she said, before he asked. 'I'm perfectly fine.' It was the most he had yet hurt her. Her back hurt where she had scraped it against the edge of the stairs, and her head where she had bumped it. There were more pains to come, she knew – already a throb in her cheekbone told her that. It was always impossible to do a full tally straight away. But if you told yourself, and everyone, that you were fine, then mostly, you were.

'Are you sure you're all right?' he asked. He sounded sorry, she thought with relief. Even if he wouldn't say it, he sounded it.

'Yes,' she assured him, 'perfectly all right.' She straightened her coat and twisted to brush at the back of it, as though specks of dirt were her main concern. The twisting was very sore and she might have winced because she saw his face twitch. She pushed her hair back into place. 'Shall I make us some stewed rhubarb?'

'Good idea.' He took her arm again, below the elbow, but gently now, and walked her carefully down the remaining flights of stairs. At the entrance to his floor, he picked up the rhubarb, still leaning in the corner, and carried it for her to the door of his flat. Once or twice he looked at her, without saying anything, as though to check her expression. And so she kept her face cheerful, a small, carefully upward tilt to her lips. Everything was perfectly, perfectly all right.

Chapter Forty-Two

Kick

'What have you done to the peace and harmony of our flat?' Edie asked Kick, only half joking. 'Ever since you and Billy decided to get married, it's like living in a very odd kind of railway station. There are trans-atlantic phone calls, cables and letters all day and all night, and now priests everywhere.'

'Some are priests, some clergymen,' Kick tried to explain.

'It's all one to me.'

'But the point is, it's not all one. Billy's lot are clergymen and our lot – Mother's lot – are priests. And they aren't at all the same.'

'But they all want the same thing?'

'Yes, at first. They all want us not to marry,' she said gloomily. 'But thereafter, they want very different things. I have tea with archbishops, telephone calls with deacons, walks with Jesuit priests, and we talk around and around and around until everyone's head is spinning. My Church insists that Billy convert and I be married as a Catholic. Otherwise I'm not really married, and therefore living in mortal sin.' She blushed hotly at that, faltering on the word 'mortal'. 'They say that any and all children must be brought up Catholic. Meanwhile, Billy's lot want me to convert to the Church of England and the children – at least, any boys – to be Anglican. It's all very tiring.'

'And you are never tired.'

'I'm never tired. Until now. Now I am tired. Because I just cannot see a way through. No one can. Sometimes I think we'll both go nuts with this.'

Edie put a plate with a slice of toast down in front of her. 'You're flapping about like a spring-time duck,' she said. 'All day with the GIs, all night out with Billy when he's on leave, up and down to Chatsworth, lunch with the duchess, and now meeting priests and pastors—'

'Clergymen,' Kick repeated.

'Church folk,' Edie said firmly. 'No wonder you're worn through. Can't you let it all alone for a while?' She sat down beside Kick on the battered sofa.

'It won't let me alone,' Kick said as she drummed her fingers anxiously against her collarbone. *Worn through* was exactly what she was. Like cloth that has been handled and washed until it is faded, thin, stretched.

Ever since the engagement became known – and they still hadn't announced it formally – there had been a storm of talking. Talking to her father, her mother, Billy, Billy's mother. Not his father. The duke let his wish be known, that Kick would convert, and left it to Billy and the duchess to do the talking. But no matter how much they all talked, there didn't seem to be any fixing the problem.

'*Please try to discover loopholes*,' she had begged her parents in the letter she wrote telling them the news. Her father's first response was to insist that nothing needed to be done.

'If we can have the first-ever Catholic President of the United States of America – and we will when Joe hits his stride – then a Catholic Duchess of Devonshire is nothing,' he'd said to her, booming down the transatlantic line in a phone call during which he had held the receiver far from his ear so that Rose might hear too.

'It's not the same,' Kick had tried to explain. 'Being a Devonshire *means* not being Catholic. It's what they are. *Not* Catholic. They are the ones that all the others look up to. It would be like . . .' she clutched for an example they would understand '. . . like the Pope not being Catholic,' she said. 'Being Protestant.' Behind her father, she heard her mother's sharp intake of breath. 'I know you'll laugh at that, or think it's blasphemous, but I promise you, the way they see things, it's the same.'

Her mother took the phone then. 'Kathleen, I will talk to Archie Spell,' she said. Archie Spell was Bishop Spellman. 'And in the meantime, I would ask you to do nothing. Nothing at all. Until this is resolved correctly, you must do nothing.' Kick promised, confident that her mother, as always, would find the right words, the right person, the right pressure to smooth the way.

That had been several weeks ago, and still no loopholes had been found. Rose, who had people everywhere, had rustled up a Jesuit priest in London, Father Martin d'Arcy, and Kick had taken tea with him in his house, where he had been kind and unrelenting. Over cups of Earl Grey and thin oatmeal biscuits he had painted a picture for her of a godless life: if she married

Billy anywhere but in a Catholic church, she would be living in sin in the eyes of the Church, unable to go to Holy Communion or make an Act of Confession. Neither she nor her children would go to Heaven. To every alternative she proposed, he said a gentle, weary no, so that Kick had felt she was being pursued by a large, soft cloud that seemed to yield and change shape, only to re-form around her with pressing grey dampness. Except what the cloud promised – threatened – was hot and angry and mortal, rather than damp and soft.

'It's like one of those conundrums we used to study at school,' she said now. 'A puzzle with only one solution that is near-impossible to land on so that everything one tries leads one right back to zero. I wish Brigid was here. She's good at puzzles.'

Brigid was in Hertfordshire, on a visit that had something to do with the hospital, or maybe a sick friend – Kick wasn't sure – and not back for several days. It was her third visit there in as many months. Each time, she came back pink-cheeked and brimming with a new kind of energy. 'Country air,' she said, when Kick asked her why. 'I'd forgotten how I missed it.'

The doorbell went. 'That'll be Joe,' Kick said. 'He's on leave from Cornwall and promised to come and help me with the puzzle.'

Edie went to open the door, and came back not with Joe but with Sissy. 'I lost my key,' she explained.

'I'd forgotten you had one. Do you still live here?' Kick asked, mostly as a joke, but Sissy's face fell.

'Yes, I live here,' she said. 'Of course I live here.'

'We never see you any more,' Edie said.

'You do,' Sissy said. 'You saw me a few days ago.'

'For about five minutes,' said Edie. 'You came in, stuffed some clothes into a bag—'

'Mostly my clothes,' Kick said, but with a smile.

'– and you were gone again. It's not exactly seeing, is it?' Edie continued.

'Busy,' Sissy said evasively.

'Busy putting on make-up?' Edie asked, taking in Sissy's over-powdered face.

'I'm trying for a more sophisticated look,' Sissy said. Kick was about to tell her, gently, that so much make-up made her look older, but not more sophisticated, when the doorbell went again. This time it was Joe.

'Came to see how the Holy War was coming on,' he said, hugging Kick. With him he brought a feeling of air and space and distant horizons, the way he always did. Almost, she could smell the salt tang of the Atlantic and the brisk wind that set the boats dipping and tinkling in the harbour at Hyannis Port. The memory made her long for those summers when they had been children and the most important thing on anyone's horizon was winning at tennis or sailing and not being caught out in Rose's nightly dinner debates.

'Badly,' she said. She stared at her mug of tea. The milk wasn't very fresh and there were bits floating on top now that it had cooled. Joe pulled a wrapped packet out of his coat pocket and gave it to Edie, then took off his coat and draped it over the back of the sofa.

'Everyone is "terribly, terribly nice" and "terribly, terribly sorry",' Kick continued, 'but no one will give an inch. And Billy and I are in the middle and we both so much want to do the right thing but no one can even say what that is.'

'I dare say it changes depending on the perspective,' Joe said wryly. He sat beside her. 'Who would ever have thought that Pa, who always has everything his own way, would come up against the one man in the world as stubborn as he is?' Kick gave a hiccupy sort of laugh.

'I know. And the duke so bashful and unassertive and *implacable*. Just like Billy.'

'Open that,' Joe said to Edie, who was holding the packet politely on her lap. Inside was a silver and blue box of Charbonnel et Walker chocolates. 'Squadron leader gave them to me. His wife got them as a present.'

'They're just beaut!' Edie said. 'I'm going to keep them.'

'What does Billy say?' Joe asked then.

'I've hardly seen him. He gets hardly any leave any more because they're about to be sent to the front, and when I do see him, he's just the saddest because he doesn't see any way out either, so I feel I've done that to him, and then I feel even worse.' She was crying now, though trying hard not to.

Joe gently wiped at a tear that rolled down her cheek with the sleeve of his jacket. Edie went to get a tissue and handed it to him. He passed it to Kick, who mopped her eyes furiously then clutched it.

'I'm sorry to be a drip, only it's all a lot bigger than I thought it was,' she confessed. 'I didn't realise how serious it would be back home too. And serious in a way that's beyond even Mother and her worries about my immortal soul. Why, in Boston they're saying it's the worst kind of betrayal. A betrayal of me being Irish. Since Pa found that out, he isn't so keen at all. Now when he says he wants me to do what's right, he means give up Billy and this whole idea.'

'And Mother?'

'Like steel, of course. She says she's appealing to Pope Pius and still hopes to find a way. She says I must do nothing in the meantime, and that I have to trust her on this.'

'And do you? Trust her?' he asked cautiously.

'I trust that she wants the best for me,' Kick said carefully, 'but I don't trust that she knows what that is.' Joe watched her face, waiting for her to say more. Behind him, Edie and Sissy watched too.

'Since Rosie?' he asked gently when she said nothing.

'What is it about Rosie?' Sissy blurted out. 'When you talk about her – which you don't, not as much as you talk about the others – there's something . . .' Kick saw Edie shoot a warning look but it was too late. The question was out there: *What is it about Rosie?*

'Do you want to answer?' Kick asked Joe. He shook his head. So Kick tried. She told them about Rosie when she was a child, how she was kinder than any of them because she was never fastest, strongest, first at anything, so she didn't bother. And because of that, how it was her they went to when they were unhappy or sore or in trouble. How they had been told the operation, the lobotomy, would make Rosie happy again, the way she had been. How it had not.

'*Lobotomy* . . .' Sissy repeated the word, trying it out.

'When I go home, I'll visit,' Joe said, when there had been enough silence. He spoke to them all but he meant it for Kick.

'Do,' she said. 'Please do.' He reached out his hand then, took Kick's, squeezed it hard and let it go. It was enough.

'I'm going to open those chocolates now after all,' Edie said.

Kick smiled her gratitude. She didn't want to talk about Rosie any more. 'So,' she said, when they had all taken a chocolate, 'what do I do now about Billy? It's an awful pickle.'

'I think you need to stop listening to everyone, kid,' Joe said. 'Just listen to Billy. And let him listen to you.'

Chapter Forty-Three

Sissy

After Kick had talked about Rosie – a story that grew more terrible the more Sissy thought about it – Joe insisted they go for a drink. It seemed too early for the Ritz, so Sissy suggested cocktails at Belgrave Square. 'Chips will be delighted,' she promised.

And indeed he was. Mixing drinks, passing round cigarettes, proposing toasts and celebrating the return of Caroline, who sat with them. She was once more staying at Belgrave Square, going as a day pupil to a school in the city. Maureen too was back; 'One can hardly blame her,' Chips said. 'Clandeboye at this time of year . . . It's as though spring withers at the boundary wall.'

Caroline was as silent as ever, although Sissy suspected she missed nothing, watching everything with those huge silvery eyes. Sissy went to pour her a drink from the jug without gin that Chips had mixed. As she poured, the sleeve of her dress fell back. Exposed was the pale softness of her inner arm, and three yellowing marks, old and no longer painful, under her elbow.

'Such bruises,' Caroline said. 'Just like Nanny used to make.' She turned her eyes upwards then and held Sissy's gaze for long enough to make her feel itchy.

'Clumsy,' Sissy said, jiggling her arm so the sleeve fell down. 'Always was.'

'Me too,' Caroline said. 'Although I've never bruised myself there.' Again that look. 'That was Miss Allie's favourite spot. Just inside the elbow. She would pinch and pinch. Something about the softness of the skin, and the grip provided by the bone . . .' she mused. 'You get used to it, though, don't you?'

'I suppose you do,' Sissy said. 'It doesn't seem like such a shock, after a while.' She touched her face, the bruise that hid beneath the dusting of powder, and saw Caroline notice.

'No,' Caroline agreed. 'Although terribly mean all the same. Underhand too, always the soft, hidden places.' Then, 'You wouldn't want to get too used to it, would you?'

Later, when it was dark, Sissy cycled to the King's Anchor. She sniffed as she went, trying to catch hints of spring in the night air. Every few minutes, she would detect a wave of some night-flowering plant, or earth that held the promise of things growing and reaching for the light. And then it would be gone, leaving the dingy smell of wet rubble. She thought about what Caroline had said: *You get used to it, though, don't you?*

She knew exactly what she'd meant. You did get used to it. Being handled roughly, angrily, in ways that hurt, was so familiar.

Mummie, mostly, but the nannies too, even the maids when she was a small child: a sharp slap, a quick, vicious tug of her hair, sly pinches that ended in a twist of flesh. All these were routine.

The first time he had properly hit her, rather than a shove or a squeeze, things that could be denied or disguised, came only a few days after the shove down the stairs. She had thought how much more it hurt than fighting with her brother. She had been surprised by that, far more than by the fact of the punch; that hadn't seemed so very remarkable. She had annoyed him, had spotted the moment when it happened, but had not been fast enough to step back and out of the way.

Caroline understood, she thought. The others wouldn't. The bruise to her face was why she hadn't been at the flat for so many days. She had needed it to fade before her friends saw her. Or fade enough that she could cover it with make-up. Too much make-up, she knew, but better than the patch of toad-coloured skin underneath.

It was wartime, a young woman with a bruised cheek, bruised ribs too, if only they could have seen, could go about most places without causing comment. But not home to Kick and especially Edie, with her blunt questions and gruff kindness.

Do you still live here? Kick had asked. *Yes, I live here,* Sissy had said, although what she wanted to say was, *Please tell me I live here. Please let me still live here.*

She had spent the last few nights at Debo's tiny house on Eaton Square that was in fact her sister Diana's house. It had been Debo's idea.

'Where are you planning on hiding that?' she'd asked, over a vat of greasy soup at the Y, staring openly at the bruise on Sissy's cheekbone. 'Not wherever you got it, I hope?'

Sissy had been astonished. That Debo, so indirect, so reluctant to look straight at anything unpleasant – always the sideways approach, mocking and teasing to avoid painful truths – should ask such a thing. 'I don't know,' she'd confessed. 'I haven't quite decided . . .' As though she had many choices. As though she had any choices.

'You'd better come home with me,' Debo had said. 'You can lie low and wait it out. If there's anything left on the ration books, I'll buy a potato and you can put a slice, raw, on the bruise.'

'Potato? Really? Not steak?'

'There's a war on, darling . . .'

'Well, all right. Yes, please. But won't your sister—'

'Diana will be thrilled to see you. To see anyone. Since leaving Holloway, she says she may as well not have bothered, that even fewer people visit her and that there at least the prison chaplain used to call.'

'You won't tell, will you?' Sissy had said then, in a small voice.

'Tell what?' Debo had said, turning vague. 'I don't know anything to tell, silly.'

So Sissy had said a grateful yes, and Diana had indeed been pleased to see her. Or at least had behaved as though she was pleased. 'You'll have to sleep in what used to be the maid's room, but it's perfectly cosy. Half of London would kill for it now.' The way she said 'kill' and the way her blue eyes with those tiny black pupils widened as she said it, made Sissy think of an animal.

'Men are brutes, aren't they?' she had said, lightly touching Sissy's cheek with an elegant finger. She must be the only woman in London whose hands weren't coarsened by physical work, in factories, hospitals, on ARP duties, Sissy had thought, hiding a laugh. Imagine prison being the place to go to escape manual labour.

It had been, Sissy thought, as she pedalled harder now, a bit like being taken in by a witch in a fairy story. The tiny house, the secrecy, Mosley coming and going, like an enchantment.

Over the three days she stayed there her cheek had healed, enough anyway. She had wondered if Peter would try to find her, telephone her, even write to her. He didn't. She tried to interpret his silence: he was ashamed and couldn't bring himself to say it; he disliked her and hoped not to see her again; the punch hadn't meant what she'd thought it had.

This, mostly, was what she told herself. He hadn't meant it. He had been caught off-guard and lashed out. The rest was just unfortunate. Anyway, what was a bruise, a thump, at a time when people were dying, bombed in their houses, buried in rubble, battered by falling masonry? She was lucky. She only hurt a bit. There was a girl at the Y who had a crushed foot, toes hammered into each other, from a balcony that had plunged to the ground and caught her as it fell.

Her plan was to go to the pub as though she had been passing and just dropped in. She wasn't there to look for him, she told herself, hoping she would be able to tell him the same. But while she was there, she'd be able to try to understand the way things were with them now. Because she couldn't go on hoping he would ring, knowing he wouldn't. Anything was better than uncertainty, she told herself bravely, as she pushed open the pub door. And maybe he would look guilty and sorry and say he hadn't meant it, and they could go back to what they had been together.

The usual wall of smoke and beer fumes hit her. The warm wet smell of many bodies, of loud brave talk and quiet fears, plans made against the wall of 'what if' and a sense of time escaping them all. These men and women were there because they didn't know where else to be.

Peter looked up and even as Sissy dithered over what to do – pretend she hadn't seen him? – came over to her, put his arm around her shoulders and squeezed. 'Drink?' he asked.

'Yes, please.' She snuggled against him gratefully, smiling with the sheer relief of feeling him so close to her again. She realised how much she had missed him. How lonely she was without him. That it wasn't just physical pain that had left her so drained. It was also pain brought by his absence.

He made the others move up so there was space for her beside him, which they did. And so happy was she tucked in by him, his arm around her, that she stayed until she could sit no longer. She got up and went behind the bar to the claustrophobic staircase. She felt rather than saw Aurora follow her. Sure enough, when she came out of the tiny bathroom, Aurora was on the landing. Sissy smiled at her and turned sideways to squeeze past. But the sudden movement clutched at her still-sore ribs and she winced, breath hissing from her.

'What's wrong with you?' Aurora asked.

'Nothing much.' Sissy tried to get past but Aurora wouldn't move, so she was stuck, close enough to touch, with nowhere to go except back into the bathroom behind her. 'A bit sore.'

'A bit sore from what?'

'Work, I suppose. There's a lot of lifting of very heavy pots at the Y.'

'Is it Peter?' Aurora demanded.

'Peter?' Sissy said stupidly. She didn't know what else to say. 'Why would it be Peter?'

'You aren't his first girlfriend. And if it is Peter, you won't be the first girl he's been rough with. Why do you think I warned you off him?'

'I rather thought you liked him,' Sissy said.

'Me?' Aurora said. 'Certainly not. He's good company, and rather a talented painter, but there's a frightfully bitter side to him. As you've discovered. And I don't much care for being hit.' Sissy winced again, more than she had over the sore ribs. 'He loses his temper far too quickly and lashes out. What will you do?'

'Try not to cause him to lose his temper, I suppose.'

'You could try that,' Aurora said witheringly, 'or you could say a brisk farewell, a wartime farewell, and keep away from him.'

'But I like being with him,' Sissy said, in a small voice.

'Well,' said Aurora, 'that is a pity.' She stood aside, and Sissy slipped past her. 'You know,' she continued, as she moved towards the stairs, 'I'm not unsympathetic. Peter can be very charming, even magnetic, although I'm lucky and don't feel it. But it really would be better to go now.'

'It's rather too late for that,' Sissy said. The last few days had shown her something, and that was the feeling of loneliness that had sent her first to Tom, now to Peter. A sense of not knowing where else to go. And, if she was horribly honest with herself, there was something else too. A kind of shouldering-of-a-private-burden feeling that carried its own kind of excitement. He must be more, even, than her boyfriend if they were bound together like this. It was as if he had trusted her with a secret; believed in her ability to keep it for both of them. That must mean something.

Back at their table, he made space for her to sit beside him and she slid into place almost under his elbow. 'Where were you?' he asked.

'Upstairs. The lav,' she said.

'With Aurora?'

'She was there after me,' she said carefully. He nodded. And when Aurora came out from behind the bar towards them, he leaned over and kissed her. Sissy looked up to see if Aurora had noticed, and realised that Peter was looking at her too.

His face was hard to read – it was always hard to read: he kept his emotions as carefully to himself as others might keep bees – but she thought he looked a bit like the men at home did when they had signed a good contract for feed or land.

Chapter Forty-Four

Kick

Sometimes, on those April mornings, Kick woke early, called from sleep by the unexpected sun, and felt she had it all clear in her mind. In her dreams she had solved the puzzle of her and Billy, their families, their churches, so that they could be married and everyone would be happy. *Of course*, she would think on waking, *it must be like this* . . . But as soon as she tried to remember how she had solved the riddle, how she had arranged everything so that there was winning on all sides, everything would dissolve and vanish even as she reached for it.

They talked, all of them, this way and that, in the hope they might find new paths, but nothing would yield. The objections were so deep, so dug in, that talking only made them worse. Billy had made his grand gesture – he had asked her to marry him – and now that gesture rotted in the ground because they couldn't make it good.

In late April, the duchess took her to lunch at the Ritz and explained that it wasn't her or even the duke. Not any more. 'You do know nothing will happen to Billy if he gives in,' she said, over thin watercress soup. 'There will be no dramatics, no disinheriting. It isn't us, you know. It's his own conscience that won't allow it.'

Kick already knew that. Impossible to love Billy and not know it. 'I have my conscience too,' she said. She wanted Billy's mother to know that.

Afterwards, she walked back to the club, where Edie and Sissy were setting up the room for dancing. Sunlight poured in, the jaunty sun of late spring, and the room spoke of the same hope and energy that was everywhere. 'A final push,' they said to one another, as they passed in the street or waited in queues. An invasion was being prepared – secretly, so of course everyone knew – that would bring about the end they hardly dared long for.

'Well?' Edie asked. 'How was the duchess?'

'As kind as ever,' Kick said, taking off her hat and shaking her hair out of its neat pins. 'Wants the best for everyone and feels utterly helpless to bring it about.'

'I've never known so many people be so perfectly, impossibly unselfish,' Sissy said. 'If even one of you had said, *This is what I want and I will accept nothing else*, the whole thing would have been resolved long ago. Instead you all stand around asking only what others want and absorbing disappointment like sponges, soaking it up and pretending always to have space for more.'

'Maybe we do,' Kick said, 'but that seems to be the way we are, me and Billy. Certainly it's the way we are together.' Watching the GIs spin their girls about, Kick thought she must be the only person in the country who felt not hope but quiet despair. She knew her parents believed the engagement was off again, buried beneath the intractability of the problem. Her mother had written to her about fortitude and grace, promising that 'God doesn't send us a cross heavier than we can bear.' *How can you be sure?* Kick wanted to ask.

'When I think of life without Billy, it's no life at all,' she said to Joe, when he rang her that evening from Cornwall. 'It's like looking out over the sea on a misty night when you can't see the lights of the harbour or any of the houses.'

'Whatever you do will be the right thing,' Joe said, as he had said before. 'I know that and Pa knows that. It'll be right because you do it. You aren't capable of doing a wrong thing, Kick. Of anyone I ever knew, you're not.' In the background Kick could hear the noise and fuss of his air base: shouts and laughter, an engine somewhere, the bluster of the Cornish wind that came in hard off the coast. 'I wish you'd tell me what you're doing down there,' she said.

'You know I can't do that. Top-secret mission, sir!' He was almost giddy, she thought. 'What I can say,' he continued, 'is that after this Jack won't be the only Kennedy with a war record worth reading about.'

'Joe, you wouldn't do anything crazy just to catch up with Jack, would you?'

'He should be catching up with me,' Joe said, no longer giddy but sombre. 'It isn't right, this way round.'

And then came the news they had all been waiting for and hinting at: the Allied invasion of France was afoot, and Billy's regiment was mobilised at last. 'We're off,' he said to Kick, unable to disguise his excitement.

'What will you do now?' the duchess asked, ringing the flat a few hours later. She sounded quite different from the woman Kick had met at the Ritz just a few days earlier. 'You know that Billy will soon go?'

Kick could hear the knot in her voice, like string pulled tight. She knew that Billy's mother felt as she did – that if he went away without the protection of her love, of their marriage, he would be exposed, weak and vulnerable. Kick knew it, deep and undeniable within her. How could his mother not?

Knowing brought a dizzying urgency where there had been apathy. She thought again of the house on Francis Street she had visited a week earlier and the man she had met there, Bishop Mathew. He was her own find, not someone deputed by her mother or the duchess. Over tea and biscuits he had talked to her in a way none of the others had. He had considered her problem in silence, and then, impatiently almost, 'No, that's wrong. It is not a mortal sin you contemplate in marrying this man. Nothing of the sort. You are not wilfully turning away from God. A sin is done from a selfish motive, and no one can say you're doing that. Are you doing that?' he barked.

'No,' she had answered. 'I do not believe I am.'

'In fact,' he continued, steepling his fingers, 'I would suggest that whatever you do is entirely from unselfish motives. You've turned yourself inside out to avoid sin.'

'I have,' she agreed gratefully. It was what her mother couldn't see, she thought. In all Rose's communications, she had assumed that Kick wanted this marriage only as one might want a particular dish on a menu: because it was the most appealing from a wide selection. And that not to have it would be no real hardship, simply a matter of making a different choice.

She listened eagerly to what Mathew said. He was pragmatic

and sensible. He agreed that a dispensation was impossible, but said, without prompting, that if Kick went ahead and got married, it might be granted at some point in the future. Even more compelling was his view of mortal sin: his belief that her marriage, even in a register office, wouldn't bring her into any such state. She had been scared so often by now with the threat of fornication, a sin of 'grave matter', that, almost, she couldn't believe what he said to her. Not a mortal sin. No excommunication. No condemnation to eternal damnation.

She had carried his views with her for many days now, turning them over in her mind, scared to put her trust in them. Until now. *What will you do?* The duchess's question settled the matter. She knew what she would do.

When she told Billy, he was at first wary. For her. 'Are you sure you won't come to see this as a capitulation? As losing?' He spoke the word hesitantly.

'I'm as sure as anything,' she responded. 'This isn't a battle, not between you and me, and not even between our faiths. We have a way out of a maze that's confused us for the longest time, and I vote we take it. We can't not, darling Billy. I can't not.'

'Nor me,' he agreed quietly. 'Not now.' So they cabled across the Atlantic to say they would be married in seven days.

Rose was disbelieving and frantic, whipping up another round of intervention from Bishop Spellman, Father d'Arcy, setting them on Kick like – she felt but would never say – the winged monkeys dispatched by the Wicked Witch of the West in that film they had all watched and loved, *The Wizard of Oz*.

Rosie, especially, had loved that film. She had even started calling the family's terrier Toto, until Rose insisted she was confusing the dog and was to stop. Remembering that prevented

Kick giving in to her mother's wishes, so Rose turned to Joe, insisting he work on his sister.

'Mother wants me to have nothing to do with this,' he said to Kick. 'Told me to think about how it will play in Boston – that you're marrying not just a Protestant but one from a family dedicated to the spread of Protestantism.'

'That's not Billy,' Kick said. 'It's not me either. Why can't everyone understand that we're just ourselves?'

'Because you aren't,' Joe said kindly. 'Not really. Which is hard luck for you. Sure, you are yourselves, but you are also *America*, and he is *England*. You are *Catholicism*, he is *Anglicanism*. There's more – his family, your family—'

'*Our* family,' she corrected him.

'Our family. Pa's money, Billy's acres, this war, the last war, Irish independence . . . Why, you've raised a real hornet's nest, kid, just by falling in love. It's a lot bigger than just you and Billy. You know what the newspapers are calling it?'

'I try not to read them . . .'

'*The Kennedy Affair.*'

'How the duke must love that,' Kick said, with a half-laugh.

'I'm sure,' Joe agreed. 'Pa too. Especially when it's the Boston newspapers.'

'You will come, though, won't you? To the wedding?' she asked, anxious suddenly. 'I couldn't bear it if the only Kennedy there was me.'

'Of course I'll come, kid.'

'It's not the wedding I ever thought I'd have,' she said then.

'It's not the one any of us thought you'd have. I saw you with Lem, or Peter Grace, or any of those guys you used to hang around with back home. Any one of them would have married you in a heartbeat. You'd have had St Patrick's

Cathedral and a dress of Irish lace, handmade by the nuns of Kylemore Abbey.'

'Instead, I have Chelsea register office, a dress hand-made almost overnight by Sissy and Edie using material from everyone's ration coupons, and a fistful of pink camellias from Chatsworth, if they arrive in time on the train,' Kick said. 'And I'm as happy as I ever thought I could be.'

Chapter Forty-Five

Brigid

Leaving Little Hadham became harder, Brigid found, especially as spring turned to summer and the countryside outside London grew green and soft. By her second visit, Little Hadham became the only place she felt right in. In London, she felt responsible for everyone – for Chips's loneliness, Caroline's silent misery, Kick's cycle of despair and hope over the engagement to Billy, whatever it was that had subdued Sissy, her patients – so much so that she thought she might be crushed under the weight of it all. Even the people not yet wounded whom she saw on the streets and buses seemed to Brigid merely injuries waiting to happen. In Hertfordshire, on the farm, she felt none of that. The yield wasn't her concern, or the pests that attacked the crops, or the ancient machinery that should be replaced only there was nothing to replace it with. All she saw were wide-open fields; all she smelt was clean air. She heard birdsong and cattle lowing. She ate food that tasted as it used to and slept deep and dreamless. And there was Fritzi, who followed her about the house and garden, while pretending not to.

His patent need for her made her tender towards him. He gave her responsibility for his happiness, and she accepted it. Or that was how she phrased it to herself when she thought about it. Mostly, she didn't think. Not too much. She slept late and wandered the fields, read and helped to prepare dinner, which meant scrubbing carrots and slicing onions, not queuing for hours to wheedle extra suet out of the butcher.

And then it was time to leave again, usually after just a few days, and each time she felt as though she had swallowed lead that pooled in her feet and legs and made her heavy and slow, dragging her backwards even as she forced herself to move forwards – forced herself to drive to the train with Fritzi, or go with the vicar's wife's pony and trap to save the petrol, to say her goodbyes as cheerfully as she could, get on the train and allow it to convey her to London even as she longed to stay behind.

But it wasn't yet time to stay. *There's a war on*, she reminded herself. And then there was a wedding on. When she rang Kick to tell her that of course she would be there, she said, 'I still can't believe that you and Billy won't find yet another moral barrier to be all concerned and good about.'

'I know you're mocking me,' Kick replied, 'and I don't mind at all. Now that I'm marrying Billy all the mockery in the world can't hurt me. I know we must seem crazy to you, raising so many objections . . .'

'Not really,' Brigid said. 'I'm teasing. It's admirable that you said no to the one thing you really want. I don't pretend to understand the finer points of doctrine, but I do understand you, Kick. And I knew it mattered.'

'It did,' Kick said. 'They all mattered.'

'And now?' Brigid asked, curious. 'How did you make it all come right?'

'It's not exactly right, but for the first time I believe we can be married and it someday will be. Billy's going to war. Nothing else is important.'

The night before the register-office ceremony, Brigid went to the flat, to help with 'any last things'. She brought a basket with a picnic dinner that Chips's cook had made, and Caroline came with her. Reluctantly. 'No, thanks,' she'd said, when Brigid suggested it. She was lying on her stomach on her bedroom floor, reading a book.

'It's a wedding,' Brigid had said, astonished. 'A bride.'

'I'm all right here,' Caroline had insisted.

'You may as well try to chat to Pugsy,' Maureen said, walking past the open door of the room, wearing a fringed evening dress and trailing a cloud of *Femme Rochas* after her.

'I need help to carry the basket,' Brigid had said, even determined to bring her after that, even if it meant lying to her.

And now here they were, handing out sandwiches with ham and cheese and cress, and scones with jam – 'Rhubarb,' Sissy said regretfully, 'but jolly nice all the same.' She and Edie were sewing furiously at pink crêpe-de-Chine, pausing to make Kick try it on, then resuming stitching the hem and lining.

The dress was far less flattering than most of Kick's dresses, Brigid thought, not as well cut – how could it be? – and in a colour that didn't suit her. But she supposed that any bride would want something new for her wedding, even if it was home-made.

'It was all we could get with the coupons,' Edie said, of the pink crêpe-de-Chine, through a mouthful of pins. 'Everyone chipped in.'

'Aren't people just dandy?' Kick asked, beaming. She sat on the old sofa in a dressing-gown so she could put the dress on and take it off with ease. 'Especially you three. Especially you, Brigid, coming all the way back from – where is it again? – to be here.' She grinned.

'Very well,' Brigid said. 'I'll tell you. You remember Fritzi?'

'Prince Friedrich, the burnished young man?'

'Exactly. Only not so burnished now. Rather worn, in fact.' And she told them all about Fritzi. The internment camps, the letters, the wound, Little Hadham.

At the end, Kick said, 'But why didn't you say anything?'

'I couldn't. I never expected to become engaged to Fritzi and suddenly it all happened. And there you were, wanting and hoping and longing to marry Billy, and nothing was happening . . . Also,' she giggled, 'I haven't told my parents yet. Or even Chips.'

'Will they be furious?'

'I don't know. Mama doesn't really think about that sort of thing the way other people do . . . And Chips knows I've been visiting Fritzi and has already begun to remind himself that Fritzi, even in disgrace, is a prince . . .' She giggled again, filled with the lightness that seemed to be with her always now. 'Anyway, I find I care a great deal less for what they think than I thought I did. You understand that, don't you, Kick?'

Kick nodded. 'I do. Though I'm still nervous as hell.' She took a bite of a cheese sandwich. 'Billy says there'll be tons of press.'

'Of course there will,' Brigid said. 'But they won't all be hostile. Not everyone wanted you and Billy to fail, you know.'

'It sure felt that way . . .'

'That's because they were the noisiest,' Brigid said wisely. 'Plenty of people quietly hoped you'd make a go of it. What is it the papers have been calling it?'

'The "Kennedy Affair" . . .' Kick said. 'How I have hated reading that . . . It's just me and Billy.'

'Except it isn't,' Brigid said. 'It never was. You know that. But it doesn't matter, because the "Kennedy Affair" is resolved, and in your favour.'

'Could it ever have been otherwise?' Edie asked wryly.

'It could,' Kick insisted. 'It nearly was. Truth is, I still can't believe that something won't go wrong, come along to stop us, even now . . . I keep looking over my shoulder, like I've forgotten something. Joe says it's just wedding jitters, but it's more than that. It's like I think we never should have got this far – that we somehow snuck something over on everyone because of the war, that they'll realise at the last minute, and stop us.'

Brigid was about to say, *Nonsense, no one will stop you*, when Caroline piped up, 'I know what you mean.' It was so unusual for her to volunteer anything that everyone turned to her. 'It's like you think you've tricked the world but that you'll be found out,' she continued. 'Some giant hand will pull you back just as you think you've got away with it.'

'That's it exactly,' Kick said. 'Aren't you clever?'

'I usually feel like that,' Caroline said, staring at the floor, 'and usually I'm right. The giant hand does come along, Mummie's or Miss Allie's. I thought I had escaped by coming back here, to London, even for a little while. But then Mummie came back too.'

'It won't always be like that,' Brigid said gently. 'An awful lot changes when you're grown-up. You'll see.'

'You have a war,' Caroline said, with feeling. 'Lucky things. That forced everything to change. By the time I'm old enough, the war will be over and everything will go back to the awful way it has been.'

'It won't,' Brigid promised her. 'You'll see.'

Caroline's gloom seemed to cast a sort of spell. The room felt darker, for all that the evening was slow and sweet in fading.

'What about your parents?' Brigid asked Kick tentatively. She knew that the flurry of telegrams had only grown more frantic, not less.

'I thought they would have come around, but they haven't,' Kick said sadly. 'I just know Mother still thinks she can do something – persuade me, stop me – but she can't. Not now.'

'Do you miss her?' Edie asked.

'I do. Being here without her, without Eunice, without Rosie, on the evening before I marry, well, it makes me realise how far from home I am in a way that nothing else ever did.' Kick drew her feet up onto the sofa and wrapped her arms around her legs. She rested her head on her knees and said, 'It feels like the end of all that. And even though it's the start of something new and wonderful, it's hard to say goodbye to the other when there's no one here to do it with me. No one to talk about our summers and school at the Sacred Heart Convent and ice creams at Katie's and tennis tournaments that went on for days . . .'

'Joe?' Brigid asked.

'Will be there tomorrow, bless his stout heart.' She unhooked her knees and sat up straighter. 'He's the best brother a girl could have, and if anything good can be said to have come out of all this trouble and upset, it's him. We talk now in a way we never did. I feel I can say anything to him, and he'll know what to say back. We're friends in a way we never were before when it was all competitions and so many other kids around.'

'What about Billy's parents?'

'They'll be there tomorrow too, "in best bib and tucker", as the duke says. And I think they're just so pleased that Billy will be married before he goes to the front that nothing else matters right now.' That made everyone fall silent again and the gloom that had lifted a bit threatened to descend again. Brigid was considering how to dispel it when the telephone rang. It was Billy.

'He wants to go for a walk,' Kick said, when she had put down the receiver. She was smiling again. 'I'm going to meet him at the corner now.'

'Aren't you supposed not to see him on the night before the wedding?' That was Caroline.

'It's Billy,' Kick said. 'I'm always supposed to see him.'

'Your dress isn't finished,' said Edie.

'Sissy can be the tailor's dummy. You've worn all my other dresses so you may as well make yourself useful and wear this one,' Kick said. She threw on a tweed skirt and promised, 'I won't be long. I can do the final fitting when I'm back. You don't mind, do you?' she asked, anxious suddenly.

'No. Go,' Edie said. 'You're too fidgety anyway. Sissy will be much better.' And then, when Kick had gone, 'Sissy, strip,' she ordered.

Sissy took off her dress and stood in her underwear.

'Arms up,' Edie ordered, gathering the pink dress and holding it above Sissy's head, trying to put it on without the pins scratching her.

'I see the bruises are back,' Caroline said. How strange, even chilling, to be so matter-of-fact, Brigid thought. Sure enough, there were livid patches of blue and purple on Sissy's arms. She wasn't what you'd call black and blue but there were enough. Too many.

'Oh, they're the same bruises,' Sissy said casually.

'Can't be,' Caroline said doggedly. 'I know bruises. Those are new. And there are old ones as well,' she said, stepping closer to Sissy who stood still, caught in the glare of attention. Brigid wondered if she should send Caroline from the room. But it was too late now. Edie had removed Sissy's dress and laid it back on the sofa and Sissy, in her slip, was held fast as they all stared at her.

'That's enough,' she said, reaching for the dressing-gown Kick had taken off.

'More than enough, I would have thought,' Edie said. She lit a cigarette and offered it to Sissy, who shook her head. 'Given up?' Edie asked.

'Yes,' Sissy said. 'I realised it's not for me.'

'Seems like it's not the only thing that's not for you,' Edie said. She was brisk, but her voice shook a bit. Brigid was impressed that she could say so much. Even as the hospital-trained part of her assessed the bruises and considered her approach – a compress, arnica – the rest of her felt queasy. Violence and destruction might be all around them, but this was somehow different.

'Don't fuss,' Sissy said.

But she sat close to Edie, dressing-gown drawn tight around her, and didn't object when Edie said, 'I'm not fussing, just asking what you've got yourself into. Those bruises aren't from the Y, like you said the last ones were, are they?'

'No,' Sissy admitted. 'They're not.'

'So where are they from?' Edie persisted. And when Sissy didn't answer, more gently, she asked, 'Peter?'

'Yes, and I already know you don't approve.'

'If we don't approve,' Brigid said, 'it isn't because of money, or his war record . . . Sissy, darling, we care if he isn't kind to you.'

'Oh, he's not so bad,' Sissy said. 'Mostly, we get along very well.'

'And when you don't?' Edie asked. 'What then?'

'I suppose this . . .' Sissy admitted. 'Sometimes. Not always. We argue . . .'

'And do you argue in a way that leaves *him* with bruises?' Edie asked.

'No, I suppose I don't.'

'Doesn't seem very fair, does it?'

'Maybe not.' She hung her head. Then she rallied: 'But when we aren't arguing, he's such fun. A whole gang of them meet at the King's Anchor. Painters and poets and writers, and there's always a pot of stew, with things in it that anyone has brought so you might a get a sausage alongside a piece of pheasant, some lamb.'

'Do they all think this Peter is "such fun"?' Edie persisted.

'Well, not all of them. There's one girl, Aurora, she doesn't like him much. She doesn't want me to like him either. But they do think he's terribly talented.'

'And do you agree?'

'I don't know. He won't let me look at any of his paintings. I tried. I won't make that mistake again.' She attempted a laugh that came out rather wobbly.

'If it isn't that mistake, it'll be another,' Edie said briskly. 'Because it isn't what you do, don't you see? It's what he does. And there's not much you can change about that.'

'But he says there is,' Sissy said. 'He says he's not used to having someone like me around – so clumsy and noisy and nosy.' She laughed. A wobbly laugh. 'It's true, I am all those things. He says we'll both settle down, and I'll learn to be less, well, less *everything*, and then we'll rub along very nicely. He is sorry, you know, when he cools down.' For a moment Brigid tried to imagine Fritzi boiling with anger, acting in rage, then apologising. She couldn't.

'Sorry you made him cross,' Caroline asked, 'rather than sorry for what he did?'

'Well, yes . . .' Sissy said.

'*That* sort of sorry. I see,' Caroline said. How horribly wise she sounded, Brigid thought. No one said anything for a few minutes, and Edie went to switch on a lamp, snapping them out of the half-light.

'Remember I said I want to feel everything?' Sissy said. 'Even the bad stuff? Well, I am.' Then, as Edie went to say something, she shook her head. 'Kick will be back soon and this dress isn't finished so we'd better get on.' She stood up and took off the dressing-gown. 'Come on, Edie, we're like the shoemaker's elves. Only at this rate the shoemaker will be back before we're done!'

Edie looked at her a while, then said, 'OK. Turn around,' and put the dress over Sissy's head. Somehow, it was better when the pink crêpe-de-Chine covered the blue and burgundy marks. As if something had come unstuck in the room.

It allowed Brigid to stand too. 'I suppose I'd better get Caroline home. It's late.' Sissy gave her a grateful smile, although she looked like someone who regretted having said so much.

Caroline buttoned her cardigan, then turned to Sissy. 'I know you're used to it,' she said kindly. 'I am too. It's not as shocking for us as it would be for Brigid or Edie.'

'What a wise little owl you are,' Sissy said. She hugged Caroline, who submitted awkwardly, even raising her arms to hug Sissy back.

'But you mustn't let being used to it make you think it's all right,' Caroline said, from within the circle of Sissy's arms.

Where were the grown-ups? Brigid thought, as she and Caroline went down the dark stairs and out into the evening. All the freedom that had been so intoxicating suddenly felt too much. Where was Honor to insist they all needed a few nights in, 'supper on a tray and early bed'? Or Mama to frown and say, 'I think *not* . . .' Anyone at all to pronounce, 'That man is not suitable. I would prefer not to see him any more' and instruct Andrews to say 'not at home' in his most freezing tones if the man was unwise enough to ring up.

The usual protections had fallen away. The walls that had been built to keep girls like Sissy safe were no longer in place, but those girls hadn't yet learned to do without them.

And now Kick was to be married, Brigid too, eventually. The thought gave her a warm secret glow. But marriage changed things, she knew. Who would be there to watch out for Sissy? For Caroline? There was Edie – the thought gave her great comfort – but it wasn't enough.

Chapter Forty-Six

Kick

The storm of reporters around the register office was worse than Joe had led her to expect. They clicked and shouted and the sound of their camera shutters opening and closing was a cradle for the questions they called at her, at Joe.

'Is the marriage definitely going ahead?'

'Why aren't your parents here, Miss Kennedy?'

'Where will you live?'

'When does Lord Hartington ship out?'

'What will Boston make of this marriage?' That, from a man with a pencil moustache.

'*London News*,' Joe muttered to her, as they went up the shallow steps. 'The Parnell guy.'

Kick nodded, remembering the headline from the paper two

days earlier: *Parnell's ghost must be smiling sardonically*, it had trumpeted. *A Hartington is to marry a Catholic Irish-American who comes from one of the great Home Rule families in Boston.*

'I'm sorry,' she whispered back, squeezing the arm that held hers.

'There go my hopes of being President,' he said, with a laugh. 'I'll be finished in Boston for this.'

'People will forget. Once they know you like I know you, they'll see there isn't a person alive better suited to being President than you. And now that Pa and Mother have accepted it . . .'

'Mother sent a telegram to Archie Spell this morning,' he said wryly, 'asking that he get Archbishop Godfrey to persuade you to wait.'

'This morning?' she asked, incredulous. 'This very morning?'

'This very morning.'

Inside the doors, crowds of Red Cross girls and GIs from the officers' club, all in uniform, mingled with Billy's parents and relatives. There were so many that Kick's eyes stung with sudden tears. All these people for a marriage that so few were certain of. That so many were suspicious of. And yet here they were, to cheer on her and Billy. She had spent the night, the morning, missing her mother. Missing Rose's cool hands and certain voice. Her calm in the face of everything, as though calm were the ordained response. She had imagined her mother's distress at being so far away. But now that Joe had told her about Archie Spellman . . . Kick threw back her shoulders, stood up straighter on Joe's arm, and looked around for Billy.

And there he was, in his uniform, face a little anxious. His hair, she realised, was so much thinner than when they had first met and fallen in love: it had drawn back from his forehead and temples, exposing the pale smoothness of his brow. How long it had taken them to get here, she thought. 'I will take the very best care of her, I swear it,' he said to Joe, as Joe took his arm out of Kick's and gave her a tiny push because she stood there, momentarily bewildered at what was happening.

'I know you will,' Joe said, 'or I wouldn't be here.'

In ten minutes, they were married. 'That didn't take long, did it?' Billy said, when the registrar had pronounced them man and wife. The cheers were so loud he had to lean right in to her.

'After everything,' she said, 'after *everything*, ten minutes . . .' And they looked at one another and burst out laughing. All the dread Kick had felt – dread at her defiance of family, at placing her trust in Bishop Mathew and not Father d'Arcy, in deciding to believe that she could marry the man she loved and keep the faith that meant so much to her, because what if she was wrong? What if Bishop Mathew was wrong? What if this thing she had done was a mortal sin? – all that fell away and all she saw were Billy's blue eyes, crinkled up in laughter and the way his smile lit his face, taking away the stiff look it held in repose, filling it with mischief.

Chapter Forty-Seven

Brigid

First there was giddy elation at the successful Normandy landings, and then came a new terror. Flying bombs called V1s that came not from planes but were propelled by their own power, pilot-less, with a menace that was impersonal. Each carried a ton of explosives and there seemed no way to stop them. No way to predict them. They came in swarms like savage insects, falling according to some directive only they understood, setting fires and destruction in their wake, splitting the June sky with orange fury.

Where there had been hope there was terror again. Londoners who had laughed during the Blitz, who had staunchly insisted, 'No Hun will chase me from my home,' now packed quietly and fled the city.

All leave was cancelled and instead of giddy talk of 'the end', people spoke grimly of Germany's determination to destroy the country so entirely that even if England won the war there would be no England to come home to. Privately, Brigid thought that Mr Churchill had damned them all by saying the war would be won in a week. After the success of Normandy, he had given voice to hope, and permission for celebration. For a few days, a week. Then the V1s came and hope retreated, back into the place they had all learned to store it.

'Isn't that just like a Hun?' they asked each other, in queues and on buses. The land girls in Hertfordshire asked it too, called it to one another through open doors and across fields full of soft green abundance. They asked with scornful knowing, as though they had, all of them, vast experience with these 'Huns'.

Fritzi begged her not to go back to London. 'Please,' he said, 'stay here.'

'I can't. You know I can't. You must be here, producing food to keep the shops open, and I must be in London, tending the wounded.'

'When will you be back?'

'I don't know. Maybe not until it's all over.' One way or another, it would soon be over. It had to be. They all knew that. There was nothing left. No resource that had not been already drained. And now these rockets that killed with remote and chilly intelligence. The sting in the tail of Hitler's dying war machine.

'And when it's over, we'll be married.' He spoke with quiet confidence.

'We will,' Brigid agreed. Although the word 'over' chilled her. It could mean so many things.

She returned to London and found the remnants of their little group tattered and frayed at the edges. Kick was gone, in

Eastbourne with Billy, where his regiment waited daily for the order to leave. Joe no longer came to London, which left Sissy and Edie in the flat.

'Mostly just me,' Edie said, when Brigid called. 'Isn't it interesting how you think you're at war, but then you realise that wasn't *real* war, not really? Not now that I see there's way worse than that was.'

'Things are bad,' Brigid agreed. 'Now, it feels more like it did at the start, before you and Kick arrived. Before America. When bombs landed every night and it felt like all of England might simply be swept into the sea.' She shook her head to dispel the memory. 'How's Sissy?'

Edie rolled her eyes. 'Impossible. Refuses to budge on anything. Says she's perfectly happy and there's nothing anyone needs to do.'

'Well, if she loves him,' Brigid began, 'maybe he will settle . . .' She didn't believe it even as she said it, but what else did one do when faced with such stubborn insistence as Sissy gave, only hope?

'No, Brigid. Men like that don't.'

'She's lucky she has you to look out for her.' Then, peering at Edie, 'You really do look tired. Couldn't you get away from London for a few nights? Go to my parents in Elvedon? No one is firing deadly rockets at them. You could sleep all you wanted.'

'I'm fine,' Edie said. 'I don't even mind the doodlebugs that much. And when Billy's regiment goes, Kick will be back. We'll wait out the rest of the war together.'

'What will you do afterwards?' Brigid asked. It was the first time she had ever asked Edie such a thing. 'Will you go back to Virginia?'

'I don't think so. Not right away, anyway. I want to see some of the places you all talk about. Other places where this war was fought. France, Italy, even North Africa. It seems like there's a lot more to discover. What about you?'

'It'll be a while before Fritzi and I can get married. Which I'm rather glad about, because it means plenty of time for everyone to get used to the idea.'

'And will they?'

'Oh, they will. Mama and Papa don't really care for things like that. And already Chips is starting to come around. I can hear in his voice that he's already thinking of him as *dear Fritzi* again. Being royal trumps *everything* with Chips.' She chuckled. 'And Maureen is advising him about the wedding, quite as if she has married a dozen princes herself.'

'A prince . . .' Edie said. 'Isn't it just the silliest thing? Of all the girls in England, and all the Dollies on that great big ship, I end up being friends with a princess and a duchess . . .'

'Not yet, either of us,' Brigid reminded her.

'As good as,' Edie insisted. 'Not that I care anything for that. So what will you do as a princess?'

'Live very quietly in the country and have lots of babies, I hope,' Brigid said. 'I feel as though I've had enough of being busy, enough excitement and trouble and everything, for a whole life. Fritzi's the same. I think maybe what we like so much about one another . . .' she felt awkward, talking about herself like that but ploughed on '. . . is that we both want things to be quiet. Waking up to days that are the same, knowing what is to happen every week and every month ahead; that seems like perfect Heaven to me.'

'You always did seem more reluctant than the others,' Edie said. 'Like you were making the best of it, not throwing yourself into it, like Sissy, or tussling with it, like Kick. I hope you get all the quiet you want, Brigid. You've earned it.'

It felt, Brigid thought, like a kind of blessing. And exactly the kind she wanted. 'It's a relief to be sure in one's mind,' she said. 'I feel as though I understand rather more about what I want than I ever have. And even though it isn't what others want for me,' she shrugged, 'now that I see what it is, I mean to follow it. I've started to understand it's the only way.'

She walked back to Belgrave Square where Andrews told her, with carefully concealed surprise, 'Mr Channon is out. Her ladyship is in the library.'

Brigid went to find Honor at Chips's desk, writing busily. She looked up as Brigid opened the door and said, 'One minute, while I finish this. Nearly done.' Brigid stood in silence, breathing the heavy, still air. This room always seemed the least mobile of anywhere in that house. As though the weight of Chips's business affairs held it down. A clock ticked loudly in the silence and she found herself following the sound: *nearly . . . done . . . nearly . . . done.*

'There.' Honor laid down her pen. 'I might as well tell you, darling, that I won't be back after this.' Only then did Brigid spot the overnight case by the corner of the desk. 'Just a few things,' Honor said, following her eyes. 'I'll send for the rest later.'

'Are you really sure?' Brigid asked. 'What if you change your mind?'

'About Frankie? That's his name. I won't. And even if I did, I couldn't come back. Not now.'

'I'm sure Chips would allow—' Brigid began.

'Oh, he would. Indeed he would. He would allow any number of indiscretions, if only I'll stay here with him. But I can't, darling. Not now that I've seen what it can be like.'

'What *what* can be like?'

'Love.'

Brigid twitched. To hear her sister – so reserved in everything she did and said – speak of love without mockery, was a surprise.

'I never expected it,' Honor continued. 'I didn't even believe in it, not really. All those people doing the *strangest* things, saying it was for love . . . I thought they must be exaggerating. But now I see they weren't. I see that one would do anything for it. So I cannot stay here. And I cannot come back to Chips, no matter what.'

'What about Paul?'

Honor's face twisted. 'We'll arrange that when the war is over and he comes home from America. But, you know, Chips always was far better with him than I . . .' Her eyes went pink for a minute and sadness made her voice deep. 'Sometimes I feel I hardly know the boy. And, yes, that is my fault.' She was silent. Then, 'If I was to tell you anything, Brigid darling, even though you're not the sort of person one tells things to . . .' by which Brigid understood that Honor found her to be reserved and distant, just as she had found Honor '. . . it would be this: expect love. Look for it. Seek it out. And don't let any of them tell you it doesn't matter.'

'I think I may have found that out already,' Brigid said awkwardly.

Honor looked at her, then smiled. 'I'm glad, darling. I really am. I worried that you might be rather too like me – not enough romance behind those charming features, all practicality and duty. It took me far too long to see past all that.' She folded the flap of the envelope, wrote *Mr Channon* on it, and placed it square in the centre of the desk. 'I must go. Will you be here when he reads it?'

'I'll try.'

'You're a dear girl, Brigid. And then, when he has read it, you must not let him keep you here. He would. In fact,' on a laugh, 'I'm sure he'd exchange me for you in an instant. But you mustn't let that happen.'

'I won't. I can't. I have other things that will soon happen.'

'I'm glad,' Honor said again.

Chapter Forty-Eight

Maureen

'**A**re you upset about Billy and Kick, Mummie?' Caroline asked. For once, Maureen thought, with irritation, she spoke clearly and audibly. She even laid down her book and sat up straighter in the armchair by the window looking onto the back garden at Belgrave Square.

'Why should I be upset?'

'I know you planned with the duke to make sure they didn't marry. Must be rather disappointing, no?' Her clear tones carried easily, even with the windows open.

'What's this?' Duff, seated at the other end of the sofa from Maureen, folded his newspaper in half down the middle and put it on the table beside him.

'Nothing, darling. Caroline's being silly. Where shall we go for dinner? I rather thought the Savoy.'

'What did you mean about the duke and planning?' Duff asked Caroline.

Caroline, Maureen saw, made a show of looking from one to the other, then said, 'The duke rings up every day. He and Mummie spent such a long time talking about ways to keep Kick from marrying Billy, but now they're married and I thought, How very disappointing for Mummie after all her efforts.' Then, in a return to her more usual mumble, 'I thought you knew.'

Duff, Maureen saw, looked at Caroline. She could see his top lip twitch in the way he had when he was trying not to laugh. 'Did you?' he said. 'Think I knew?'

'I think I did . . .' Caroline said, head bent over her book again.

'Maybe you'd run upstairs, darling, and let me and Mummie talk.'

'Of course.' Caroline closed the book and went out, without looking at Maureen. She shut the door quietly behind her, and when she was gone the room was perfectly silent, although from outside came the busy evening sounds of birds. How surprising they were, Maureen thought suddenly. After everything of the last few years, the nightly bombs and now the rockets splitting the skies and setting fires that raged for days, bringing noise and smoke and filth, the birds still gathered at evening to chirp and sing out the day, closing it behind them with full honours.

She waited for Duff to speak. When he turned to her, any hope she'd gained from the twitching lip died. His face was dark and his bushy brows drawn tight down over his eyes. 'Well?' he said.

'I don't know what the child is talking about.' Maybe if she could emphasise Caroline's youth, her childishness and unreliability . . .

'Does the duke telephone you here every day?'

'Not every day, darling. That would be terribly tedious.' It was the wrong tone. She had known it would be.

'Answer the question, Maureen.'

'He does telephone.' She shrugged and leaned back against the sofa, careful to look straight ahead rather than at him. Duff in such a mood could be frightening. 'You are gone a great deal, you know.'

'What do you talk about?' And, when she didn't answer, 'Billy and Kick?'

'Sometimes.'

'Was Caroline right? Were you plotting with Eddie Devonshire to keep Kick and Billy apart?'

'He asked if I would help and I said yes. I did it for their sakes, as much as anyone else's. They do not understand how difficult marriage can be,' she looked sideways at him as she spoke, 'and how much more difficult if there is so much against them from the beginning. It has come to nothing, but I felt it only right to try,' she said, with as much dignity as she could bring to the words. But if she hoped to distract him by dangling *duty*, she failed.

'It was – is – none of your business. What would possess you to do such a thing? Unless . . .'

'Unless what?' She kept her eyes away from his. Her heart beat faster and higher so that she felt it in her throat. Almost she wanted to put a hand up to see if she could feel it hammering there, but she stayed completely still. For one moment, she felt as a pheasant or rabbit might, certain that to stay still was to be unseen, unnoticed. And yet, how very often they betrayed themselves, she thought: the twitch of a white tail, the swish of a speckled feather.

'Unless,' his voice was like gravel falling into water, 'this was only an excuse and there are other reasons why you and Eddie might talk? And even meet? Because I cannot see otherwise what possible reason you would have to be so busy in someone else's affairs. I know you like to break things, Maureen, but even for you, a marriage that has nothing to do with you is rather too much.'

'Well, if Billy didn't marry Kick, perhaps it *could* have had something to do with me. Or, at least, my family . . .'

'Brigid?' he said. And, when she said nothing, 'You really thought . . .?'

'Perhaps. A little. We all thought how much better suited she and Billy would be.' And that was true, she told herself. It wasn't the only true thing, but it was true.

'We?' he asked. 'You mean you and Eddie. Why him, why not Moucher?'

'She couldn't bring herself to do anything. She's too fond of Kick.'

'But she knew all about you and Eddie scheming together?'

'I don't know. You'd have to ask her that. Anyway,' quickly, 'what does it matter now? Caroline is right, we failed. They are married.'

'Failure doesn't make your trying any less frightful.' He got up and shut the window, and only then did Maureen realise the birds had fallen silent except for a few sleepy twitterings. It was almost dark. She wondered if he would leave the room, the house, but he sat down again. 'I think it's time you went back to Clandeboye. Caroline can follow when her school term finishes. I don't like either of you to be in London now. When I leave, I want to know that you're safe, at home with the children, not rattling around London in harm's way.'

'When you leave?'

'Yes. It will not be immediately, but it will come. There is a mission I wish to volunteer for.'

'Because of this?' She spoke into the gathering gloom. 'Because of the duke . . .?'

'It is nothing to do with this.'

'I thought I could make you stay,' she said softly, 'I was so sure I could.'

'You always think you can do anything.' He spoke with affection. 'You think it is enough to want something for you to achieve it. I envy you that.'

'Except, if it was true, it isn't true now,' she said. 'And of all things, *this* that I want so much – for you to stay – is the thing I cannot have.' Then, 'I wonder if Caroline knows what she has done?'

'Caroline hasn't done anything,' he said sharply. 'Anything that has been done, you have done it.' Then, more gently, 'I will go, because I must, but, darling, this has nothing to do with you. I was always going to go. This row has been unpleasant, and I'm ashamed to think of you colluding with Eddie in a way that is so unworthy, but it has no bearing on my decision. None at all.'

'Please,' she said. 'Please don't.'

'I've never heard you say that word before.' But he took her hand as he spoke, reaching across the sofa to find and hold it.

'Don't joke, darling, not now.' She moved closer to him so that he could put his arm around her. He drew her close in towards him. 'I'd do anything at all to persuade you to stay. I'll give up anything, be however you want me to be, if only you'll stay.'

'It isn't anything you can do, darling.' He rested his head

against hers and spoke into her hair. 'It's what I have to do. But I cannot do it unless I know that you and the children are safe. At Clandeboye.'

She thought of refusing, of saying she would remain in London, live in the highest building she could find, on the top floor, and shine a light through her bedroom window every night, if he left her. But she didn't. Not that she wouldn't have done it, she thought. To keep him, she would do that and more. Only he would hate it. And hate her. And sometimes, she found, even when you didn't want to, even when you had no habit of it, you found you had to do what was right.

'I'll go home,' she promised. 'And I'll wait for you there.'

Chapter Forty-Nine

Kick

Within days of the wedding, Billy's regiment was told to prepare to ship out. They had known it would be soon. And then it was. 'We seem to do nothing but say goodbye,' he said, when he told Kick. 'I'm sorry, my darling, to leave you.'

'You'll be back,' Kick said, putting all the effort she could muster into making those words sound true. 'And then we'll have the glorious rest of our lives. I can't wait for you to see Jack again, and meet Eunice, and Pat, and the Little Boys . . .'

'We've had so little time.' He held her close. 'When I'm back, we'll have a second honeymoon. A proper one.'

'We had five glorious days,' she said. 'Maybe the five most glorious days of my life.' And it was what she continued to tell herself after Billy had gone: five glorious days. These she weighed against the days that followed, the days without him. And they were enough. They held true as she came and went from her duties at the club, through afternoons spent with Edie in parks now that summer had arrived, or with Brigid in the garden of Belgrave Square in that last, increasingly precious hour when dusk was drawing down but not yet advanced enough that they needed to hide indoors from the Vis.

It was as though, without Billy, without Andrew, without Joe mostly now too, they settled instinctively into a different rhythm. One that was quieter. Subdued, even. They clung closer together in a city that was emptying.

'One million evacuated I heard,' Edie said, one day, as they walked slowly in Hyde Park with Debo, Sissy and Brigid. 'And more still clamouring to go.'

'You can almost see them draining away, like bathwater,' Sissy agreed. Despite the beauty of the day, there were no children in the park. No nursemaids with prams, and not many of anyone else either. A few dawdling soldiers, nurses on their break, an elderly couple walking slowly hand in hand.

'London feels so empty. It's like a party where everyone has gone home and you see only empty glasses and overflowing ashtrays,' Sissy said.

They drew near to the fountain. Two of the jets weren't working and in the basin there were just a few inches of muddy water. Apollo, high on his plinth, seemed no longer the lofty figure who surveyed the world beneath his feet with bemusement, but rather someone washed up beyond the tide line, far away and lonely.

'The Ritz bar was deserted last night,' Brigid said, sitting on the stone rim. 'All that feeling of fun and being together despite the enemy, none of that was there. The men are almost all gone now. You know Duff is going too?'

'So he did it? What does Maureen say?' Sissy asked.

'She's beside herself but she's agreed to go back to Clandeboye. She leaves almost immediately, Caroline too. Belgrave Square will be jolly quiet.'

'Poor Chips,' Sissy said. 'He'll hate that . . . Will you go out tonight?'

'I don't think so,' Brigid said. 'It doesn't feel right any more.'

'Something about there being no men makes it hard to go out,' Kick agreed.

'No one to dance with?' Sissy asked.

'No. Like it isn't fair to them, or as though, if one takes one's mind off them even for a moment, something bad will happen. That they're only safe as long as one keeps thinking about them.'

'It's not like you to be superstitious,' Brigid said.

'And I'm not. Not much. Only in this. It doesn't feel like superstition. It feels like common sense.'

'It feels like waiting for the end,' Edie said. She trailed her fingers in the dirty water. The day was hot enough to make even muddy brown water appealing. 'It's over. Everyone knows it. Now, it just needs to end.'

'It's almost exactly a year since I arrived here,' Kick said thoughtfully. 'A year and a few days. What a lot has happened.'

'Do you remember ghastly old Meredith, that first night at the 400 Club?' Debo asked. She lit a cigarette and blew smoke at one of the bronze turtles that were supposed to spit water at Apollo. Without the spitting, the poor turtle looked very old and helpless. 'Demanding to know if you were back to become a duchess? And then what did she say? *Just because America has joined the war doesn't mean you can come over here and help yourself to anything you want*,' she mimicked. 'I guess that's what most people thought. Yet here you are.'

'Not a duchess,' Kick pointed out.

'As good as. One day to be the most important woman in the country, next to the Queen.' Kick saw Edie and Sissy blink at that. 'And, what's more,' Debo continued, 'the family all adore you. Andrew tells me they never stop singing your praises.'

'How perfectly sickening for Meredith,' Sissy said, with a grin. But talking about Meredith wasn't much fun. Her fiancé had been killed in North Africa.

'And she's unlikely to find another,' Debo said.

'Hush, Debo,' said Brigid. 'Don't be unkind.'

'I must go,' Sissy said, stretching her arms above her head and yawning.

'Where? That wretched pub, I suppose?' Brigid asked. Sissy nodded.

'The only place in London where young men are still to be found, I believe,' Debo said scornfully. 'You'd think they'd have the decency to stay at home like the rest of us.'

'They didn't all choose not to fight,' Sissy said gently. 'Most of them were turned down.'

'All the same,' Debo insisted, 'they should have the wit to know not to be there, in plain sight. And so should you.'

'I wish you wouldn't go.' That was Edie. 'Why not just come back to the flat? I have a late shift, but you and Kick could be company for one another.' But if she'd hoped to persuade Sissy with this sideways appeal to Kick's loneliness, she failed.

'Don't worry,' Sissy said cheerfully. 'I'll be perfectly all right.'

'You'll certainly say you are,' Brigid agreed; 'although you know it isn't exactly the same thing,' and, when Sissy had gone, 'That girl terrifies me.'

'She terrifies all of us,' Edie said. 'But I'll watch her. Something will get through to her, you'll see. She's young, something has to.'

'A year,' Kick said again, leaning back on the thin rim of the fountain, 'and everything just as different as can be.' She trailed her fingers in the murky water and flicked some at Brigid. 'For both of us.' She still found it hard to believe that so much of what she wanted had come to pass. As though, even now, her mother, Billy's father, someone, would say *There's been a mistake . . . Of course you cannot be married . . .* 'I just wish the next bit would hurry up.'

'What next bit?' Edie asked.

'Ending the war instead of just talking about it, everyone coming home. Instead of waiting.'

'Yes,' Brigid agreed. 'I don't like this bit. It's not quiet, not at all, but it still feels like the lull before something.'

What a lot had happened indeed, Kick thought later, alone in the flat, watching the sun disappear behind the buildings outside the window. And not just Billy and being married. It was nearly two months since the wedding, and still her mother hadn't spoken to her. Kick had sent so many entreaties, direct and via her brothers and sisters, but Rose's silence had a granite quality. Smooth, unyielding, a surface that reflected your need back to you but always out of reach.

Being outside the circle of her mother's approval was hard, especially as Joe wasn't there to laugh her out of her sadness, or Billy to tell her earnestly, 'It'll all come right, you'll see.' It was the longest Kick had ever been at odds with her mother. She was worried that, if Rose didn't give in soon, she would get used to the distance between them, become accepting of it. Because somewhere, buried beneath the disquiet at Rose's silence, a little voice said, *See? The world didn't end . . .*

As though Rose had read her mind, and been jolted from her

stony resolve, two days later, as Kick readied herself for her shift, a letter arrived. Recognising her mother's neat hand on the envelope, she went back up the stairs to the flat. Whatever was in the letter, she needed to read it properly, not while she was walking or on one of her short breaks at the club.

Almost, it was an apology. Rose pleaded shock, and Kick wondered what had persuaded her even to give a name to her behaviour; *but that is all over now*, Rose wrote, *and as long as you love Billy so dearly, you may be sure we will all receive him with open arms.* She wrote about how much they looked forward to having Joe home after his time with the RAF ended, and how they wished they could welcome Kick and Billy too.

Knowing she was forgiven, that her mother was once more on her side, as she read her words about welcoming Billy, Kick felt a great sense of peace. Sitting at the worn table, the letter in front of her, she conjured a vision of Hyannis Port on the best kind of day – clear, breezy, sunny but not so hot it scorched your feet to walk barefoot along the dock. Days longer than nights, to be filled to bursting with all the things she loved.

She imagined Billy there, and thought how alien he would find it, then of how quickly he would discover people and things he enjoyed, how interested he would be in everything he saw. She could see him, Joe and Jack together in any one of half a dozen places, talking, laughing. How proud and happy she would be alongside them. She didn't mind waiting, she thought, because she had so much to wait for.

Rose's forgiveness acted on her like a sedative, and some of the agitation – the longing for 'the next bit' – quietened. She found she was more content to go about her days at the club, the flat, visits to Billy's parents, with a kind of calm that was new and wonderful. 'It's like everything is resolved,' she confided to Edie, one day in early August, as they went home to the flat together, 'and the play is about to begin. The lights are dimmed and the curtain is about to go up, and I'm settled comfortably.' She stretched her arms above her head as they walked, releasing the strain from her shoulders.

'Sometimes that's the best bit,' Edie said.

'How fast time goes now. Can you believe that today is the Glorious Twelfth?'

'What's glorious about it?' Edie asked.

'Grouse shooting begins. Don't ask me why that's glorious but apparently it is. And I can't believe I know it.'

'Feels like fall already,' Edie said. At the flat, she opened the front door with her key, then scuffed at a few dry leaves that had drifted into the narrow hallway, kicking them out into the street. Kick went ahead up the stairs and was in the sitting room when the doorbell sounded. 'That'll be Sissy,' she called down, in exasperation. 'Why does she never have a key?'

She had taken off her coat and was tidying her hair when Edie came up. 'It wasn't Sissy,' she said. 'A telegram. For you.' She held out the yellow envelope.

'Mother must have changed her mind about forgiving me,' Kick said lightly. Edie nodded but Kick saw that she stayed right where she was, beside her, as Kick tore through the yellow paper. And when she couldn't find words to say what she had read, Edie took the paper from her with a hand that shook like Kick's own.

'Joe?' she said. 'Joe.' It was a question. And then it wasn't.

His plane, they said, had exploded over the North Sea. The secret mission had gone wrong. The way in which he had planned to even up the score with Jack had failed him.

Kick wished he could have understood that it didn't matter.

Not as much as he thought it did. She had defied their parents, refused their instructions, even lived with Rose's fury for two months and the world hadn't ended. *Not everything is the way we were brought up to believe it is*, she wanted to whisper to him. It was what she had learned – that you could go your own way and it could be a different way from the one you'd been given, and it could work out just fine. But there was no telling him now.

She tried hard not to believe the news. Tried to be one of those people she'd heard of who denied the truth when it was ugly and hateful, who lived in a state of unreality. But she couldn't. The black words on the yellow paper would not allow it. They took possession of her completely, so that even as she passed the paper to Edie and watched a grey tide wash over her friend's face, she was already planning what to pack and how to travel. What to tell Billy's parents.

'Let me help you,' Edie said.

'Thank you. Pa has arranged an army transport plane. I leave immediately.' Then, bitterly, *'Plan for Good Times . . .* This is what I should have prepared for.'

'You cannot prepare for this. It wouldn't be right even to try.'

As they were packing, Sissy came in. Edie swiftly took her into the small bedroom – afraid, no doubt, of what chatter Sissy might launch into, and told her. When they came out, Sissy was crying, as neither Kick nor Edie could. But instead of her easy tears being an affront, as they might have been, Kick found them comforting. 'He was the best in the world,' she said. 'I'm glad you knew it.'

'We knew it,' Edie said.

'Being here, just him and me, away from everyone, it changed him,' Kick said. 'Changed both of us. It's not easy to see, when your nose is pressed against the window all the time, what's really around you. And I think we were like that – noses too close to the window. Growing up with Pa and Mother didn't leave much time for finding things out by ourselves. There were always so many things to do and not do, and even the things to do had to be done the "right" way. It's only being here – for me and I think for Joe too – that we got a bit of a breather and could look around more. See the way other people do things . . . And, well, I think he liked that. I know I did. He was different, these last months. A bit kinder. Joe was always the best, but he could be mighty heedless. Because he was always first at everything, he didn't often see what it was like for those who weren't. He started to learn that, and he liked learning it.'

She took a deep breath to keep the tears where they belonged, not spilling out. 'You two showed him that, you know. As much as anything it was you two.'

'Edie mostly,' Sissy said.

'Yes, that's true, but you as well. It was something different for him, having friends who were girls. Not girlfriends, not love affairs, just friends.'

'I wish I could come with you,' Edie said, repacking the top layer of Kick's case more neatly.

'There isn't to be a funeral,' Kick said. 'Not yet. There's an investigation needed first. And it'll take time to bring him home. Maybe when that's all done, maybe you could come then?' She looked at Edie.

'I'd like that,' Edie said. 'You only need to let me know and I'll be ready.'

Chapter Fifty

Sissy

When Kick had gone, Sissy, crying even harder, admitted, 'I'm crying for myself too. Am I going to Hell for that?'

'Sssh. Don't talk about Hell,' Edie said. 'Not now. It's foolish, when there's death all around. Why are you crying for yourself?'

'Well, for all of us, I suppose. It felt like we'd get right through this war without anything so very terrible happening. I even started thinking about afterwards, what we'd all do, which I never did till recently because I didn't dare. And now this . . . Almost, I feel it's my fault. That I jinxed us all by letting myself make plans.'

'You didn't jinx anyone, Sissy. Don't be crazy. Making plans isn't what killed Joe.' Even as she said it, Edie flinched. It was too soon to speak it. 'In any case, you should make plans. You need to.'

'Why me especially?' But she knew why.

'Because you can't keep on as you are. Surely you can see that.'

'It's not so bad,' Sissy said. 'Actually, not bad at all. I think he's changed. No fights for ages.'

'Men like him don't change,' Edie said. 'It's a real shame you can't see that. In the meantime, I don't like you staying out in that pub. It's not safe. Not now. To be out so much at night.'

'Oh, but Peter says there's a fail-safe way to know. He says it's a question of listening to the engines. You hear the doodle-bugs – such a pretty word for such a horrid thing – come in over the city. When the engine cuts, you count four seconds and wait for the explosion. That way, you can work out whereabouts they are and make plans.'

'All very clever. But what if the explosion tells you they're close by you? You aren't going to get very far in four seconds.'

'No, I suppose not,' Sissy said thoughtfully. 'I suppose it's not much of a strategy really but—'

'Do not say, *it's all we have*,' Edie said fiercely. 'There are better strategies. Don't be out at night. Go to a shelter. Leave London. Make an effort, Sissy. Stop drifting. Stop meeting that man – a man who can't be good to you and doesn't even pretend to try. I can't bear to watch any more.'

'I promise I will try,' Sissy said after a moment when she saw how serious Edie was. It was the best she could do.

*

That evening in the King's Anchor, the room was quieter than usual. There were empty tables all around them and the nicotine-stained wallpaper, the boarded-up window seemed grimy, not exciting. Sissy wondered if it was the place itself, or Joe's death that coloured it so differently. Joe's death, Edie's fury with her: these things took light and colour from everything. Perhaps they always would, she thought. She felt old, and wise, and so terribly sad.

There was no sign of Jim. Aurora breezed in, but only for long enough to say she was going home, to her mother who was sick. 'Compassionate leave from ARP duties,' she said. 'A few days just, but I'm jolly relieved to be getting out of London. There's something rather sinister about the place now.'

'Do you think of leaving?' Sissy asked Peter, when Aurora had gone. Mostly she spoke to fill the silence.

'Either the rockets have your name on them, or they don't,' Peter said, with a shrug. He took a deep drag of his cigarette and blew smoke towards the ceiling. 'It's your time or it isn't, that's all.'

'At home they say, "What's for you won't pass you by,"' Sissy said. 'I don't suppose this is what they meant, but it's certainly apt.' She took one of Peter's cigarettes and lit it. She still hated the taste, but the moment seemed to demand some gesture to express how she felt – irresponsible and cynical and . . . sort of *contained*, she thought. Partly it was Joe's death, and partly it was the way Peter so often made her feel. As though there was no before, no after and nothing except being with him, beside him, close to him. It was as though something about him made time move slower.

'If it is my time, it may as well be here,' she said, leaning in to him. She didn't mean it – of course it wasn't her time – but it seemed the right sort of thing to say. Grown-up, worldly. She tucked a strand of hair behind her ear, wondering what the maids at Ballycorry would say to see her, with Peter, a drink in one hand, cigarette in the other, while outside London trembled with uncertainty.

Later, she would wonder if it was at that moment, that very moment, that the rocket struck the house on Portland Street. The house where their flat was. The place that had been home to her, for all her coming and going and fudging, for more than a year now.

Later, when people said, 'Just think, you might have been there . . .' she knew what they meant: *Be thankful you weren't there. What a lucky escape.*

But she wasn't thankful. That they said such things was grotesque and made her wonder about all the times she had done something similar – said bland, vile things because she hadn't bothered to think through what she was saying or, more likely, hadn't understood what her words might mean. Because she should have been there. Or Edie should have been out somewhere with her. Either of those things. Neither was preferable to the other, she decided: to save Edie, to die with Edie; either of those things. Not this.

She imagined her friend, listening to the sound of the engine cutting, then counting four seconds. Her final four seconds. Counting, hoping; because Sissy had told her this piece of foolishness. Why had she repeated the stupid thing Peter had said to her, as though it were of some use? Why had she been with Peter when she should have been with Edie? Instead, Edie had been all alone. Alone not just in the flat but in the whole building. Kick gone, Brigid away, Sissy out. Just Edie, when the bomb with her name on it had come.

Peter shrugging, breathing smoke towards the ceiling. *Either the rockets have your name on them, or they don't. It's your time or it isn't, that's all.*

What nonsense that was, Sissy realised. What silly, dangerous rubbish he talked. The doodlebug hadn't had Edie's name on it. It just happened to land where she was so it killed her. Just like so many others had been killed because they were in a particular place at a particular time. Nothing had anyone's name on it. They just were, when they could so easily not have been.

Edie could have been out – at the shops, at Belgrave Square, at the club, in the park, anywhere at all. It would have been so easy. Perhaps she already had her coat on and was about to leave. Perhaps she was in the act of taking her coat off, having just that minute arrived home. That was the worst of it. How easily it could not have been.

Stop drifting, Edie had told her. *I can't bear to watch any more . . .* When she said it, Sissy had promised she would. She hadn't meant it. She hadn't really understood what Edie meant.

But now she did. Edie dying showed her that. Because Edie didn't drift. She had left home, same as Sissy had, but she had done it with fierce determination where Sissy had simply allowed herself to go where she was pushed. Edie had worked hard, made friends and learned about a new country. She had looked in all the right places and found out the person she really was.

She had done all these things and they hadn't saved her. Sissy had done none of them, and here she still was. That wasn't right and she must do something about it.

Brigid rushed back from Little Hadham as soon as she heard, and Kick telephoned from America, but in those first hours, it was just Sissy, all alone. She went to Belgrave Square, but

Caroline and Maureen were gone, and when she realised Chips didn't understand – he had never taken to Edie – she shut herself in the pale green bedroom. This, she realised, as she got into bed, still fully dressed, because she was shivering, this was what being a grown-up felt like. Not sitting with Peter in the King's Anchor, playing at being sophisticated and worldly. It wasn't a question of hemlines and high heels, of smoking without coughing, of having a lover. It was this: quietly accepting the kinds of blows you would once have said you could not survive. Seeing before you a path that was hard and without much jollity, and knowing you must take it.

Chapter Fifty-One

Kick

Kick had been home almost a month and in that time she had played more football, more tennis, swum more and sailed more than ever before. Every hour of the day, from the clear dawn through to the spectral evenings, was filled and filled again. It was August, then September, and every day was shorter than the one before. Autumn closing in. It was a relief to know that each day her efforts would be a few minutes less than they had been the day before. That dusk would come quicker and release her from the need for action.

She knew their friends were shocked by the ceaseless activity but, as she said to Jack, 'They didn't know Joe like we knew Joe. He would never want us to be sad and gloomy. Can't you imagine him asking, "Gee, can't you all get along without me?"'

Jack smiled as she'd known he would. He had to. There was

no joy in the smile and none in hers either. Just as there was no joy in the games they played. They ran and jumped and sailed and squabbled over wins and points and even laughed. And in none of it was there any mirth. But they were the eldest now – no Joe, no Rosie, or not really – and this was the example they had to set. And set fast. Before being a Kennedy turned into something else entirely.

So they gathered every day and planned what they would do, and they did it. Even though the friends were shocked. Even though Jack was so thin he was almost hollow. The two of them stayed together as much as they could. There had been four, the Big Ones, and now there were just two. Only with Jack close beside her could Kick feel that she might learn to bear it. Her sin picked and plucked at her. Her sense of fault. *Mea culpa,* she found herself thinking when she didn't make an effort not to. *Mea maxima culpa.* The sin of wishing Rosie dead, or at least of thinking she'd be better dead, had that killed Joe? Surely God wouldn't do that. But who knew, these days, what God would do?

At night, she wrote to Billy, every night, even though she knew he would receive the letters only intermittently. She liked the idea of him getting a bundle all at once, an out-pouring of the things she did, and how she missed him. Again and again, she told him she would see him soon, 'when all this is over'.

In late September, the family went to New York. Kick was soon to return to England. She didn't want to go – with Joe gone, with Edie gone, London was no longer London. She would go to Chatsworth, she decided. She would wait out the rest of the war quietly with Billy's family. Without Edie, she knew she couldn't cheer up the GIs. She couldn't bring a sense of home or comfort to them. Really, Edie had always been so much better at that. Kick just copied what she did – that blend of kindness and gruffness that was so unlike anyone else she knew.

'You need new things,' her mother encouraged her when the New York trip was planned. 'You need nice things. Every woman does.' Kick and Rose trod so carefully around each other now, and the treading was so tiring that Kick agreed. Of course she needed nice things. There was rationing in America too, but not like it was in England. In any case, Sissy had most of Kick's clothes.

She thought of the letter Sissy had written: '*I cannot stay in London. Not now. And I won't go back to Ballycorry. Might I come to America, do you think? I will do anything . . .*'

Kick had asked her father if he could find the girl a position. 'Maybe she could have my old job at the *Washington Times-Herald*?' Kick said. Washington, Kick thought, would be well away from Peter. In case Sissy's determination to stay away from him should waver.

'Let me see what I can do,' her father had said.

Sissy would be far better at that job than she had been, Kick thought. If she could only get to Washington, she might be all right. 'She can't be comforted,' Brigid had told her on one of their transatlantic calls, her voice coming and going between the crackling. 'She's convinced it's her fault Edie was in the flat when the rocket hit. It makes no sense. If I nurse a patient and the patient dies—' Her voice disappeared. '. . . responsibility,' she was saying when Kick could hear her again. 'But for Sissy to believe this, well, it's wilful, if you ask me. But you know Sissy . . .'

Kick agreed that she did. 'Once she gets out of London she'll be OK,' she said.

Brigid had begun to make plans for her wedding, Kick knew, telling her family quietly about Fritzi. She wanted to ask, but found she couldn't. And Brigid, as if she knew, said nothing of that. 'It's true Sissy believes that going to America is what Edie wanted her to do,' she said.

'I think she might be right about that,' Kick said. She must write to Edie's family, she thought. To her mother and sister, her father the doctor. Try to tell them what Edie had been to her in London, what she had been to Joe. How much they had all admired her and the grit that had made her travel halfway across the world 'to help out'. She would tell them that.

Kick chose to shop alone, in a department store on Fifth Avenue, where she debated between a darling dress in lilac and one in buttercup yellow, knowing she would probably buy both. She was to meet Eunice for lunch afterwards, and later they would take tea at Rose's suite at the Plaza. Her parents stayed in different suites in different hotels. They always had. Only now that Kick was married did she think how strange that was. She would never want to be anywhere Billy was not.

There was Eunice now, early. 'I'm not quite ready,' Kick said, as she stepped out of the elevator. She stood still so that people behind her had to step around her, *tsking* crossly.

'You ought to go back to the hotel and speak to Pa,' Eunice said.

'Why? What's happened?'

'You need to speak to Pa,' Eunice said again. 'I'll come with you.' She tried to take Kick's arm but Kick twitched her hand away. She couldn't bear it.

She didn't ask anything more. They stepped out onto Fifth Avenue and walked the few blocks to the Plaza in silence. She was careful not to say a word that might allow Eunice to speak. Because doing so would shatter the very last of the moments she understood. As long as nothing was said, nothing had happened.

I will buy the yellow and the lilac, she told herself. *Because when Billy is back there will be a need for both. There will be so much to do together. The second honeymoon he promised. Duties at Chatsworth, a place to make in the new world he spoke of where dukes were not so welcome. Although what world would ever not welcome Billy?*

And all her thoughts were gentle and swift. As long as she did not try to catch any of them and look too hard at it, as long as she did not speak and Eunice did not speak, they could play around her head like swallows in a barn, swooping this way and that, quick and graceful, always half from sight.

At the entrance to the Plaza she tried to keep walking, to carry on briskly down the street, keep moving, stay in motion, accompanied by the gentle happy thoughts. *The lilac dress would be perfect for a garden party, the yellow for lunch . . .*

But Eunice took her arm and this time held it fast. 'You need to speak to Pa.'

That evening, her father Joe took them to dinner at a Park Avenue restaurant. They sat at a large round table in the centre but the restaurant was empty so there was no one to see the maître d's triumph. It was 11 September, and Billy had been dead for twenty-four hours. Most of the world still did not know, Kick realised, yet already it was a different place.

They talked of plans for Palm Beach, of Roosevelt's speech. They did not talk of Joe. And now they did not talk of Billy either. Only once did they approach it and then indirectly. 'When will you go back to England?' Eunice asked.

'As soon as I can,' Kick said. 'I need to be there now. Not here.' She was sorry for that to be true. She had come home to be a comfort to her family. Now she needed to go. To seek comfort. She needed to be with Billy's family, to be with those whose hearts were broken just as hers was.

'God doesn't send us a cross heavier than we can bear,' Rose said firmly. She reached out on either side of her and clasped Kick's hand and Eunice's in each of her own. The feeling of those thin hard fingers in hers, the way her mother pressed her certainties into her daughters so that they might take root, expand, crowd out everything else, caused Kick to tremble.

God doesn't send us a cross heavier than we can bear. This was what Rose wanted them to accept. And in accepting, to suck life from all the doubt, the questions, the horror that lay in the space after the word *why*. Rose's pressing hands offered to take all that away. Close the shutters on *why*. Shut the doors on *how*. In their place, put pious certainties.

Kick felt sick. She felt as though, if she didn't say Billy's name, Joe's name, Rosie's name, Edie's name, right then, that no one would ever speak them again.

She opened her mouth.

'There'll be no tears in this house,' her father said, staring right at her. He looked old, and almost frail. But not so frail that she could speak when he had ordered her to be quiet. Because that was what it was. An order. She bowed her head. There would be no crying in that house. She knew it. They all did.

You'll be the ones to write the story of the next generation of the family. That was what Pa had said to her and Joe and Jack, the last summer in Hyannis Port. Joe couldn't, she wouldn't – she knew this for certain now. Rosie had never been included.

That left Jack. She hoped he would be enough. She looked at him and tried to smile.

'Will you stay there?' Eunice asked then. 'After?'

Kick thought about it. Billy was gone and England would never be the place she'd hoped. She would never be Duchess of Devonshire, or mistress of Chatsworth. The future she had planned – all the changes Billy wished to make, ideas learned from his failed political campaign – was empty now. 'Isn't it all just like a beautiful dream?' Jack had asked her, before she went back in her Red Cross uniform. And, yes, more than ever, those days now felt dreamlike, unreal. A piece of time too perfect to endure.

'Maybe,' she said. Really, she had no idea; 'After' was too far away.

It wasn't her country. They weren't her people. But she would go to where Billy's family were. To Brigid, to Debo, to Sissy. Because she couldn't be here. There were too many empty places at the table. She looked up to find her parents watching her. She would go.

Afterword

Rose Kennedy herself said the relationship between Kick and Billy contained 'enough material for a novel'. It has now given me enough material for two novels. It may feel at times that I have overstated the religious objections to the marriage, but these were really very profound. A future Duke of Devonshire marrying a Catholic girl was a matter important enough for the then-king, George VI, to say to Billy's father, 'I am very glad you have gone into the matter of her religion so carefully . . . and that she herself may come over to the Church later . . . I am sure the girl takes after her mother and not her father, as his behaviour here as ambassador in the early days of the war was anything but helpful.'

Meanwhile, over in Boston, the idea of Joe Kennedy's daughter marrying into a family that had provided so many of the instruments of colonial rule in Ireland was just as unpopular. Kick was sent anonymous hate mail, so was her family. The match was seen as a deep betrayal of her Irishness (and therefore genuinely represented a hitch in Joe Snr's presidential plans).

The third Duke of Devonshire was Lord Lieutenant of Ireland, so was the fourth; the fifth duke was one of five peers resident in England but with large estates in Ireland who protested a proposed absentee tax. The eighth duke was Chief Secretary of Ireland, and his brother, Lord Frederick Charles Cavendish, who was appointed Chief Secretary after him, in May 1882, was murdered by a splinter group of the Irish Republican Brotherhood in the Phoenix Park only hours after he arrived in the country.

This wasn't any old parental opposition, this was deep-rooted and visceral.

And yet, somehow, Kick and Billy did it. They managed to marry, without alienating any of their families, which I think is testament to their patience and courage, and the extent to which they clearly loved one another.

Rose Kennedy proved the hardest to bring around. She didn't talk or write to Kick for nearly two months after the wedding – and even on the morning of the ceremony was still working behind the scenes to get it called off or, failing that, later annulled. But by the end of June, she wrote to Kick to say 'that is all over now, dear Kathleen, and as long as you love Billy so dearly, you may be sure that we will all receive him with open arms.'

She was far less forgiving about Kick's later relationship, with Peter Fitzwilliam, who was, again, Anglican, but also – worse! – married. He planned to divorce his wife and marry Kick. Before that could happen, they were both killed in a plane crash in 1948. I have heard that Peter's wife, Olive Dorothea Plunket, kept his bedroom exactly as he had left it for many years after.

Only Kick's father, Joe, went to her funeral. She was buried quietly at Chatsworth.

The mission that killed Joe Kennedy also earned him the Navy Cross – just as he had wanted. His death was a bitter blow to Kick. They had become much closer during the months together in England; 'he was the best guy in the world,' she wrote to a friend.

Because of Joe's death, she was back home with her family when news of Billy's death came through, just a month later. A friend, going to see her in that time of tragedy, was shocked to find her family carrying on 'as normal'. 'God doesn't send us a cross heavier than we can bear,' was indeed Rose's response.

I often wondered about Kick's defiance in marrying Billy, and later taking up with Peter Fitzwilliam. Yes, she was motivated by love, in both cases, but I always found her determined defiance of the family she clearly adored intriguing. Along with her decision to be in England and stay in England – far away from them all.

For me, the answer to why she put so much space between herself and them lies in the criminal violence done to Rosemary Kennedy.

There are theories around the lobotomisation of Rosemary – including the suggestion that Joe Kennedy had been abusing his daughter, and the lobotomy was his way of making sure she never told anyone. I don't know of any actual evidence to support that. Instead, it seems to me that Rosie, who had suffered oxygen deprivation during a difficult birth and had mild cognitive impairment as a result, had the same kind of sex drive as her brothers. Quite unlike Kick who herself said to one boyfriend, 'I don't want to do the thing the priest says not to do.'

She couldn't even say the word.

Rosie, on the other hand, liked men. A lot. When she began running away from school and home, and meeting strange men, Joe Kennedy seems to have decided she would bring shame on all the family. And he acted to shut that down. Kick herself researched lobotomies in autumn 1941, while she was working for the *Washington Times-Herald*. The conclusion – one she shared with her mother – was that it wouldn't do. It was too much. The patient would be 'gone as a person'.

Apparently Kick believed that was that. Rose may also have believed the same thing. Joe, however, had other ideas, and in November 1941, Rosemary was given a local anaesthetic – she needed to be awake during the operation – and neural connections severed.

She was left severely brain-damaged, unable to walk or communicate.

Did Rose know Joe had planned this? Apparently not, although that seems hard to believe. In any case, in that year's round-robin letter to all the children, Rose didn't mention her eldest daughter at all. The family never spoke of her again. Although Rose had enough understanding to later write, 'Rosemary's was the first of the great tragedies that were to befall us.'

I don't know whether Kick saw Rosie after the lobotomy – Joe, her brother, certainly didn't. But in this book, I have given her the chance to see her sister in the aftermath of the terrible thing that was done to her, because I believe this great tragedy is what sent Kick back to England – away from America. Away from her family. The complicated emotions of loving the people who were responsible for such an atrocity must have been considerable. I also think this is what allowed her hold firm in the face of her parents' opposition to both her matches.

My version of Brigid Guinness is, of course, based on a real person too. She really did work as an auxiliary nurse during the war, and go to look after Prince Friedrich, then living as George Mansfield, after an accident with a tractor. And they really did then marry and have five children.

Sissy and Edie are both invented, based on memoirs and biographies of young women living in London during the war years. Chief amongst these, certainly in creating the character of Sissy, were Theodora FitzGibbon's *A Taste of Love* and Leland Bardwell's *A Restless Life*.

Both those books made me think about the intoxicating freedom these young women must have felt – and I have tried to create that feeling here – but also the very unprotected nature of their lives. They could do anything they wanted, but there was no one, really, to look out for them. Here, I have given them each other to do the looking-out.

Edie came to mind as I read about the 'Donut Dollies'. President Roosevelt's administration was concerned about maintaining US troop morale, seeing this as a major component of victory – so the Dollies were asked to provide emotional support. They were young American women, aged between twenty-five and thirty-five, who were carefully selected to have a decent level of education, and be 'healthy, physically hardy, sociable and attractive'. Only one in six would-be applicants were chosen. Once picked, they were outfitted in neat Red Cross uniforms, and engaged in basic training on the history as well as policies and procedures of the Red Cross. Considerable attention was paid to properly representing the United States on the world stage (which involved constantly smiling and wearing no earrings, nor excessive use of cosmetics). Over three hundred Dollies were transported to Europe in early 1944 (my thanks to https://history.delaware.gov for this).

I have given Caroline Blackwood, Maureen's eldest daughter, a small but occasionally pivotal role in this story. This aspect is purely my invention, brought about because I am so fascinated by her, and wanted to write her into things. One nice thing that happened while I was writing the book was the re-publishing of her book *The Fate of Mary Rose*, kindly sent to me by my editor Ciara Doorley. This was first published in 1981, but was long out of print by the time Virago Modern Classics re-issued it. I like to think (ridiculously) that I might have had a tiny part to play in this because I tell everyone, at every event I do, what a wonderful writer she was.

I have depicted the relationship between Maureen and Caroline as cold and fractious, because that is what I believe it was. Caroline, as an adult, once said that her childhood was too painful to speak of. Interestingly, the first pages of *The Fate of Mary Rose* carries the line, 'Damn that little dead Maureen!' Maureen Sutton is the name Caroline has given to a character in her novel – a murdered child, which struck me as interesting. I would never write my mother's name in such a sentence.

I should say that the affair I hint at in this book between Maureen and Billy's father is presented as fact in Paula Byrne's book *Kick*, but I have chosen to make it ambiguous.

By mid-1945, almost all the men in this book were dead. Joe and Billy, but also Brigid's brother, Arthur, who was killed in the Netherlands in February 1945, and Basil Blackwood – Duff – who was killed in Burma in March. Kick herself was dead three years later. Knowing this, you will see that it really wasn't possible to give the novel a happy ending.

Acknowledgements

A quick whip-around of the people I owe the greatest thanks to – these are by and large the same as previous books, and I hope by now you all know just how much I rely on you.

My agent, Ivan Mulcahy, for being always enthusiastic and having great instincts, and a breadth of knowledge I have come to rely on. My editor, Ciara Doorley; some books are hard, some are easier (I'm not saying which this was . . .), but you are always there for whatever is required. You put so much into these books, and I am very grateful.

All my pals at Hachette Ireland, especially Joanna Smyth who patiently deals with all manner of irritating questions from me (thank you!), and Breda Purdue.

I started this book – as I have now started many books – at the Tyrone Guthrie Centre in Annaghmakerrig, and I owe a huge debt of gratitude to that serene and inspiring place. I set myself ridiculous goals every time I go, and somehow the unique atmosphere means I always come good. Thank you!

The wonderful people I meet at readings and writer events, who come and listen and ask questions, and often tell me of their own encounters, with Guinnesses and Kennedys, and other related folk. Everything you tell me adds a little to the landscape I have built in my mind containing these characters.

My family, for keeping me sane and driving me nuts. My mother, most of all, for being almost (but not quite) impossible to please, with standards close to unattainable. I think I probably put the extra 10 percent into everything I do, because of you. It's always worth it.

David, Malachy, Davy and B – it is a joy to share my life with you.

Bibliography

In researching and writing *A Kennedy Affair*, I read books about the family, about Kick, and also about London in the years of the Second World War. Some of those I found particularly interesting are:

Kick, Paula Byrne

Black Diamonds, Catherine Bailey (about the family of Peter Fitzwilliam)

Dangerous Muse: The Life of Lady Caroline Blackwood, Nancy Schoenberger

Henry 'Chips' Channon: The Diaries (vol. 2) 1938–43, edited by Simon Heffer

A Taste of Love, Theodora Fitzgibbon

A Restless Life, Leland Bardwell

I was also guided by many of the wonderful novels of the time, most particularly Elizabeth Bowen's *The Heat of the Day*; Elizabeth Jane Howard's brilliant *Cazalet Chronicles*; and Evelyn Waugh's *Put Out More Flags*. Also on my mind were the many wartime books I read as a child – especially Nina Bawden's *Carrie's War* and *The Silver Sword* by Ian Serraillier.

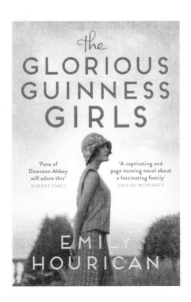

The Glorious Guinness Girls are the toast of London and Dublin society. Darlings of the press, Aileen, Maureen and Oonagh lead charmed existences that are the envy of many.

But Fliss knows better. Sent to live with them as a child, she grows up as part of the family and only she knows of the complex lives beneath the glamorous surface.

Then, at a party one summer's evening, something happens which sends shockwaves through the entire household. In the aftermath, as the Guinness sisters move on, Fliss is forced to examine her place in their world and decide if where she finds herself is where she truly belongs.

Set amid the turmoil of the Irish Civil War and the brittle glamour of 1920s London, *The Glorious Guinness Girls* is inspired by one of the most fascinating family dynasties in the world – an unforgettable novel of reckless youth, family loyalty and destiny.

Available in print, audio and ebook

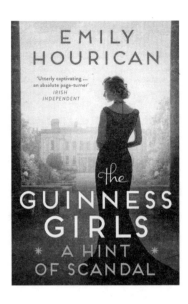

As Aileen, Maureen and Oonagh – the three privileged Guinness sisters, darlings of 1930s society – settle into becoming wives and mothers, they quickly discover that their gilded upbringing has not prepared them for the realities of married life.

At Dublin's Luttrellstown Castle, practical Aileen has already run out of things to say to her husband. Outspoken Maureen is very much in love but feels isolated at the crumbling Clandeboye estate in Northern Ireland. And, as romantic Oonagh's dreams of happiness in London are crushed by her husband's lies, she seeks comfort in her friends – but can they be trusted?

As the sisters deal with desire and betrayal amidst vicious society gossip, their close friends, the Mitfords, find themselves under the media glare – and the Guinness women are forced to examine their place in this quickly-changing world.

Inspired by true-life events, *The Guinness Girls: A Hint of Scandal* is a dazzling, page-turning novel about Ireland and Britain in the grip of change, and a story of how three women who wanted for nothing were about to learn that they couldn't have everything.

Available in print, audio and ebook

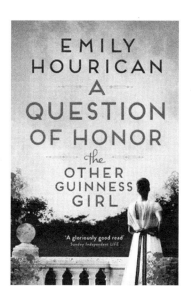

Surrounded by wealth, glamour and excitement, Lady Honor Guinness is a reluctant wallflower. But that all changes when she married Henry 'Chips' Channon, a charming and ambitious American. On his arm, she finds herself at the heart of 1930s London's most elite social circles, mingling with aristocrats, politicians and royalty. But it's not too long before Chips begins to prioritise his aspirations over all else, and Honor begins to wonder who exactly she has married.

By her side is her best friend Doris, a young woman eager to establish her place in society. A social butterfly who keeps the details of her family background to herself, Doris is hopeful her beauty and charm will win her a suitable husband, but she has no interest in a romantic attachment. Until she is introduced to 'the most devastating man in London'.

Inspired by true-life events, *The Other Guinness Girl: A Question of Honor* is an elegant, captivating story of two young women navigating friendship, loneliness, love and desire as they try to find their places in a society where the rules seem to change every moment.

Available in print, audio and ebook

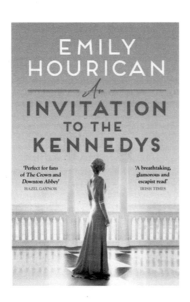

London 1938: Daughter of the US ambassador, Kathleen 'Kick' Kennedy is a huge hit in society's most elite circles, though she isn't always sure she fits in. While Kick is falling for duke-in-waiting Billy Cavendish, a man her parents will never let her marry, across the city Lady Brigid Guinness has no interest in love or society connections. But her ambitious brother-in-law has other ideas and seems determined to engineer a match with a German prince.

When they are invited to an exclusive gathering at a country estate, the young women soon form an unlikely friendship: the stuck-up aristocrat and the brash American. Then Billy and Prince Fritzi join the party, and tensions rise as Kick and Brigid discover that beneath the group's façade of politeness, nothing is as it seems.

As the days at Kelvedon Hall pass in a haze of sunshine, secrecy and surprising revelations, Kick and Brigid begin to rethink their hopes and plans for the future. Do they still want what they once did? And with the world around them constantly shifting, as war in Europe looms, will they ever be able to have it?

Available in print, audio and ebook